We Were Beautiful Once
Chapters from a Cold War

Joseph Carvalko

We Were Beautiful Once

Copyright © 2013, by Joseph Carvalko.
Cover Copyright © 2013 by Joseph Carvalko.

For information about special discounts for bulk purchases, please contact Sunbury Press, Inc. Wholesale Dept. at (717) 254-7274 or orders@sunburypress.com.

To request one of our authors for speaking engagements or book signings, please contact Sunbury Press, Inc. Publicity Dept. at publicity@sunburypress.com.

FIRST SUNBURY PRESS EDITION
Printed in the United States of America
February 2013

Trade Paperback ISBN: 978-1-62006-171-8
Mobipocket format (Kindle) ISBN: 978-1- 62006-172-5
ePub format (Nook) ISBN: 978-1-62006-173-2

Published by:
Sunbury Press
Mechanicsburg, PA
www.sunburypress.com

Mechanicsburg, Pennsylvania   USA

Dedicated to

The soldiers who end wars
leaving on the battlefields
their bodies,
minds or spirits,
and
their loved ones who
live without an answer
to where they may be found

Author's Note

This book is a work of fiction inspired by real events and real people. It draws upon the experiences of soldiers who served in the Korean War and the families they left behind. I have taken liberties with names, places, and geography, to weave multiple stories into a cohesive whole to explore the burdens ordinary people take on in times of war and carry for the rest of their lives.

Prologue

When the Monsignor died, Sister Annagail, his housekeeper for 60 years, discovered a manuscript in his dresser that contained names, places and events she thought she recognized, and although it read like fiction, it included the following prefatory letter:

Nature consigns to every child a body, a mind and an emotion and sets them adrift to sow that one feature claimed exclusively theirs alone: their identity, the essential part of them, the self, one human and one soul that congeals and anneals under the weight of events, tempered by the good and the bad, actions and reactions, objects and subjects, by which life exposes and draws together its parts. And, the possibility exists that through the carelessness and perfidies of others, an identity so formed can be deformed and finally denatured to evaporate into naught, zero, a cipher. I bore witness to the destruction of such a self and now within the limits of time granted by the powers of the Almighty, I am duty bound to explain, in disregard of that sacred trust vested in me as confessor, my complicity in a well-deserved killing.

Mgr. Francis X. Ryan, S.J.
Enders Island, 2010

Too Far To Bridge
November 1983

IT WAS LATE IN THE AFTERNOON WHEN DRESSED in the only suit he owned Jack walked to St. Patrick's, its luminous steeple and lesser spires guarding the sanctity of the old neighborhood, where priests had flung open the doors from the stronghold allowing faint voices from a practicing choir to waft into the street. He climbed the granite stairs, entered its massive doors and blessed himself in holy water from the eight-sided font, the gateway to a cavern of pews, crosses and an assortment of saints iconized in marbleized plaster. At the foot of the altar he folded his long legs and knelt beside three wrinkle-faced ladies in black babushkas, rosary beads tangled between the fingers of their boney, translucent hands. Jack listened to Acts of Contrition coming from the dark stall where penitents left their sins behind, and when the prayers fell silent, he lifted himself from the company of the old ladies and entered the confessional to speak to God through a priest's ears, to try once again to dissolve the most grievous of his sins. The church bell struck eight times when Jack's turn came to enter the confessional.

"Bless me Father for I have sinned. It has been three weeks since my last confession."

"Proceed my son."

"I'm not sure where to start, but I'd kept secret from Julie what I knew about Roger Girardin. She waited for him her whole life." Jack sat quietly, head down looking at his hands. "Like I said, I don't know where to... "

"Tell me, what is it?"

The words stuck in Jack's throat. "I lied, I lied to Julie, I lied to myself... ."

The hour passed, and Jack felt he had purged himself from the sins and guilt of a lifetime. He took three short breaths.

"Father, Father, I have this dream where I'm at a station. I hear laughing, then it sounds more like horns, sorrowful ones, a locomotive, whooshing out of time, a stationmaster hollers arrivals of men coming home. Roger steps off the train. I'm standing there. He doesn't see me... walks right passed and I lose him in the crowd."

"Jack, what can I say? Put all that as far behind you as you can. You have regrets, but they're about things in the past you cannot fix. Every man regrets something."

Following the string of Hail Marys meted out by Father Ryan, Jack kneeled in the rearmost pew taking swigs from a pint of gin he had tucked in his back pocket. He prayed to St. Cronan for deliverance, feeling he had come full circle, not knowing much more about the great mysteries of life than he knew as a child. The bell struck the half-hour and Jack crossed himself again. Through a haze of perfumed incense and candle smoke, he walked past a relief of Magdalene borne by the angels to the exit where Father Ryan waited to lock up for the night. He gave Jack a stiff pat-on-the-back. Jack stopped, took in a yawning breath, and slowly exhaled.

"Father, we're like air to the world, it breathes us in, faults and all, to keep itself going and when it takes what it needs... it simply breathes us out."

White shirt opened at the neck, sleeves rolled above his elbows, Jack walked away from the church looking down to avoid cracks in the sidewalk. Street after street passed unnoticed: South, Kossuth, River, then left up Asylum, mumbling, "... how fitting, sanctuary or nuthouse." He reached the soot-laden red bulk of the railway station, where at its entrance a blind bum in 101st Airborne fatigues cried out, "Hey, buddy, got two bits?" Rather than take the darkened stairwell to the upper platform, Jack took the promenade dotted by lamps encased in fog-like cysts, two hundred yards of poured concrete, straight ahead, long strides, no cracks leading directly to the edge of the dimly lit eastbound platform—quiet and empty except for two men in a far corner in London Fog raincoats with briefcases. The stationmaster's wooden bellow broke the peace.

"Westbound Track Two, New York, Philadelphia and Washington D.C."

In the background, running heels tapped against the hard surface. He looked back before stepping to the sharp edge of the platform. He gazed into the bed of silver rails reflecting parallel worlds running four feet apart: the gap too far to bridge. Each occupied a different space, each channeled that blinding light, a sun, a god, the erratic flash from the one-eyed locomotive, candlepower, china blue sliver, bedazzling, a frozen eye staring without seeing. The chasm met him at the gate of Eternity, hurling the remains of a man onto the vacancy of a roadbed. Except for the squealing brakes and the fading rhythm of leathered soles against concrete, the station resumed its incandescent solitude.

The Terrifying
July 1983

"8, 7, 6, 5... 8, 7, 6," JACK MUMBLED, "... 5, 8, 7... 6, 5... "

Suddenly a soldier in a brown parka jammed the butt of a Russian carbine into his shoulder blades hollering something in Chinese."

"What's your bitch!?" Jack snarled.

"He's telling you to shut the fuck up," the guy next to him grumbled.

A loud explosion followed and two men were seen sprawled on the ground, one missing legs and the other missing his brains now covering a fresh layer of snow in a splash of grays and reds.

Jack saw himself walking to a chicken wire fence where a man stood with a .45 caliber pistol, standard Army issue. "Give me that goddamn thing," he yelled.

"Trent, I'm Trent, Jack. I'm Trent!"

Jack grabbed a chunk of the man's hair and pulled him against the barbs.

Men in brown parkas approached. Jack straight-armed the one closest. The other came from the side and hit him with a night stick, sending a wood block wallop reverberating through the frigid air. He fell limp, unable to wake up as he was dragged across an icy field, where an ever-enlarging fresh snowpack filled his nostrils, his windpipe, to play out the recurring nightmare and panic of suffocating in a forgotten hell hole.

Suddenly, Jack opened his eyes to silver light and hissing from a TV that had lost its reception. He stumbled to the front window, lifted the slat in the blind and looked out where rain poured down in velvet sheets, vertically twisting in the orb of the street lamp, and in the near distance he could see the dim lights from the badlands

5

where urbanized junk, junkies and speculators inhabited the night's shadow as they slipped past stripped cars, the strip joints, empty cans of Sterno and Spam, fifty-gallon drums, tin garbage cans, and fast-food wrappers blowing freely. And, he saw beyond where gulls with dirty wings flapped over rain soaked tenements he knew as a boy. It was different then—before Bridgeport had been left behind the rest of the America, before her colors faded, before her tired humanity became hidden in shadows black and white, to waste away in deflowered flatlands, among factories in rubble as far as the eye could see.

He looked up Willa Street and saw the Ford still parked with blue-gray smoke coming from the muffler. Trembling, he poured himself a tumbler of gin, gulping it down before slumping on the couch, to wait it out.

Jack Be Nimble
July 1983

"C'MON, C'MON, SOMEONE'S GOTTA KNOW SOMETHING. Everything points to him being there. Somebody's gotta know what happened to him," Nick shouted just before closing the office and letting Mitch and Kathy go before Jake's happy hour ended. They hadn't managed to track down Jack O'Conner, but it dawned on Nick to let up on what were essentially two college kids: Kathy a final year law student and Mitch a recent law grad awaiting his bar results. And, his other reason for shutting down the office was to have supper at home with Diane, with whom he hadn't exchanged more than a dozen words since an argument about why she paid for their son Jamie's Boy Scout trip to Lake George, rather than the electric bill. As tensions thawed over dinner, Nick and Diane watched a segment that Nick had helped the local station put together covering the upcoming trial.

"Well, you're certainly getting attention," Diane conceded, as she cleared the remains of a tuna casserole.

"It might just help tie up some loose ends."

Later, Nick reflected that Diane was right. The case was getting attention and he knew that fact could play for or against him. Reaching down into his desk drawer, he pulled out a dusty glass and a bottle of Glenmorangie single malt he reserved for those times when he was about to don the chainmail and poleaxe of the gladiator. He knew enough about the game to have an idea of how it would play out, but in little more than a week, and for the first time, he'd step into the arena for the other side. In pursuit of what? Truth? Justice? So far it hadn't felt any different than battling on the side of the king he'd gotten used to in the VA cases.

7

He had poured his fifth shot of the 25-year-old scotch by the time he thought back to the blindfolded chess tournament his father had taken him to in Brooklyn in the fifties. He remembered the frisson of excitement surrounding the Hungarian mastermind, which had stemmed as much from his ability to keep straight the moves of a dozen ongoing matches, as his being the latest prize in Cold War defections. Nick was thinking through the possible permutations the trial could take when the phone rang. With an unsteady hand he grabbed it before the second ring could wake up Diane.

"Nick, Walter here, from WNVS. Did I wake you?"

"No, it's okay."

"I just thought you might like to know we've had several calls tonight."

"Oh?" Nick sat up, alert.

"Lots of the usual stuff, support and thanks for remembering the vets, but you know there's always a couple of 'em out there with too much time on their hands, real sticklers for getting the details right."

"Yes?"

"Yeah, this guy must have been out there, too. I've got a name. Hold on."

Nick could hear papers rustling.

"Here it is—name, name, oh yeah, name: Johnny Fitzgerald. Let's see, he complained about it being the 24th Army Division and not Regiment, he said that O'Conner was on the left, not the right in the photo and goes by the name of Prado, not O'Conner, and, let's see, that Pyoktong, Korea was 57 kilometers, not—"

"Wait! What?"

"That it was the 24th?"

"No, the O'Conner bit."

"Oh, that O'Conner was on the lef— "

"Yeah, yeah—"

"... and goes by the name of Prado and that... "

Now Nick was fully awake.

"That's it, Walter. Walter, thank you very much. I owe you one."

By Tuesday morning Mitch had located a "Jack Prado" on Willa Street, but all attempts at calling him proved fruitless. Later in the week Nick drove over, rang the bell, knocked and peered through the dirty front window. He would have been more surprised had someone answered. Because the trial was about to start, Nick did not have time for cat and mouse games, so he asked Mitch to prepare a subpoena and his secretary Sophie to find a sheriff to park in front of the house to serve him, if he showed-up. All Nick needed was to talk to O'Conner, aka Prado, to see if he had anything useful to say.

***

It was nearly 9:30 when Jack took his last swig from his usual one cup of coffee at the Silver Streak Diner. As he turned the page in the *Bridgeport Post*, the heavyset waitress whom he had known since high school poured cup number four. "Ya want some breakfast Jack?"

Without taking his eyes off the sports page he answered, "Nah, not today, Mol."

"Jack, if you get any thinner, you're gonna blow away."

"Yeah, just ain't much hungry these days." He reached for his cigarettes, pulled one out, put it between his lips.

"It's not my business, but ya need a good woman."

Jack grinned, the cigarette butt dangling from the side of his mouth. "Yeah, that's it, Mol, a good woman. Ya ready?"

"Huh! I wouldn't have ya... too moody."

Jack lit the butt, rolled up the half-pack into his tee-shirt sleeve, paid his bill and started back to the house, hearing in the distance the dog across from where he lived barking up a storm. Within fifty feet of his door he saw an older model, black, four-door Ford parked in front. It looked like a retired state police car, the kind people picked up at auctions. On his porch stood a giant of a man in a brown suit. Jack slowed down, put his hands in the back pockets of his Levis, kept his eyes on the man, and within a few feet of the porch, yelled, "Yo, Mack, can I help ya?"

The man turned. He had a flat mug with jowls that made Jack think: St. Bernard.

"Yeah, lookin' for Jack Prado O'Conner, you him?"

"Who wants to know?"

The man stepped toward Jack. "I'm here to hand him something."

As the man got closer, Jack backed up. He had to be 6'5", three hundred pounds, probably a football player, he thought.

"You O'Conner?"

"Whatcha got?"

"You O'Conner?" he insisted, stopping within an arm's length of Jack; too close for comfort.

Jack surveyed the hulk top to bottom. "Yeah, so who wants ta know?"

The man stretched out his arm. "It's a subpoena. Appear in court tomorrow at ten."

"What's this about?" Jack asked, pulling in the envelope.

"It's all there, much as I know."

Before he opened it, Jack grumbled, "My goddamn wife again, what the hell's she want now?" He tore open the envelope, letting it fall to the ground, and read the document, top to bottom. Reflexively he gulped, "Can you tell me why they want me?"

"Can't tell you much, Mister."

"Well who wants to talk to me?"

"Can't say for sure, but probably the lawyer that hired me."

"What's his name?"

"Nick, Nick Castalano, over on Main and West."

The man looked on for a few seconds. "Here's a buck to make sure you've got enough to get ya there," he said matter-of-fact. He got into his car, drove away, noise from his faulty exhaust swamping-out the dog's bark. Jack, taken aback by what he had in his hand, ambled to the house in a stupor.

The Barnum Line

LATER THAT DAY AN ORANGE BUS APPROACHED the corner of Willa Street and Barnum Avenue, on the same side of the street as the Silver Streak. Julie stepped off the bus and squinted at the slice of pinkish sun about to set into the warm July night. While she waited for the light to turn green, a breeze blowing off the sound flapped her full skirt. With one hand she held the hem against her knees, so it would not work its way up her thighs, and when she stooped over, the wide patent leather belt around her waist dug into a midriff thickened with middle age. She had bought the beige silky rayon outfit from Goodwill, where the saleslady, in a nearly identical dress, had told Julie it accentuated her small bust line. In the fitting room's full-length mirror, her eyes were drawn to the shadow beginning to form beneath her jaw line, so she missed how the dress flared out at the hips. She ran her hands over her cheeks. She was still pretty, but because of her age, more times than not, only annoying men with large bellies asked her to dinner. She always refused.

It normally took five minutes to walk from the bus stop to Jack's house, but Julie's bad leg forced her to walk slowly. On a dare she'd once walked blindfolded and backward from St. Patrick's on the corner, landing right at her front door. Blindfolded or not, Willa Street constantly drew Julie back. Here, her grandparents had raised her mom. Here, her mom had returned when pregnant with Julie's older brother Jack, and again a dozen years later, after she'd divorced their dad.

Julie climbed the stairs to a warped stoop, faced a wooden storm door with half its screen in tatters and knocked lightly. The door creaked open, and she pushed it wide, a spider's silk snagging her face and the stench of rotting garbage and stale cigarette smoke making her gag.

"Jack, you home?"

11

Julie peered into a small darkened hallway. Straight ahead, an open door showed the kitchen, its sixty-watt bulb reflecting off a pile of dirty dishes. To the right, a short landing led to a flight of stairs.

"Jack? Where are you?" Julie ventured the two steps to the landing, and with a diffuse shaft of light piercing the small, stained-glass window behind her, she cautiously followed the varnished hand rail until the shape of a body sitting on the top stair stopped her. Tremulously, she whispered, "Jack, that you?"

In jockey shorts, his bearded chin resting on his bare chest, Jack sat with his arms folded across his thin, naked thighs.

"Jack, you okay?" she asked gently.

"Julie?"

"Yeah, what're you doin'," she asked, her voice tentative.

"Go 'way, don't bother me!"

In the shadowed stairwell his face appeared like a dark gray blot, but she knew her brother's throaty voice.

"Get outta here. Don't come any closer!" Jack barked, as Julie put her foot on the next step.

"Jack, what's the matter?"

"Nothin'. I got business to do."

"Business? What business?" Jack hadn't worked in months. Not since Anna had left with their daughter.

"Sheriff came. Couple days ago. Tacked papers to the door. Did you know that Anna wants a divorce? Irreconcilable differences. All I did was call her to say three solitary words: 'Will is dead!' Julie, he ain't never coming back."

"I know, Jack, let him go. It's been ten years. Jack, she's a good woman, she loves you."

"Just go away, I gotta take care of business."

The stairwell was quiet. Julie looked it up and down like a mouse looking for a place to hide. She broke the silence. "So why are you sittin' in the dark?"

Jack ran his hands through his graying hair. "Dark's natural. It's always dark, otherwise ya wouldn't need light. Anyway it helps me think things out."

"Jack, you're not making sense. What's the matter? What things?" Slowly moving closer, Julie was hit by the stench of whiskey.

"Nobody's business, for Christ's sake."

"How can I help?"

"Can't, unless you want to pull the trigger!"

Julie saw a flash of silver as Jack quickly lifted a small revolver pressing the barrel hard into his temple. Julie clutched the handrail, fell a step back, and struggled to catch her breath.

"What the Christ you goin' to do with that?"

Jack's thumb rubbed the treads on the hammer pulled halfway back. "I'm squeezin' it and... Whammo!"

Inevitability Postponed

WHEN JACK DRANK ENOUGH HE INEVITABLY went from ranting to babbling and back again, mostly about how Anna, his soon-to-be ex-wife, was making a record for the divorce, broadcasting her disappointment that he never rose above middle management despite his relationship with the company president. Julie had heard it countless times. "Jack's turning points" she'd labeled it: Korean War, marrying after Korea, raising his wife's son William, their daughter Mona's arrival after he thought they could not have kids. William's death. But, this was different, he had never pointed a gun to his head. And, she was not so sure he would not pull the trigger; Jack was definitely capable of that.

"Jack, wait. Let's talk! Why you want 'a go an' do that?"

Julie saw the gun shaking in Jack's hand.

"Because I'm fucked up, that's why; can't get out of it."

"Get out of what? Tell me what's goin' on, what's buggin' you?"

"I'm spinnin', woman, spinnin'. Can't face it no more."

"I don't understand. What do you mean—spinning?"

The hammer half-cocked, Jack began sobbing, his shoulders shaking. "I been drunk too long. Forget what's real. Lost it. Other day I heard Dad's footsteps doubling up the back stairs. Then I was standin' at the head of his grave. I don't even pass out no more. My eyes stay open. A bad dream?" Still clutching the gun, he rubbed his eyes with his knuckles.

"Jack... Jack."

"Ah, ah, murderin' bastard, a fool—drunk—freakin' freak, man, I'm floatin' away   from everybody—and everything."

14

"What do you mean, murderin'? What're you talkin' about?"

"I'm bringing the man down, ya hear?"

"What man?" She wondered if Anna had been having an affair.

"Yes, sir, I'm bringing the bastard down."

Julie took two steps up. "Jack, put down the gun; let me help—promise I can, know I can!"

"You can't, no one can. I'm unstuck from everything, mother fuckin' earth and mother fuckin' god—everything is —out of control! Do ya hear? Ev... everything. My mind goes in one direction, my body's stuck here. I know one thing. Hamilton's going down."

"Hamilton? What are you talking about? Trent Hamilton? What does he have to do with anything? You haven't worked for him in over ten years." She begged in an unsteady voice, "Put the goddamn gun down. Please. Please, Jack, please!"

She took another step closer. "Come on, now, let me help. You're not well. I'm calling the VA. You can get some sleep, some coffee, something decent to eat."

Julie tried looking in his eyes, but he bowed his head, dropping the gun to his side. He grunted, "I lost it. Lost it. Can't get my timin' right, no how. I'm fuckin' slippin' deep. Ain't got no options. Gotta remember, but gotta forget, man, day by day. Ain't got no choice, but to blow it all away—puff."

Julie wrapped her arm around his bent shoulders, took a deep breath and gently took hold of the gun barrel. Jack slumped his head between his knees and wept quietly, seemingly resigned to his survival.

For the moment, all that had to be said had been said — dust motes twirled lazily in the yellow, red and green shafts of light shining through the stained glass window. As Julie shifted, her brother slumped back onto the top landing.

"What happened, Jack? What brought this on? Today, I mean," Julie enquired softly.

"Life takes on its own rhythm, doesn't it?"

"What's that, Jack?"

"I still need to find my place. I can tell you it's not on this fuckin' earth."

Julie reached back and stroked Jack's head. "It'll be all right. I'll help you. It'll be better tomorrow."

"Tomorrow, I gotta go to court. Got subpoenaed."

"What for? Is it Anna or something?" Julie asked.

"No, the Army."

"The Army? It's been thirty years since you were in the Army."

"Might be the past, but it never stops. It's tracking right behind me all the time. That's the thing."

"What thing?"

"It ain't important."

Jack and Julie sat in a silence broken only by the dog barking from across the street and little girls giggling and jumping rope under the street lamp. *Cinderella, dressed in yella, went upstairs to kiss a fella, by mistake she kissed a snake, how many doctors did it take, 1, 2, 3... .*

Suddenly, everything went silent and Julie changed her focus from Jack to a name lost in the vacuum of war thirty years ago. Then and there she decided to call in sick to work, something she rarely did, and follow Jack to court.

"What time do you have to be there?"

"At ten down on Lafayette, at the federal court over there."

"I'd like to go."

"What's that?"

"I'm going with you."

"I don't need you there; it ain't important. Sorry I mentioned it."

With Julie next to him now, Jack's headache began to subside, but an unbridled palsy took hold of his hand, arrhythmic palpations took hold of his heart, a storm of low pressure shuddered through his body, the thought of the subpoena, its consequences, pushing everything else aside. He licked his lips, tasting the ghost of a stiff shot that might still quell the thought that Julie could bear witness to what had happened to Roger Girardin—a man lost in a winter of mayhem, a man whose fate he had withheld from her, a man about whom she filled a three-decade long diary of solitary conversations. A man, for all intents and purposes, present but invisible.

One-Lung Law Practice
1981–1983

NICK CASTALANO RAN WHAT THE LOCAL WHITE-SHOE firms called a one-lung law practice, a two-room office over Zorba's Luncheonette, where he could set his watch by the smells that wafted up the ventilation shaft, where the only items he actually owned were a few law books, a chess set and a phone with an extension that sat on the secretary's desk. Everything else, the desks, the credenza, a side chair and a gray steel filing cabinet was leased. Over the past few years he had done contract work for the VA, defending the agency when it had turned down claims and veterans sued. That work had dried up, so Nick resorted to advertising divorce, DUI and debt collection. Most days he stayed holed up in his office, working on cases, reading and playing chess with a few luncheonette regulars he had gotten to know, but on Fridays, to get away from the smell of fried fish, he left the office early and walked two blocks to the American Legion Club. One particular Friday, while Nick sat at the bar watching a Yankee shutout, Art Girardin, an infrequent patron, took up the stool next to him, ordered a beer and began to tell him a wild tale about his brother Roger, last seen twenty-seven years ago in a North Korean POW camp along the Manchurian border.

Art told Nick about the day a letter came from the Army notifying the family that it listed Roger as MIA, somewhere in North Korea. Four years later another letter arrived, indicating that the Army entered a presumed finding of death, based upon having received no further reports. Art never believed that his brother could simply have vanished. And years later, when families were raising issues about Vietnam MIAs, he began his own investigation by perusing declassified Army records. He told Nick he believed that

Roger was then, and now, a POW. Art, picking up on Nick's curiosity, excused himself, went to his car and returned with a battered briefcase full of "evidence" gathered over the years. Intrigued by what little he had read—an International Red Cross report listing Roger Girardin as a POW, and a later, official Army letter stating Girardin was MIA, presumed dead—Nick invited Art back to his office to make a better assessment of Art's collection. More than curiosity, though, Nick's instinct told him that this could be one hell of an opportunity for his struggling practice.

Art Girardin, slightly overweight, early-fifties, had worked in the Department of Transportation for the past nineteen years, spending most of that time inspecting roads throughout Connecticut. He had a ruddy complexion and thick muscular hands that did not go with the image of a guy who had painstakingly rifled through the arcane records of a complicated war. Now seated in Nick's office, he started from the beginning.

"Yeah, this old bastard at the National Archives told me I was wastin' my time. But I said to this little prick, get the goddamn records out, an' let me decide. That was the middle of, no, beginning of '77 when I first went to D.C. The fucking Army was, well, they were worse than the guy at the Archives."

Nick perused one document after another while Art briefed him and let off steam.

"For almost three goddamn years I went back and forth to the Archives, running down leads going nowhere, others pointing to people who vaguely remembered a Girardin, writing admirals, generals, staffers at the Department of Defense, the U.N. Military Armistice Commission and the CIA. Then the minute I found a guy, out in California, who definitely could place Roger in Camp 13 in '52, he turns up dead two weeks later. It was like either collective amnesia, or the thing was hexed."

Nick tried to size up this man, who had worked himself into a lather, to make sure he wasn't some whacko on a crusade.

"Yeah, useless politicians mostly humored me. Promised more than they delivered," Art continued sullenly. "And depending on who was in, they talked to one or more of these asshole bureaucrats in the Defense Department."

"Which ones did you contact?" Nick asked.

"Oh, Goodsmith, from Georgia, Walkovich, Welsh, Connecticut. Yeah, these suckers have short-term attention. They read from a patriotic script and eventually move on. But, I never let them forget me, what it means to find some poor foot soldier, the gullible kid who drank the Kool aide and enlisted. And who now may be living in hell somewhere."

"Have you been in touch lately? With the politicians?"

Art threw his arms in the air. "No, these jerks all called it quits after a little publicity." Art looked at his puffy hands. "I wished I had a crystal ball, so I could see what goes on in those bureaucracies."

"They hide a lot, Art, they hide," Nick commiserated.

Bemoaning, Art continued, "Now, well, the Pentagon dropped us. Like a sack of shit. They don't even take my calls." He slammed a fist into his palm. "Goddamn it, I want my day in court. This is my last chance. We gotta get them to listen, Nick. Can you do that?" he was pleading now.

"Art, before I say yes, I need to know what you're trying to do. I mean, your brother's been gone thirty years. A lot of boys didn't come back. What is it, Art?" Nick looked deep into the man's eyes.

"Listen, Nick, on my dad's sixty-fifth birthday, I made him a promise that I'd find out what happened to Roger. My brother, dead or alive is over there, unclaimed. I've come to bring him home, the only way I know how."

Nick had a military habit of standing ruler-straight in his 5'11", one-hundred and fifty pound frame, which as of late shouldered the gathering disappointments of life. But tonight he rose from his chair, shoulders curved and an unmistakable weariness in his eyes adding ten years to his already advancing forty. He had grown up not far from the town center in a working-class family; his father had hammered home the idea that hard work built character. Yes, he knew about fathers, the heavy burden of expectations, the hopes unrealized, and the torment of those that lose or come close to losing their sons altogether. Drifting to the window overlooking West Street, he saw that the stores were dark, and his eyes focused on the reflection of his face—sunk behind a five o'clock shadow. At street level, people scurried for home. He took a deep breath.

Directions Decided
1981

NICK PUT THE KEY IN THE BACK DOOR OF THE SPLIT RANCH that sat isolated at the cul-de-sac of Coswell Street, feeling that what might appear to be the wrong move to the rest of the world might turn out to be the right move after all. He'd decided to take the case, despite having represented the government's interests against veterans, despite Art's inability to pay but more than a fraction of what it would cost to prosecute the claim. Nick told Diane his decision after dinner, when she and the children—Trish, seven, and Jamie, fifteen—were all seated on the tall chairs that surrounded the kitchen bar. The conversation turned to an obligatory appearance at the Bennetts' next Saturday evening, to his son's petition for new sneakers and his daughter's recitation of the day's playground politics. Finally, left alone with dirty dishes and over the endless murmur of the television in the corner, his rationale to Diane was that his practice needed a boost, and one of the things he knew well was the ins and outs of veteran claims. As she dried the pots, she nodded her head—more a sign that she was listening, rather than approving. Nick said he thought representing veterans rather than fighting them had a better business upside. What he had not shared with Diane was his curiosity about the apparent dismissive treatment Art got from the Army, especially in light of the reports of his brother's sighting in Camp 13.

Later on, when the children were in bed, Nick peeked into Jamie's room to listen to him breathing, something he did every night since nearly losing the boy to an asthma attack as a baby. Nick recalled the hours spent watching Jamie sleep in a clear bubbled hospital croup tent, a speck in the Universe tenaciously clinging to life. Three days and three nights he had stared through the tent enveloping this human lump of flesh, whom he had only known for a few days but for whose life he would have traded places. He left Jamie's door open a crack as he walked towards his study, mulling over his reasons for taking the case. Reasons beyond those he had given Diane, and not simply because he had developed a soft spot for veterans. Reasons to do with that image Art painted of his dad, how he had lost the will to live when the government marked the death of his son in a registered letter. Recalling how he had nearly lost Jamie and experienced an uncertainty no father should, Nick knew his reasons had to do with a man's grief, a son unclaimed. Nick knew about feeling helpless and hopeful at the same time as he watched Jamie's doctor pull an all-nighter—his stethoscope to the boy's chest, palpating, peering deep into the body; running blood to the lab, scribbling on charts, searching for the pathogen destroying his son's lungs. Jamie survived. This, he knew, was what drove him to undertake the quest for Roger, because he, like Jamie's physician, was now linked to a son's fate.

***

Five weeks later, Nick filed suit in Federal Court. The government responded by assigning Bertram Harris, Assistant U.S. Attorney for the District of Connecticut, a seasoned lawyer that oozed oily success and a smug confidence in his ability to play the game, making him an ideal advocate for the army litigation machine. When after nearly six months, Nick had obtained a court order obligating the Army to turn over its declassified files, Harris, playing for time, made high-sounding arguments that the records were scattered between Washington and Seoul, and it would take an army to reassemble them. After several court hearings, Federal Judge Joe Lindquist observed that the Army was, after all, "an army" and told the government's lead defense attorney that if they did not produce, "some Army record's custodian is going to be hauled into my court to face contempt." But, the best evidence would be kept from Nick under the heading of "national security."

23

Witnesses to What?

THE YEAR 1982 WAS COMING TO A CLOSE, AND NICK was up against a fast approaching trial scheduled for the summer of '83. He had made little progress tracking down and talking to potential witnesses. This was caused partly by government stonewalling, partly by a lack of funds and partly by lack of help. Nick reached out to the local law school and found Kathy Rutherford and Mitch LeBeau willing to work for a stipend. They helped him painstakingly sift through a redacted CIA list of Camp 13 POWs that he had hoped might shed light on what happened to Roger. Kathy, a stout woman with a Norman Rockwell face, had celebrated her twenty-fifth birthday the week before Nick hired her. She dressed thirty-something and behaved forty-something, with a speech pattern shaped by a blue-blooded Yankee upbringing. Mitch, with hair banded in a short ponytail, proudly wore thick glasses that lended credence to a New York lefty, skeptic persona that forced Nick to justify his every out-of-the-mainstream machination.

Nick took his first really deep breath in late January 1983 when, in one of a mere handful of files submitted by the army, he discovered Roger Girardin mentioned in an Army Intelligence memo about an operation called Little Switch in April 1953. Entitled *"Missing in Action"*, it read: *Several sources in Camp No. 13 report date Girardin last known alive: February 1953.*

Nick did not need witnesses to confirm what had happened in the fall of 1950, between October 26 and December 11, when the North Koreans and Chinese Communists had captured tens of thousands of Americans, but he did need someone who could talk about what had happened to the men, and Roger in particular, from when they were captured until the Armistice in mid-1953.

"I need one or more of those guys who saw Roger in the camp," he said, "then we could possibly win a reclassification. Go back over the Army intelligence reports from Panmunjom to see who else might have slipped through the crack." Though Mitch and Kathy were diligent, they were coming up with a big fat zero. Nobody remembered Roger Girardin.

Mitch burrowed through the short stacks of government released files, phone books and maps while Kathy pored over Art Girardin's notes made during his needle-in-the-haystack searching at the Archives. Meanwhile, Nick interviewed the POWs from Camp 13 his team had found. The men who had been in Camp 13 all related the same inhumane conditions—bone-piercing cold or brain-searing heat, coupled with starvation and sicknesses without medical assistance—but only vague memories, if any, of a guy named Girardin, or was it Jardin? Or Giardino?

Nick looked at his watch, it was after 9 p.m. on Wednesday. He dropped the phone back into its cradle, pushed back his yellow pad, loosened his tie, and growled in frustration, "Who is left, Mitch?"

Stretching his long skinny legs and cracking his knuckles, Mitch responded, "Well, I've got Simmons, Forte, and Ciuci left, who were in Girardin's company, November '50, but not at Camp 13. But no discharge papers, so nobody's located yet. And, some Montoya guy who *was* at Camp 13, where his DD 214 discharge form lists New Mexico as his home address—thirty years ago." Nick lifted an eyebrow.

"Leave him. Who else you got?"

"A Sonny Reiner."

Kathy, who had been listening to the rundown while rifling through a tall stack of reports interjected, "That's a no-go. He's dead."

Nick and Mitch looked at each other in disbelief.

"Do you do this in your spare time?" teased Mitch.

Ignoring the jibe, Kathy continued, "Art Girardin and I tracked him down to a small town north of Osage, Washington and talked to him for about 10 minutes. Guy claimed he didn't know Roger, but we told him in '53 he'd

25

told the interrogators at Panmunjom he did, and that he knew him from Camp 13. Then, he said he wanted to think about talking any further. When Art called back later two weeks later, the guy's wife said he'd drowned. Art freaked. Said this was like when he'd found the guy in California, and the next thing he heard, the guy was dead."

"Nobody mentioned this to me," said Nick, mildly irritated.

"Didn't think it was that important," Kathy brushed it off.

"We can try Jaeger again," suggested Mitch.

Nick was annoyed and pensive at the same time. "Where's Jaeger out of again?" Nick asked.

"Pennsy."

"Man, doesn't anybody live close by? We're not even on a shoestring here, more like a piece of thread, and that deadline for naming trial witnesses is fast approaching," Nick complained while picking up the phone and handing it to Kathy. "Get him on the line."

Kathy called the number listed in the file. "Message says the phone's disconnected."

"Call information, see if he's relocated or something," Nick said, wondering if taking the case was such a good idea. "Mitch, it's after 9 here, so it's still early in Washington State. See if you can get Mrs. Reiner on the wire... put her on speaker."

Ten minutes later Nick was expressing his condolences to the widow Reiner and delicately segueing into her husband's military service. She knew little, because the man never spoke about the war to his wife. As to his recent death, she was still mourning, one month to the day he'd washed up on the shore of Lake Wanapipiti.

She said, "Retired after 25 years as investigator with the state welfare office. Only 56, good health, went out hundreds of times... to fish, wouldn't even tell me, but I'd guess where he was, good swimmer. Clear day, too."

"Did they do an autopsy?"

"Coroner did. But even after the investigation, police couldn't figure it out. Drowned, a big gash on his head... said he must of hit the edge of the boat, fell over. Didn't make sense to me. What do I know? He's dead."

"Do you have children, Mrs. Reiner?"

"Nope, had no kids. We didn't have a lot of friends, either... living way out here by the lake all these years. I tried calling a couple of men that came by just a few days before he passed, but didn't even have their names. Friends from the Army, Sonny said. He'd left a number on a pad in the kitchen. I tried it, thinking it might be someone who should know he died."

"Were they friends from the Army?"

"Think so, but I didn't have their names. Maybe Sonny told me, but I didn't remember with all that went on. A woman answered, said something like 'Army defense.' I had no idea what to ask. I hung up."

"You didn't meet these gentlemen, then?"

"No, was out shopping, and when I drove up the driveway, they were driving out. Sonny said they were buddies from the Army."

"Do you have the number you called?"

"Oh, I don't know. I can look, but I threw out a lot of scraps Sonny kept."

"And that was all? No further contact?"

"No, put it outta my mind, 'til now."

"Do you remember the car they were driving?"

"Not really. Sonny only said they'd be back."

"If you run across the number will you call us back?"

After Nick hung up, he turned to Mitch and Kathy. "So, what's odd about that conversation?"

Mitch chimed in, "I would think the wife would have gotten more from Sonny or remembered who those guys where. It's not like he had a lotta friends."

Nick turned to Kathy, who was standing by the large window overlooking West Street. "Kath?"

Without turning in Nick's direction, she said, "Friends, Army buddies, or buddies from the Army, which was it? I think that 'Army defense' is the key... suggests, 'buddies from the Army.'"

"Witnesses can't be found, some dying off. Trial's a few months down the line. Folks, something's gotta break our way or we are in deep... "

27

Kathy interrupted Nick. "Hey guys, across the street, that dark office right across from us. I thought I saw someone looking in our direction. Whose space is that?"

"That's an empty office. Hasn't been used in a year."

Nick walked over to the window. "Was that a flashlight that swept across? Mitch close the lights."

The three stood back and looked across the street for about 10 minutes, saw nothing, and decided to call it quits for the day.

The Dog Waits
1981

ON THE OTHER SIDE OF TOWN, HARRIS and his staff had begun their investigation by interviewing the Army Board for the Correction of Military Records chairman, when Art Girardin's petition had been denied. Having access to all the records without court orders, Harris's team was far ahead of Nick. One Congressional from the mid-50s listed over 400 names, but rather than locating and interviewing each of those men they focused on a file, which had not been turned over to Nick on the opinion of the security counsel, that the report be withheld on grounds of national security. The file known as the Broadbent report listed as the names David Bradshaw, Harry Sheer, Kenny Preston, Juan Montoya and Sonny Reiner. Kenny Preston could not be located by Harris's Justice Department investigators, but the others were and were eventually contacted. Except for Reiner, whom a senior official in the Department of the Army decided should be interviewed by a little-known investigative unit referred to simply as DA, under the umbrella of the larger Defense Intelligence Agency.

A search of FBI records turned up Juan Montoya, aka John Montoya, as an inmate in the New Mexico State Penitentiary serving a twenty-five-year-to-life sentence for a bank robbery in 1959. In a phone discussion with Montoya, they had learned that he had been in the 32nd Army Special Forces assigned to working behind enemy lines. After being captured, he had been put into Camp 13. When the name Girardin was mentioned, it rang a bell. He had claimed that the last time he remembered seeing him was in the late winter of either 1952 or 1953.

Montoya had been moved from Camp 13 in June 1953 the following year. But he recalled an American officer who spoke Chinese as being familiar with what went on in the camp: he thought his name was Tad or Tray or something unusual. Harold Foster, the young JAG officer working for Harris, went in two directions: setting up an ex parte deposition, to which Castalano wasn't privy, to obtain an official statement from Montoya and locate an American POW officer that spoke Chinese. Although there were several Chinese-American POWs in Camp 13 that spoke the language, none were officers. However, based on a DD 214 service record of First Lieutenant Trent Hamilton, it was learned that he spoke Chinese and had been in Camp 13 during the last year of the war. He was easy to locate; he had a secret security clearance, because his company did work for the Defense Department. Harris's staff arranged a conference call. The discussion did not produce anything pertinent to their investigation and they moved on.

Harris's next step was to fly to New Mexico and interview Montoya. Foster arranged to have Montoya's statement recorded, but the government had no intention of sharing it with Nick under the "work product privilege" attorneys use to conceal things lawyers create in the course of litigation. Phone interviews of Bradshaw and Sheer had pointed to the fact that Girardin may have been a POW. But the interviews weren't exhaustive and Harris remained skeptical about much of what the men had to say after thirty years. Montoya seemed to be the last in the line of those who may have had contact with Girardin.

Montoya, a small-shouldered, dark-complexioned man wore the tan shirt and pants of an inmate. At the end of a long table, he seemed lost. Crammed in behind him sat a stenographer from the U.S. Attorney's office at Santa Fe. Suit jackets removed, shirt sleeves rolled up, Harris sat at one side and Foster the other. Harris, balding man standing well over six feet tall, did not have enough room to stretch his legs. Near the door, a prison guard in short sleeves sweated profusely, water streaking down his pancake-shaped face.

After introductions, Harris asked, "Mr. Montoya, do you have anything you'd like to say before we get started?"

The man ran his fingers through his crop of dark gray hair, then smiled through large, amber-stained teeth. "Hi Mom," he giggled.

"Mr. Montoya, this is a serious matter," Harris cautioned.

"Yeah, yeah, got a weed?"

"Neither of us smoke. Anything else?"

"I wanna make sure we gotta deal."

Foster interjected tersely, "I think we discussed that fully."

"Yeah, but tell that man over there," Montoya countered, his voice tense. He nodded in Harris's direction. "He's *el jefe,* no?"

"So there's no misunderstanding, you tell us what you think we talked about," Foster said.

"Well, if I tell you what I know, Justice will recommend I get good time added for parole. You talked five years."

Foster, a man in his late twenties, lowered his voice, "I think we talked along those lines."

Montoya flipped his head in the direction of the stenographer. "Mr. Reporter, get all that?"

The stenographer, a slight man in his fifties with black pencil mustache banged on a few keys. "Yes."

Harris began by having Montoya recount his training and early combat missions. He said he was in-country almost nine months, on his way to Japan for R&R, when at the last minute he'd received orders transferring him from the 101st Calvary to the 32nd Army Special Forces.

"There came a time when you were captured by the Chinese, right?" Harris asked.

Before he answered, Montoya looked at the guard. His eyes were closed. Montoya's shout of "Yes!" startled the man out of a catnap. The prisoner hee-hawed.

Without blinking, Harris followed up, "Tell us what happened."

Montoya put his head between his hands. "On my fifth mission behind the lines, late summer '52, ground was shit soft. Ten of us parachuted in near the Yalu. Raining. Chinese spotted us. Was surrounded. Marched thirty miles to a camp."

31

Montoya told about interrogations and attempts at indoctrination. Harris moved to the question that brought him to the Southwest in the first place: "Did you know Roger Girardin?"

"Sounds familiar, think so," Montoya answered coolly.

"What can you tell us about him?"

"Was in my hut. He was there first. I came in the middle of winter '53, so I didn't get to know him good. I was beat up. But, these guys all looked dead."

"What did he look like?"

Montoya's face turned somber. "Dead, like I said."

"Color hair, remember?"

"Unh-uh." The prisoner had a vacant look.

Foster handed Montoya a picture. "From the file, when he was drafted."

"Looks like a convict," he snickered.

"Was he talkative?" Harris looked up.

"Can't say." Montoya seemed bored.

Harris clenched his fist. "Well how'd you know if he was there if you can't remember anything about him?"

"Man, I dunno. My brain knew 'im."

Harris exploded. "Goddamn it, I flew 2,000 miles to learn nothing." Foster avoided eye contact. A moment passed. Harris cooled off.

"Mr. Montoya, you told Mr. Foster that you and several hundred POWs were transferred to another camp. Explain, please."

Montoya looked up. "Yeah, June '53."

"How were you selected?"

"Hell, I don't know, orders came from the commandant."

Harris laid his pencil down. "Do you know who that was?"

"Yeah, Jo or Chao, something like that."

"Did he come out and say, 'You men are... ?'"

"No, nothin' like that. Guy who spoke Chinese, a first louey, his mouthpiece told us."

Harris sped up the pace, "What'd this guy, the 'spoke Chinese guy' look like?"

"Big, big mother. Well fed," Montoya giggled.

"Hair color?"

32

"We wore Mao hats. Even inside."

"How were men selected?"

"Guys that seemed hard-headed, like me, seemed to be on it."

"Hard-headed?"

Montoya, squirmed, then sat straight up. "We couldn't be taught, brainwashed. Them that refused to go to sessions was beat up, put in dog houses. I was put there once. Maybe that bought me a ticket. Don't know." He looked at Harris and blurted, "*Chinga a su madre!* I need some water."

Harris looked at the guard who had shut his eyes. "Officer, it's got to be ninety in here, open the door and get some water, please?"

"Yes, sir! Be right back, sir." He ran out as if he had been ordered by the warden himself.

Harris twiddled his pencil. "Who stayed behind?"

The prisoner put his hand to his forehead to wipe away the sweat. "I only know from my hut. I had names for everybody, Waltz, I called 'im Missouri Waltz, was a guy I called Jamestown Races, real name Jameston, and Jack-Be-Nimble—can't remember his whole name—real nut bag, never stopped rhymin' and countin'. Don't remember his last name, 'cept that's what I called him." Montoya hesitated, "Wait, now, wait, no, not Jack-Be-Nimble, cause he was a sick fuck, disappeared sometime before it got warm. There was another couple 'a guys, ain't good at remembering names."

"Why were they left behind?"

He raised his hands in the air. "Couldn't be sure, maybe brainwashed, signed papers. You know?"

"Remember the men you went with?"

"Don't remember but a few."

"Did Girardin go?"

"No, he went on a detail in... oh, winter maybe. Never came back."

"Why is that?"

"I have no idea."

"Do you recall if there were any officers with you when you shifted camps?"

"Yes and no. I think the first louey went, and maybe one more."

"Why did you remember him?" Harris glanced across at Foster, but could read nothing from his expression.

"Cause when I was captured, I was sent to the dayroom for grilling."

"Was the officer there?"

"Yeah, he translated. He was comfy with the Chinese.

"What'd you mean translated?"

"Spoke Chinese, like I said, so if the chinks wanted to talk, they used him."

"Tell me about the day they came and got you."

He shrugged. "When they came an' got us, we didn't know what they were up to. But it wasn't unusual that they'd line us up, bring us to this big opened area an' try an' brainwash us."

"Any other details come to mind?"

The guard put a pitcher of water on the table. Foster poured three glasses. Harris continued, "Any rumors what they'd planned?"

"Nope, they rounded us up, four, five hundred guys."

"Where'd the rest of the men come from?"

"When we fell out in the yard, there was lines of men. It was humid, dark, nobody shootin' the shit."

"What happened then?"

"Nothing. We waited. Couple hours, hot... humid like I said. Marched us out of camp four across." He walked his fingers on the table.

Harris felt the sweat dripping off his back. "When'd you reach your destination?"

"Half-day, maybe five, six hours."

Harris inhaled, slowly letting his breath out again. He looked at Foster, wondering what to make of the story. "You say you never saw Girardin again?"

"Never. Positive."

"Did you imagine he died?"

The room went silent for about thirty seconds.

Montoya asked, "What time you got, Mister?"

"You going someplace?" Harris ribbed.

Catching on, Montoya countered, laughing. "Yeah, wanna join me for lunch?"

34

"You imagine he died?" Harris asked again, straight faced.

Montoya's smirk vanished. "Man, I ain't never 'magined about nobody."

"So you never saw Roger Girardin after the winter?"

"Nope."

"What'd you think the move was for?" Harris asked, returning to the mass exodus.

"You mean to the Death Valley?"

"Death Valley? What's that?"

"That's the name we gave the camp we was marched to."

"How long did everyone stay in this Death Valley? 'Til the switch in August?"

"Don't know really. After about three weeks, I slipped out one night. Ran about twenty miles. Stayed close to shore."

"So you escaped?"

"Uh-huh, then got caught."

Harris seemed respectful of Montoya's moxie. "How long were you gone?"

"A week. Couldn't find no food so—look at me, I could pass for gook, right?" Montoya chuckled. "So, I got closer to the villages to get food and got caught."

"By whom?"

"NKs. Took me back to Camp 13. Put me in a hole. By then it was near August. One day a guard just let me out, out of the hole. Went to my old hut. What a fucking homecoming."

"Who was there?"

"Guy I called "Fartin' Arsen" and another guy. Can't remember names. Just the three of us now."

Montoya looked at the guard: he had his eyes shut. "*Ay, cabron! Es* too mucha work! Needa break!" He starting laughing and then coughing.

"Do you remember what he looked like?" asked Harris, annoyed with the banter.

"No, can't say."

"And, I take it you stayed till Big Switch?"

"Yeah, first came Little Switch in April, and we figured that the wounded would finally get home. A lot of guys left in bad shape. I had no idea if they was going to let the rest of us go."

"And you? When'd you leave Camp 13?"

"Late August, put us on trucks, drove us outside of Panmunjom."

"Did you see the guys from Death Valley?"

"Nope, not one, but then all the POWs weren't in Panmunjom at the same time."

"Did anyone question where they were?"

"No. No one knew where these other guys were, and... "

"When did you realize these guys didn't come back?"

"Wasn't till you and me talked and you told me you were looking for Girardin."

"You didn't try to find any of these guys after the war?"

Sounding a note of regret, Montoya explained, "Look man, we was young. When I got out in '53, was twenty-two." He looked down at his hands. "I came back here to New Mexico to get my life started. I was pretty fucked up. Drank, smoked everything I could get my lips on, weed, peyote. No, never tried to get in touch. Tried to forget, figured they did too."

Foster rose from his chair, took out a hanky, wiped the sweat off his face. Montoya cackled, "Hey, homie, make ya cry?"

Putting his hands on the table, Foster asked, "I'd like to ask a few questions."

"Fire away, Harry," encouraged the senior lawyer.

Foster looked at Montoya wryly. "Sir, tell me, the man you refer to as Roger, could his last name have been Garden or Jorden?"

"Well, hard to remember now."

"But, pardon me for asking, is your first language English or Mexican?'

"English."

"You have a very thick Mexican accent."

Montoya laughed. "No shit, college boy, we spoke Spanish when I was a kid."

"Well isn't it possible that what now you think is Girardin could have been Jorden, Garden, or even Gardin —like the flower without the "ya" at the end?"

"Or Geronimo?" Montoya giggled. "Maybe, could 'a been. I got it right."

"Can you spell it for me, I mean Roger's last name. The one you knew."

"I ain't no good a speller."

Foster insisted in a low, mocking voice, "Try."

"F-U-C--" laughed Montoya.

***

Back in Washington, Harris and Foster headed for the Pentagon to debrief John Russell. Sloppily dressed in a short sleeved white shirt and shiny red tie, Russell—all 5'5"—stood in his office doorway eyeing Harris through washed-out gray eyes. He breathed heavily through a globular ruddy nose, "Come in, have a seat." He moved behind his oak desk, flopped his wide ass on a soft chair. Behind him, Old Glory and the Army Flag drooped to the floor; to the right a picture of President Reagan looked past the men. He dispensed with small talk.

"Gentlemen, what'd you find in New Mexico?"

"Sir," Harris began, "There was a suggestion that Girardin was in Camp 13 and likely disappeared after some detail, sometime in the winter." He followed with his analysis of something more troubling—at least to Harris and Foster. "Mr. Secretary, if Montoya is telling the truth, there is a strong indication that a war crime was committed. We have more than one returning POW mentioning in the Panmunjom reports that the last time they saw so-and-so was June '53 and never returned. I'll bet we have counted a few hundred guys that went unaccounted for. This is over and above the guys that died throughout '51, and the ones we accounted for that likely died in Camp 13."

"Well, Harris, 'war crime' is pretty strong. Why, what those bastards did in not caring for the sick and wounded in that camp was a war crime. We lost maybe 3,000 men."

"I realize that, but it looks to me like a couple hundred men disappeared, most sent to a place called Death Valley. Disappeared off the face of the Earth."

"Yeah, and one of our officers may know more about this," Foster added. "May have been involved in the transfer of prisoners to this place."

37

Russell looked at Foster annoyed. "What are you saying, Counselor?"

"I'm saying that Montoya keeps bringing up some officer that spoke Chinese. Thought he was 'comfy with the Chinese' were his words. Closest I could trace it was to a lieutenant by the name of Hamilton."

Russell shot back, "For Christ's sake, get off that. Trent Hamilton is no more a collaborator than I am."

Shrugging his shoulders sheepishly, Foster replied, "Just telling you what I heard."

"Well knock it off, you hear, knock it off, that kind of talk isn't helpful."

Russell had a scowl on his face. "Gentlemen it looks to me like Montoya's recollection only leads to more speculation and *only a suggestion* Girardin was even in Camp 13."

"Yes, sir, that's about right," Harris added. "The guy seemed pretty flip about all this."

"How credible is he, anyway?"

"He's a convict," Harris said forcefully.

Russell looked at his overfed hands. "Yeah, yeah, suppose he wouldn't make the best witness."

Harris supported Russell's instincts, "No, sir, he could do damage if he continued to only have a vague recollection." The men fell silent, and Harris used the pause to make his departure.

But Russell had one last question. "What about this Montoya guy? Can the other side get to him?"

"Well our questioning will be protected; we don't have to turn it over."

"I mean, *can* they question him?"

"Sure, if they can find him."

"Well let's see what we all can do to make sure they can't," Russell said, in what Harris thought sounded an unmistakably sinister tone. The men were quiet. Then Russell asked, "Who is this Nick Castalano anyway? An ambulance chaser?"

"I've known him for some time. He used to work as a Veteran Affairs contract lawyer, handling their Agent Orange defenses. You know, the Vietnam vets would make a claim for disability based on Agent Orange, the VA'd deny them, and they'd send the cases to this guy if the vets appealed."

"What the hell would he take a case like this, if he's a defense lawyer—against veterans to boot?"

"The VA stopped sending him cases about a year ago because the vets started a class action suit, and they hired some big firm. He lost the work."

"Was he good? Did the VA win on his watch?"

"Yea, old Nick had no mercy. Won twenty-five out of twenty-five, as I can tell. He's no tree hugger."

"Can we make him a deal?"

"It's possible. Anything's possible."

Harris and Foster were halfway down the hall before when Russell yelled out, "Harris, come back here a minute. Not you Foster, just Harris."

"Sir?"

"Step in. This is for your ears only. For reason's I can't go into, we have a record indicating Girardin and another soldier were wanted by CID and the CIA. We need to be careful. Under no uncertain terms is any 'so-called' order to apprehend this man to come out."

Russell put up his hand to stall the questions he saw in Harris' expression. "That's all I'm permitted to say at this point. Let's just dispose of this case in the most efficient way possible."

Amber Waves of Grain
1983

ON THE MORNING OF JULY 28, 1983, Julie rose from a restless night in her brother's spare bedroom. Jack had already left the house—probably he was on his way to court to answer the subpoena. She phoned Jack's wife Anna to tell her what had transpired the night before, and they talked about whether Jack was on his medication and how they could get him back into the VA to see the psych doctor. They hung up without a plan. She then phoned the hospital where she worked as a nurse and called in sick before slipping into a plain white cotton outfit she'd found in the closet. She made no attempt to hide the puffy bags beneath her large, round eyes with makeup. Passing by the hallway mirror she adjusted a small-brimmed reddish hat she found in the closet and walked to the bus stop.

She saw Father Ryan—two dark olive eyes on each side of a pugilist's nose staring back. He patted the empty seat next to him. In his rough Irish brogue, he bid her good morning and returned his attention to his newspaper. But after a few stops, he folded it in his lap and started a conversation, one which Julie found hard to follow. It wasn't the first time the gray haired Jesuit looked into her lime-green eyes and mused about the unfathomable—this time how life flowed, sometimes fluctuating slowly, sometimes going "bang bang," outside our control.

"All things happen for a reason, Julie. Happenings are really signs."

"Father, I take things as they unfold, don't question much, maybe don't even see the signs." She fiddled with her hat, wondering if it smelled musty, like the bedroom where it had laid untouched for years.

The priest rolled the newspaper into a hollow tube, tapping it on his palm, putting it to his eye, and looking through it like a telescope.

"From the time you were a little girl at St. Pat's Grammar, you charted your own course."

She could not tell if he was teasing or serious. She clutched her purse and squeezed her knees tight to avoid touching him. Then she looked over and smiled without cracking her lips.   "I can't put no finer point on it than that, Father. Guess I learned early in life not to reach for the next moment when it wasn't time."

Julie looked out the window. "But I wonder, wonder if the Lord always gives us a sign. You know, that it's coming." She heard the buzzer signaling the driver to pull over at the next stop. The bus changed lanes and slowed down.

Ryan twisted the rolled up newspaper with both hands. "He always gives us a sign, Julie. Sometimes like a message inside a bottle bobbing its way to shore, and sometimes it comes like the ocean itself, pounding the rocks in the throes of a storm. We have to want to see the sign."

Julie rose grabbing the overhead strap as the bus crawled to her stop. She smiled at the priest, this time showing the fullness of her perfectly straight teeth. "You've made me self-conscious of the bus pulling on me while it slows."

"Yes," he said waving goodbye (or giving benediction? she wondered). "We go through life mostly unaware of what's happening to us, but if we have faith, we'll surely see the signs."

Julie gingerly stepped from the bus one foot at a time and walked to the courthouse, where the doors were still locked. She sat on a bench in a courtyard lined with zinnias and black-eyed Susans. It reminded her of a secret garden she'd once had. She pulled her diary from her purse and wrote:

Father Ryan thinks hidden forces move us through the simplest and most complex parts of life, birth canals, hospital beds, graves, purgatory and maybe hell. These are signs. Maybe today's bus takes me to the place where *those hidden forces connect the part of me left behind to the part of me that I see in the mirror every day.*

Julie waited until a Federal Marshal unlocked the outer glass doors. "Sir, can you tell me where the trials are held?" she asked. The Marshal lifted his thick arm and pointed down an empty hall. She walked down the wide granite corridor, her low heels making a sharp, tapping sound that echoed off the walls. She stopped at a brown cork bulletin board next to the clerk's office. And she gasped when she saw *his* name: *Roger Girardin versus the U.S. Army—Courtroom 6, 10:00 a.m.* She hadn't seen it typed out since she saw the notice from the Army in the Girardin family living room thirty-three years ago. It was eerie to see the name posted, impersonal, not like she saw it, written out in his handwriting on Christmas or birthday cards, on letters tucked into the shoe box she had kept in the back of her closet in a bed of silvery dust balls. In that same place, she kept her high school graduation pumps, next to the galoshes she wore to the beach the day she and Roger whispered goodbyes, the week after he unbuttoned her dress in a New Haven hotel, the same dress hanging over the collection of footwear.

Another Bite at the Apple

WITH NO EYEWITNESS TO GIRARDIN'S ULTIMATE disappearance, Nick had little choice but to reconstruct, through three or four witnesses, the events that took place from 1951 through 1953, in POW Camp 13. Together, he and Kathy were putting the final touches on the brief that would support Art's claim for damages while Mitch organized and copied the exhibits Nick would introduce into evidence. It was close to quitting time and Nick and Mitch were wrapping it up for the week, but Kathy, with her elbows planted on the desk opposite Nick, wasn't quite ready to leave.

"Nick, what's our approach anyway? How do you think you can overturn the Army Board's decision that Roger was MIA."

"Good question. We know that the Board has jurisdiction in these cases, but *no agency* can just wave their hand like some Omnipotent, and without the slightest attempt to carry out their Constitutional mandate— you know due process and all that— proclaim such and such without some legitimate basis."

"But they didn't Nick. Girardin petitioned, gave them what he had, the Army investigated and the Board decided that the record didn't support a finding that the man was a POW. Case closed. Sounds like he got his day in court."

"Yeah, but, if they'd called those witnesses in, if they'd heard them live, with Art there to exam, cross examine, create a *real* record for Christ's sake, and then said 'sorry Artie,' his goose'd be cooked. But they didn't, didn't give him the time of *day*, he didn't get to examine one single witness, treated him like he was some *crazy*. He's *got* to be given an opportunity to be heard, plain and simple."

Mitch stood up and stretched his arms. "Isn't the judge going to reach the same conclusion? He's bound, after all, only by the thin evidence the Board worked with. The

Board was the... the fact finder, and he's stuck with those facts. That's Agency Law 101. The witnesses, if they can still remember, won't say much more than what they told the interrogators at Panmunjom, thirty years ago, when it was fresh. How much better will it sound now, thirty years later?"

"Right, Mitch, but that's where this gets interesting. We're asking for a trial *de novo*, in other words we want the judge to assume the role not of an appeals court, which looks at only the facts developed below, but as a trial court, developing its own evidence. And the dilemma for the government and the beauty of all this is that for the judge to determine if the Board was arbitrary and capricious, he has to hear all the evidence we present, old and new. Now, if— and it's a big if— *if* he accepts the proposition that the evidence we bring to him *was available* to the Board, but they ignored it, in the process of this consideration, he'll have given us the trial *de novo* we're looking for."

Mitch sat back down. "So, we are claiming 'arbitrary and capricious' and we're allowed to prove it by presenting evidence the Board did not look at?"

"And if after the judge hears the 'new evidence' and decides, hopefully, the Board was unfair, then what? He'll remand it to the Board for further consideration?" asked Kathy.

Nick thought about what Kathy had said, because that also had occurred to him. "Maybe, but I doubt it. I think with all the evidence before him, he'll just rule on his own, and it's over."

"Unless the government wants to run this up to the Second Circuit," Mitch added.

"That's always a possibility," Nick conceded.

***

The morning of the trial Nick carried the boxes of evidence to his car, but before he even reached it the white, starched shirt his wife had pressed the evening before had gray sweat spots around his armpits and a wide wet line down the middle of his back. As he walked up the courthouse steps, Kathy materialized at his elbow, carrying a large leather trial brief case in one hand and a coffee in the other.

44

"Good morning, Nick. Ready?"

He snapped out of his daze and smiled, comforted that he wasn't walking into court all by himself. "Kathy, you surprised me. Yeah, I'm ready. Let's take no prisoners."

One of the two guards checking IDs at the entrance waved Nick and Kathy by, a courtesy extended to the attorneys he'd come to recognize by their black briefcases, pinstriped suits and swagger. Unlike Nick's other forays into this forum of nonphysical violence, today, dozens of people lined up along the hallway, calling to mind boxing fans with cheap tickets waiting for the main event. Marshal Picolillo, a man who in his younger days fought Joey Pepe to a draw in the Bridgeport Athenaeum, saw Nick struggling with his bags. He rushed to hold open the twelve-foot door that led to the ring where men fired off words in lieu of jabs, where round by round standings would advance on the blows of proffered evidence, where truth would battle the deception of grudges, and unsportsmanlike conduct.

"Morning, Marshal. The heat never keeps the gadflies away, does it?"

"That's right, Mr. Castalano, heard they drove in from New York and Boston."

Among the spectators were the national press and plainclothes functionaries from the army and the CIA. Most of those assembled had been sitting quietly for at least a half-hour before Nick's 9:30 a.m. arrival.

Castalano shouldered people aside with his leather bags as he moved to open the gate to the well. Huffing, he dropped his bags with a resounding thud next to Art Girardin. Art had already hung his sport jacket over the back of his chair and put his beefy freckled hand on the long, oak table in front of him. He was nervously leaning his chair back to reveal light spots at the knees of wrinkled pants, an un-starched white shirt with sleeves barely above his wrists, and a red-plaid, clip-on tie fixed to a tight collar around a bull neck.

"Mornin', Nick," Art said, looking away.

At a table of the exact dimensions, style and quality as Nick's, U.S. Attorney Bertram Harris rubbed his delicate, nearly see through hands. From a distance, Harris's

45

overweight mass looked off-balance, because his completely bald, smallish head seemed oddly attached to his large shoulders. Harris wore a three-piece pinstriped suit, complete with a chain strung from a buttonhole on his vest to a pocket watch he would lift from his trousers to check the time every fifteen minutes. In addition to Foster, the Pentagon had assigned another JAG Captain, Jeffery Townsend to help Harris. He wore Army dress greens to court. Nick walked over, hand extended.

"Bertram, I see you've got some help."

The lawyer ignored Nick's hand, "Nick. This is Captain Townsend and you know Foster." The two sandy-haired, crew-cut Germanic men did not budge, but almost on cue, they pursed their lips.

"You guys gonna appear before the court?"

"No, these men are just assisting."

Harris did not tell Nick that in executing their official duties, the captains, helpers or lawyers would report to Russell at the Pentagon several times a day. In turn, Russell would report to an interested constituent, one who would take the matter under careful consideration.

Walking back to his table, Nick nodded to Amy Dusseldorf, a reporter with the *Bridgeport Post,* who sat in the open jury box— since a judge, not a jury, would be hearing the case. She proudly sported the crabby newsroom scowl that comes with working a deadline until the wee hours of the morning. For weeks leading up to the trial, she'd fed information to veterans organizations interested in MIA/POW issues who in turn fueled national interest in the first-ever POW-MIA trial. Today, plain white blouse, gray knotted hair, she disappeared between two television reporters. Sitting at the far end of Amy's row were media artists from three national TV networks.

"Hear ye, hear ye, in the U.S. District Court for the District of Connecticut, the Honorable Joseph Lindquist presiding."

"All rise."

The echo from the marshal hadn't died down before Federal Judge Lindquist entered from a door behind the bench. At sixty-two, he had grown into a large, robust (his doctor would say overweight) body. His longish white hair accentuated his naturally tanned skin, giving him the appearance of a royal Spanish magistrate, but one that clipped his words like a Vermont Yankee and hinted at French Canadian when he let his guard down.

The raised platform and black robes gave Lindquist a larger-than-life appearance. Nevertheless, the first impression of those who stood before his Eminence was that of a wizard with a disdain for toadying lawyers. He surveyed the place where the polity obeyed his rules and paid rapt attention to what he said, how he said it, and where he fixed his flinty eyes. A place where, without pity or passion, men were vindicated or punished according to the law and the predilections of the man who appeared to see, hear and, eventually, came to know all. His eyes fell on Nick for several seconds.

Lindquist sat down and addressed the occupants as if he were master of ceremonies. "Ladies and gentlemen, air conditioning does not seem to be workin' today, so occasionally I may ask the marshal t'open the doors in the rear of the courtroom. His gaze fell on Nick a second time. Nick folded his lips between his teeth and pulled his cuffs out from his jacket sleeves. Sweat poured down his chest, further sweat soaking the shirt that hadn't dried from the walk to the courthouse.

"Counsel, are you ready?"

The judge already knew the contours of the case, so the attorneys did not need to make opening statements. Lindquist wanted to see how Nick would prove his bizarre claim that Roger hadn't been MIA, but the victim of a stubborn Army bureaucracy that refused to acknowledge him as a POW. And that he might still be alive after thirty years.

Nick picked up a pad from the table and fumbled with it. "Yes, your Honor."

"Call your first witness!" Lindquist bellowed.

Art Girardin lumbered to the witness stand tugging on his lapels. He turned toward the assembly of busybodies that waited to be entertained by the telling of tragic events. The clerk shuffled over to Art and completed the first of many steps in the ritual of testifying, asking him in a high voice to swear to tell the truth. Art nodded, "Yes sir, I do."

Nick, standing behind a blonde oak lectern threw down a cache of notes and pushed his fingers through his longish, brown hair.

"Mr. Girardin, may I call you Art?"

Art ran his tongue over his lips. "Yes, sir."

"Art, this case is about your brother, Roger Girardin, a soldier who fought during the Korean War, correct?"

The witness put his hand to his mouth and turned in the direction of Lindquist, "Yes, sir."

"Tell us about your brother."

Art remembered the last time he had spoken to Roger: it was his eighteenth birthday and he had called from boot camp. The boys were four years apart, but they were always close. Art was in the kitchen, standing anxiously by until his mother handed him the phone. The subject of the brook behind the house overflowing came up, and Roger recalled spending summers as a kid on Lake Memphremagog, Vermont, where they had caught pollywogs. These were parts of the conversation Art would spare the court. Instead, Art gave the court a brief history of Roger's boyhood, where he went to school and where he worked before being drafted. He testified to the letters his family had received before he shipped out to Japan and the last letter sometime in mid-September 1950, with the address, *APO, Pusan, Republic of Korea.*

Walking in Art's direction, Nick said, "Art, I asked you to bring the correspondence your parents received from the Army."

"Yes, sir." Art reached down to pick up a folder.

"Let me have them, please."

Art removed the two letters his parents received from the Army, wrinkled and marred, a white shock of hair falling to the floor. Art resisted the urge to pick it up.

"These were the notices my parents got that Roger wasn't coming back. I promised my Dad... I wouldn't stop looking."

Art testified to the unexpected finding of a Congressional Resolution in the U.S. Archives, where Roger's name appeared along with hundreds of men that were unaccounted for, but had been listed as POWs, and how Congress never again considered the subject of Korean

KIAs, MIAs, POWs. He told how he'd contacted the men mentioned in U.S. Army Intelligence reports from Panmunjom, North Korea, in 1953 and those named in reports the International Red Cross recorded after visiting POW camps.

When Nick completed his examination, Harris stood up to say he had no questions. The judge looked in Art's direction, "Sir, you're free to go."

Art lifted himself from the witness stand feeling worn. For six years he had shoveled the past into banker's boxes labeled A through Z, had spoken to scores of people from veterans to senators, lawyers to archivists, privates to generals, and it had all come down to two short hours, a hundred plus spectators, a cabal of government lawyers and a judge who, from what Art could sense, was skeptical of a man dragging in skeletons and relics from halfway around the world.

The clock on the wall ticked past 11:50. Lindquist looked at the crowd, "Let's take a five minute recess."

The marshal cried out, "All rise."

***

At the precise moment when both hands on the clock pointed to twelve, Lindquist, for the second time, addressed the occupants, "Ladies and gentlemen, air conditioning still not working. I've asked the marshal t'open the rear doors. Counsel, you ready?"

"Yes, your Honor," Nick said rising from his chair. "Your Honor, if you recall six weeks ago, you handed down your ruling that, with considerable redactions for national security reasons, the Broadbent report was to be turned over to us by the government. The report, dated April 24, 1953, summarized the interrogations of several individuals who in one way or another mentioned the name Roger Girardin. Only after receiving the report did we speak by telephone to David Bradshaw and Harry Sheer, two men we plan to call as witnesses, and until two weeks ago were not included in our witness list. We ask the court to grant us leave to proceed with these witnesses."

"Proceed, Counsel, I am aware of the late production of the document."

"Your Honor, I call Mr. Harry Sheer to the stand."

From the box unoccupied by a jury, Ed Armstead, the newscaster from CBS, watched a man in the second row of benches make his way to the aisle. While the man shuffled along, Armstead whispered to the fellow next to him, "About six feet two." The man, a CBS sketch artist who earned his living capturing faces, drew the outline of a countenance creased and drawn. He started to draw, a thin face, aquiline nose, fair hair parted to one side, and as he immersed himself in his work, he felt that his subject had spent considerable time in the unforgiving outdoors.

Had either man known Harry Sheer, they would have known that he lived alone on a farm in South Dakota, where on a typical summer day a searing sun could hastily disappear behind thunderheads that would heartlessly dump tons of wheat-flattening hail, or where in winter, winds blew snow horizontally— plunging temperatures into dead zones where the molecules that energized life forces slowed, thickened, and crystallized. And, along the latitudes and longitudes of this meteorological tempestuousness, his farm sat at the end of a rutted road, where every morning for the past thirty-odd years— save the years in Korea— Harry would put on a pot of coffee at four, milk his cows by five and by six head out to the fields. Yesterday, Harry had milked the cows and returned to the farmhouse and then did something he had never done before. He'd dressed in his holiday suit, drove his '65 Ford pickup fifty miles over dirt roads to Valentine, Nebraska, and boarded a plane to Connecticut.

His scuffed cowboy boots now tapped against the oak floor, echoing off the twenty-foot walls enclosing the forum. Armstead turned to the artist and muttered, "A rancher or a farmer."

Sheer met the clerk at the witness stand.

"Sir, please raise your right hand." Sheer turned away from the lanky clerk and raised a thick, calloused hand toward the flag behind the bench, where he gave his present address and swore to tell the truth, the whole truth, and nothing but the truth.

"Mr. Sheer, you're a veteran of the Korean War, are you not?"

Harry lifted his head, "Yes, sir."

50

"Mr. Sheer, as I explained when we spoke by phone, we're trying to determine the last location of Private Roger Girardin, a soldier listed as MIA during the Korean War. Did you know Private Girardin?"

"Yes, sir."

"You learned that his brother Art was searching for the whereabouts of Private Roger Girardin, isn't that true?"

"Yes, I would say almost a year and a half, maybe even two years ago."

"Let's say about two years ago. Did he call you?"

"Yes, he'd called me. Asked me straight out."

"Alright. Did he tell you where he got your name?"

"No, told me his name, that his brother was lost in the Korean War. Asked if I knowed him."

"Did he say right off, 'Did you know Roger Girardin?'"

"When I heard him say he was Art Girardin, the name Roger popped into my head. He hadn't mentioned the name 'Roger.' It was me saying 'I think I knew a Roger,' or 'I knew a Roger Girardin.'"

"You're absolutely sure of that? That he didn't say, 'Did you know Roger Girardin?'"

"No, he asked me if I knowed his brother. I'm the one who came up with the name 'Roger.' Tell you the truth, didn't know how I remembered that."

"Had you thought about it since you first talked with Art Girardin?"

"Yes, sir, I have."

"Please tell us what you later thought about that made that response likely?"

"I figure I remembered because I'd gotten orders from the Company Commander that the soldier was to get down to regimental headquarters in the morning, ASAP."

"Any idea why they wanted Roger?"

"Nope, no idea."

"Well, did he go to the regiment at that time?"

"No, it didn't happen."

"Why not?"

"We got nailed that night."

"Would you tell us what happened? Why didn't Girardin report to headquarters?"

As Sheer started to answer, the hundred odd spectators stopped shuffling and leaned forward. Amy Dusseldorf adjusted her glasses and muscled her way free from the bodies on either side of her to sit on the edge of her seat.

"Well, was November '50, a few days after Thanksgiving. I was a Second Louie in charge of a squad in Company C, 19th Regiment, 24th Division, on recon patrol outside of Usan along the Ch'ongch'on River. We were retreating south, tryin' to see if the way in fron' of us was clear. Orders were to follow the river southeasterly and destroy any enemy we encountered. But we were more interested in runnin' from the Chinese coming at us heavy from the north. Lots of us lacked seasonin'. Heck, I only had a couple of months in; I wasn't lookin' for a fight.

"You see we moved through the ravines and through the woods stayin' clear of paddies. During the day we hid in irrigation ditches. So the night before Girardin was to find his way back to regiment, a message came down the line from our point man. It must have been two in the morning. Point man walked ahead of us so we didn't bump into the enemy, you know, by chance. He'd spotted NKs or Chinese about 800 meters in fron' of us. Maybe they were headed to eventually outflank us. Didn't know."

Head down, Nick silently read from a letter Sheer had sent him detailing the events. A few coughs came from the crowd. The clock ticked loudly, filling in the auditory gap. He laid the letter on the lectern. The big hand swept past 12:45.

"Did you plan to engage?"

"The short answer's yes. We were pretty banged up since the day after Thanksgiving. Already winter. Low teens. Guys had the runs. You forget what stink means."

"What happened?"

"Master Sergeant Horowitz, the top non-commissioned officer in the company; fought in France and Belgium. We called him Arrow— you know, putting his first name Aaron and his last name together. Told us we had to figure where we'd set an ambush."

"And, then what?"

"He got a squad together and told'em to go out half-mile and find out what direction they're heading. How many."

At that moment, Harris interjected. "Your Honor, may we have a five minute break? I need to attend to something."

"Mr. Harris, if you plan on interrupting, we'll never get through this case. But very well, let's break for lunch."

As Harris bolted from the courtroom, Nick walked back to counsel's table where Mitch had returned after preparing a subpoena for Jack O'Conner, aka Prado. Nick vented in Mitch's direction. "Let's hope Harris doesn't end up directing this show."

"What happened?" Mitch asked.

"Too much to get into right now. Did you get the subpoena drafted?"

"Here it is."

"Get the clerk to sign it and tell Sophie to find a process server to serve Prado, or O'Conner or whatever the hell his name is today."

***

The ex-pugilist marshal stood in the front of the bench and hollered, "All rise, court is back in session."

Harry Sheer recalled the night that he had replayed over and over during his three years in a POW camp, every move he made, the faces of the lost, the mistakes, and the remorse that followed that night the men huddled on their haunches, hands under armpits, waiting for the squad that was reconnoitering the enemy's position to return. He spoke of how he had checked his green fluorescent watch, but not that he had wiped off the ice that clung to his honey colored mustache with his leather glove. He said there was a clear moon and light smoke wafting in from the forest fires, but not how badly he had tried to ignore the shakes that had taken over his legs, or that the saliva on his tongue had thickened and made it hard to swallow. He told them how Arrow's long, frost-bitten face seemed fixated on the few stars that twinkled through a clearing in the trees, but not that his hearing became sharper as his hands and feet grew colder.

Nick walked to the podium waving his pad. "Mr. Sheer, you'd dispatched a squad to determine what path the enemy was on. Did the squad get the information you needed to mount an attack?"

53

"Girardin and Velez returned and told us thirty or forty NKs were traveling west, diagonal towards us. Figured we might catch 'em if we headed on an opposite diagonal. Told my radioman to send out our terminal position to HQ, start Medivac. Wanted it timed so that shortly after we opened fire, the copters would be in earshot."

Harry began to shake as he replayed the plan that he had concocted based on a faulty report that there was just *one* enemy unit converging. Working on a farm had taught him how nature took over in situations where fear takes hold. Lots of things were outside his control that night, like the stiff, frozen grass that resisted movement; the night shadows that magnified and camouflaged his band of grunts beneath rising smoke and a moonless sky. As the troops advanced, the line tightened, compensating for the insecurity the men felt. Jones remained nearly fifty meters in front, backed by Richey Pittmen— the second oldest vet in the squad. The lieutenant's position was fifteen yards out front. Arrow took center stage to keep the line ruler-straight. The column advanced as one and what happened to one happened to all, but every man would remain alone in his own skin, the place where he packed his fears, his weaknesses, obsessed in the mantra "safety off, ready, lock and load."

Boots fought against taut grass, the narrow path and dark spaces. The men moved elegantly, intent, a relentless prowl to meet— one hundred meters to the right— a serpentine line of figures as fearless and as fearful, each pursuer slithering and slicing through the same murky smoke, rising into the same dark sky. Multiple military columns traveling without knowing the precise flash of contact, the vertex, the point where life and death would join. They closed ranks to meet the convergence, seconds away. God had no stake in this — He informed men on all sides to freeze. One bolted from the line like a pulling lineman. Others, spooked, scattered like darkened roman candles launched in random directions.

"You met the enemy, Mr. Sheer?"

Snapping back into the present, Harry spoke into the cavernous silence. "I heard shots coming from the other side."

Nick watched Harry's eyes. They leveled somewhere beyond the spectators. In a flicker, lasting tenths of seconds, Harry added, "Piercing whistles, bugles... a huge force... Chinese Reds."

Then like that night when the saliva thickened, the words in Harry's throat stuck, words to describe the enemy officer running at right angles, away from the charge, following the impulse to escape death. Another pop and a . 30 caliber slug tunneled deep into the man's shoulder. He staggered, his limb flopping aimlessly. His band lost all semblance of order, scattering randomly, some hitting the ground. The officer wobbled toward the wooded blackness that crumbled under the mass of retreating mortality. Hector, a seventeen year old L.A. Pachuco who carried a picture of himself dressed in a zoot suit jitterbugging, tumbled forward, neck twisting, his heavy frame hurrying his descent into the frozen ground. Slow-motion-like he fell and lifted like a half empty flour sack before resting. Behind him, the enemy appeared; apparitions out of a smoky miasma.

Following the deafening carbine chatter, Harry ran toward the right of the line where the action boiled. Enemy reinforcements populated front, rear, and center. Corporal Franklin first trailing him, flew passed him. He fired without direction, shooting Franklin in the back, but before hitting the ground, the man's face caught shrapnel and unwrapped from its skeleton underpinning. Blood, bone, gristle, a man with no face, the horror of twenty-five, fifty, a hundred or more Chinese charging across the paddy.

Reports from a machine gun syncopated whatever empty intervals weren't filled by small arms fire and bugles; men appeared and disappeared like cascading dreams, darkly magical, deadly real. Two grenades exploded within tenths of seconds, and Harry felt warm blood flowing over his cold pubic bone, down his left inner thigh. He ignored the sensation, turning toward a silhouetted mortar opening up on the left. Arrow's booming charge ordered the men to retreat into the dense woods, a Tommy gun droned on in the roaring chatter, until the Browning automatic rifle opened up, stuttering, spraying staccato-like over the full terrain, crisscrossing back and forth, pounding out the rhythm of a tom-tom played to a frantic crowd of beboppers. The sky sizzled with yellows and reds from the ever widening mountain fires. Dillard, a guy who nobody had believed when he had claimed to be an Olympic athlete, ran by like a gazelle for no apparent reason, except to maybe knock out the mortar single handed. He folded, doubling over, hitting ground face first, tumbling, coming to rest, peaceful, imagining starry constellations over Lookout Mountain, just outside of Cheyenne. In the next instant, he closed his eyes to the stars and the ghoulish condensing cloud that emanated from the entrails exposed to the cold black air.

"Mr. Sheer are you okay, sir?" Lindquist asked.

Sheer stared beyond the well, to the open rear doors of the courtroom, standing room only, war voyeurs, vacant eyes staring back, heads upon necks stretched forward, suspended in poses of expectancy, one-hundred-fifty pairs of eyes, blue, gray, brown, rained in on him. Eyes empty of the terror few men know, full of the starry visions of bloodthirsty citizens and generals, men in black suits who wallow in the glory of battle.

"Mr. Sheer are you all right?" Lindquist asked again.

"Yes, sir, guess the trip made me tired. Lost my concentration."

Harry remained quiet. The courtroom remained still. The afternoon sun shone through the windows, casting a beam of light in the center of the well. Four to five seconds ticked off the clock above the jury box. Lindquist uncharacteristically cut in, "Mr. Sheer, is there more you would like to tell us?"

Sheer's eyes opened wide. "What's that?"

"Is there more you'd like to say?"

"Yeah, we were scattered to the four corners. Some in the ravines."

"Is there more, sir?"

"Yes. Marched my men into a situation, that I not been... had I not — ."

Lindquist motioned to the clerk, "Let's take five minutes."

***

When Lindquist again assumed the bench Harry continued where he had left off— as if he started a tape recorder that had been paused. "Somehow, I got separated. Then the lights went out. No idea where I was or what happened; hands were tied, pants were like cardboard, stiff frozen blood, crotch was numb. I was later told... "

Harris jumped up. "Objection. The witness is about to offer hearsay testimony."

"I will allow it. Proceed, Mr. Sheer."

"They told me copters came, scooped up the wounded. Two days later, the copters returned, bagged the dead... like cakes of ice. That night, I guess the Chinese were pullin' us out of cricks, puttin' us in groups, marchin' us in circles, movin' us all night. You could see the men against the snow, so travelin' in the daytime was dangerous. At daybreak, they'd put us in another ravine, kept us there all day."

"You reached a permanent destination, correct?" Nick asked.

"Yeah, came upon this camp, looked like a little city."

"Did they tell you what camp you were in?"

"No, sir."

"Did you ever see Roger Girardin after that?"

"No, sir."

"It is possible he was captured like you, right?"

Harris jumped up again. "Objection. Speculation."

"Sustained."

"Mr. Sheer when you were repatriated in August 1953, is it not true that you discovered you'd been listed MIA?"

"Yes, that's right. My parents did not know I was a POW, even though it seemed I was on a Red Cross list."

Nick turned and read the judge's unusually weary face. "Your Honor, no further questions for Mr. Sheer."

Lindquist rubbed a lump on his neck. "Mr. Harris proceed."

Harris stood up to cross-examine. "Mr. Sheer you never laid eyes on Girardin again, did you?"

"No sir," responded Sheer emphatically.

"It is your testimony, sir, that you never spoke to anyone who saw Roger Girardin after that skirmish?"

"Yes, sir."

"Tell me, sir, did you speak with the plaintiff's Counsel before you testified here today?"

"Yeah," he said, feeling that somehow he'd violated the law.

"Isn't it true that Mr. Castalano discussed how you were going to testify, what you'd remember, how'd you say it?"

"Yes, for about an hour."

"Isn't true that your speaking with Mr. Castalano is the reason you can so vividly recall what happened thirty years ago?"

Someone in the crowd groaned. Lindquist instantly raised his head. The crowd drew back, warned.

"No, sir!"

"No further questions," Harris sneered, turning from the lectern.

Lindquist adjusted his glasses and looked at Nick.

"No follow up, your Honor."

The judge turned to Sheer. "Sir, thank you, you are free t' go."

When Sheer was halfway across the well, Nick rose from his chair. "Your Honor, I'd like to call my next witness."

Lindquist rubbed his cheek, the corner of his nostril, checked the clock on the wall above the jury box. "Counsel, we have several motions scheduled, so let's adjourn for the day. Marshal, see what they're doing to fix the air conditioning!"

***

That night, Julie could not sleep. Two floor fans droned on, sweeping side-to-side across a thick layer of humid air. Tractor trailers fell noisily into potholes half-mile away, the couple on the fourth floor fought over infidelity, the cats scratched the already badly shredded chair in the corner. She tossed in bed, soaked from stifling heat and the adrenaline that shot through her every time she imagined Roger dead and bagged like the cakes of ice Sheer described. The images now came to her in flashes and flickers like a frightful black and white movie playing to an insomniac who lives in profound solitude, obsessing over where it all began.

Cold Workings
1940s

MARY, CHARLIE AND THEIR TWO KIDS— Jack and Julie— lived in a three room, cold-water flat with a community toilet from 1931— right after Julie was born— to the beginning of World War II, when overtime helped them move to a five room cottage with hot water. When war broke out, Charlie had been working at a lipstick factory that seamlessly converted lipstick cases into brass cannon shells. Scrawled on the mirror in the women's toilet in Max Factor Red was "make war, not love," but for these warriors— "essential to the war effort"— the monotonous hum and occasional clang on the factory floor were the only war sounds they would ever hear.

When the war started, the company Mary worked for converted bedsprings into barbed wire. She felt she did important work during the national emergency, and though it was not necessarily recognized by others, it was important to her. Six days a week, precisely two minutes after the 6 a.m. whistle, she would flick a switch to send electricity into the controls of an extrusion device and pull a lever transferring molten steel into a die that formed filaments. After waiting thirty seconds she would press her foot on a pedal to engage a five fingered, claw-like device that pulled, coiled and cut the steel into a long thin wire. The barbs were added later. If the machine jammed, she would gingerly push on one part or another to dislodge it from its fellow rotating members and concentrate on not entangling her fingers—certain amputation. By the time the war ended, she had aged two years for every one — but she, at least, had all her fingers.

After the first few years of marriage most people learn the mechanics of a fair swing: occasionally striking out, occasionally getting on base. But Mary and Charlie would never see the ball coming or see it too late and swing to exhaustion. In place of managing life's changing pitches, they became neurotics waiting for a catastrophe— the next inevitable, life-altering event. In anticipating the next bad thing, they sensed the slightest curve and overplayed it, flailing until the no-win, no-way-out inning passed. And these eccentricities, as if caused by genetic defect, would eventually afflict Jack and Julie.

Charlie had a gloom and doom about himself. He felt powerless and drank too much on payday, which probably conditioned his paranoia and extreme jealously. He was also quick with the rod, especially when it came to Jack. Sometimes several nights in succession, for infractions major and minor, Charlie would charge into Jack's room, strap in hand. Jack would clasp his hands around the back of his head and tuck his knees into his chest. Crack across the skull! A right arm moved forward. He would shut his eyes. Head slammed to the right. He'd open his eyes. Crack! A fist would come from the left and he would close his eyes, sometimes traveling to a different world, one where the pounding was only a distant thunder. A hail of assaults would rain down until Charlie no longer felt powerless and Jack again heard the sound of his own voice mumbling numbers— adding, dividing, multiplying, and questioning the odd results.

Jack did not intellectualize how he survived in an asylum that periodically went haywire. Years later, a VA-appointed psychiatrist told him that he stored the aftereffects of Charlie's brutality in damaged dendrites and synapses— crippling his psyche by leaving him unable to speak his mind and by ingratiating himself to overcompensate for feelings of worthlessness. Well into adulthood, when the world sometimes caved in on Jack, he would curl himself in a fetal position, take quick, short breaths, blink rapidly and count backward—replaying that stroboscopic view of reality that got him through those long moments of suffering.

Farewell, My Plebe
1945–1950

MARY LOOKED TO THE LORD TO MAKE HER son strong and her husband sober. In Charlie's case she would have settled for tolerable, within the margin that close friends and relatives will allow closet drunks. She worked hard on both accounts until Charlie left Jack with a black eye. She took one look at his shiner and declared, "The Lord leads us through signs that can't be ignored." When the war ended in 1945, she quit trying to fix Charlie's problem and moved in with her parents on Willa Street, two miles across town but nearer the schools were Julie and Jack attended.

The month after she left Charlie, she quit the factory and put her hands to work at Hilltop Hospital. Her first assignment was the polio ward— kids in iron lungs. She emptied bedpans, salved bedsores, helped the miserably sick in a factory town whose thrift paid for no more than one nurse per hundred patients. Jack felt that the "fat cats," as his grandfather called them, took advantage of his mother's empathy. And he worried she would get sick if she worked long enough in the polio ward. She told Jack, "I'd rather die in the fever than crushed in the gears of one of those presses." Jack knew there weren't any good options for his mother, but his own salvation could come if he could find another world.

Jack enrolled at Ridley University, a state-run school, where he signed up for ROTC and the promise of joining the Army Reserves as a second lieutenant at graduation. Mary wanted this, but Charlie felt differently. He told Mary, "Kid's tryin' to prove he's smarter than me. Well he ain't. Never gonna be." When Jack asked his Mom why Charlie was cool when he got the acceptance letter, she told him that his Dad didn't want him to get too big for his britches. His reply was, "Mom, all I ever want is for people to say, 'There goes Jack O'Conner. He's no freeloader; he's no draft dodger.'" Jack's deeper drive, one he would not admit, was conquering the fear that he could not stand up to guys like Charlie— the ones who had made it hard for him to speak his mind.

***

For one month during the summer, ROTC students went off to Camp Davis to join hundreds of budding officers from dozens of colleges throughout the northeast. At the end of freshmen year, arriving the same day— Jack O'Conner by bus, Trent Hamilton by car—, the two ended up among eighty other plebes in the same barracks, and, although they had never met, Jack recognized Trent from the football team. Walking into the mess hall that night, the two boys talked and discovered that they were from adjoining towns. In parting, Trent hollered back in an unexpected flash of solidarity, "Ridley guys stick together."

Two regular army drill instructors ran the unit, and the custom was to assign an upperclassman as a barracks chief, who with help from four underclassmen squad leaders, took charge in their absence. The DIs appointed Donny O. Greun, a twenty-two-year old, 5'5", thick runt with a long, crooked nose and chipped teeth. "I don't respond to no Donny, Greun, or Sir... you guys call me Dog," he snarled.

Dog took charge at night, putting the troops to bed by 9:30. The recruits were into their second week when a cabal of Dog and his four squad leaders began holding kangaroo court after lights out. Each night at ten, in a windowless room next to the latrine, Dog, wearing creased fatigues and spit shined boots, sat feet up on a wide oak desk, barking orders to his squad leaders. "Hamilton, get Grabowski. Let's see what he knows about Article 15."

"Yes, sir!"

Hamilton went to the end of the barracks where Grabowski bunked above Jack. He whispered in his ear. "Wake up, Grabowski. Dog wants you... pronto."

Grabowski sat straight up. "What? What's goin' on?"

"Dog wants to see you... now."

"'Bout what?"

63

Jack opened his eyes. "What's up?"

"None of your business, Mister. Go back to sleep. Come on, Grabowski, let's not keep 'im waiting."

Three minutes later, the tall, lanky, milk-white kid from New Jersey, stood in skivvies and a tee shirt before Dog and shivered.

"Grabowski, what's a summary court martial?"

"A way of givin' out punishment for small stuff. A conviction that doesn't put ya in the brig... . Sir!"

"Good, dismissed," Dog snapped.

After a week of holding court, Dog began probing the soldiers' sense of respect. Dog turned to Lowell, a tall, quiet, undernourished kid with pinkish skin. "Bring in O'Conner."

Following Lowell, Jack stopped at the threshold separating Dog's quarters from the large bays. He knocked once on the open door and waited.

"I can't hear you," Dog clamored in a commanding voice. "I can't hear you!"

Jack knocked harder.

Dog raised his voice to match the sound of the knock. "Still can't hear you!"

Jack pounded with the side of his fist, cracking the wooden panel. Remaining resolute, eyes forward, Trent appeared impassive. Four rounds of pounding later, light burst through the fractured door.

"Enter, soldier," Dog barked angrily.

Jack stepped over the threshold, blood dripping from his hand.

"Trent," ordered Dog, "get a goddamn towel. He's gettin' blood all over the floor."

Flushed, Trent pitched a towel in Jack's direction, and said, "Hey, man, I've had enough of this bullshit. Dig?"

Leaping to his feet, Dog peered up at the 6'4" recruit, howling, "You ain't with us, you're against us. So fuck off, *comprendo!*"

With his head, Trent motioned to Jack. "Come on, man."

Dog hadn't finished. "Stay where you are, soldier. And you, big guy, get the hell out of here, now."

Trent stopped. Jack stood in front of Dog blinking rapidly. "O'Conner, polish my boots," Dog ordered.-

Jack wanted to tell him to screw himself, but could not get the words out. Dog jumped from his chair.

"Polish my fucking boots," he roared.

Jack crouched as if to obey, but instead drew back his left hand and punched Dog's soft belly. Dog's fist dropped onto the back of his neck. Stunned, Jack fell to one knee before shaking off the blow. Dog backed up. He reached for the polished hickory stick he used when he walked around the barracks. Trent threw himself between the two as Dog sliced the air. Missing Jack, the stick grazed Trent's head, forcing him into the wall. Later, one guy said, "Felt like the barracks was shelled." The other squad leaders joined the fray, subduing Dog. Jack applied the bloody towel to Trent's head.

Trent went to the infirmary for stitches. Forty-eight hours later, Jack and Trent were cleared of any wrongdoing, and Dog lost his job as barracks chief. One night over beer, Trent told Jack, "The brass knew what was going on. They wanted it that way; we did their dirty work."

"Dog should've been booted out," Jack said hardheartedly.

"Nah, the big deal was he got caught."

"I suppose that's why there's boot camp— to get us into a frame of mind. How red-blooded American boys learn to kill... I suppose."

Following the fracas, the boys bunked together until camp ended, and when school started, they told war stories about the night court and how it ended in a minor mutiny. What was left unsaid was that the incident joined the boys— about to turn men— into a brotherhood. The kind against which scripture admonishes: because brotherhoods bonded in blood can unravel through births, deaths, jealousy, and shame, and in this case, the added brutalities of a war half-way around the globe.

***

Mary's high pitched voice echoed in the upstairs hallway. "Jack, Jack!" It grew louder and more insistent. "Jack, where are you?"

65

"Yeah, what?"

"Aren't you supposed to be leaving? You're gonna be late." After a few seconds, she added, "Don't forget to stop by Berell's and pick up Tracy's corsage. She closes at 8:30."

Jack admired himself in the mirror, combing his hair straight back and rubbing his hand over his cheek. Tracy hated coarse five o'clock shadows like the one he had inherited from his grandfather Libero Prado. But, even a heavy black brown beard did not change the fact that at twenty-two he could pass for eighteen. Maybe it was the cowlick that he could not hide despite a thick dab of Brylcreem.

Julie saw Jack coming down the stairs.

"Well, man," she said, "you look pretty swanky, hair straight back. Look almost twenty!" She pressed her finger into his cowlick. "A little greasy, Jack?"

He would not be seeing Julie for the months he would be on active duty, so Jack let his eyes sweep over her. She was becoming a young woman.

"So, Tracy's folks are having a send off for you and Trent — you look a little nervous."

"Me? Nervous? Not me. But, I wish you'd come."

Jack remembered how much they depended on each other as kids to get through the nights Charlie went half crazy. Besides his mother, Julie was the most important woman in his life.

"Well, let me see that O'Conner grin," Julie said, wanting to savor it before Jack pushed off for the Army.

"How's this?" Jack raised the corners of his mouth.

"Oh, Jack, stop, that makes you look scary. I don't think I'm gonna see ya in the morning. I'm gone by 6 to New Haven."

"How come so early?"

"I have a recital in two weeks at the Klein Memorial— first violin. They have me practicing double sessions. If I don't see ya, stay safe, brother."

"No sweat, Julie, I'll be home in no time. Take care of things while I'm gone." He looked in the hall mirror and resmoothed his hair. "Have you heard from your boy Roger?"

"Of course. Writes me twice a week. A real writer, he is. He thinks he's shipping out to Japan."

The idea of the Orient passed through Jack's mind. "Boy, lucky guy, I wish I could go over there, they say... " He stopped, thinking his sister might not take kindly to what he was about to say.

Instead, Jack put his hands on Julie's shoulder and looked her in the eye. "Love you, Sis." He pushed her long brown hair aside, brought her close, breathing in her washed hair. The two hugged for a few seconds, something they hadn't done since their mother had left Charlie.

"You take care," he said in a spirited tone, as he opened the screen door to the porch.

"Goodbye, Mom!" he yelled. Then added, "Can I drop you off at church?"

"No, I'll walk, it's a short service. I don't know if I'll stay. Have a good time, an' come home safe and early... . Wait!"

Mary ran from the kitchen.

"You're not a little boy anymore," her voice cracked. Jack, self-conscious, shrugged and smiled. "And by the way, since you'll be the handsomest guy at that party... don't let that go to your head!"

"I won't." He grinned, feeling awkward.

"And, make sure you stand up straight, 'look 'em in the eye,' like your grandfather says."

They hugged, and Jack felt her gently resist when he tried to let go. As he walked away, Mary's eyes sparkled. She shook her head, suddenly feeling melancholy.

"Jack, be careful."

Driving Mary's black '37 Ford up Route 11, he thought how it would feel to be free, no longer having to answer to his parents or some prof' chasing him down for overdue assignments, yokes lifted by the Army, finally feeling like a grown up, like someone who could make his own way, his own decisions. Deep in thought, he drove past *Berell's Flower Shop*.

Hamilton's main house sat three-quarters from the top of the highest of three hills that formed a semicircle around the colonial village of Fairview. At night, from the mansion's second floor balcony, Bridgeport appeared as a sulphurous stain between the topographic vacancies of black lumps. In daylight, it lay hidden behind a forest of hardwoods that blended into the far off leaden waters of Long Island Sound, a geography and environment separated by class and economics: someone who had never ventured beyond Fairview could understandably be apathetic to the existence of its industrial neighbor to the south.

Quarter, Sift and Lay Asunder

TRENT DANA HAMILTON, AN AMALGAM OF grandfathers Hamilton and Dana, believed he could have things his way. At Chalmers, ten miles north of Fairview, Anglicans taught him Protestant conceit and a clear separation between those with whom he shared a similar providence and those who served his ambitions. For all the pedagogical advantages bestowed, he recorded no notable academic achievements, but racked up a record related to "comportment" for bullying, a behavior his father chose not to discourage since he saw it as constructive in someday dealing in a competitive world. When time came for college, the boy insisted on attending a state school because it had the best football team in the Northeast, rather than Yale, his father's alma mater.

From infancy to adolescence he had a governess, Karen, a petite, meek Chinese woman, who had been educated in Shanghai, at Ginling College, run by a consortium of American Presbyterian denominations. Karen, who had learned English at the college, had a desire to see America after she graduated and the president of the college, who knew the Hamiltons, arranged a visit. Linda Hamilton, pregnant with Trent, liked her and offered her a position as a governess.

Karen spoke English well, but held her homesickness at bay by speaking Chinese to Trent when they were alone. Before he went to kindergarten, he spoke Mandarin as well as English, and rather than drawing pictures of misshapen houses and dogs larger than life, he learned to draw Chinese characters. Trent's parents were delighted to let the boy acquire a second language in the way many immigrant children learned the dual languages of the homeland and the new society.

As Trent entered his senior year in college he had that age-old urge to search for 'who knows what.' He

69

remembered how handsome his wimpy uncle Ronald had looked dressed in his WWII uniform. Duty was neat, but he told his friends he wanted the Army to get away from — in order of priority — his father, mother and Fairview where his family's banking fortune lay secure beyond the reach of disastrous random events, economic and otherwise.

Trent had the personality of his old man, especially his need to be in control, on top. He dominated all the sports teams in high school, but not in a friendly, sociable way that made room at the top for anybody else. His classmates respected his prowess on the tennis court, the football field, the skating rink, but he had a way of doing things— of going for blood— that did not always sit well with his peers. Lagging behind in a run for Ridley class president his sophomore year at college, Trent had poked his finger in his rival's face over a policy of drinking alcohol in the dorms, reinforcing his bully image. Bobby Morris was an academic overachiever who stayed out of the sun and starved himself, but spoke impeccably. Trent, very much his opposite, towered over him by a foot. When a classmate's wallet was found minus the driver's license in Morris's locker, Morris claimed innocence, but resigned his candidacy nevertheless. His supporters believed that Trent's reputation for winning at any cost played into the mess somehow. The day after Morris's resignation, Trent defended his ex-opponent, saying he was a kid of spotless integrity, publicly urging him to reconsider. Morris declined, but the student body, taken by Trent's high-minded gesture, moved him into first place.

At the end of the year, when Jack and Trent were cleaning out their lockers, a small blue-green card fell to the floor. Before Jack could get it, Trent swept up the dog eared document.

"Hey, is that... Brown's—?"

"What're you talking about?"

"Whoa, man, sorry I asked." Jack turned back to his own locker.

Trent stuffed the card in his pocket. There was no way of knowing what Jack may or may not have seen but he wanted to know how the wind blew.

"Jack, come up to my place next week. We're having a pool party. I'd like you to meet my folks."

Jack shot a look across at Trent, but if he had something to hide, his face did not show it.

"Who's coming?" he asked.

"A few friends, Gallagher from high school, guys like Steve Boddie, my sister with a few gals she hangs with."

"Yeah, all right."

The following week Jack's mother drove him to the Hamilton estate and dropped him off at the gate. He walked up the gravel driveway to the back of the house where he found Trent and his friends. Trent, beer in hand, grabbed Jack's arm.

"Come and meet my sister."

At first Jack could not tell which of the three blonds standing together was Tracy, until Trent said, "Tracy, this is Jack O'Conner, the guy I told you about."

"Hi." Tracy, beaming, pushed her hair off her face.

"Nice to meet you. Trent talks about you all the time."

She laughed. "Nice to meet you too. But Jack, let's get something straight: Trent never talks about me."

Jack blinked a few times and forced a grin.

"Did you bring your suit?"

"No, but I'm not much for swimming. I'm more for tennis, myself."

Trent looked for a way out. "Hey, I need another brew. Jack, make yourself at home. Beer's in the cooler."

After exchanging the obligatory pleasantries with Mr. and Mrs. Hamilton, Jack stayed in viewing distance of Tracy. Every so often he saw her glance back. She was small, with perky breasts and thin legs, the kind of woman Jack never figured he had a chance with. Later, when the crowd was leaving, Tracy and Jack talked briefly. She was eighteen, unattached, and headed for Radcliffe in the fall. She invited him to play tennis the following week and from that point on, holidays and summers, they were a couple, and although Jack did not date while at school, he put no restriction on Tracy dating the Harvard boys.

***

Jack had a mile to go before reaching the mansion, all the while thinking about how the night would go, how

Tracy's dad would welcome him: civil, but distant, inquisitive, but sour, not making Jack feel "at home." He remembered how Father Ryan felt about the Hamiltons. His mother had invited the priest for supper, and while Jack sat on the porch, he overheard her remark, "My son's been dating the banker Hamilton's daughter." With the bluish aquarium tank gurgling in the background, Ryan told Mary things Jack was certain she needn't hear, like how the bank was mixed up in a judge fixing scandal in the thirties. Ryan waxed on, his ruddy face puffing on his briar pipe, "The old man wasn't the first Hamilton to live in the mansion; the great grandfather was. And before him, the first Hamilton in the area emigrated from England. Started the Congregational Church across from the old town green."

"You don't say," said Mary, frowning.

For the first time she noticed that two to the priest's fingers were bent—paralyzed or bent in position—when he tapped his pipe on the edge of the ashtray, and he had a little difficulty pulling out a pack of tobacco to refill the bowl. She looked away as he fired up his Ronson and puffed hard until smoke poured from his lips. The two were quiet. With the pipe clenched between his teeth he quipped, "Yeah, your boy's girlfriend's great-grandfather preached on Sunday, rest of the week collected rents."

The next day, Jack told his mother that he had overheard the conversation.

"Jack, I have no reason to dislike the Hamiltons, regardless of what Father Ryan may or may not approve. You only get a few chances in life. Do what's best for you, for you Jack... if it means sticking close to the Hamilton's then don't pay no mind to Father Ryan... do you hear?"

***

Jack shifted into second gear helping the Ford climb the final quarter-mile to the mansion—its front portico held by four pillars, glowing yellow and white beneath a three-quarter moon in a star filled sky. It was nearly 9:00 when he passed the doorman and walked into the powder blue foyer. To his right he saw the large art deco living room, beyond which six glass doors led to a veranda, a marble patio and the swimming pool. To the left, a thin Negro with a narrow white mustache mixed drinks behind a marble top bar. At the far end, five white-jacketed musicians from the Fred Bacon Quintet played Lester Lanin society music. Though the party hadn't been billed formal, men came safely dressed in dinner jackets with satin lapels. Women with short hair, curls and jeweled bracelets clutched clear martinis between their pinkish fingers and smiled without parting their lips. Most dressed to the neck in beige or light pastel dresses, a few with quivering sequins reflecting hues from flowered vases, designer lights and abstract wall hangings.

Ordinarily, Jack avoided the inside of the mansion, preferring to stay by the pool, but tonight he had little choice. He meandered to the edge of the room where he heard small talk: who was marrying, who was divorcing, who was sick with what, who was building a house or running for office, why Truman didn't nuke Moscow. He smelled stuffed mushrooms. A maid with obsidian eyes held up a silver plate with hors d'oeuvres.

"No, thanks."

From across the room, Jack caught Tracy's eye. She smiled coquettishly as she walked toward him. He admired her rosy white All-American face, thin model-like body dressed in a high necked green brocade gown tightly fashioned about her tiny breasts, tailored past her boney hips. Under the lights, her hair looked the color of honey and was tucked neatly behind her flat ears, which were adorned by pearls that picked up the emerald in her gown. Jack beamed an easy, natural smile, one that complimented a strong jaw and near perfect teeth. Beneath it all, though, he was edgy, feeling that Tracy's father would be watching him all night.

"Hi Jack." She leaned in for a kiss.

"Hi." Eyes darting he puckered his lips and brushed her cheek. "I forgot your corsage."

"Oh Jack, you didn't. I wanted that—to save it."

Jack knew she could be overly romantic, sometimes comically so. "I'm sorry, I'll give you something else to remember me by."

Smiling devilishly, she cocked her head. "Like what, Jackie boy?"

73

Jack blinked fast several times. "You'll see." Jack did not intend to give her anything. Over time he had come to know her and her friends, and he felt that they were spoiled—not in the affections of their parents, but by an overabundance of everything material. All Tracy had to do was wish and it appeared, like the 1948 green MG roadster in the garage. But that was only part of an aroma of resentment, jealously or what his friend Rossini called "social differences."

***

By the middle of summer '47, Jack began spending Saturday nights at the Hamilton pool, where his friends would drink beer, listen to music and disagree about sports, religion, politics, you name it. They argued over whether Truman or Dewey would make a better president: Jack for Truman, everyone else for Dewey.

Tracy said, a wry look on her face, "If I were voting, I'd vote G.O.P. Don't pay taxes now, but pretty soon I will. And, like Daddy says, we don't want our money going to deadbeats."

Jack calmly replied, "I don't want my taxes going to welfare, either."

Tracy nodded agreeably.

"On the other hand, I'd gladly pay taxes that go for defense, or things like that," Jack continued. "Some of us pay higher taxes, sacrifice so that our neighbors live decent, and... "

Gallagher interrupted, "Jack, you're a goddamn socialist. The whole idea's Marxist. If you give to those pulling at your coattails, they'll never get off their ass. It's common sense, man. Dig it?"

Jack did not think much of Gallagher. He was a gawky clumsy kid in the frame of an adult; his strongest talent was imitating his uncle, who had given him a job.

"But, Tom, we give and take. To get the balance right we need to do more, I don't know... " Jack said, trying to be conciliatory.

Trent, with a touch of sarcasm, chimed in. "You're saying if I work hard, make more, then government should take more?"

Tracy, not wanting to get further into the row, went to the radio and dialed in Dinah Shore howling "Buttons and Bows."

Ignoring the blast of music, Jack turned to Trent deferentially. "No, I ain't saying that. But my grandfather was a socialist from Europe, my father was a New Deal man. A little like religion—once you are what you are, it's hard to change."

Trent crushed his cigarette in an ashtray overflowing with butts. "Ain't that the truth," he growled. Then blowing out a plume of smoke deep from his lungs, he added, "Let's have a beer and screw politics." With that, Trent walked over and pushed Jack in the pool. The guys laughed, the discussion ended and Jack, blinking rapidly, looked up at Tracy, who stormed into the house. Trent took a long swig of beer. His friends were onto a different topic.

When Jack went home that night, he had met his mother coming in from work, beaten down from two shifts at the hospital. He thought about how different his friends were, not because they were rich, not because they weren't Catholics, and not because they were Republicans, but because they worked differently and thought differently. They'd never had to witness mothers trekking miles of greasy factory floors or Lysol scented hallways. They had money, power, call it what you will, but it guaranteed that they'd never fail.

***

Tracy thought that Jack seemed lost. "Jack, Jack, are you in this world?"

"Sorry, I was looking at the band."

"Look at me, please."

"Trace, I'm a bit overwhelmed. Guess I didn't expect this many people."

"Relax, you look really handsome. I've never seen you in a tux before." She touched his cheek. "Monkey Cliff," she said, teasing him with what her girlfriends called him. He blushed like when he had first heard it.

"You look swell. I mean beautiful." He'd never said this to a girl before and was afraid it sounded phony.

Smiling now, Tracy looked Jack straight in the eye. "Well, Mr. Jack, I think that's the first compliment you ever gave me."

"You know I get tongue tied." He put his hand on the small of her back and looked past her where he spied her old man next to the bar. A large man with thick silver hair, he could easily be mistaken for an ex-pro football player. Tracy followed Jack's gaze. "Let's say hi to Daddy." She grabbed his hand. "You're cold, Jack," she said, "you're not shaking, are you?"

"No, just... " Jack did not press the thought. He knew Tracy played games with her father, bringing him all sorts of things—from wounded birds to weird friends—to get a reaction; maybe Jack was one of those "things." She either tried getting his approval or shocking him, depending on her end game. At this point, Jack fit somewhere, but he didn't know exactly where. Maybe she wanted the old man to see him dressed in a tux.

Jack was aware of heads turning as they walked across the floor. Athletically built, within a quarter-inch of six feet, he looked military trained, head back, eyes straight ahead. Although this was the first time, he wore the tux with the confidence of a man who had worn one countless times—impeccably creased, without fold or wrinkle, from bow tie to black shoes.

Hamilton was a man accustomed to having other men hang on his every utterance. Surrounding him were two local politicians Jeb Brookfield, Fairview's alcoholic selectman, and Gerry Mason, listless Town Clerk. Both were shaking their heads.

"Daddy!" said Tracy, insistently.

Jack felt from when he had first met Hamilton that the old man did not like him, or at least did not like him dating Tracy, so when Tracy confessed that, "Daddy thinks I'm too young to be dating you," and a month later, "Daddy thinks I need to find someone closer to home," Jack wasn't surprised. When he was with the pool crowd, Hamilton never gave Jack the chance to talk, cutting him off before he'd get to the end of a sentence. Jack had told Tracy, "Your father can't stand me, Jack Prado O'Conner, dating his only daughter."

She had replied, "Jack you're imagining what's not there. Daddy just isn't that warm of a guy."

"Daddy," Tracy persisted, in a voice loud enough to hear over the band.

Focused on the politicians, Hamilton either did not hear his dear daughter or pretended not to. Sidling up, Tracy asked, "Daddy, may I interrupt?"

Hamilton stepped aside. "What is it, my girl?"

The old man ignored Jack.

"Daddy, Jack wants to say hello."

As Hamilton extended his large, soft, banker's hand, Jack could not tell if the man was looking him directly in the eye or over his head. In a deep voice, he said, "Oh... hello, Jack." He took Jack's chilly hand and drew him into the perimeter guarded by the two sycophants.

"Hello, sir," Jack used his deepest tenor. When he spoke he usually impressed listeners by his maturity, although they were soon aware of his hesitating speech, which by some was assumed as a sign of respectful diffidence.

"Jack, I'd like to introduce Mr. Brookfield and Mr. Mason, our First Selectman and our Town Clerk."

Jack shook hands and nodded. " How'd you do, sir."

Brookfield let go his hand like he had touched a hot stove. "Well, son, tomorrow's a big day. By noon you and Trent will be in Uncle Sam's Army. It didn't take you boys long to grow up, did it?"

"Yes, sir, really lookin' forward to... "

Hamilton interrupted, "How tall are you, six feet?"

"More or less, sir."

Jack felt Hamilton studying him, though he could not tell what he was looking for.

"I remember when I first met your folks, about '42, yes, maybe eight years back when they came to the bank. You must've been about fifteen, high school age I guess. A skinny kid. They needed a mortgage. For a bungalow." He smiled and then added smugly, "Still there?"

"No, sir." Jack stood stiffly at attention, and Tracy touched his arm. Hamilton's eyes momentarily shifted to Tracy's hand and back to Jack.

77

"And how're your mom and dad? Will they be at the station tomorrow?"

"Yes, I guess so." Jack knew that his mother would be there.

Hamilton looked away. "Fine, I'm hoping to see them."

"Yes, sir, I'll tell them you said hello."

"Good. Now you and Tracy have a swell time." He turned to Brookfield, who smiled, pleased that he had won the greater man's attention.

"Nice meeting you both," Jack said earnestly.

Always looking for a vote, the First Selectman replied, "Good luck, son." Mason only needed Hamilton's vote, so he fixed on Hamilton stuffing a wiener into his beefy face.

Tracy steered Jack toward the foyer. "Come on, let's walk through those fox trotters and say hello to Mom."

Tracy's mother was welcoming guests, smiling, mentioning their children or hobbies in a few words. She invited Congressman Bickford and his young wife Nina to help themselves to cocktails before she acknowledged Jack with an arched brow and a turned up smile, "Hi, Jack, enjoying yourself?"

"Yes, Mrs. Hamilton, the party's terrific, I never expected so many people."

"I did hope your mom and dad would be coming."

"I'm sorry, Mom isn't feeling well, and Dad has to get up at five."

Jack and Tracy had been making the rounds for an hour before they ran into Trent.

"Jack, what do you think?"

"Well, a little more fucking sane than the last frat party."

"Sane ain't the word for it. Let's blow this joint. Gallagher and the guys are makin' a dent in our beer supply out back."

"I want to introduce Jack to Congressman Bickford, then we'll come out," Tracy said.

Jack watched Trent walk in the direction of the pool and, having been in the old man's presence a short time ago, saw in him the mold of his father, aloof, deciding by the numbers, trusting only what he saw and touched, gravitating toward reality, repulsed by the ideal—not a dreamer. Between detached and emotional, Trent chose the former, even to the degree that he didn't have a steady girl, so there would not be any tear jerking goodbyes in the morning. Trent told Jack the day before the party that Anna, his on-again, off-again girlfriend, wasn't coming to the party, but that he would see her just before the train came—not for some soppy farewell, but to make sure, "things were settled before he left."

Tracy and Jack danced a few numbers, then she drifted off to her college friends and Jack found himself alone among guys he had come to socialize with over the past few years, but in reality had remained distant. The band played until one. The honored guests and their friends sat on the veranda around a circular glass table. Jack remained quiet, drowned in the sounds of beetles throwing their bodies against the ceiling lamps, the buzzing of mosquitoes close to his ears and the crickets chirping in the stuffy summer air.

Tracy's mom appeared, thumb in the air, signaling that the party had ended. She pursed her lips.

"It's time to call it quits. Trent has an early start, people."

Old man Hamilton, having walked the last of his guests out, appeared in the doorway and laid eyes on Jack, before rubbing his chin and bidding everyone good night. Linda followed saying, "Goodnight, all, don't stay up. You have to be at the train by eight."

***

After the guests left, Trent lay in bed painting thoughts on his bedroom ceiling— thoughts that could no longer be delayed by graduation exercises, soirees and going-away-parties. Thoughts of tomorrow's reality, adventurous military operations, foreign cities, alluringly strange women. Out the bedroom window, Bridgeport's sulfurous lights cast an orange halo over the black hills. With sunrise, the hills would be forest green again and, in a few short months, red, russet and gold. Trent would miss Fall's wild asters, goldenrod and gentians in the fields behind the stables. Like the birds that migrate south after the first frost kills most of the insects, Trent's time had

79

come. He would fly away and return at the end of the season. Neither he nor anyone in Fairview could know that the next season would not be that of a bucolic New England countryside, but that of a foreign place, where the hills would be painted brown, black, and white, a less than Impressionistic selection of color. He went back to bed, shut his eyes, and dreamed of the good life, until the 5:30 alarm that would send him to Anna's.

Dawn had barely broken over the southern hills leading to Bridgeport when Trent drove out of his driveway down the two lane highway and by the old gravel quarry that brought back memories of the years he and his friends raced cars around the field, took girls there to make out, played chicken and, occasionally, crashed perfectly good cars.

***

During the '49 summer break, Trent went to work for his father's loan department, where he inspected the condition of collateral before the bank loaned money. Albert Staples and his wife Rebecca, a couple in their mid-sixties, needed $2,000 to buy a tractor, and they applied to Hamilton Bank. Every morning he hitched up two huge brown Percheron work horses, mother and son, to a small two wheeled wagon, and depending on the season worked one of three fields until supper. In the spring, Albert decided to buy a used John Deere after the gelding broke its ankle and had to be put down. The remaining mare could not work alone.

The Staples' farm with its dilapidated, unpainted barn sat a quarter-mile at the end of a dirt road twenty miles north of Fairview. The couple was on the porch when Trent Hamilton pulled up in an open convertible.

"We've been expecting you, young man," said Albert.

"Well, where should I start?" Trent asked in business-like fashion.

"In the house. I can take you to the barn, the chicken coop. We can go to the field if your car don't mind."

Mrs. Staples bowed her head slightly when Trent entered the front hallway, where he opened a notebook and jotted things down. When he finished inspecting inside, the men walked to the barn. Inside, it smelled of horse manure and piss, and except for the horse stall, the place hadn't been used in some time. Behind a pile of hay at the far end, was a 1929 four door, yellow and black Studebaker.

"Nice car."

"Yep, haven't driven it in years. Belonged to my boy."

"Well how come he don't get it on the road?"

"Didn't come back from war. Lost in '43. Over Germany, bombardier, B-17."

"Probably worth a little."

Pointing in the direction of the car, Staples complained, "Yep, who wants an old car?"

"I'd take it off your hands."

"Well, don't know. I didn't mean... . If you're serious. We'd have to see how we felt about it."

After looking at the barn, Trent headed for the bank.

That night the phone rang at the Staples house.

"Staples here... oh, Mr. Hamilton."

"I'm calling to ask if you're interested in selling the car," said Trent.

"How much?"

"Well, I can make it worthwhile. Hundred bucks. How 'bout it? Take it off your hands?"

"Well, son... I'll ask my wife. Call tomorrow." Albert hung up and sat down at the kitchen table. "Well, offered hundred bucks for Scooter's car."

"I'm not ready to let it go."

"Maybe I can get more. But, you know if we give the kid a break, I'm sure he'd put in a good word with his old man. We need that loan or this time next year we're out on the street."

Rebecca slumped her shoulders forward and picked up a wet dish. "Do what you want, you always do." Albert went into the bedroom, Rebecca finished drying, patted her hands on her apron and went out on the porch to watch the sunset.

The next night the phone rang. Albert picked up. "Yes, Mr. Hamilton. No sir, we haven't come to a decision on the Studey, yet."

"What's he want?" Rebecca whispered.

Albert waved his hand at his wife to keep her from distracting him. There was a pause while he listened to Trent. "We need to get more than a hundred," Albert countered forcefully. He listened and reiterated his position, "No... it's worth more than a hundred."

There was a hesitation in the conversation. Rebecca looked at Albert for a clue to what Hamilton was saying.

"Did you say that the loan officer asked to go over our loan on Friday?" Albert smiled at Rebecca. He cupped the phone and whispered, "Looks like they're going to decide this Friday."

There was another hesitation. "Alright, Mr. Hamilton, hundred." Albert hung up and turned to his wife. "He's picking up the car in the morning."

Rebecca went to the barn after supper, opened the doors and walked past the mare bedded down from a long day of hauling stones. She climbed in the car and let out a grief-stricken scream, flung herself down on the Mohair seat and bawled until she had no more tears left inside.

Early next morning, Trent, dressed in a tan Palm Beach suit, and a skinny, acne-faced kid in blue overalls came to revive the old car. The kid popped the hood, installed a fresh battery, and while Trent punched the gas pedal and turned the key, the kid sprayed ether down the carburetor's throat and fiddled with the butterfly. When the car cranked over, Trent pressed his foot to the floor, sending a black cloud of smoke into the horse stall. Trent stared vacantly ahead as he drove the car through the barnyard and down the dirt road. Rebecca watched it disappear around the first bend.

On Friday, Trent met with the bank loan officer.

"Trent, tell me what you can about the condition of the collateral out at the Staple farm."

Trent slowly opened his notebook. "Let me see here." He passed his finger along the margin of the opened page.

"Glad to see you took notes," the officer said with an approving look.

Trent smirked, lifted his head. Wiping the grin off his face, he looked at the loan officer squarely. "Ben, the place is a wreck. Those people have nothing. You'd be looking to hire a collection agent if you loaned them more than a hundred bucks."

***

Anna lived with her mother among Polish immigrants, small stores and antebellum storied houses, interleafed among metal-working factories. It was a tight ghetto bordered on one side by the Pequannock River and on the other by the railroad yard. Below Anna's bedroom a small dry cleaning store started its machines at 5 a.m. On the floor above her were a dozen small, cold-water flats let to families that came and went when the factories ramped up production or cut back. Her bedroom window faced the gated entrance to the Remington Arms Company, a Civil War-era red brick factory that made ammunition, where she, like her mother before her, would someday work the 4 to 11 shift.

When it came to women, Trent acted like a self-centered little boy in the body of a virile man, never feeling the kind of emotions that led other young men to that thing most called love. As long as Anna lived close by, he would come around—even when he dated other girls — because she made him feel manly. She helped Trent explode when he had to. Otherwise, he had no strong ties to her. In fact, he felt no strong ties to anything: not to the town or the people he grew up with. There were no defining moments, outside of football, and no special places, except perhaps the Fairview countryside and the mansion. Anna would not be there when he entered the future; he could find others to satisfy his sexual desires, and he knew that she had no illusions about that.

As Trent got closer to Anna's house, he started working himself up, imagining Anna slipping into panties, a full length silk slip and her white cotton dress. He pulled up in his red '48 Merc coupe, the fender with the black Chinese ideogram signifying 'fun' facing the house. Trent tooted the horn and saw her peek out from the drape. The moan of the factory horn signaled a new day. Across the street, the usual cast of workers marched through the company's gate.

As she came out, she grasped the brass doorknob with both hands, gingerly shutting it. Running down the stairs

83

toward the car, the heels of her white pumps hardly touched the ground, and her crisp white dress pressed against her slim legs. Her short, caramel colored hair was neatly pinned behind her ears with a gold-plated barrette.

A few minutes later, Trent drove through the granite pillared entrance of Lamb's Park and to an elliptical pond at the far end of a dirt road. Wisps of dew hung over still water—green with algae—trees bordering the pond were reflected in the ripples caused by the breeze. He knew this was Anna's favorite spot, but neither had ever been there this early in the morning.

Trent did not need sex if something could substitute, like hunting, drag-racing, gliding or skiing. His favorite pastime was chicken. Lights off, he and his buddies sped around in old or stolen cars doing curly cues, careening over rough ground and fissures, yelping, caterwauling, then straightening out toward the embankment. They never thought about the certain death that would come if a hand slipped or a leg tangled within the steering column. If the jalopy—with them trapped inside—completed its journey to oblivion. Last year he'd played chicken, jumping out seconds before his 1929 Studebaker dove off a fifty-foot cliff, crashing like a wingless bird into the pit of an old stone quarry. Running over to precipice, the guys cheered its eruption—first into flames and then exploding. It cast an eerie, sapphire haze that reflected off low-hanging clouds.

"What a rush, man, dig it, what a rush," Trent had howled.

For Trent the rush was any stunt that produced its own aphrodisiac, adrenaline high, like mainlined heroin to a junkie. Sex, too, brought on the rush. He could feel it coming long before he had his way: sweat flowed, face flushed, a wild urge reached deep, deep into his loins, his stomach twitched, twitted and wriggled—insufferably euphoric, bursting, releasing. He turned toward Anna, lifted her dress to the bottom of her panties. She closed her eyes. He took a long hard look at her white legs. She put her thighs together, he pulled her panties down her legs to the floorboard, and she opened her eyes to see his reaction. He unzipped his pants and put her hand on his

84

boner. She pulled it from the top of his shorts. He lifted his leg over her hips and momentarily suspended any analytical thoughts until he penetrated, and in a few short minutes released an uncontrolled passion and recovered in her tight grasp.

The dew dissipated. Everything stilled. Trent saw her staring at the nearly de-flowered dogwoods at the far edge of the pond. He imagined that she wanted him to tell her he loved her, or that he would miss her, or that he could not wait until he got home again.

"I feel great!" he whooped. "Can't wait to go."

Anna spun her head in Trent's direction and glared.

"Thanks a lot!" she said.

Trent pulled a pack of Lucky's from his shirt pocket, tapped the open end and pulled out a butt. He lit up and took a long, deep drag before blowing out a puff of gray smoke. "I didn't mean it to sound that way. I'll miss you, Anna, but I gotta go. Got to find what's outside this burg."

He pretended he did not notice her eyes welling. She turned and sat still, lips pursed. She had dated Trent on and off since high school. What he liked about her, besides the sex, was that she never pushed him for a commitment.

Pushing her hem below her knees, she started to say, "Well, I feel, I don't know. I feel sad, and maybe... " She stopped short.

What he did not like about her was that she always searched for meaning in things. He puffed on his cigarette. Pulling down the mirror visor, she dabbed her eyes with a tissue.

"We're so lucky to have the park to ourselves," she remarked, yet sounded somber.

Trent pulled her in close. A cat stalked a large raven across the pond. A slight breeze kicked up and blew leaves near the cat, which forgot the raven and began to chase the leaves.

"Will you at least write me?" she asked, looking for some scrap of sentiment.

"Sure," he agreed. To Anna, it sounded too easy.

"Like waiting for Fall to end it all," she said.

"What's that?"

"Oh, talking to myself. Do you think you'll forget me?"

"How could I forget you? No, I won't forget you," he answered, sounding like he was trying out for a school play.

***

Jack had been the last guest to leave the Hamiltons' the night of the farewell party. He grabbed Tracy's hand and led her to the stables where he'd parked the Ford. They leaned against the car beneath a moon held in place by a cotton-like ring that forecast rain and stared across the graveled driveway into a field bordered by an ancient stone wall. Jack caressed her, moving his hand toward her breast, until she casually reached up to hold his hand. "Jack, remember the first time?"

August '47. Two weeks before Tracy and Jack would return to school, the couple had left their friends at the pool, wandered toward the stables and beyond, through the tall grass—a half-mile to the lake. They followed a deer path filled with branches and twigs, and every so often Jack had to clear the way to reach the secluded overlook of the lake.

Leaning against a large boulder she'd gazed upon the water with her legs stretched out, unusually quiet.

"You look a little down, what's up?" Jack had asked.

"Well it's Daddy; he's pestering me."

"About what?"

"It never ends, wanted me down at the bank. All summer he wanted me to learn the ropes, he says. Wanting me to meet Harvey Baxter, some guy working there for the summer."

"Make him happy," Jack said, annoyed.

"I'm just not going. Too much to do with what's left of summer."

Jack noticed Tracy pouting. "You make me laugh."

"You never take me serious."

She brought her legs in close. Jack straddled her thighs. "What do you mean?"

"You know what I mean."

"What're you talking about?"

Her trademark coquette smile crossed her face, "One of these days I'll show you."

86

"I'll bet you could. How's about now?... Ouch! The goddamn mosquitoes, look at you, ain't got much cover."

Her eyelids narrowed, her lips puckered. "Jack, *I said*, I can show you. Wanna watch them take a bloody bite?"

Jack kissed her. He tasted her warm mouth. He pressed against her as he had done many times, but this time she slid down, putting her head against his crotch. He moved on top of her. She spread her legs around his hips and started to rotate. Jack felt the pliant crease between her legs, something she had never let him feel before.

"Wait, Jack. Get off me."

Jack moved aside. He slapped a mosquito that had drawn blood from his leg, but was instantly distracted when Tracy pulled off the bottom half of her bathing suit. She laid back in a clump of ferns and closed her eyes. "What do you think?"

He put his hand on her belly and slowly moved it to her honey-colored, wiry crease. He slipped off his suit.

"Jack, you have anything to put on?"

"Like where would I carry it?"

"Oh, Jack, never mind, hurry, hurry."

Jack pressed on top of her. This time pliant became penetrable.

"Oh Tracy... squeeze your legs tight 'round my waist."

He pushed her top above her breasts, put his full lips on her tan nipple, and then moved his lips up her neck, past her chin, burying his tongue deep into her opened mouth. "Oh, Jack!" Jack could not control the jolt of lightening that jerked his body. When they finished, they sat against the rock, letting the mosquitoes feast on their bare skin.

Jack broke the silence. "What would Daddy say now?"

Tracy giggled. "Jack, if he didn't want me dating you before, he'd be absolutely bullshit now... wouldn't he?"

***

On the night before he went into the Army, Jack wasn't interested in sex. He wanted to tell Tracy something that she would remember, but his lips quivered, and she never heard what he had in his heart: that he loved her, and that she should wait until he returned, when they could get

87

engaged. She hugged him firmly and kissed him, her lips tightly sealed. With her head on his chest she whispered, "Jack, take care of yourself." He started the car and drove toward the main entrance, while watching Tracy through the rearview mirror. When she reached the front door, she walked in and never looked back.

Jack took a last ride around Bridgeport, surveying the avenues, factories and old neighborhoods that, like a vault, held all the better emotions he had ever acquired. Driving past the plant where his father still made lipstick cases, he wondered if he was working the night shift, wondered if he would see him at the station. A vacant lot to the south of the plant marked the spot of the first town post office—torn down after World War I—the lot ensuring that every new generation of kids had a place to play ball. Next to the lot was a dock where a half-dozen rowboats listed in the river, a wispy mist making them appear like they floated above the water. Across the street, a lamp illuminated the clapboard side of a little theater and the mossy green of lichen mold that attached itself to the buildings facing the river. In this part of town, there were no grassy lawns or flower beds. The factories and their fulmination had long reduced the trees to wearing nothing more than ragged sweaters of leaves.

Except for the out-of-town students he had met in college, Jack only knew people from Bridgeport, and, oh yes, Fairview, where in summers he mingled with the rich kids, made love to Tracy and flirted with skinny debutantes in blue dresses. He tried hard to be one of the tall, white skinned beaus with black and white saddle shoes, but never felt he had succeeded. In the morning he hoped to forget much of this for a while and experience the great country that lay beyond the rivers and fields that separated the vigorous from the spent. But in his heart he knew he could not let most of it go: the feeling that he had yet to overcome his childhood pain, the feeling he would always be connected to Bridgeport, as rundown as it was, the feeling that his mother and sister would always be there if he needed them. He could not think of a more important virtue than loyalty to the town he grew up in, his friends and those he loved. These were the sentiments that held him together. Under the fullness of the May moon, Jack headed home, his childhood landmarks committed to memory one last time so that someday when he returned, unlike Odysseus, he might recognize that from whence he came—a place where everything was familiar, quiet and old.

Boots, Camps and Commissions

THE ARMY HAS A PATENTED RECIPE to transform a green lieutenant into a fighting specialist in the space of five weeks. Take any aggressive, obedient, red-blooded American ROTC college grad, presumably between the ages of twenty and twenty-five, short, tall, skinny, chubby, fit, unfit, cocky, unsure, timid, rich or poor, smart or dumb, and in thirty-five days they can be made to dress, act and think like the previous class of second lieutenants, and the class before that, and the class before that. The process reforms young men under the repetitive jack-hammering of induction, examination, regimentation, humiliation, subjugation and brutalization, into one solid whole.

In spite of the drill instructors who kicked his ass, hollered obscenities, forced him beyond physical, emotional and mental tolerance, Jack loved it. Most guys did not. More than one cried to sleep. Only two out of three survived this trial by ordeal. The unfit third were either too weak or too smart or too screwed up. Jack and Trent, reservists, had finished boot camp before graduating, but needed another round of Army orientation—a post graduate officer's leadership course of sorts—before being assigned to a unit for five months and then return home as weekend warriors to serve out their enlistment.

None of the soldiers had passes to leave post, but since Caesar's time, soldiers have tested the system in search of the nearest tavern and the eternal hope that they might "get lucky." One Friday night, Trent and two Texans that Jack did not have much truck with were being picked up by Dawn, a not so attractive thirty-year-old, who considered it her patriotic duty to bus GIs to the nearest bar on her nights off from Ho Jo's. At the last minute, the Texas boys decided to drink 3.2 beer on the post, so Trent invited Jack to the off post outing. Trent's buddy Wally

Potter was pulling charge-of-quarters duty and would cover if bed checks were ordered.

At nine, the boys snuck out the barrack's backdoor and walked to Dawn's orange '39 Plymouth sedan. Her brown hair hung loose below shapely shoulders, large shadowy eyes, and a round face plastered in pancake makeup that glossed over a few noticeable pockmarks. Dawn was unperturbed by the change, saying whimsically, "Why not? Y'all wear the same uniform."

They drove off past the guard house and the MPs. Five miles from post they stopped at Robbie's, a cement-block beer joint with red, blinking lights and a sign that read *Country Music Every Fri. and Sat.* Blue-dungareed townspeople and GIs in brown uniforms crowded a bar littered with beer bottles and empty shot glasses. Jack got his first full view of Dawn when she sidled up to Trent. Her head came to his shoulders—she was large boned, probably of Russian stock. Trent had his body bumped up against Dawn's, claiming her. She appeared surrendered.

Jack fidgeted with an assortment of nickels and dimes on the bar listening to the bartender tell a story about the time he and his high school buddies celebrated his WWII homecoming and drank a quart-sized flask of white lightning. After two beers and bored, Jack dropped a nickel in the Red Rocket pinball machine—setting in motion chrome balls, bells, and flashing wonder women dressed in patriotic themes. A heavy-set girl with stringy blonde hair and a low cut pink blouse walked over and leaned on the glass platen, while Jack jostled the machine. He took his eye off the ball to gawk at her generous cleavage, and tilted out. Annoyed, he excused himself to use his nickels in the jukebox.

Trent and Dawn danced every number and by eleven o'clock, her pink lipstick dappled the front of his khaki shirt. At the bar, the cleavage-girl moved close to Jack. She snapped her fingers while slowly rotating her hips to the music. She lit a Camel, and Jack breathed in the smoke. He studied her huge hungry eyes in the mirror. She brushed against his arm. He looked at the Schlitz clock over the bar.

"Yo, Trent, look at the time."

91

"Yeah, time to head back."

The cleavage girl held the last inch of her cig between her finger and thumb, inhaled deep and tried to make eye contact via the mirror. Jack turned away.

Outside, a light rain shined the asphalt. Depositing Dawn in the front, Trent swung himself behind the wheel of the Plymouth. Jack fell asleep still upright in the back seat. Trent hit the wipers while, on the radio, Patti Page crooned "With My Eyes Wide Open, I'm Dreaming." Kicking off her red shoes, Dawn curled her legs under her, the hem of her powder red skirt stretching over her chunky thighs. Feeling tipsy, Dawn shut her eyes. Trent moved his hand from the rim of the steering wheel to finger her hem. He passed by the Burma Shave signs, all ten of them, but his hand was too occupied to stroke his face for signs of a five o'clock shadow. He slid her hem up her thigh, feeling the silky nylon of stockings until he felt the garter's raised clasp. His heart pounded. She sat motionless. His hand glided from the top of the nylon up her smooth porcelain skin until he felt the stiff garter belt. His hand slipped between her fleshy, white thighs. She remained motionless. His boner pushed on his zipper. His hand crawled to her crotch. She loosened her upper leg, giving permission, and he pressed his middle finger to the slit beneath her panties. He checked the road. Rain pelted the windshield, and the worn wipers swished, blurring the headlights of oncoming traffic. Encouraged by her willingness, Trent lifted her skirt to see the soft bulge at the apex of her thighs.

A mile from the post, Trent, steering with his left hand, rounded an uphill curve at fifty miles per hour. He glanced at Dawn's thighs, while his fingers negotiated the loose elastic. When he looked back at the road, he was blinded by high beams. In the strange way the mind works, Trent registered that both cars were traveling the same side of the road in a symmetry that destroys two bodies vying for the same space. He dug deep into his athleticism, steered toward a twelve-foot embankment between the road and the dark vast prairie, and jammed his foot on the brake. Back wheels locked, the car skidded—rotating right. Trent wrenched the wheel left, then sharply right to get it straight again, but the car careened toward the embankment. A telephone pole snapped into the headlights, followed by a lightening crack and blue and white sparks as power lines lashed the car's steel body. The force of impact impaled the chassis on the pole's stump and slammed Jack into the backside of the front seat, twisting his neck. Trent's head struck the windshield's side post gashing his temple as Dawn met the dashboard. She never had a chance. The horn blared into the rain-soaked, cosmic grassland. Everything stopped except the pendulum swing of a tiny pink ballerina shoe hanging from the rearview mirror.

"What the fuck!" moaned Trent.

Crawling out the back on all fours, Jack grabbed his neck, moving it side-to-side. He saw Trent, head down, hand to his forehead. Jack reached in and put his fingers on Dawn's neck; he saw she was out cold. No sign of life. Jack went to the driver's side and tugged at the jammed door until it opened.

"You okay? Anything broken?"

"No, but my knee whacked the goddamn column."

"Get out, you're smashed. Get your ass back to post. Stay out of sight. Let me take care of this... I'll catch up in a few minutes."

"Whatcha gonna do?"

"Never mind... get the hell outta here!"

Trent said nothing, limping off into the rain.

From the driver's side, Jack wrestled Dawn's limp body into position behind the driver's seat. She had an indentation in her forehead, and her eyes were restfully shut. Mascara blackened lashes and Vaseline coated eyebrows looked almost perfect.

The impact jolted a farmer and his wife out of bed. He told the police, "I dreamed that my horse was fallin' through the roof. I woke up and heard nothing."

In his gray and white striped pajamas, the farmer ran out to see a soldier tugging at a woman behind the wheel of a wreck. "You okay, son?"

Jack looked at the farmer in horror, he knew it was too late to bolt. He jumped from the wreck, "Yeah, we were driving back to the base, and... "

The bright headlights from Dawn's car beamed spaceward. The farmer peered at a body slumped over the wheel. "Is she hurt?"

Trent got back to the barracks about twelve, slipped through the back door and into his bunk. The thought of getting caught terrified him. He did not know for sure, but Dawn's stillness had been eerie. Did she need an ambulance, or would she only suffer a bad headache in the morning? He wondered if she would mention his name. Then there was old Jack. When would he get back? He figured anytime now. Minutes passed into the quarter hour and Trent began to sweat. He kicked off the covers. Adrenaline coursed through his veins the more he thought about the downside possibilities. Maybe Jack did not get away. Maybe Dawn needed a doctor. If Jack did not get away, what would he tell them? Eventually, with no sign of Jack, he fell asleep.

About one in the morning, a man in the communications shack heard about a fatal crash on the police frequency. He called the commanding officer, who ordered bed checks. Wally found Jack's bunk empty. He stuffed a pillow beneath the blanket, then searched latrines and phone booths. The CO called back forty-five minutes later asking if everything was in order.

"Well, sir, no. There's a guy missing," Wally answered uneasily.

He had hoped he might cover for Jack, but within minutes of putting down the phone, Wally heard the deep voice of a drill instructor crack the air, "Ten-hut!"

The following day, MPs escorted Jack from the hospital to the post in handcuffs. AWOL and implicated in the fatal accident, he was court-martialed. His short army career was over. Stripped of his gold bars he had a choice: a general discharge or enlist as a private.

Six weeks passed, and Jack hadn't heard from Trent. His letters to Tracy explaining what had happened went unanswered. He saw an end to more than his military career. He chose to enlist.

On graduation day, Trent donned his dress uniform, zipped his hair to the scalp and erased all evidence of facial hair. By nine, he and his graduating cohorts had assembled in front of the barracks. They marched to the parade ground, the army band leading the way with "Washington Post March." Two hundred people, mostly parents and wives, came to see their sons and husbands graduate. They were unaware that these staunch soldiers had just completed something like a mass stupefaction, a descent into Hades, to be reincarnated in this bloodless public birth. Chests out, eyes right, a military cadence guided the lieutenants past a reviewing stand, cutting the wet morning with a crispness the spectators would remember long after the troops were deployed.

The drizzle had turned to rain by the time the post commander mounted the lectern. His voice boomed over two loudspeakers at each end of the reviewing stand, "Men, the Commander in Chief confers upon each of you the authority to carry out your soldierly duties on behalf of America and our way of life." For the next twenty minutes, in a soaking rain, he spoke about duty, exaltation, adventure and imagination—ironic, given that the past weeks were spent wringing out the notion of independent thinking from each of the men, now too disciplined to come out of the rain. The lieutenants were in another world— tomorrow's—thinking about the leave that would come before their new duty posts. Trent thought about strutting amongst his friends in Fairview in full army dress, or his father taking him around the bank to shake hands with the men that he would someday manage. And, he thought how hungry he was for a woman, any woman. Maybe he would call on Anna, or any one of a half-dozen girls who would be impressed by his uniform.

The Army delayed orders for several days after graduation. The men sat around the barracks reading paperbacks and playing cards. With so much time on his hands, Trent went from cards to listening to the radio to thinking about Jack and Dawn. Nearly two months had passed since that night on Route 29, and all that he knew was that Jack had been busted down to a private and Dawn, a woman whose face he had a hard time picturing, had died.

Finally, for Trent, the wait ended. The Army took interest in his Chinese fluency and assigned him to the Military Intelligence Training Center at Fort Holabird in Baltimore. He welcomed the Holabird assignment, but for the first time, railed openly about Jack's "bad luck," as he preferred to call it.

"Shit! Goddamn. Shit!" He carried on for an hour.

That night he called his father about his new station and explained he wasn't going home on leave. Both men discussed the Korean conflict and agreed that unless MacArthur restored the 38th parallel, most soldiers would be heading to Korea. Trent asked his father if he had heard from Jack. He claimed that he had, a month or so earlier, and told Jack he had called Congressman Bickford.

"Trent, Bickford didn't sound encouraging, and honestly, after the lies he told Tracy, I'm not sure we should be too quick to follow up," his father counseled coldly. "More importantly, Bickford asked if the Army had any more questions for you."

"None, not after I called you."

"Well, let's close the book on this." The men turned to how things were shaping up around the upcoming election for governor.

The next morning Trent received his first and last letter from Anna,

Dear Trent,

It has been several months since we last spoke, that morning before you left. I cried knowing I would not hear from you again. I was right. I thought our last time would have been different. But, if I am truthful to myself, I realize that every child born of a body, a mind and an emotion must eventually be set free to discover how dissimilar things fit together. You are off on that journey. Off to find a purpose, or a sacred place, kinship, or even a mate to solve this individual puzzle. I hope you find what you are looking for. Some never do.

Fondly,

Anna

Trent rolled the letter into a ball and pitched it down the barrack's bay, unaware that Anna's swollen desire for him had slowly dissipated as her attachment to that last night stretched thinner and thinner. Over time, an icy resignation set in with the realization that she must eke out a life alone in silence, carrying the seed that could not, in her mind, be unplanted: Trent's child. She would name him William.

Between that last morning with Anna and her last letter, nations around the world had turned their sights in an ominous direction. The calendar read June 26, 1950. Men and women were dying on the Korean peninsula, and Trent's transfer to Fort Holabird was cancelled. Two days later orders were posted to "... Transfer to Army HQ, Pusan, Korea, for assignment 3457th Intelligence Service Detachment... "

Music In and Out of Tune
1945-1950

WHEN THE O'CONNERS DIVORCED, MARY took the children and moved in with her parents, Libero and Rosa Prado. One afternoon, Libero brought home a scuffed leather case containing a violin he had received for rewiring the widow Esposito's attic. Julie was setting the table and Jack was in his room boning up for a chemistry exam. Sliding the supper dishes aside, Libero put the open violin case smack in the middle of the kitchen table. "The old lady had no money. She gave me this instead. Maybe it's worth something."

Rosa moved her finger across the body, carving a line in the dust.

"We don't need another piece of junk," she moaned.

Libero held the stringed bow lengthwise to his eye studying its straightness. He shrugged. He dropped it into its case and laid it in the corner of the room. Rosa poured canned string beans into a saucepan.

"That thing won't pay the rent," she harangued.

Libero, in blue workpants and a gray shirt with Prado Electric embroidered over the pocket, sat in front of a plate of pasta, a rumpled paper napkin, glass of red table wine and a serrated knife to cut the provolone. He picked up his fork, stabbed a sardine from a can, yanked a hunk of bread off a loaf and stuffed it into his mouth. As he chewed, he jerked his head in the direction of the violin.

"Tomorrow, I'll ask Santoro if he wants to buy it. He could rent it to one of his students," he declared with an air of optimism.

That night Julie, who had just turned thirteen, asked the old man to show her the violin again. His big beefy hands lifted the featherweight instrument from its purple, velvet-lined case. He plinked the strings with his chubby fingers and held it under the floor lamp in the corner. He put his eye to one of the *f*-shaped sound holes and made out a hand written label: *Joseph Kloz, 1805.* The next day Julie and the old man went to Mr. Santoro. The evaluation was swift.

"Libero my friend, don't quit stringing wires." Santoro tuned it up and played a short Chopin mazurka. "Not bad."

He put the violin in its case and when he looked up, Julie caught his eye. She smiled. He nodded in her direction and turned to the old man.

"Libero, maybe your granddaughter might like to learn." He turned to Julie. "Would you like to play the violin, little girl?" he prodded eagerly.

A toothy smile overcame her. "Oh, yes, Mr. Santoro, I would."

He suggested, "My friend, why don't I give her a few lessons? At least you can enjoy the music, even if it doesn't put food on the table." Santoro lifted the violin from the case and handed it to Julie.

"Here, put it under your chin," he said soothingly, fitting it tight against her neck. "Now take this bow and come down across the strings, straight." She adjusted the instrument, brought the bow to the taught strings. She yanked it down. A screech reverberated off the walls. The teacher smiled and sheepishly turned to the old man. "Libero, lessons are only a dollar a week."

In the next few weeks, under Santoro's mentoring, the screeching subsided and the sound turned to something resembling music. And within the next few years, Julie played with fluidity rare among young violinists. Through a stuck-open window in the cubbyhole off the kitchen, neighbors heard her practicing at all hours—most suspected the girl was driven by the music in a not-so-healthy way. They often heard the violin and her soprano voice, such as the first part of the Concerto No. 3 in G major followed by Puccini's "Un Bel Di Vedremo," *a capella.* They never clapped. And if Julie were to meet a neighbor they would never hear a civil "hello"—merely a throat-clearing cough, while she looked away. Although they admired her talent, they thought her rude, eccentric and obsessed. Reaching out with an opened hand the old woman across the alley gossiped, "How could this uncivil creature make such beautiful music?"

Mr. Santoro knew about Julie's dedication to music, one that may have bordered on the pathological at times, but he felt his job wasn't psychiatry—it was music. He recommended that she be enrolled at New Haven's Conservatory of Music when she graduated high school. For the family it represented training by the best the state had to offer, and because of their income and her talent, the school offered a scholarship.

One Friday in mid-August 1948, after finishing her lesson, Julie decided to visit the Yale Art Museum. At seventeen, she was, by all accounts, a plain looking girl, and she carried her scuffed violin case past the young security guard unnoticed. She wore no makeup, and uncut, her hair grew to uneven lengths over her small shoulders. But behind the unadorned face, she had a well-proportioned nose and chin, a petite frame, and eyes, like two lime-green emeralds that pierced through strands of auburn hair. She stopped at a portrait labeled "Equestrian Portrait of the Duke of Lerma," and seconds later heard a voice.

"Do ya know Rubens?"

"Pardon?" She turned. A tall, thin young man in blue carpenter's overalls stood behind her. The man stepped closer.

"Do you know Rubens?"

Julie moved to the side, open mouthed. "I come here to admire these paintings, but I really don't know who the artists are."

"Well he was a master of deep color, deeply real in his portraits. This one's on loan from a Madrid museum."

She studied him, top to bottom, not sure if it was his muscular hands or his dark almond-like eyes she was more attracted to. Or not attracted, but simply surprised by his self confidence and apparent knowledge of the painting—especially since he dressed like one of the janitors she had passed in the hallways.

"I'm Roger," he said energetically.

"I'm Julie, Julie O'Conner. Do you work here?" She looked to see if they were alone.

"Oh, no, I'm a carpenter. A cabinetmaker actually," he asserted. "I come here when I have a few hours to myself." He could not take his eyes off this Venus de Milo behind the "starving artist" look.

That introduction turned into an afternoon of talking about art, music and each other. She learned he was twenty-one, born in Vermont and raised in Bridgeport—where his parents still lived, though he now lived in New Haven. With a tongue made glib by his attention, she told him about all things that fascinated her and that this past spring she had planted wild flowers in her backyard, but never told anyone. He looked at her gently, telling her in a soft voice, "A woman in love should have a secret garden where she picks her wild flowers." The afternoon buzzed by before she heard the chime of the clock fronting the steeple of the Congregational church.

"Oh my god, I have to catch the 5:30 train."

He grabbed her hand as if to shake it. She held it limp. He looked down. There was a moment of stillness between them. Julie had never gotten this close to a man outside the family, except Mr. Santoro, but she felt completely at ease, noticing that she had lost the tightness in her throat.

As she walked away she heard Roger call, "Wait! Before you go let me take your picture." She turned as he opened a case to a *Leica 35MM* camera. He pushed her hair from her forehead and stepped back. "Smile. That's it. Perfect. And by the way, on my days off I always go to the museum."

That night Julie went home in a daze. When her mother asked her if she was feeling okay, she faced her, extended her arms like she was about to belt out a number and said joyfully, "Mom, I feel I'm on the brink of something." Her mother, thinking about her music, answered, "That's wonderful Julie, does that mean you'll be ready for the recital in January?"

***

Roger Girardin lived in a loft over a woodworking shop owned by seventy-year-old Solomon Carvahal, a Portuguese carpenter who had hired him in '47 after Roger answered an ad in the New Haven Register. Carvahal had not asked to see a list of schools Roger went to or places he had worked; rather he asked to see something he made. When Roger opened the door to the shop, he heard a bell clang before inhaling an odor of wood and fish. His eyes adjusted to the natural light that funneled through a dirty skylight and lit up a floor rife in sawdust and a complement of machines: several jury-rigged saws, a lathe, drill press and three workbenches in front of a fat supply of lumber.

"Hello, anybody here?"

From behind a row of half built cabinets a small man—with a thin face and dark complexion and a *kippah* on his balding head—popped out. He spoke rapidly in an accent Roger heard only in the Bridgeport Jewish neighborhoods.

"Come, young man. Girardin, yes?"

"Yeah, that's right. I called."

He studied Roger before asking, "So what have you brought me to look at?"

Roger ripped the brown paper bags he had taped to cover a picture frame fashioned from cherry wood and propped it against a workbench, before pulling a hanky from his pocket and wiping it down. The old man moved back about ten feet and then tentatively walked forward, until he could smell the butcher's wax, and removing his wire-rimmed glasses, he knelt down to eyeball the bold turns and twisting threads stitched in curving motifs. He had small, calloused hands and thin fingers that he ran over the polished finish—letting his hand freely twist and slide down the curvature of several faux spiraled flutes. His heart beat fast as he pulled a brass magnifying loop from his pocket, leaned in, lodged it into his eye socket, and stuck his little finger into the slippery scrolls, rosettes and twisted ropes sweeping effortlessly through a maze of tiny, hyperbolic French curves. Hunched a bit, he backed up, grasped the back of his neck, and smiled approvingly. The frame was just short of a masterpiece.

"Where'd you learn the craft?"

"My father, and for this I spent lots of time at the museum—looking at frames."

"Well, young man, if I stand back, back where you're standing, sides ain't straight. Off by a few arc-minutes."

"Arc what?" Roger came back nervously.

"You know, not squared. To the left."

"I don't see it."

The man's stare made Roger uncomfortable—like he was boring into his soul. In a slightly accusatory tone, he asked, "Are you interested in seeing it, young man?"

"I think so, if it's there," Roger replied, not sure what the man was talking about.

"It's there. It's there all right." Roger heard certainty in the voice. "Are you interested in seeing it?" adding, "I need to know, up front."

Roger heard water dripping from a faucet in the corner of the shop. "Yes, I am." Then he looked at the man and this time with emphasis, affirmed, "Yes, sir. I am, sir."

The old man put the back of his hand against his brow and let out a deep sigh. He knew the boy's potential: a careful craftsman, who cared deeply, even passionately about the craft. But he had to hear him say "yes."

"The inner eye, I call it, to see arc-minutes, to become aware, to see... to believe is to see. It's not something that comes easily, takes years. Some never get it. You may never get it, ever. Takes an inner eye for things that are part nature, part us. Are you interested, young man?"

Roger rubbed his chin, not quite sure what to make of the old man's rambling. "I never thought about it. But, look I'm out of work, I wanna make something. You have enough work?"

The carpenter leaned against a workbench. "There's work enough for us who know our business. Have a seat. My name is Sol, Sol Carvahal."

He pulled up a chair in front of Roger and the men got down to what Roger would do if he were to take the job, how he would be paid and what the old man could promise.

Roger summed up what he had heard. "You pay me a dollar an hour, sometimes I work eight hours, sometimes more. I can use the loft upstairs as my apartment. I get Friday afternoon from 2:45 to Monday morning off. I got to clean up every day—including the toilet—and if you ask me, I pick up lunch at the deli on Church."

"Yep, that's it. Oh, and unload the trucks when they deliver."

"Sounds okay, I guess. I do what you tell me to."

"Yeah, that's it. Anything that needs to get done. And you learn how to be the best cabinetmaker in New Haven. I show you how to sniff out good oak from bad oak, dry from green maple... only the masters know. Sol himself will teach. You want it, young man?"

Roger looked, wide-eyed. His head, shoulders, upper body all said yes. "Yes, Mr. Carvahal, I'll do it."

"Call me Sol. I'll call you Roger, make it easy?"

"Yes, sir."

"Good, let start. Apron over there. Move in upstairs anytime, tonight, tomorrow, whenever. Oh... no women."

Roger had been working in the shop nearly six months when one afternoon he returned with the deli order and heard the table saw screaming with Sol unconscious on the floor. He phoned for an ambulance. Sol had suffered a mild heart attack. Two weeks later the doctor released him from the hospital under orders to stay home for at least four weeks. He lived downtown, five blocks from the shop, in a four room, converted storefront that smelled of fried fish. Roger visited Sol every day to take direction on what to work on and saw to it that Sol ate three square meals.

On the day the old man returned to work, he looked like gray slate and seemed ten pounds lighter. His beady dark brown eyes focused on the shop floor, which Roger had cleaned and organized. He thanked Roger for being like a son and a partner during his recovery. The discussion led to Roger telling him about the work in progress and the deliveries ahead. At one point, Sol looked over at a black walnut music stand in the middle of the shop floor.

"I don't remember an order for a music stand."

"It's for my girl. She plays violin. Thought I'd make it for her birthday."

Sol walked over to inspect it. He ran his hands over the polished members held together through a solid design and a little glue. Then the centerpiece, a platen with a mirror-like finish for the music, furrowed and scrolled, its edge a crochet-like pattern to look filigreed, affixed to an adjustable, fluted, tapered stand that screwed into a base with three hand carved lion's claws. On the back of the platen was a small engraved brass metal plate that read: "*To Julie. Forever, Roger*"

Affectionately, Sol looked at Roger. "You love her much, don't you?"

"Someday we're gonna marry."

***

During the 1948–1949 college break, Trent invited Jack to a New Year's Eve party at the Pleasure Beach Ballroom— a large big band style dancehall on an island off Bridgeport.

"Hey, I've never met your sister. Bring her along."

"Aww, she's got a fella she's goin' steady with."

"Have her bring him, too."

When they arrived, a stream of people was funneling through the door, past an overweight cop checking IDs. Looking Julie over, the checker seemed to bare his belly as he insisted, "Little girl, you ain't getting past me unless I see the right ID. Now move along."

The three were huddling from the sting of a steady wind off the sound, plotting to get Julie in, when Trent and Tracy drove up in the red Mercury. When they reached the entrance's barrel-shaped awning, they walked over to the threesome. After introductions, Jack explained the problem with the cop; suddenly it became Trent's problem, because Tracy was also underage. Without hesitation, Trent pulled a twenty from his wallet, walked over to the guard and said that he was the guy throwing the party, and he needed to have his two sisters there when his parents arrived. The cop glanced around, shook Trent's hand, folded the bill into his palm and gestured the group into the ballroom.

Though Trent had hired a six-piece band to play until the early morning hours, he spent most of his time, not on the dance floor, but sitting with Julie, Roger and Jack. He seemed not to notice Anna or the other three dozen friends that he had invited. None of them could help but notice that Trent was captivated by Julie; he would not let her out of his sight. Wearing a sapphire blue silk cocktail dress, her hair swept up on the sides with long pipe-curls and a borrowed pair of rhinestone-studded earrings, Julie was as beautiful as any girl in the room. What was more, she was in love. But seeing an opening, Trent asked Julie about school, music, hobbies and engaged her in nonstop, yet polite, conversation. Roger was usually unruffled by the attention men showed Julie. There was something special about her, for those who took the time to look twice, and he was proud that she was his girl. But when Trent asked Julie to dance—a slow dance—Roger straightened his tie and met Trent's eyes dead-on.

"You don't mind, Roger, do you?" Trent smiled, while reaching for Julie's hand.

Roger, brushing off what he knew was a pass, answered, "Mind? Julie's a big girl—she dances with who she wants."

For a split second, Julie felt the scene go tense, but her hand was already extended in Trent's direction. Roger focused on the couple as they embraced on the floor. The lights were dimmed, a rotating mirror ball in the center projected sparkling flickers throughout the hall and Julie looked for Roger as Trent spun her around, but Trent moved her to the far end of the kaleidoscopic ballroom. Halfway through "I Can Dream, Can't I," Trent asked her to a movie or dinner. It would not be possible, she explained —she and Roger were steadies. Claiming he hadn't known, Trent left the offer open should she change her mind. Following the dance, Trent disappeared until midnight, when "Auld Lang Syne" brought everyone together under a storm of confetti and favors.

Later, Trent told Jack he had not realized his sister was "a knockout." Jack had never considered Julie anything but average, but Trent suggested that the next time they returned from school that Jack and he take their sisters out for the night and get to know each other. Jack did not feel one way or the other about Trent's attraction and left it at that.

At the end of February, the boys returned home on college break. Trent asked Jack and Julie to dinner at the mansion. They had the whole house to themselves—the older Hamiltons having ventured to Palm Beach. Instead of dinner, they had pizzas and beer. For Julie this was new, as she had few friends—especially friends with homes with huge pillars out front. After eating, the group ventured into the gameroom to play pool, Trent put on some music and it wasn't long before he and Julie were dancing. Trent being Trent, he held her close, and Julie being Julie, it made her uncomfortable. She lightly pushed back, her floor maneuvering unnoticed by her brother. About mid-way through the evening, Tracy disappeared with Jack, who hadn't noticed her attempts to out maneuver Trent on the dance floor. Julie found herself alone with Trent. When she leaned over the pool table, he grabbed her by the waist and pressed against her, kissing her neck. She turned abruptly, red-faced, and pushed him off.

"No, Trent. I can't. You've been drinking too much."

"Hey, what's wrong? C'mon, girl, I can show you a really good time."

"Look, I don't know you, and I'm not interested right now."

"Is it that loser, what's his name? He doesn't have anything I don't got. Hah."

"Roger's no loser, he's a... " Julie broke off. What she saw in Roger was her treasure, hers alone, and she wasn't about to share it or justify it to Trent. "I'm saying, I have a boyfriend."

"God help you, girl, look around."

Four weeks later, Julie received an unexpected call.

"Trent? You looking for Jack? I thought he was there with you, up at school!"

"No... looking for you."

"What'd you mean?"

"Julie, about that other night."

"Trent, let's just forget—"

"Julie, hear me out, I can't take no for an answer. All I do is think about you."

"Please, Trent, that's flattering, bu—"

"Next time I come home, I'd like to call."

"I can't stop you, but I'll always be straight with Roger."

107

***

Trent invited Jack and Julie, together with Roger, to a Memorial Day pool party. Julie agreed, wanting to appease Jack and maybe even to demonstrate that she and Roger were a couple. Except for a slight twitch to his smile and an extra, unnecessary pressure in the handshake he offered Roger, Trent's face revealed nothing. He was the perfect Hamilton host. The guys talked sports and cars, while the girls, sitting on the other side of the pool, talked about school and boys. As the evening progressed, Trent and his friend Gallagher started in on a '34 Chevy that they had souped up and then crashed and ditched at the sand banks one night.

"Hey, Roger, you know anyone with a clunker they want to get rid of?" Gallagher asked.

Taken by surprise, Roger answered, "The guy I work for has a '37 Packard he never uses. It's just sitting in the lot behind his shop." Before the words were out of his mouth, he regretted having said anything at all.

The following week Trent and Gallagher asked Roger if they could see the car, and wishing again he had kept his mouth shut, Roger invited them over. If they were really interested, he would ask Sol if he wanted to sell it. On Saturday night, Trent, Gallagher and Steve Boddie drove up in Boddie's new Plymouth coupe. Roger brought them around the back of the shop where the car sat in an otherwise vacant lot.

"Hey, Roger, mind if we start it up?"

"I don't think we should do that, not sure Sol would like it."

"Come on. Got the key?"

"Inside the shop."

"Go get it, let's just turn her over, that's all."

Roger went to the shop and retrieved the key from a hook behind Sol's desk.

"The battery's sure to be dead," Roger said.

"Get that coupe over here, we'll jump it," Trent said, pointing to the Plymouth.

Roger stepped out of the way, while Boddie moved his car in position. Gallagher popped the hood on both cars. A minute later, the old Packard turned over. Trent, behind the wheel, shifted in reverse, floored the gas. The car jerked back.

"Hey, hold on there," Roger protested.

"I'll just take it for a spin, Roger-boy. Be right back, don't worry. Boddie, follow me in case I get stuck."

"Trent, get that goddamn car back here. I'm going to get fired if my boss gets wind of this."

But Trent was already halfway out the back lot, Boddie and Gallagher in tow. An hour passed, and the Fairview boys hadn't returned. Roger went into the shop and went to the loft to lie down to a restless night.

The next day, Sunday, he stayed in New Haven rather than make the weekly trip to Bridgeport. He tried to contact Trent. Later that night, Jack called to tell him that while his friends were joy riding, the car went off the road and crashed somewhere north of New Haven. The boys had abandoned the vehicle where it had come to rest.

When Trent, Gallagher and Boddie were arrested a few days later, old man Hamilton's lawyers launched a full scale attack claiming that Trent had had Roger's "permission" to take the car for a test drive. As Trent later told Boddie: "This guy ratted me out. He's gotten in my way once too often, first Julie, now this. This won't be forgotten. Next time, I'm going to beat that bastard to a pulp."

On the day Trent and his old man went to court, people with legal problems were standing in the aisles, jamming the courtroom doorway, bobbing, turning, listening for a familiar name, or even their own. A rap on the oak door behind the bench signaled Judge Miniter's entrance. Everyone stood as a diminutive, black-robed man emerged from behind a door, commanding, "Sheriff, open court!"—

The prosecutor, a skeletal young man in his mid-twenties, stood next to a shellacked wooden table with two stacks of manila files. He reached for a folder, and in the timbre of a teenager said, "Your Honor, the State calls... "

Forty minutes later the prosecutor had cleared the docket and, having no more defendants in the stack, approached the judge. "Sir, it's the Hamilton case up ne—" and whispered something.

"Sheriff, clear the room," Miniter commanded, cutting him off.

The proceedings took two minutes, but Trent—his particular sense of loyalty offended, wasn't about to let things go as easily as the judge had been persuaded to. He seethed, vowing that the time would come to get even with old Roger.

Until It's Time to Go

ONE CHILLY MID-DECEMBER AFTERNOON in '49, while waiting on the steps of the museum, Julie saw Roger a block away and started running, oblivious of the Santas ringing bells in front of red and green buckets of money and bumping past shoppers, until she threw her arms around his neck. Taking her soft cheeks in his hands, he kissed her. They took a stroll to East Rock Park on the north end of Yale's campus. She leaned against a large boulder, and Roger embraced her tightly, blanketing her body with his.

"You're the first guy I ever had a crush on, you know," she said. "Never dated anybody, except when I went to a freshman dance once." Roger listened, kissing her gently on the neck. Eyes open, looking straight ahead into a thicket of yew, she continued, "I just never drew any attention." Roger did not answer, his fingers—rough from shop solvents—moved under her sweater feeling her smooth breasts. "Always thought I was too plain. Do you think that's weird?" Roger rubbed his palms on her back then her stomach. She felt him press against her. "And in school it seemed when anybody found out I played the violin, they ran away, like I had the plague or something." Roger's body began to move slowly, arcing against hers. She pushed him away looking beyond the yews. "Roger, be careful, someone might be watching." He turned down the corners of his mouth and furrowed his eyebrows. She burst out laughing. "How come you're so attracted to me? Well, why?" Roger was at a loss, trying to regain some measure of self-possession.

"Why'd you think?"

"Maybe because I let you feel me up?" She grinned.

"Yeah, that's it," he said, unable to hide his smirk.

"I love it when you try to hide your smile."

"I ain't tryin' to hide nothing."

111

"Roger, do you think we'll last?"

Roger's look went from playful to serious. She tried looking him in the eye, but he turned away.

"Roger? You're scaring me. Will it last?"

Roger was mute.

"Well? Will it?"

"Julie, I've got bad news."

She felt a chill pass through her. Tears welled in her eyes. "Bad news?'" she whispered.

Beyond the yews a crow picked at the carcass of a small rodent. The trees were barren, and the sun was no longer visible behind high cirrus clouds.

"I got drafted."

Her brows rose as her eyes bloomed into fullness: he wasn't breaking up! Everything else could be solved. Then her brows furrowed. She drew a deep breath and prepared for Roger's explanation.

"What do you mean?"

"Means... I'm soon to be in the Army."

Her eyes swelled with tears again. Her lips tightened, her mouth went dry. "You're leaving?" she said softly.

"Ain't leavin' you. I'm going to the Army."

The old tightness in her throat returned. She moved from the boulder toward a leafless tree. Roger kicked the frozen ground, jamming his hands into his jacket.

"Right after New Year's, I'll be shoving off to Fort Dix. From there, who knows?"

"I... I suppose, you can do something? I mean get out of it, right? My brother's in ROTC, maybe you can talk to him. He might have an idea. He'll be home from college next week."

"It's no use. I already quit my job."

"Wh... Wh... " she whirled around to face him. "Roger! Why?"

"I don't have a choice."

"So you're just gonna leave?"

"Well, yes and no," Roger spoke tentatively, "Julie... Julie, I know a, a small hotel, let's go there."

Julie would remember this room—a steel framed bed with the thin, feather-stuffed pad, coffee-stained oak dresser, a maple credenza with a yellowed mirror that had lost most of its silver. A Gideon Bible was closed on a discolored doily. The window was stuck partly open at the top and a radiator creaked beneath it. The wallpaper had different patterns on adjacent walls, oddly reminding her how badly she wanted Roger, but how scared she was. It was her first time. But the credenza and dresser—leftovers from the First World War—made her think about the furniture in her bedroom, and these things made her unafraid.

Julie stood in the middle of the room, her belly pressed against Roger. She closed her eyes, felt his stiffness. Roger touched the back of her blue flowered dress and undid its row of small buttons. His calloused carpenter hands lightly lifted the dress off her shoulder; it fell to the floor, exposing the whiteness of her chest and the silver locket hanging from her neck. His thumbs slid beneath the thin satin straps of her slip. She felt like a calla lily on a naked stem—every organ inside her waking, blossoming into experience. She wanted Roger kissing every part of her that burned with desire. She saw him take stock of her smallness, unadorned and imagined he might be looking at her like one looks at a half-naked mannequin at Macy's. Never taking her eyes off his face, she sat on the bed, waiting for him to undress. She felt nervous. Fearing her teeth might start chattering she laid back and slipped beneath the covers, where the sheet felt cool on her back. Covered now, she disrobed completely.

The lavender pink sky gleamed through the translucent prism of the gritty window. She kept her eyes on Roger as he stripped off and slipped in next to her. His body was on fire. Nervous, aroused, excited, scared, quiet tears flowed down her cheeks over her lips, she embraced him, saying, "I love you so much, Roger. So afraid, so afraid... that what we have will die, if I don't see you. What if something happened to us?"

They made love, and as the lavender pink sky turned silver gray, Julie lost all sensible measure of time. Each lay in the other's limerence, her head on his shoulder, his arm behind his head. A tawny, orange-winged monarch flew from the window sill to the foot of the bed. She raised herself on one elbow.

113

"Roger, a butterfly!" She followed the insect's minute movements and reached down to coax it onto her hand.

The bug flapped its wings and flew toward the window. She drew her finger down Roger's forehead, over his nose, lips, chin. "You know, Roger, a butterfly holds a person's soul."

He squinted, smiled and turned his head toward her. "Where'd you hear that?"

"I don't know exactly, but I like to think it's true."

"Whose soul?"

"I don't know, they say it could be someone who's alive, or dying or already dead." She pulled her hand from the sheet, raised it in the direction of the creature that flew from the window to the ceiling in the far corner, where the lengthwise wallpaper stripes ran counter to the paper on the adjacent wall, the black margins and veins on its wings making the incongruent wallpaper congruous. "Maybe ours!" she said, turning over to smile at Roger.

He let out a breath of resignation. "If I were a reckless god, I'd unbuckle Nature's hair and let it fall on her shoulders, letting all the days we've had together come undone again." He put his arms around her, burying his face in her breasts so she could not see the ocean filling his eyes.

"You're a poet, you know. The way you think. Feel."

Nothing stirred. Julie wanted it that way—to freeze time if she could. She whispered, "I guess what I'm afraid of more than anything in the world, is that what we have right now may someday fade."

Daylight fell further into the horizon, the striped wallpaper disappeared, and the butterfly flapped its wings, stalled them upright, and finally vanished through a small opening into the cold void of winter. In their nakedness, they met each other no longer as strangers, in longing, in lust, no longer searching for warmth and tenderness. Roger filled the voids, erasing all Julie's perceived imperfections: her awkwardness, her loneliness, her frailty.

As they left the hotel, a light snow fell. At the corner, Julie looked back and noticed how quickly their tracks were covered.

"Roger, tell me you will always love me. Tell me, tell me and keep telling me while you're away, so I can hear it over and over. So I know you're there."

Roger stopped and pulled her close. "Julie, most things in life are figments of our imagination. They only exist because we're conscious of them. Music's that way. If we disappeared, music would only be noise to the universe. Love's different. It is beyond our conscious being, it's that place where beauty, song, the spirit live. If we accept it, it never vanishes. Never."

The light turned red and Roger loosened his grip, but she grabbed and held onto his coat, afraid to let go—aware how close she was to a new order of time, when all things emotionally temporal would suspend until her man returned.

On the train home that night she wrote:

I know now that I will never have to hurry through life searching to feel what we have at this moment. If for no other reason than today, I shall always love you. If for nothing else, I shall always know that whatever I do, wherever I go, it will be not futile or in vain, because all things will be forever cast in this moment—be it my music or that unnamed thing which I have yet to meet, or that unknown thing, for which I claim to live. From this moment, it is you.

The next week Julie and Roger met in Bridgeport for the last time. Outfitted in navy blue pea coats and rubber boots, the couple spent the day walking arm in arm along the beach at Seaside Park. Gray and white gulls flew overhead, shrieking open-throated for a scrap of bread. Except for the gulls and two resolute fishermen casting off the stony breakwaters, they had the foamy lips of the ocean to themselves. The January tide ebbed and flowed— the long moments of silence marked by the breaking waves that kept time like brushes against the drumhead of a lonely snare.

"I used to do a lot of fishing when I was a kid, right out there," Roger said with a longing in his voice. "My dad and I, we'd get there at dark so we'd see the sun come up. The ocean and sky would wake up across that span of 180 degrees. And depending on the way the earth turned, every day was a new brilliance. Blink and you'd see patterns within patterns in a world that brought us a day that had never before existed."

Julie loved the poetry in him, and the utter freedom it allowed her own words—words that for most of her life were inside her, tied at the base of her tongue. "I see that in us, Roger. It seems love invents a new splendor every morning since the day we met." They walked until the new tide came in and the sun found its way to the western sky. A strong gale roiled the ever-darkening green gray waves and stung their faces.

A weathered old man in a black woolen overcoat walked toward them. "Sir, would you take a picture of me and my girl?" Roger asked hopefully.

"Sure," he said, in a gravelly German accent.

Roger pressed the camera into the man's oversized hand. "Look in here and press this."

Roger grabbed Julie's bundled waist, and they posed in a mist blowing from an up-tick in wind. The man stepped back, and Julie imagined how they filled the eyepiece: two faces, hers under her mother's paisley kerchief, Roger's under a black pea cap. The man's finger located the small silver button. He steadied the camera. "*Lächeln. Sagen Käse, eh.*"

Feeling Julie shiver beside him, Roger squeezed her. "I think he means smile."

The shutter snapped, a frame of silver halide exposed two smiling lovers in the light of a low, winter sun. As the man handed the camera to Roger, he smiled widely, and Julie heard him say, "Lucky man." Roger thanked him. Julie blushed, then lifted her chin, smiled, staunchly feeling in that moment a woman invincible to her core.

The two lovers moved away from the shore, avoiding the occasional wave that broke free to chart a new high, washing away all earthly footprints. The gulls vanished one by one. Roger and Julie walked into a headwind for nearly a mile to the five story, arched entrance to the park where she would take the number 5 bus to the Barnum line and where Roger would take the number 2 to the train station. Alone at the stop, they held each other, wordless.

It started to rain. A number 2 came and went. Then, too soon, a number 5 came into sight. She boarded, finding a seat adjacent to where Roger stood against the wet wind, promising to be resolute. She focused straight ahead, but then at the last moment turned her head and Roger appeared on the other side of the rain streaked glass, mottled and sparkling. The bus hissed and lumbered forward, until the lovers, one from the other disappeared. Slumping beneath the sill, Julie let all the tears she had dammed flow like the rain slipping passed the slippery glass, imagining the lonely winter ahead—the long one, the one where only the nature of things outside human influence would decide if she were to ever see Roger again. And believing with the passion of first love, that of course, she would.

***

During the first five months of Roger's Army life, the couple exchanged dozens of letters. On June 2, 1950, Roger read orders posted on the bulletin board: *Private Roger Girardin, San Diego, California, Naval Station, port of embarkation. Assignment: 1st Battalion, 21st Regiment, 24th Infantry Division, Japan. Arrival estimated June 21, 1950. Report to Command H.*

Julie had written to him often about her loneliness, and he felt answerable for her sadness, but just before he embarked on his new assignment, he wrote:

Yes, yes we do have better days ahead. Days when we can pick morning like a wild flower again, when we can love life again (when I know you are there, I truly love life), when we can spend our days with each other and grow old. Right now I cannot see you, your smile, your nakedness. It's empty here because I can't hear you whisper, laugh, or moan, or even hear your beautiful complaints. These things are what fill me up.

The barrack's lights went out promptly at nine. Roger placed the letter in the outgoing mail. Twenty days later, he received her reply:

Roger, you speak of our love so wonderfully. See, this is why I love you so much & why it's so hard to ever move on —each day is a struggle. Last night I played the violin from three till dawn. The workers leaving to make the six o'clock whistle must have heard me all the way to the bus stop.

After he read Julie's letter he noticed a small crepe paper with something hidden inside still in the envelope. He unfolded the paper and found three blue-button wild flowers neatly pressed and pasted to a tiny card that read: *From My Secret Garden.*

That evening, Roger, Julie and millions of Americans picked up their newspapers. The headlines all read: *NORTH KOREA INVADES THE SOUTH.*

Road to Suwon

ON JUNE 25, 1950, IT RAINED HARD ALONG the invisible line separating the two Koreas. Sometime in the early morning, rumors flooded Seoul that the North Korean People's Army (NKPA), had crossed the 38th parallel. Three days later, the NKPA stormed into the capital killing, wounding and capturing thousands. Taken by surprise, the Republic of Korea's (ROK) government based in Seoul set up operations twenty miles south, in Suwon. President Truman ordered troops flown into the country, in what he described as a police action—giving the impression he was sending forces in for crowd control. Less concerned with how it played at home, General Douglas MacArthur ordered the 1st Battalion, 21st Regiment, 24th Infantry Division to Suwon, to hold the line of advancing NKPA. Under the command of Lieutenant Colonel Brad Babcock, a contingent of four hundred and six men departed from Itazuke Air Base, Japan on the morning of July 1. Included among the troops were a few war horses, like WWII veteran Sergeant Joe Johns, a burly thirty-year-old with one ear, and a large contingent of green privates—like Roger Girardin, the lanky twenty-three-year-old.

Accounts of well-orchestrated troop movements going awry litter military history, and Korea was no exception. Instead of flying to Suwon, the Air Force dropped the men on a landing strip outside of Pusan, hundreds of miles south of the intended destination. Babcock quickly organized a caravan and moved seventeen miles to board a train that would take the troops partway to Suwon. Since the train wasn't ready for boarding, Babcock ordered the mess sergeant to break out a chow line, but when his adjutant informed him that, except for the sergeant, the rest of the cooks were left in Japan, he revised his order— C-Rations. The troops were off to a shaky start.

Roger and his fellow neophytes deploying to the front for the first time did not dwell much on food but on the abstract anticipation of combat. They feared the unidentified, saw a boding evil in everything—from the orderliness of lines to the simplest staccato commands— that seemed loud and exaggerated. On the platform, waiting to board an old steam train, Roger watched the officers, hushed and heads lowered, sluggishly moving toward the rickety, wooden second-class cabins.

Sergeant Johns stood at the front of the formation.

"This fucking place smells like shit," he grumbled.

"Smells like rotten cabbage, Sarge," blurted the man next to Roger.

"No one asked you, soldier."

A local high school band played a Sousa march near the locomotive, as commands were shouted over horns, calling for the men to climb aboard. In the brown boxcars coupled behind the officer's second-class cabins, the stench of cabbage gave way to the smell of hay, piss and animal crap. Each man found a spot suited to his level of anxiety: edgy talkers and listeners, readers (comics, novels, bibles) letter writers, poker players. Most men were sweat-soaked to the bone. Roger chose a corner strewn with hardened nuggets of dog shit, pushed them aside, and flopped down onto floorboards suspiciously stained with dried blood.

A steam whistle blew. The cars jerked forward as the locomotive chuffed from the station, spitting and spewing a silver-white vaporous exhaust, its sound swallowing the oompah-pah of the golden tubas. A steady acceleration, a repetition of articulating connecting rods, the mechanical growls as the wheels bore down on the tracks—muffling the bass drums that had earlier drowned the shouts of the officers bringing the men to order. In due course the train relaxed under a steady quickening, its cadence eventually calming Roger's unease. He pulled Julie's last letter from his knapsack, and his eyes closed before he finished reading the last line.

At 0800, July 2, the train pulled into Taejon, its whistle startling Roger out of a restless sleep. Some diehards were still playing poker. The men jumped from the cars and

120

assembled in rows ten feet from the tracks. On command, they broke formation, found a dusty space alongside the dirty, gray, clapboard station, opened rations for a second time and shot the breeze—reminding Roger of the Boy Scouts he once saw headed for summer camp.

While the men bivouacked, Colonel Babcock and a band of soldiers, including Roger, drove jeeps north to Osan to survey and choose a location they would defend if the NK headed toward Pusan as predicted. A few miles south of the village of Suwon the colonel found what he was looking for: a group of small hills that crossed a road—a pinch point for troops moving through. He designated one—a three-hundred foot elevation, Hill 116—to serve as his "vantage point." That night the troops boarded another train to Pyongtaek, leaving them with a ten-mile march that began at midnight. Three hours later, in a light rain, they reached a muddy flat one-half mile south of Hill 116, where men from the 52nd Field Artillery Battalion were setting up artillery armed with high explosive anti-tank shells.

Roger woke at dawn to the sound of radio chatter. "T-34 tank from the interior. Look to the north, sir." Two lookouts about twenty feet away heard the report, too. One of them poked his head out of the brush, scanning the horizon through field glasses blurred by a steady downpour. Handing the glasses to the man next to him, he snarled, "It's crawling like a motherfuckin' bug." Thirty minutes later, other tanks were visible. The radioman reported, "I think there are eight, maybe more, sir."

"Recoilless! Recoilless rifles!" Babcock hollered. Johns repeated the order, and men on the forward slope fired the first American rounds of the war—sending a shudder through the troops huddled behind boulders dotting the hill.

"A splash of mud, sir, the mark's short. Tank's advancing," reported a veteran.

Babcock radioed the bazooka men lodged in a drainage ditch alongside the road, "Hold your fire until they're on top of you!" When the lead tank came within twenty yards, an explosive fire and thunder shot out from the turreted gun. A second later, a concussive vibration rattled the hill, followed by a sharp cracking sound from several toppling hardwoods. The radio chattered. "Tank's still coming." From another direction, "Medic, medic." Roger saw three men covered in branches sprawled in a clearing next to the felled trees.

The men of the 24th crouched or leaned behind the trees and large boulders. A short while later the point man spotted twenty-five more tanks moving from the north, outside the range of small artillery. A howitzer from the south encampment blasted off two rounds in succession targeting one of the six forerunners.

"Bug's on fire!" shouted the point man. The five remaining tanks turned to outflank Babcock's howitzer 105s. Within two hours, the first of the group of twenty-five T-34 tanks had completely bypassed Hill 116. Roger heard chatter again.

"Sir, one o'clock." Roger lifted his head from behind his rock and through the rain saw a column of trucks and troops that stretched out as far as his eye could see, reminding him of the panic he felt the first time he saw a five-foot water snake slithering along the ground at his uncle's farm. He felt like shitting his pants.

Another hour passed before he heard the rattled pulse of sprocket driven tracks; fifteen minutes later the metallic cadence stopped. Enemy infantry emerged like green ghosts out of the downpour. Three hundred yards north of Hill 116 an NK tank faced the troops. It raised its turret and fired. Following a thud, screams of "Corpsman, corpsman." Babcock's bazookas returned fire, but the shells bounced as they fell short. Roger saw the colonel, a few lieutenants, a dozen noncoms and as many grunts zigzagging toward the top of the hill. He followed, bolting up a narrow path and tripping over a man gurgling in his own blood. "Corpsman," someone yelled. Roger kept running until he saw a three-boulder fortress, and he fell safely into a cranny, shaking as much from fear as from the cold rain coming down in sheets.

From his new position, he saw a steady stream of enemy infantry, arcade-like, crossed the base of the hill, two hundred yards out, firing blindly. The Americans fired back at phantoms—partly due to the rain and partly due to the enemy darting in and out, but the firing seemed to retard an all-out assault. Roger, like most of Babcock's new recruits, did not conserve the two hundred rounds of ammo issued in Pusan, and by late afternoon, he had less than thirty rounds in the extra two magazines he carried in his field jacket.

As the afternoon passed on, rain limited visibility to feet rather than yards. Over the staccato rifle fire, Roger heard garbled orders shouted out in the distance. About an hour later, in the last light of day, he saw hazy figures of men fleeing their positions. To his astonishment, he and a few men had been left behind. The yelling earlier had been orders to retreat. Everything was still, and he felt the enemy was waiting for dusk before charging murderously. When he could not see farther than the end of the barrel, he heard the bugled death-knells and a swell of fire from the base of the hill, followed by horror-filled shrieks that filled the air—the sounds that living things make when impaled, sliced and blasted in the soft extremities. Guys in front of him were being massacred. He held fast—frozen with the dry heaves—but he knew had to get his jelly-like legs moving. He started running away from the screams, south by southwest, where the hill flattened into a murky no man's land. At the edge of an open rice paddy, there was a gully where he found Sergeant Johns crouched. Together, they headed away from the gun fire, turning east, south, southeast following a half-frozen muddy irrigation ditch. Three feet apart, they now most feared losing one another in the desolate night. Only when near-terminal exhaustion set in and Johns said he could not go another step, did they stop.

The pair crawled into a dry part of the ditch and slept. Next morning, the horizon began to reveal what seemed like the end of the Earth, a long, flat, empty plain. The men followed the narrow channel as it wound through the outskirts of several adjoining paddies. In the distance, Roger thought he heard small-arms fire—.45 caliber.

They followed the trench, and the shots got louder. A half-hour later, Roger poked his head over the edge. About two-hundred-fifty clicks, a steam shovel was parked near mounds of dirt, and next to it a pair of diesel trucks and three black cars with silver emblems, and milling about, were a dozen South Korean grunts. Beyond them were a half-dozen men in black suits standing on top of a long levee, firing into he figured was a creek.

Neither man could tell what was happening, and they stayed put. Fifteen minutes later the firing stopped. Soldiers got into the unmarked trucks, and the men in suits got into the cars and drove off.

Roger and Johns waited another half-hour before approaching the levy, which turned out to be dirt-piles ten feet high. As they climbed the pile, their boots sunk to the tops of the laces. When Roger came within a few feet of the top, he gagged and had to cover his nose in his field jacket. Smelled like a rotting carcass. At the top he saw wide trenches. Inside a large hole, were dead bodies, white shirts, suits, women in dresses. His stomach turned upside down. Johns fell to his knees, stuck his head between his thighs and puked.

Roger, hands shaking, pulled his camera from his belt and, holding his breath, clicked off half-dozen frames of hundreds of bodies heaped one one another, arms and legs tangled. Gray tones, dirt, matted hair, black sludge, exposed bones, bared nipples, twisted, doubled over, eyes facing all directions. Innards and entrails reminded Roger of the time he bagged a buck and sliced its belly open. Snap. He wound the next frame. Snap, snap, exposing the blacks and whites of the devil's work against condensation —threads lazily rising from the pit.

Roger and Johns laid back behind the elevated berm habituating to the sweet stench of death.

"Holy Christ! What the fuck?" Johns grumbled, in a voice just above a nervous whisper.

"A bloodbath."

"Koreans."

"Korean Commies, maybe?"

"Maybe the guys who shot 'em were... who the fuck knows... we better not hang round," Johns advised, grimacing.

Roger, committing to memory what logic rejected, looked into the pits one more time. Thoughts raced back in time trying to connect things he had read, stories he had heard, pictures, paintings, bad dreams—anything that might have prepared him to process what reality dished up. No match, no reference.

Hidden as before, Roger watched three flatbed trucks hauling yellow bulldozers come bumping over the fallow ground, stopping thirty yards from the pits. He snapped three more frames. Workers in green coveralls emerged from the trucks to crank the dozer engines. In two hours, the machines had leveled the grave, its secret intact. Roger loaded more film and snapped pictures of the workers driving the dozers back to the flatbeds. When the engines were shut down, a quiet swept over the land—except for a few birds of prey.

In the distance, a brown sedan approached. It stopped, and two men got out and walked over to one of the truck drivers. From Roger's vantage they appeared to be U.S. Army officers: a major and a second lieutenant. Later, Johns would indicate he wasn't sure. They decided to stay put. As Roger finished one roll and loaded a fresh one, he quipped, "Damn, that guy looks familiar."

Johns warned, "Be careful, sun may reflect off the lens."

Rogers snapped a few more frames: the officer leaning against the door of the sedan, trucks with soot spewing from vertical exhausts, dirt road, barren field and the horizon—beyond which, the men would later learn, Suwon lay torn asunder.

Roger lifted his notebook from the knapsack lying on the ground and opened it to jot down that memory, putting pencil to paper and wiping the tears that added a residue to the carboned script:

"A no man's land, faux vacancy, methane of the dead bodies twisted in sculptured poses, pyres of flesh, wire, gas, guns, stench, cold, killed in the trench, buried... the improbable mug staring back... ."

The men remained holed up until nightfall, then followed the maze of ditches to Ansong, arriving close to two in the morning. They ran down a narrow street with darkened houses, which led to an avenue with a roadblock. Two police cars were parked across the road. Johns said worriedly, "I don't know if it's safe to just go over to the two guys sitting there. You stay here, cover me."

Roger watched Johns—carbine slung over his shoulder, pointed forward, safety off. One of the policemen jumped out of the car. Johns held his ID in front pointing to where he had come from. Roger heard him say who he was.

"GI?"

Johns nodded, and the other guy got out of the car. They took stock of Johns' ready rifle. They motioned to him to get into the car. John said he had a buddy and waved Roger out of the shadows, and the four drove less than five minutes, passing a sign that read: *U.S. Army—Post Headquarters.* MPs at the entrance escorted them to the CQ's barrack. A duty corporal poured the men coffee while Johns told him what he had seen. The CQ picked up a phone relaying the matter to the officer-in-charge. At about 6 a.m., two first lieutenants from Pyongtaek, who had been flown in June 29 from the States with an intelligence unit, woke them. Lieutenant Jacoby, the apparent leader, was a five-foot-five talky guy from Texas. Roger thought he looked like Napoleon. Lieutenant Samuelson let Jacoby take charge. Johns described what he saw. "Blood looked like it was still wet. Most were men in white pants. Women there, too. Bodies over bodies in all directions. I wanted to puke even before I knew what I was lookin' at."

"Could you tell how many, Sergeant?"

"Figured four, five hundred. Mostly guys. All dead, I figure. Saw one, two move, but I'd seen the dead move before. Had to be... dead."

"Were they wearing any special clothes, anything odd about them?"

"Don't remember. Mostly peasants. Lots of them doubled over, poor buggers. Saw lots of white. Probably remember because," he paused. "Honestly?" He paused again. "There's lotsa, lotsa blood... a few men in white shirts. Few women in long dresses."

"Could you tell if they were mostly shot in the head?"

"No, sir, could not." He paused. "Honestly? Remember a young girl, stared straight up. Didn't look that long. Saw what I saw, didn't need to gawk."

"What about you, Girardin? What'd you see?"

126

"Sir, can't add nothin'."

"You must have seen something."

"Yeah, but you know, was like a bad dream, a picture of hell." He hesitated and added, "The 'Souls of the Wrathful.'"

"What's that soldier, what'd you say?"

"The Souls of ... it's a painting. Dante's hell, bodies lying all over the goddamn place."

Samuelson and Jacoby looked at each other.

"Dante who?" asked Jacoby.

"Never mind."

Lieutenant Samuelson, the more introspective officer, dropped his gaze to Roger's waist. "Take any pictures?"

Caught off guard, Roger replied straight away, "No... " Then remembered the *Leica* tied to his belt and quickly countered, "... 'cept for the film that's in there."

"Let me have the camera."

Samuelson rewound the film, opened the back and removed the film Roger had loaded earlier. He returned the camera. Roger's hand passed over his pocket—he felt the rolls of film he had put away and wondered if he should turn them over. He looked at Johns, got no sign; he left things where they were, one roll for them, three rolls for himself. Later that day, Roger and Johns hitched a jeep ride to Pyongtaek, where Roger bundled the film rolls into a package and had the mail clerk send it to his father's attention. The note read: "... *hold until I return.*"

***

In August and early September, victory continued to elude the Americans. At one point, the better conditioned NK soldiers captured nearly the entire 19th Regiment, leaving dozens of American POWs shot in the head, hands tied behind their backs. This hit the newspapers. American sentiments about the U.S. engagement sank precipitously, and the political arm of the CIA considered it all the more essential that any atrocities be kept top secret.

Based on the interrogations of Johns and Girardin, the intelligence officers generated an incident report. They wrote "*Secret*" on the envelope and inserted the report, along with the photos they had developed. The package was delivered to Major General Church, in Pyongtaek, fifty miles away. The general would emphasize its importance in his cable to Washington, but the matter of the pits did not register in the organizational mind of military intelligence or the CIA until mid-September, nearly two and a half months later. Meanwhile, forces south of Seoul could not push the NKPA back from the advances made in August. But on September 15, 1950, U.N. forces under MacArthur's command launched a surprise amphibious attack at Inchon—well above the NKPA units in the south —effectively severing their connection to the northern supply lines. By the end of the month, MacArthur's forces had recaptured Seoul and pushed the enemy back across the 38th parallel.

In late September, when CIA chief Walter Smythe learned about the pictures, he fumed, imagining the political consequences if anyone learned that the ROK, under orders by President Rhee, had massacred thousands of political prisoners and citizens suspected of being friendly to the communists. Smythe ordered Paul McCallister, the U.S. Embassy military attaché operating out of temporary headquarters in Seoul, to have Staff Sergeant Joseph Johns and Private Roger Girardin immediately brought back to HQ X Corp for sequestration and questioning.

On September 30, two senior Army officers, thirty-year-old G-2 Lieutenant Colonel Herbert Barclay, twenty-seven year old a G-2 Captain Sonny Reiner, and CIA operative thirty-five-year-old Robert Perrone from Langley Field, Virginia were under secret orders to find the fast moving reconstituted 1st Battalion, 24th Division, 19th Regiment and return Sergeant Joseph Johns and Private Roger Girardin for questioning. The instructions were specific: "... *Confiscate all cameras and film the men might have in their possession.*" There was a supplemental order:

"... *if it is deemed unfeasible to secure the subjects under the control of the military police or otherwise return the men for sequestration and questioning, then any member of the Barclay Task Force is empowered to take necessary and sufficient action to prevent Private Roger Girardin or Staff Sergeant Joseph Johns from falling under control of the enemy.*"

By mid-October, the U.N. forces north of the 38th parallel were situated along a line from the North Korean capital, Pyongyang, inland to Wonsan—a seaport forty-five miles to its east. Under MacArthur's leadership, the U.N. forces were heading straight for the Manchurian border. The 24th Division, with Johns and Girardin, crossed the Ch'ongch'on River and came within fifty miles of the Yalu River, separating Korea from Manchuria. But in November, an ominous turn stopped the relative ease with which the U.N. had penetrated North Korea.

Surprising Army Intelligence on Sunday, November 26, 1950 stated an estimated 300,000 Chinese Communist troops crossed the Yalu River. They overran Allied forces, cut off escape routes and drove them thirty miles south, killing, maiming and capturing more than 40,000 U.S. troops. On December 2, the U.S. 1st Cavalry lost a battalion in a battle with soldiers wearing Mao apparel. The next day, the 24th Infantry hit heavy resistance and, alongside large numbers of other U.N. forces, began a hasty retreat south. The men of the 24th Division again crossed the Ch'ongch'on River. The end of the war was a long ways off.

Silence of the Mail Call
Fall 1950

A POSTMAN DELIVERED A LETTER FROM THE Army to an old man painting a green fence. The next day, the man visited a barbershop with the red, white and blue pole spinning out front. The barber, bloodletter of older days, was now the unofficial sympathizer to eight blocks in the west end of Bridgeport. Trimming straw-like hair from the old man's ears, the barber said gloomily, "You son's missing? He might be found!" On that note of hope, the barber seamlessly passed the scissors to his left hand, which held a comb, so that he could make the sign of the cross.

The clip, clip of the scissors cutting short strokes across the man's thin, white hair echoed off the hard, mirrored surfaces. The barber moved behind the patron. For a fleeting moment, he lifted his gaze into the full length mirror, and the men locked eyes. The barber stepped back and inhaled the smells of soap and alcohol that saturated the air—odors that served the barber as a poor man's incense, a way of suffusing an inner sanctum filled with hushed grief. For fifty years he had listened to men like Girardin while cutting their hair and watching them through the silvered mirror, searching for words that might console them.

"*Pazienza.* Gone in the middle of the nowhere they say, between *il presidente* and *la Madonna a mia,* and you read this, from a big a shot in a Washington, somebody you willa never see... *Madon.*"

The barber, like a local crier, shared the news that Roger had disappeared with patrons and with those who stopped by to catch up on news. They, in turn, passed it on to their wives. The next day the wives ensured the reliable propagation of the account, and in a short while, all eight square blocks had learned of the old man's tragedy.

The next Sunday, under a steady rain, friends bearing baked breads and cold cuts stopped by the white house with the green fence to commiserate with the Girardins. The old woman kept a clean and neat place that carried within its walls the smells of cleaning fluids and moth balls, and all who came were careful to wipe their feet at the door. But a child lost at any age, under any circumstance brings with it a stench of casualty, a dark dampness in a room filled with people neither mourners nor well wishers—fatalists sober in the face of uncertainty.

***

By late October, Julie hadn't received a letter from Roger for seven weeks. She waited for the postman. Nothing came. Outside, the rain pelted the house, the last leaves of fall abandoned their branches, the clock ticked past 5 a.m. and Julie had already written for ten minutes.

Dear Roger,

I hope this letter finds you safe and warm. The picture of me is from last May with my brother Jack (in case you're wondering who that guy is). We have not heard from him in almost eight weeks. I'm frightened. But I refuse to give in to it, and lose faith that he, and you, are okay and doing what needs getting done to come home as soon as heavenly possible. I know there are thousands of our boys over there, but if you run into him, tell him his mother is worried, and he should write. I read about the war twice a day, can't take myself away from the radio. Mrs. White has a new TV & lets me watch the news when I want, & it's always on Korea.

To let space separate her from the page, she poured a cup of coffee and went to the small room where her violin laid in its velvet case. She plucked the strings—so, re, la, me—and imagined the sound of Roger's voice. She returned to her letter.

The newspaper tells us the Army crossed the 38th Parallel, so I guess you are in North Korea. It had an article on Oscar Hammerstein that said he was against the

131

government setting up a group to censor entertainers. The world's gone crazy.

It was 6 a.m. when she heard her mother turn on the shower. Not wanting to let go the quiet time she had with Roger, she penned one more thought before starting her day.

Oh Roger, it might be years before I see you again. I can't stand to bear it. I heard you call my name a little while ago when I plinked on the violin, so I tell myself, you are, at least, in my music.

In late November, newspapers reported that the Chinese invaded Korea, but Julie's attention to the day to day war reports was diverted when Nonna Rosa had a stroke a few days before Thanksgiving—confining her to a wheelchair. Grandfather Libero had passed away the year before, so Mary, who worked at the hospital, and Julie, who faithfully practiced her violin, managed to take care of Rosa around the clock. Eventually the calendar flipped into December and Julie found her rhythm again—waking before sunrise, writing and posting letter after letter to Roger's last known APO, Pusan, Republic of Korea.

Julie went to Sunday mass the week before Christmas. The air was crisp, like the day Roger told her he had been drafted. Leaving church, she bumped into a high school friend and they talked about Roger's long silence. Her friend suggested she visit his parents. Julie had never met them, but knew they lived somewhere across town. She went into the Silver Streak Diner to look up Girardin in the white pages and saw one listing, Jean Girardin, First Avenue. She called the number and a man with a French-Canadian accent answered.

"Hello."

Julie's throat tightened, and she hung up, afraid to learn what may have happened to Roger. She walked to the counter, ordered a coffee, but before she took her first sip, she was headed for the door and the address listed in the phonebook.

The Barnum line dropped her at the one room Greyhound terminal on Center Street, where she transferred to the Oxford line that took her to the West

End. She found the house on First Avenue, a white Cape Cod with a green picket fence. At first she walked past the gate, thinking that Roger might be all right, that he and his parents were in touch, or that she might learn Roger had another girl, a sweetheart, a Canadian beauty, engaged, married—who could tell? She returned to the bus stop and waited a few minutes, but the house and those inside who had the answers she desperately needed drew her back.

She knocked. A plump, white haired woman in a cardigan and a over a flowered housedress came to the door. The woman smiled, revealing several crooked teeth.

"Yes?" she asked. Her voice put Julie at ease.

"Is this the home of Roger Girardin's parents?"

"Yes, I'm his mother... and you are?"

"I'm a friend... of your son."

Mrs. Girardin wrinkled her brows, tightened her lips, and gave Julie the once-over. "Come in, let me take your coat."

Sitting on a red, tufted sofa, Mrs. Girardin leaned forward. She moved her foot over a frayed spot in the red and gray circular rug.

Julie sat in a stiff side chair next to a maple coffee table adorned with a bouquet of fake blue irises, and surveyed the sparsely furnished room: a bulb was missing in the small, plastic chandelier in the center of the room, but otherwise the home was neat, with a hint of mothballs. Above the sofa, a lithograph of a huntsman with brown and white hounds in an ornate gilded frame suggested a different time and place.

The old woman stirred. "Can I get you something? Water, coffee?"

"Oh no, thank you."

"How long have you known my son?"

"Oh, we go back to August '48. Was a Friday. I saw him for the first time at the art museum in New Haven."

"Roger wanted to be an artist, then a writer. His father wanted him to learn a trade. He'd helped his dad from the time he could carry a hammer."

"Told me he made cabinets." Julie smiled faintly and tried to see Roger's face in Mrs. Girardin's.

133

"A cabinetmaker, like my husband. Do your people live 'round here?"

"My dad works at Colt Cosmetic Cases. Mom's a nurse."

"And, you? Do you work?"

"I play violin. And my grandmother, she had a stroke, so I take care— " Julie could not hold out any longer, "Mrs. Girardin, have you heard from Roger?"

"Oh, my dear, Roger is missing!" She plucked a tissue from her sleeve to dab her eyes. "I suppose you had no way of knowing."

"Missing?" Julie could not make sense of it. She bent forward. "Missing?"

"Yes, my dear."

Julie cocked her head, struggling to get the words out. "What do you mean? How do you know?"

"About ten days ago, we got a letter from the Army. Said he's missing. Let me get it."

When she rose from the couch, Julie saw that the woman wore an apron stained with blue or blackberries. She heard Mrs. Girardin blow her nose. Water flushed. A door creaked open and the woman called, "Come upstairs, we gotta friend of Roger's here. I think you should meet her." Julie heard someone climbing stairs. Roger's mother returned with a brown envelope.

"Julie, was it?"

Julie straightened her back. "Yes, Mrs. Girardin."

A white haired man with horn rimmed glasses appeared, dusting off brown overalls.

"Jean," she pronounced it in the French way, "This is Julie. Roger has a girlfriend." She smiled.

"How do you do, sir?"

"Very, very pleased to meet you, young lady," he said with the French-Canadian accent she had heard on the phone. He sat next to his wife. He raised his eyebrows, and Julie felt a familiar warmth in the soft, blue eyes behind his thick glasses. "You know my son?"

"Yes. We were going out." She wondered how she seemed to him: neat, polite, pretty enough.

"Oh, we figured Roger had a girl," he chuckled, "didn't we, Lisa? But he's so private, that one."

Mrs. Girardin plucked a letter from a wrapper with an official government seal. "I told Julie we hadn't heard nothing," she said in a clear-cut manner. Reaching across the coffee table, she handed it to Julie. "Well, here it is... from the Army."

Julie unfolded the paper thinking it was stiff in an official way, like the letter saying she had been accepted to music school. This one used fewer words to say much more.

Dear Mr. and Mrs. Girardin:

The Secretary of the Army has asked me to express his deepest regret that your son, Private First Class, Roger Girardin, has been missing in action in Korea since the 24th day of November, 1950. Casualty code D-- Jonathon S. Wortz, Major General of the United States Army.

Julie laid the dispatch on the coffee table. She twisted her hands, digging her nails into her palms. She closed her eyes and moved her lips almost imperceptibly, quietly spelling the word "missing" forward and backward. She pictured him alive, walking a no man's land, strong sun to his face, determined to find home. If she opened her eyes or raised her head tears would follow. She did not wish to make it any harder on the couple than it already was, but finally she could not hold back the emotion. "Did you know Roger and I would meet at the art museum? Did you know we used to take long walks? Did you know... ? He was such a gentleman to me."

All was quiet when a cuckoo clock sounded. Julie glanced at her watch. An hour had passed trading small talk of the kind that all polite and decent people do linked by common interests in an uncommon tragedy. The afternoon enveloped three lost spirits, joining them to the one they cherished. The cuckoo clock again signaled them to bid sympathies and well wishes. And as people do in such times of grief, each expressed invitations to stay in touch, to let one know should the other hear something, to stay well, *ayez une vie heureuse, bon soir.* She gave a hug to *madam* and a handshake to *monsieur*, and left for the East Side the way she had come, via the Oxford line transferring to the Barnum.

135

Familiar neighborhoods rushed by, but to Julie the streets and buildings were from another place. At the end of the line, she walked across the street to the fortress-like church. Beyond the foyer, candles drew her to an alcove where she beseeched the Virgin Mary to intercede in the matter of Private First Class Roger Girardin, missing in action, Korea, last seen the 24th day of November 1950.

***

Father Ryan heard weeping coming from the direction of the blue and white Holy Mother statue.

"Julie! Whatever is the matter?"

Startled, she turned. "Oh Father, it's Roger, my boyfriend. He's missing in action."

Expressing both sympathy and alarm, Ryan took her by the arm. "Let's sit down."

Julie explained how it had been months since she had heard from her brother and her man, and how she had just learned that Roger was MIA. Ryan fingered a strand of prayer beads that he often carried in his pocket, wondering how he could console his young parishioner. He stared up at the cavernous ceiling where shadows danced from scores of yellow votive candles lining the alcoves. He searched for words that would be meaningful or comforting. He had neither.

"Julie, God hears you, and maybe Roger hears you too. Do not lose faith, my child. Hope, yes, hope, and keep listening, you will hear, you will hear the Lord in good time." He knew this was just another Jesuit sop, for he knew, he could no more speak for the Lord's predilections than he could explain his own shortcomings on such occasions. He knew the absurdities of war, the promises of honor and glory, the poor who fight for the rich, the bizarre earthly deceptions, ironies and ambiguities that boys with good intentions fight and die for. Yes, if this were a wake, he would have the right words, but few men of the cloth were prepared to offer condolences for a life that may be far from dead, that may be lost and never be found.

***

The Jesuit knew about violence, love and loss long before he emigrated to the U.S. In Ireland, he was Frank

136

Kennedy, part of a band of social radicals in the Irish Republican Army. The IRA had recruited him and his friend Kevin McLoughlin in 1934 to fight against the fascist Blue-shirts. During the next three years, the two, not yet having reached their twentieth birthday, brawled in the streets of Dublin, disrupting social gatherings and political meetings whenever they could. By day, Frank lived in a shack in the back lot of a sympathizer and by night, wreaked havoc on the fascists, if conditions were right. It was in this revolutionary atmosphere he met Abaigeal Quinn at a dance one night and immediately fell in love. In a week's time they were living blissfully in Frank's one room shack. In early '37 Frank's cohort Kevin went missing after a raid on the O'Dougherty Social Club. Suspecting that his friend had been kidnapped, Frank spent every waking hour searching the backstreets. The rumor was that Blue-shirt leader Ian Finn knew what had happened to Kevin. One night while looking for Finn, Frank and his gang busted into O'Farrell's—a pub in Ballyboden parish. Frank was shot in the leg and Finn was killed. The Blue-shirts plastered Frank's face on every signpost in Dublin's poorest neighborhoods, so he went into hiding, seeking refuge at St. Conan—a church fifty miles away—under the alias Aloysius Ryan.

Abaigeal was cautioned not to make contact with her boyfriend, because she was being watched. After six months of dipping into the poor box, Frank had steerage for a tramp that would take him and Abaigeal to Boston. He was returning to Dublin to find her when he was informed that his arrest was imminent. Without hesitation, he headed for the port, where he boarded a departing ship. When he landed in Boston, he tried reaching Abaigeal, but she had disappeared. Six months after landing, the parrish priest at St. Conan provided a letter of introduction that would grant him admission to St. Cyril, a Vermont seminary. He took his vows in 1942. His first and last assignment was St. Patrick's.

Broken Hearts, Broken Bodies
1951–1954

ONE NIGHT IN MID-FEBRUARY 1951, WHILE JULIE serenaded beasts burrowed in the snow-filled yards behind the houses on Willa Street, Nonna Rosa took her last breath. The funeral director from *Piagente's Funeral Parlor* spared the family the high cost of dying and laid the old woman's body in the front room so the few people who remembered her could pay their respects. Following Rosa's burial, Julie decided to keep a lilied wreath from the coffin, but in less than two weeks the bluish-white flowers turned brown and stiff. After the death, winter stayed long, dark and cold, and Julie hardly left the house—except to buy a pack of Pall Malls at the pharmacy every other day. Months had passed since she had heard from either Roger or her brother, adding to the slowly rotating lamentation of late winter blues a resurgence of the introverted obsessive patterns that had plagued her childhood.

Her mother worried about the incessant singular arpeggio Julie practiced and the odd vocalizations she heard when the music stopped. She arranged for Julie to visit her older cousin upstate—a recent divorcée who lived in the woods to escape people's problems and not be bothered.

With the physical reminders of her loss left behind at Willa Street, her mother told her she would eventually escape her long moment of suffering, but she could not. After three weeks at her cousin's place, she still muttered under her breath. Not only did she imagine Roger in all kinds of peril, she missed her brother—though she was grateful that they hadn't gotten a letter from the army saying he was missing, or worse, dead. She made fruitless attempts to tell her cousin what she was feeling, but dealing with her own problems, the woman remained distant.

For Julie, the world had ripped from its moorings one year to the next. No one noticed. To add to her distress, she woke one morning with flu-like symptoms: a recurring nausea, headache, a nagging back pain, stiffness in her arms. To feel better, she decided to walk down the dirt road beyond the next farm, which turned into a murky backcountry trail, and back again. She did not remember passing out. Her cousins Abel and Mathew found her folded along the side of the trail when their flashlights swept across her body. She did not remember the white-uniformed ambulance driver and his assistant porting her through the woods on a stretcher, or the thirty mile race to Danbury Hospital.

Julie woke up three days later, with two doctors at the foot of her bed. She had been diagnosed with a mild form of polio. After several weeks in isolation, she was transported to Taylorsville Rehabilitation Center where she learned to walk with a limp, where she clutched a broken spirit with a partially paralyzed hand. She never asked what would become of her, but in the weeks and months that followed a new reality set in. She accepted that she would never play the violin again, that she would never run again—like the time she ran into Roger's arms. She would be an invalid, never quite normal, someone that even Roger would not want to look at.

Three years passed, and Julie, once the goddess of late summer, beautiful and jubilant, a Persephone who had held a violin in one arm and her lover in the other, fell into a long winter of solitude. The violin slept in its scuffed case and neighbors no longer heard her play at all hours. Her mother brought her flowers and new dresses, but she refused to look at them; brought her music and a canary, but she refused to hear it; spoke to her about a new life and times, but nothing changed her outlook. When the armistice ended Korean hostilities, she hardly noticed. All was quiet on the Eastern front, all was quiet on Willa Street.

139

Three-Piece Suits
1955–1979

IN PANMUNJOM IN 1953, WARRING FACTIONS IN spotless three-piece suits turned in their licenses to kill for a paper armistice. Prisoners of war were repatriated. One day passed into the next, seven days turned into a week among many, and turned into years that cast an indelible pall over the Girardin household. Over time, the news of Roger's disappearance dissolved into the plume of history and the woe and sympathy expressed in a casual hello faded. An all-pervading conviction took root among mother, father, daughter Berta and son Arthur, that Roger remained alive, lost someplace on the other side of an unreachable underworld.

In 1955, the parents received a final notice:

Since your son, Private Roger F. Girardin, RA 22 006 482, infantry, was reported missing in action on November 24, 1950, the Department of the Army has entertained the hope that he survived and that information would be received dispelling the uncertainty surrounding his absence. However, as in many cases, no information has been received to clarify his status. Full consideration has been given to all information bearing on the absence, including all reports and circumstances. Accordingly, an official finding of death has been recorded under the provisions of Public Law 450, 77th Congress, approved March 7, 1942, as amended.

"Damn it!" hollered Girardin, so loud his wife came running.

"What's the matter, *cheri?*" she asked, drying her hands on her favorite, thinned apron.

"Those idiots are giving up," he clamored, flapping the letter. "I know Roger's out there somewhere, they're just giving up. I'm calling Congressman McKnight. We need answers."

Lisa rushed to the kitchen, her head in her hands. She wept inconsolably. Jean wondered if she would ever stop. He sat in the living room and later heard a pot boiling in the kitchen, but Lisa's sobbing persisted. Thoughts about what he might possibly do raced through his head. He wanted to comfort his wife, but thinking about what to do next, while fighting his own grief, took all his strength. He went to his room, threw the letter on his desk, and sat, head on his chest. He waited while the letter faded into the silhouettes of late afternoon, waited while the moon cast its penumbral light on the last letter he would receive about his son's fate.

The next day, Girardin called McKnight's office. A staff member listened politely and promised he would get back in a few weeks. He received a letter from the congressman the following month telling him there was nothing he could do. To McKnight, Girardin was a potential liability to the image he was polishing up for the '56 campaign. In fact, his re-election manager told him to avoid the subject of MIAs at all costs. What McKnight did not share with anyone, including his staffers, was that he attended a meeting between the Military Personnel Subcommittee of the Committee on National Security and President Eisenhower, where the President said, "We have had long, serious discussions with the Chinese Communists, trying to make them disclose where our approximately 450 prisoners are being held. We might be making progress. Just last month four F-86 pilots were returned. They'd been shot down in Manchuria. Gentlemen, I trust you will keep this to yourselves."

Art Girardin never discussed the idea that his brother Roger might still be alive beyond the occasional commiseration with his parents when Roger's birthday rolled around. But it wore at him through his college years, then his marriage, and the death of his mother in 1976. Following the Vietnam War, a new controversy erupted over claims that Americans were still captives in Vietnam and Laos. In March of 1977, Art was listening to the radio in his living room, when he heard a newscaster report that a U.S. commission had traveled to Vietnam to make inquiries about GIs missing in action and to lay the groundwork for diplomatic relationships. During the visit, the Vietnamese surrendered the bodies of eleven identified American servicemen. Art could not stop thinking about what he had heard. The next month he took time off from his job at the Department of Transportation to travel to the U.S. National Archives in Washington D.C. to investigate whether there was anything that might shed light on Roger's disappearance. Under the heading "*Korean War*" he found a yellowed folder on POWs/MIAs, including something McKnight apparently did not share with his father: HR Resolution 1957-3544 titled *Korean War POW Initiative-A309* demanding an account of 450 POWs. He leafed through dozens of official documents. The papers came in a variety of forms, from thick, brown thermographic paper to an occasional onionskin carbon copy. A document in the last category listed more than 400 names under the heading POW. His fingers trembled while he scanned the list. Under "G" he saw *Girardin, Roger. Pvt. RA 22 006 482, infantry.* How could Roger have been listed MIA if the government knew he was a POW? Struggling to contain his wide-ranging emotions, he managed to calmly ask the clerk for a Xerox. He went back to the carrel where he was working and held the copy under a lamp, studied it like a Dead Sea scroll, praying it would lead to answers about whether or not Roger might still be alive.

Armed now with a piece of evidence concerning his brother's possible fate, Art wrote the Army requesting the last known whereabouts of the men who had information about his brother. He received a tersely worded letter signed by an Army captain, indicating that such a review or hearing would be "impracticable." The refusal came in a four-line letter read to him by his wife when he spoke to her one afternoon from a payphone on a noisy street.

"Yeah, Art, the letter just came. It says... "

"I can't hear you, Marge, talk louder," he yelled anxiously.

Raising her voice she continued. "It says, your letter doesn't provide 'sufficient specificity'... it says that 'if it did, we have insufficient resources to gather up information of this kind for matters long since disposed of... We appreciate your request... "

Art finished the sentence, "But unless you have political pull, we'll dispose of your request in the circular file." At that moment, an eighteen-wheeler raced by.

"I can't hear you," Marge yelled.

"Goddamn it!" Art yelled back, hanging up the phone.

The following week, Art made a trip to Stamford to visit Dave Walkovich, his congressman, who held Saturday "Meet Your Representative" forums. When he arrived the congressman was out of town, so he only spoke to a clerk. But through the clerk's efforts, Walkovich did send a letter to the Office of the Secretary of the Army to ask if the Army might provide a "better answer" than the one Art had received. August and September passed. In October, Art received an envelope with a transmittal letter from the same captain he had heard from earlier, that began, "Dear Mr. Girardin, The army has reconsidered... " Attached was a freshly typed list naming two soldiers, Broadbent, who had died in 1960, and Montoya, who had seemed to have disappeared.

The following June, Art went back to the Archives. In a dark corner of the public vault that he had passed by on prior visits, he found a 1952 account by the International Red Cross (IRC) following its inspection of North Korean prison Camp 13. Again, Roger's name was listed among the other POWs. This time he thought Roger might still be alive. After all, he reasoned, the IRC does not list as "alive," someone who is "dead," despite having been "pronounced dead" by the Army.

In April 1978, Art filed a petition with the U.S. Army Board for the Correction of Military Records requesting an amendment to the record, from the *presumptive finding of death* to that of *prisoner of war*. Even after several appeals by Congressman Walkovich—the last one in 1980—the Army refused to change the record. A short time later, on account of fried fish, one might say, Art met Nick Castalano.

Presumptions and Points of View
1983

BEFORE THE TRIAL RESUMED ON the second day, Nick met Mitch and Kathy for breakfast at Zorba's Luncheonette. He took a sip of black coffee from the bone white, chipped mug that Annie saved for her best customers.

"Wow, you missed a good day in court yesterday!" ribbed Kathy, as she poured syrup over her French toast.

"All right, no need to rub it in. Nick, why am I point man for the library?"

"Because you're the best."

"You're the only one he's got, so it's a shoe-in," smirked Kathy.

"Next assignment, 'presumptions.' Let's see what Connecticut law is on that. The judge has to take certain things for granted. No one has to prove that the Korean War happened. But that's also a problem—the system takes things for granted."

Mitch, pushing aside the remains of a browned Spanish omelet covered in ketchup recalled his evidence class. "You mean legal presumptions, right?"

"Exactly, like the presumption that the government's actions are reasonable. Sometimes a judge, who let's not forget is a government worker, stretches this too far. Like, in our case, Uncle Sam would not forget to repatriate a POW. Would they? He might answer, 'No, they wouldn't' and that's what I'm afraid of. The court's letting the Army get away with this. It happened when the Feds locked up thousands of Japs during WWII. The Supremes held it was constitutional because the government had the presumption of legitimacy, though looking back, it's hard to believe."

"Japanese, Nick, Japanese," Kathy chided.

144

"We have to lay it out step by step, to show how it could've happened, how outrageous it was to leave a red-blooded American hanging out to dry."

"How can you keep the judge from lowering the bar?" Mitch asked, as he chewed on toast covered in globs of jam.

"We need good witnesses, that's how. We need men like Sheer, like our next guy Bradshaw, who can testify about what they saw over there. Bradshaw's experience is Roger's. And he's got to come across as credible, the eyewitness who'll testify for those who didn't come back."

"What's he look like? Will he make a good witness?" Mitch asked.

"No worse than you would, with a good hair cut."

"Ha, ha. Come on, you know what I mean."

Nick smiled. "Never laid eyes on him, just talked on the phone."

"Nick, how confident are you that these guys will remember?" asked Kathy.

"They were there."

"Yeah, but most eyewitnesses are not *that* reliable," Mitch interjected.

"I suppose, but that's all we have. Their recollections, as faulty as they may be. But I'm afraid you're not going to get to see him."

Mitch groaned and dropped his fork with a clatter.

"I've got an errand for you."

"Aw, Nick."

When Nick and Kathy arrived at the courthouse the clerk indicated that the judge was running a few minutes late. That's when Harris approached him.

"Nick, I need to call my witness Jaeger out of turn. He has to get back to Pennsy for an operation later this week."

"Isn't it something he can postpone?"

"No, it's heart surgery."

"Christ, that means... ?"

"Nick, I don't have much choice. Lindquist will understand. The guy drove up from Pennsylvania last night."

"Do what you gotta do," Nick conceded. To Kathy, he explained tersely, "Change of plan. Let's hope it's not Harris using Jaeger in a cheap move at primacy."

"What's heard first is believed most?" Kathy asked.

Nick nodded. He knew, as did Harris, that getting one side of the story out first placed a burden on every story that followed.

Lindquist had been suffering from a pus-oozing abscess on his gum, making it impossible to bite through the hard roll he had for breakfast. And while the lawyers would take the witness through hours of testimony, he would half-listen, distracted by his pain and hunger. He brought his gavel down and declared the court back in session. "We will go until four, today. Mr. Castalano, please proceed."

Harris interjected, "Your Honor, may Counsel and I approach?"

Lindquist nodded, brought his lips together and twisted his mouth from side to side. Lindquist leaned forward, looking at Harris and asking in an irritated tone, "Well, Counsel, what is it?"

Harris began to speak rapid-fire. "Your Honor, the government needs to call Mr. Jaeger out of turn and regrettably break up Mr. Castalano's presentation. Mr. Jaeger is scheduled to return home tonight, because... "

The judge interrupted. "Slow down, Counsel... "

"He... Mr. Jaeger, the defense witness, needs open heart surgery later this week. There might be times when his testimony will seem disjointed or lack foundation, but I'll connect up before I rest."

"Any objection, Mr. Castalano?"

"No, your Honor, we've discussed it."

"Very well, but let's keep surprises to a minimum."

Harris assumed the podium. "Your Honor, I wish to call Mr. Thomas Jaeger to the stand."

A woman in her mid-fifties stood up in the front oak pew. Next to her sat a man wearing dark glasses. He rose when the woman placed her hand on his shoulder. He clutched the woman's arm. She wore a plain, blue rayon dress, buttoned close to her thin, long neck. She opened the chrome-over-wood gate leading into the well, and together they walked toward the witness chair. Although the courtroom had a hundred occupants, the only sounds heard were the click, click, click that the woman's matronly high heels made on the mottled, gray granite floor. Even with the woman at his elbow, the man walked toward the stand straight up. He appeared older than she by many years, though not as weary. Perhaps the shock of thinning, gray-blond hair falling over his forehead or his ruddy complexion made him appear so. One artist in the jury box imagined that he had labored hard, but only the elderly stenographer saw a workingman's rough hands.

The man looked like he had been poured into his suit—a brown wool, two-button that had seen days at fifteen pounds lighter. His neck protruded out of a loose collar with a green tie, the same outfit he would wear when he and Marlene, the lady next to him, and their two teenage daughters attended the Marysville Lutheran Church on Sundays.

Jaeger took his place to the left of Lindquist's maple perch, a perch from which a skilled magistrate detected all manner of prevaricator. The white-faced clerk planted himself to see into the usually anxious eyes—something he had done to a thousand witnesses—but this time, he only met the reflection of his own gaunt image. Unfazed, the clerk continued to study the dark, reflecting receptacles, while reciting the oath: "Raise your right hand, sir. Do you solemnly swear to tell the truth, the whole truth, and nothing but the truth so help you God?"

Jaeger responded in a deeply resonant smoker's voice, "I do."

"Sir, please state your name and address for the record."

"My name is Thomas J. Jaeger, and I live at number 15 Mifflin Place, in Marysville, Pennsylvania."

Rattled by the witness's blindness, Harris unconsciously left the security of his oak chair and moved to the lectern angled toward Jaeger. He became oblivious to the crowd that packed the courtroom, the reporters scribbling notes, the sketch artists scrawling the visage of a man in dark glasses. He threw his papers onto the lectern.

Jaeger had called Townsend just two months before the trial began, indicating he had read about the case in a local veteran's newsletter. Harris had had two phone conversations with him, never imagining that he was speaking to a blind man. Townsend and Foster, his two Army beagles, were supposed to ferret these things out. Nevertheless, he asked the obvious, "Mr. Jaeger, are you able to see?"

"No, sir."

"Mr. Jaeger, you were a member of the Army, right?"

Jaeger mechanically turned his head toward the voice. "Yes, I was in the Army for twenty-six years," he answered, swollen with pride.

"When'd you retire?"

"January of '75."

"At what rank?"

"Master Sergeant. I was also First Sergeant in my company."

"So when did you join? What year?"

"Well, was the day after the eighth anniversary of Pearl Harbor, the exact date, December 8, 1949."

"Did you enlist or were you inducted?"

"Enlisted."

"All right. And what did you ... ?"

"Army infantry."

"And you remained with the infantry throughout your career, is that—?"

"That's right."

"Any tours of overseas duty?"

"Yes, one tour in Korea and pulled one in Germany after Korea, two tours in Vietnam."

Harris caught Lindquist moving his head up and down as he made a note, and supposed the judge must so far be impressed with the witness. He had no way of knowing that Lindquist was only moving his head to relieve the stiffness in his neck.

"Have you ever seen combat?"

"Am credited with five years. Three in Korea, two in Vietnam."

Lindquist nodded again.

"You mentioned you did one tour in Korea, correct?"

"Uh-huh."

"When did you first go to Korea?"

"The early part of August '50. I'd been stationed in Kumamoto on Kyushu, Japan, with units of the 19th Infantry Regiment, 24th Division."

"And you went from Kyushu to Korea?"

"About 200 men ferried out on small transports—called 'em Gooney Birds. When we arrived, we were put on the firing line."

Out of the corner of his eye, Harris saw Lindquist wince when he picked up the pen. He dismissed it as a random tic, but the abscess would cause Lindquist's face to grimace more and more as the day wore on.

Harris looked at the Judge. "Your Honor, at this time I wish to produce a certified partial duplicate set of Roger Girardin's military records and offer them as an exhibit. For the record, among other things it shows that Private Girardin was assigned to the 19th Regiment during this period."

"Any objection, Mr. Castalano?"

"No, Counsel and I stipulated to its admissibility."

"Very well, mark it as a full exhibit."

"Mr. Jaeger, your unit moved north, right?"

Facing dead ahead, Jaeger continued, "Train took us about three hours away. Where we camped. We was fed. Next day, moved us out on a train."

"Where exactly did the train take you, relative to Pusan?"

"About 50 miles north, a staging area, near the Yongsan."

"You were still assigned to the 19th?

"Right."

"Did you immediately come under fire?"

"Oh, yeah, the regiment had retreated from its position, but we was trying to hold the line at the river, the Naktong. We lost guys. You heard Air Rescue Squadron, you know, M.A.S.H. copters 'round the clock."

Jaeger let his head drop down and repeated in a low voice, "Yeah 'round the clock."

"Sometime in September, you and the 19th moved north past Seoul and beyond the 38th Parallel that had

149

separated South Korea from North Korea before the war, is that correct?

"Yes, that's right."

"Sir, let me turn your attention to, let's say, mid to late November. You and the 19th were well inside North Korea, not far from the Manchurian border, correct?"

"Yes, I guess we got within 50 to 75 miles."

"Isn't it true that sometime in mid-November, the North Koreans helped by the Chinese turned the U.N. forces back? And, that the 24th Division generally, and the 19th in particular, were in full retreat from the Northern territory of Korea above the 38th Parallel, headed south?"

"Yes, sir, that's right. After the Chinese entered the war."

"And you were in full retreat through early December?" asked Harris.

"Yes, sir."

"Was the 19th Regiment experiencing any reports of men killed-in-action or KIA, during this time?"

"Yeah, casualties went up pretty fast. Because normally when you're withdrawing like that you always try to keep some contact with the enemy."

"If you're retreating, why'd you maintain contact?"

"You're fightin' a delaying action."

"And what about your company from, say, late November to early December? During the retreat, how many were lost?"

"Far as I know, more than a dozen wounded and killed, six or seven disappeared."

"Did you know for a fact that at that time the enemy was capturing 19th Regiment personnel?"

"Heard that... big numbers... a half-dozen guys in my company couldn't be accounted for, from late October to, say, near Christmas, more or less."

"What do you think happened to them?"

"I assumed, as did everyone, that the men that couldn't be found were captured, got disconnected, and they'd eventually show up."

Townsend rifled noisily through a pile of papers an inch think. Glancing over his shoulder, Harris saw Foster motioning him over to the defense table.

"Your Honor, I need to speak with my colleague." Harris walked over to Foster and turned to Lindquist, "Your Honor, defense counsel would appreciate a five-minute recess."

The judge scowled, "Counsel, we just got started!"

"Your Honor, I need to make an urgent call to my office. I apologize. It won't take more than a few minutes."

"Very well, be back in five minutes!" Lindquist rubbed his cheek hard, before amending his order, "No, instead let's take our mid-morning break."

To Nick, Lindquist's behavior was becoming more atypical by the minute.

Rushing into the corridor Harris took the stairs two at a time. He opened the office door to a sparsely appointed suite for government lawyers. A middle aged receptionist looked up.

"Mr. Harris, come this way. There's a line in here. I'll put your party through."

Harris sat back in a large, black chair and rolled it back and forth, arms crossed, hands thrust under his armpits. The desk had a clear, reflective finish and was empty, with the exception of an unlit lamp. He waited nearly five minutes before he heard a nasally voice coming through the intercom. "Mr. Harris, Mr. Russell on line one."

Seeing that the receiver had a greasy sheen to it, Harris picked it up by his thumb and forefinger and held it away from his ear.

"Hello, Mr. Secretary." The caller seemed miles away. "Sir, can you speak a little louder? The connection is bad... Oh, yes, things are going well. Our witness is up— Jaeger, guy I told you about. Nothing remarkable, no." Harris listened intently. "No, I don't think that they'll concede on this. What're the chances of the status change, if we can take their mind off the money-bit, the damages, you know the back pay since 1950?"

The man on the other end raised his voice and could be heard in the outer office. Harris held the receiver further away from his ear.

"Yes, sir, yes, I understand. We'd have to do it in confidence, but they've refused that condition, and they've said they want information on where the guy was last seen. So it's not a matter of money." Harris listened. "Yes, sir, we can't set a precedent, but I was thinking that we could do this without shaking the hornet's nest." Harris was quiet, listening to the concerns of the man on the other end. "Well, yeah, I know there are at least 400 to 500 of these same situations, and you wouldn't want a flood... I can understand that. Yes, you're right; we'll put this one to sleep."

Harris listened, then responded, "Yes, they won't see that. If it comes up, I'll get the judge to redact, on national security grounds, the part about the CIA and references to the Girardin film." He put his hand to his head, squeezing to alleviate a pounding headache.

"Correct, we've decided that it's not in our interest to bring in Montoya from New Mexico. He's too vague, and he doesn't help our theory." Harris got up from the chair and took a step to his right. "Yes, I appreciate that I'm not to mention CIA and Girardin in the same sentence." The man could be heard still coming through the receiver. "Well, sir, we'll do our best. I think there's only a small chance that things will turn out different than we've predicted." Two minutes passed while Harris shifted back and forth—one foot then the other. His face reddened.

"Thank you, sir. I'll stay in touch if anything develops."

Harris walked over to Jaeger before the session resumed. "Tom, nice to finally meet you. I'm sorry, I didn't know you were blind. If I had, I could've had someone drive you up from Pennsy."

"Nothing to be sorry about, Mr. Harris. I've been like this for a few years. Hard getting used to at first, but you know something? Once you can't see, you soon realize everybody's got a blind spot."

"How'd it happen?" Harris asked with concern.

"Well, after Vietnam, you know. It came out about Agent Orange leading to permanent blindness."

"Ole Nick there, he was a VA lawyer handling Agent Orange cases."

"For vets?"

"For Uncle Sam. Was pretty good at it, too."

"What do you mean?"

"Never lost the VA one case for the government. Were you given a medical discharge?"

"No, the blindness happened about two years after I retired in the late seventies. VA denied the benefits. Back then I'd been workin' as a part-time guard at Lewisburg Federal Correction. I have a small farm that me and the wife grow corn on and one day in the field the green stalks turned brown for a few minutes, then everything turned black. Last thing I saw, corn stalks. Now, I ain't able to do much. I mean, I can dig a hole or get eggs, feed chickens, you know, the things that are like the back of my hand."

After a few seconds passed, Harris remarked, "Well, I can't tell you how much we appreciate you coming all this way to set the record straight."

Hunters and the Hunted

WHEN COURT WENT INTO RECESS, Lindquist returned to his chambers. It had an oversized desk, a small library of books and several ornately framed pictures of judges that had once occupied the room. He picked up the phone and called his dentist. "That's right, soon as you can. Can I get some pain meds at the drug store? Good, then yes, this afternoon... that works. What time? ... Fine, see you then." He pushed on the intercom and asked Alice, his secretary, to find him an ice pack.

"My father would have sent me for some pain killers," he mumbled. He sat back and closed his eyes.

Unlike the vast majority of men and women who have opinions on war, Joseph Lindquist formed his while living through one. When he returned from Europe in '46 he went to college and studied history in a vain attempt to intellectualize what he had experienced. He never found an answer that completely satisfied him.

Lindquist and his friend Tom Aspinwall, a judge appointed under Nixon, had many a discussion about politics. Lately, when the men had nothing better to talk about, they would discuss what the government's response should be in matters of its overseas interests.

The day before the trial started, the men walked to *The Rex*, a men's club where judges could drink outside of public scrutiny after work. They sat in overstuffed leather chairs, in a room with dark oak paneling and gilt framed oil paintings, mostly of men at sea—a reminder of where many patrons would rather be. Aspinwall brought a glass of merlot to his lips and took a sip before holding the glass aloft and twirling it so the wine coated the inside.

"Well, Joe should we retaliate for the Lebanon Embassy bombing?"

"Not a good idea, Tom."

"Don't you think we go in and take them out?" Aspinwall asked to provoke his friend.

Lindquist stretched his legs. "Tom, you'd risk starting another war."

Aspinwall ran his hand through his thinning white hair and straightened himself to better face Lindquist. "Sure, but we can't let them make us look like fools in the eyes of the world."

"Well, that's a new one, 'fools in the eyes of the world.' Countries go to war to conquer territories for riches, to defend nations, to bring civilization to heathens, to convert infidels, but now we have 'fools in the eyes of the world.'"

"People have gone to war for reasons far less noble than that."

Lindquist lifted his empty glass over his shoulder to get the bartender's attention. "Yes... rape and pillage, I suppose. And, there're men who would go to war if they felt their honor were at stake. I think we should sit this one out and see if the diplomats can't handle it."

Aspinwald, a chubby man, leaned forward and, in a low serious tone, he opined, "You know, Joe, unless we deal with these dictators with an iron fist, we'll find ourselves in deeper trouble. Look at Hitler. We should have taken him down two, three years before we actually got into the war."

"Blame it on Republicans."

Aspinwall laughed. "Oh, let's not go down that road."

"I don't know. We're always looking for reasons to go to war. There's something basic in our makeup, motivates us to wage war. Man's genes, maybe. Yes, what man does by way of organized killing of his own kind is something copied into his flesh."

Lindquist was sipping from his glass when he saw Paul Morris, the judge who occupied the office next to his. "Eh, Paul 'ow's it goin' der?" he said cheerfully, adding, "want a join us?"

"Hello, Joe. Sorry, can't. Meeting an old college friend."

Aspinwall looked at the large painting behind Lindquist, the one with a man hooking a fish the size of a great white. "I think there's some truth to that if you want to look at it philosophically," he said. "We can no more stop war than stop making babies."

Ever since his wife Mattie died five years earlier, Lindquist spent Sunday morning reading the *New York Times* and the *Bridgeport Post* with his cat Red. At some point he usually put down the newspapers and picked up an album full of photos of him and Mattie. Then he would turn on the TV to watch the Sunday political shows and, if nothing particularly interesting was on, he would read trial briefs for the cases in the weeks ahead.

The Sunday before the Girardin trial started, he read the briefs. After an hour, he put down the paperwork, walked over to the pull-down stairs to the attic and ventured into the place where old memories were archived. In the far corner of the attic his eye caught a twelve-by-twelve picture of Robby O'Halloran dressed in a khaki colored army jacket, the kind of picture the boys took right after boot camp—before they were put on liberty ships and sent to North Africa. He found an album of pictures his father took on his first hunting trip. It was 1937, up Vermont way near the Canadian border. His father had spotted the buck and was close enough to his son to whisper, "Aim slightly higher than the buck because he's going to leap into the clearing." Bam! Four legs slowly buckled under the 500 pound frame of a beast that offered no resistance and did no harm. Now, it shadowed the memory that all dead innocents cast in the executioner's mind. In time, Lindquist became both the hunter and the hunted. It was during that cold winter of '44 in Belgium where he accrued a soldier's inventory of menacing memories, where he came to know death, not through the oblique angle of a hunter's sight, but as a man intent on killing other men.

Later that night, Lindquist picked up his pen, and in the habit formed from watching his father, he made a notation in his diary:

What justification do boys have for going to war? Maybe it's patriotism, or maybe it's because they are dead ended in life and war promises status, dignity. Regardless, in time their sacrifices or their ends are forgotten.

Federal Judge Joseph Lindquist would never forget what happened forty years ago, in another place, where men woke up every day with the full intention of killing one another. The final journal entry for that night read:

Can there ever be such a thing as the unimpassioned observer exercising objective reasoning in recounting war? For in war, that thing called reason gives way to that thing called Nature, and more precisely the Nature of Man. Under the circumstances of my own experience, can I still judge things by that standard of judicial objectivity that my oath of office demands?

Blood on the Field

THE LANKY CLERK LIFTED HIS CRANE-LIKE NECK and, in his naturally high voice, shouted in the direction of the lawyers, "Are you ready to proceed?" Hearing joint confirmation, he motioned to the boxer-turned-marshal that the stage was set for the next round.

"Please rise."

Having heard the marshal shout and the long familiar sound of people getting off their duffs to pay their respects, Lindquist, in black robes and trademark frown, eyebrows pinched at the furrow, turned the doorknob of the door directly behind the bench.

"Be seated," Lindquist barked. He turned to Jaeger waiting in the witness chair. "Mr. Jaeger, you are still under oath. Mr. Harris, proceed. I hope we're finally getting to the end of the war."

"Yes, sir, I'll be finishing up in a few minutes."

"Now, Mr. Jaeger, can you recall where you were on or about the morning of November 27, 1950?"

"The regiment was near Kunu-ri, close to the Ch'ongch'on river. We were still well north of Pyongyang, the North Korean capital, but now we were heading south again, as I said before."

"Why would you remember a particular date like November 27, 1950?"

Jaeger paused, touched his chin and seemed to stare in the direction of the audience.

"Mr. Jaeger, did you hear the question, sir, the morning of November 27. Can you recall what happened next?"

"That morning I went scouting. I had heard two, three shots fired in the distance and decided to move in that direction to see what I could. I found a stray North Korean, or maybe it was a Chinese, and I shot him. I also found two GIs on the ground near one another, and one of our guys standing over one of them."

"Can you please elaborate for the court, let's start to what led to the shooting?"

Jaeger hesitated. The word "shooting" reduced the politely hushed din. "Well, that night a wet snow had passed, leaving us soaked. The unit was headed south and scouts were dispatched north of the bivouac to figure out if the enemy was comin' from that direction. Wasn't my job, but 'cause the scouts were north, Lieutenant Billingsly ordered me to recon the area south to see if the enemy'd moved 'round the unit—you know, out-flanked us. Was half-mile south when I heard a noise like maybe a pheasant. Caught movement out of the corner of my eye."

Jaeger would not tell the court that when he stopped, his heart beat wildly. He was acutely conscious of condensation forming phlegm with every lungful of air, and he needed to cough. Through his breathy fog, he saw a soldier in the foreground. The man had moved slightly and sniffed the Siberian air. Jaeger crouched into a prone position and removed his leather gloves. The man turned in Jaeger's direction. A glint of an emerging, rose-colored sun reflected off his glassy pupil.

Jaeger set his carbine into the crease between his shoulder and pectoral. He released the safety, squeezed the cold metal grip, taking a slow deep breath. White air spilled off his lips and he froze a moment to steady his weapon, panning along the line defining life within the "V" of its bore sight. He pressed the curvature of the trigger, releasing a firing pin into the backside of a .30 caliber bullet. The rifle jerked upwards as the bullet crossed the vacancy separating the two warriors.

"Saw an enemy. Fired. Missed! Man looked left, spotted me. Fired again and hit 'em. His head jolted up... jaw unhinged." Jaeger was quiet, thinking he had said more than he should have.

"Mr. Jaeger, what happened next?"

Jaeger was quiet.

"Mr. Jaeger, besides the enemy you engaged, were you alone that morning?"

"I thought so, but I'd a couple of angels with me."

"What do you mean?"

"Well, I thought I was firing at one, but he had back up. As I fired, his backup was ready to drop me. But a couple of guys from another company were apparently on scout patrol, too."

"What exactly happened?"

"I heard the crack of another rifle. I looked right. I wondered if someone was shooting at me, but I saw a GI on a small knoll. I realized that he was firing at somebody stalking me."

"What happened next?"

"Well, laid as close to the ground as I could. Heard more shots, but wasn't lifting my head. Let at least ten minutes pass. A pheasant flew into the woods, and I finally felt it was safe to move toward the GIs who'd helped me. But, as I got close I noticed one guy was kneeling next to another guy on the ground. Tryin' to stop bleeding. His whole side was bloody, right through his jacket. Like I said to you the other day, he looked like he was gone."

"Did you talk to the guy trying to stop the bleeding?"

"Yeah... after a while. We was both pretty shook."

"Do you remember the name of the man who you met that morning?"

"He asked my name. Told me his name was, and I'm guessing now, it's been a while, an O'Connel or O'Conner, can't remember exactly... but it's the one you and me talked about."

"And, did you learn about who the other guy was?"

"The man said he was Girardin or Jardin."

Nick rose from his chair, "Objection, hearsay."

"Sustained."

Undaunted, Harris charged ahead, "Was there any other way you confirmed the identification?"

"Yes, sir, dog tags."

"What did they indicate?"

"Best I can recall, they confirmed what I'd heard."

"Was it Girardin or Jardin you read?"

"Now, I am not sure, but at the time, I was sure it was the same as what the man told me."

Nick and Kathy exchanged glances. One of the interrogation reports from Panmunjom actually mentioned a man by the name of "Jardin," but they had passed it off as just a phonetic spelling of Girardin. And now each knew what the other was thinking: was there really a guy by the name of Jardin?

"You're sure now that the name was either Girardin or Jardin and the guy that saved your life was O'Connel or Conner?"

"Yes, sir, on the two. But the guy I first came across, no didn't get his name."

Harris turned away from the witness, contemplating his next question. He looked over at the jury box where artists busily knocked out drafts for the evening news. Later, when he walked over to see what they had drawn, he saw cartoon-like sketches of Jaeger with a shock of blondish gray hair and large oversized dark glasses. He seemed like a man on vacation, a musician or maybe a blind man who wanted to keep the rest of mankind from seeing the two white, gelatinous marbles that once saw the splendor of a bright orange Korean sun in the dead of winter.

"Mr. Jaeger, I have no further questions. You certainly are to be commended for your service. Have you anything else you would like to add to your testimony?"

"No, sir."

"Thank you, Mr. Jaeger. I have no further questions at this time. Counsel, your witness."

The judge leaned forward and was about to tell Nick to proceed with his cross examination, when the clerk handed him a brief note from his dentist: oral surgery, 3 p.m. Lindquist did not know how he would manage until then—the pain was now affecting his concentration. "Mr. Castalano, proceed with your examination," he snapped.

The irony of what he was about to do was not lost upon Nick. Hadn't he switched sides precisely to avoid impeaching veterans? But, one last time, he found himself contemplating what could he possibly do to cast doubt on a soldier's claim that he remembered the names Girardin and O'Conner from an encounter that had lasted less than a few minutes thirty years ago. He was quick to understand that Jaeger did not need to see the audience to make his performance believable. But even blind men of good intentions might dissemble reality. Nick knew that to tell his story, he needed to find the lines, the dialogue. He needed to find the right words, so that regardless of one's blind spot, they would separate reality from fiction, truth from superstition. He tightened his jaw, turned to the podium and opened his three-ring notebook of pleadings, depositions, briefs and bios—in short, the dirt on each witness. On top of every page he had penned in red what he told Mitch was Napoleon's maxim, *"The art of war requires being stronger on a particular point."* Mitch had looked for the quote in the library but had come up empty. Nick responded, "It doesn't matter, it reminds me to look for the one piece of evidence the judge cannot ignore. That piece of evidence that separates the real from the unreal, the wayward memory from the irrefutable logic that it had to be *the other way.*"

"Sir, on behalf of my client, I want to commend you on your service in Korea. Please do not take my questions as a personal affront; we just have to get to the truth. During the month of November, you testified that you encountered heavy fighting?"

"Yes."

"Tell me if the regiment at that time was contained in one area, fully?"

"In most cases."

"At some time during November you encountered the Chinese in large numbers. Is that true?"

"Yes."

"How far from the Yalu were you, say around the 25th or 26th?"

"We were near Chongju, west coast. About fifty miles. My own estimate. I may be wrong."

"Now... you were experiencing battle casualties?"

"Oh, yes, like I said. Early November, then a lull until the end of the month. Then all hell broke loose."

"When, more or less, was that?"

"Had to be after Thanksgiving, on the side of Hill 336. About daybreak. It had been quiet for about 24 hours, no big guns."

"If there was a skirmish, say, involving the 19th Regiment at that time, and if somebody were killed, would that have been discovered by fellow soldiers?"

"By the company the man was assigned to."

"That was the only way?"

"Unless he had a friend in another company or something. Usually only his own company would know of his KIA status, because these reports were fed back through the battalion, the regiment and the division."

"How spread out were you?"

"A company could cover a front of, oh, four or five hundred yards, even a thousand yards—just one company."

"So KIAs and MIAs were limited to the basic unit, right?"

"Unless it turns into something major. If one company has a little firefight your other units might hear about it, but they don't know the number of casualties you suffer, or who, or anything like that."

"The companies stayed contained within a thousand-yard area?"

"Right. Your company's always the basic unit."

"In your experience, if you lost someone from the company, was it likely that you would find them dead?" Nick asked.

"Oh, yes, unless you got beat out of your positions. Now, many times the enemy would overrun your positions. Even wounded... had to leave 'em, and if they didn't die from their wounds, they probably froze."

Nick cringed. "Were there times you might retrieve the dead and wounded if you were beaten out of position?"

"If you were lucky enough to take back that territory—the hill, or whatever—you might find your dead there. You might evacuate 'em if you had time, which we were runnin' out of."

"And if you couldn't evacuate? Would they become MIAs and eventually POWs?"

"The wounded? The enemy would shoot them or take them prisoner or, like I said... they'd freeze. That's the part that you can't forget, leaving 'em to freeze."

Again, Nick knew he had asked one question too many.

"Let's turn attention to your earlier testimony that you remember hearing a name sounding like the plaintiff's in this case—Girardin." Nick's eyes momentarily shifted in the judge's direction. "Sir, over the course of time, there were but a few names that you recalled from your tour of duty in Korea, isn't that true?"

"I remembered lotsa names. When I read that in the veteran's newsletter that there was a case involving a Private Girardin, I remembered immediately where I thought I'd heard that name before," Jaeger answered indignantly.

"You're familiar with the power of suggestion?"

"I think so."

"Isn't it true that but for Mr. Harris, or Captains Foster and Townsend mentioning Private O'Conner's name, you would never have remembered that name?"

"Well, true, I hadn't thought about that name, until Mr. Harris and I... "

"That was the first time? Strike that. Wasn't it recalled after Mr. Harris's associate mentioned the name? One of those men sitting over there?" Nick raised his arm and pointed to Foster and Townsend, forgetting that Jaeger could not see.

"Don't recall."

"Well, what if Mr. Foster tells us that you spoke to him before you spoke to Mr. Harris, would that refresh you recollection?"

"Not sure."

"Is it not true that but for Mr. Harris or Captain Townsend mentioning Mr. Connel or Conner's name, it would never have been in your memory?"

"I... can't be sure."

"You can't be sure if Connel or Conner was the man you encountered, right?"

"No, not exactly."

"Did Mr. Harris or Captain Townsend mention his rank?"

"... Can't be sure."

"Mr. Jaeger, you only had these conversations a short time ago with the government's lawyers, and you cannot retain this vital piece of information. Yet you are telling this court you remembered names from over thirty years ago, names read off a dog tag in a brief encounter?"

Jaeger sat there, virtually staring into space. "Please answer the question, sir."

"I *know* what happened in '51 because a man saved my life."

Again, Nick felt he had gone too far. "Sir, isn't it true that you were involved in a court martial and reduced in rank a year before you retired?"

"Yes, sir."

Nick knew this was a low blow and unpleasant, unworthy even, but expedient.

"The court martial had to do with drinking on the job, did it not?"

Harris rose from his chair. "Objection, your Honor. I don't see the relevance of this line of questioning."

"Counsel?" Lindquist gave Nick a weary look of 'what for?'

"Your Honor, Mr. Harris went into the ranks held by Mr. Jaeger. I think he testified that he retired as a Master Sergeant, and he was First Sergeant. The record shows otherwise. My line of questioning goes to credibility and memory."

Harris, rubbing his hands together, persisted. "Your Honor, Counsel has not laid the proper foundation for impeaching this witness based upon a so-called military tribunal decision."

"You mean conviction, Counsel?" Lindquist asked sternly.

"Well, yes, or rather, maybe. If there was a reduction in rank it might have been through Article 15, and I do not think that qualifies as a conviction."

Lindquist turned to Nick. "Do you have a certified copy of the court martial?"

Nick clasped his hands together and turned to Kathy. "Do we?"

"Here it is," she said.

Nick opened his arm wide, palm pointing in the direction of the table where the document laid in its envelope. "Your Honor, over there."

"Then let's do this by the book," Lindquist ordered.

Nick picked up the envelope, removed the paper and handed it to the clerk. "Mr. Clerk, please mark this as Defense Exhibit." He paused. "What number are we up to?"

Kathy answered, "Exhibit 78."

The clerk fixed a yellow sticker marked 'Exhibit 78' to the document and handed it back to Nick. He read it, then addressed the witness. "Sir, are you, Mr. Thomas Jaeger having a former army serial number US 13436890."

"Yes, sir." Jaeger squirmed in his chair.

Nick turned to Lindquist. "Your Honor, I offer the following certified copy of the court martial of Mr. Thomas Jaeger—having a former army serial number US 13436890 into the record."

Harris jumped up. "May I see that?"

Nick, suit jacket swung open, sauntered over, dropping the record on the table. Harris picked it up and knew he had screwed up. Sweat flowed down his chest, his face flushed. Walking away, Nick heard Harris mutter, "This shouldn't have come as a surprise. We didn't even have to go into the ranks he'd held."

Harris studied the document for a minute and handed it to Foster. Foster slid his finger along a line of the document. Harris addressed the court. "Your Honor, this is a summary court martial, Article 15. Not a conviction. I object to the offer, move to strike testimony dealing with any reduction in rank."

Lindquist stared down at Nick, "Counsel, anything you'd like to say?"

"No, sir, I've made my point. I withdraw my proffer."

Lindquist pulled his hand down the center of his face, as if applying pressure to his nostril and his upper lip. "Proceed, Counsel."

The ritual now complete, the impeachment of an ostensible hero foiled, Nick went in another direction.

"So, you were subject to an Article 15, is that not true?" Nick asserted.

"Yes, sir."

"Conduct unbecoming a noncommissioned officer, correct?"

"That's right," Jaeger replied, hardly audible.

"And the conduct, sir, was it not harassing a female subordinate?"

Jaeger felt his wife's embarrassment. What Nick was about to reveal was no secret—she had lived through it eight years ago. Jaeger imagined rightly that reporters in the witness box would turn their heads to observe her reaction. He imagined Madeline would publicly ignore the stares, remaining the loyal, military wife. An unassailable sphinx, one who had fought her own battles—not against the Army, but against what the Army did to the wide-eyed boy she had married in a time of mutual innocence. The same boy who, at the end of a career retreated into a cocoon and treated her like an intruder into a space reserved for those who carry the shame of killing men, women, children. No, this petite, weathered military wife—whom no one in the courthouse would have noticed normally—would not give clues to her feelings to those who fashion themselves keepers of the public trust.

"I think that, that... the Army didn't prove that," Jaeger came back.

Nick had drawn blood. Reluctantly, he hastened his pace. "Well, sir, in addition to that charge, were you not charged with an assault on your wife?"

Harris jumped up. "Objection! Your Honor, what does this have to do with this case?" he yelled indignantly.

"This is in the weeds, Counsel. Both of you, please approach the bench."

Lindquist gave Nick the stern schoolmaster's stare before asking, slightly above a whisper, "Why's this necessary, Mr. Castalano?"

"Your Honor, Mr. Harris put this witness forth as having a stellar army career to enhance his credibility. I'm merely trying to show that all is not what it appears to be."

"Counsel, be forewarned. I'm giving you a very short leash on this, so measure your questions carefully. Proceed."

Admonished, Nick looked at Lindquist guardedly and decided he would not press the matter of Jaeger's wife further, the damage was already done.

"Mr. Jaeger, when Mr. Harris asked, 'At what rank did you retire?' you answered, 'Master Sergeant.' You also said you were a First Sergeant. I want to clear something up. Mr. Jaeger, how many stripes did you wear on your uniform the day you retired?"

"Retired Sergeant First Class, yes one... "

"Not Master Sergeant, right?"

"No!" he answered, crestfallen.

"And you were relieved as a First Sergeant, is that not the truth?"

"Yes, after five years as a First... " For the first time, Jaeger dropped his head.

Nick quickly followed up. "But to be clear, you didn't retire in that position, correct?"

"No," he answered, shaking his head from side to side.

"Mr. Jaeger, when you went blind in 1977, you went to the VA in Harrisburg for medical treatment?"

"Yes, that's true."

"The VA medical board turned down your claim that your condition was service related, isn't that true?"

"Yes."

"You appealed, did you not?"

"Yes, I did."

"And, sir, what was the result of the appeal?"

"They turned down my claim, but the Army got involved, and they reversed themselves."

"So you now have what's considered a service-connected medical disability?"

"Yes, sir," Jaeger answered, impassively.

"Is your case coming up for review again?"

"It does from time to time."

"And you are afraid that the VA will deny your benefits again, is that not true?"

"I suppose it's possible."

"And it's possible you may need the Army to step in again, isn't that true?"

"I haven't thought that far ahead."

"But if you needed them, you would want them to help you, right?"

"Yes, sir, but the fact remains that I—and a lot of men that served in Vietnam—went blind 'cause of... "

"Do you feel beholden to the Army for turning your claim around?"

Harris broke Nick's momentum. "Objection, your Honor. Counsel is badgering the witness; he isn't giving him a chance to complete his answers."

Lindquist bore in on Nick. "Let the witness finish."

"I ain't beholden to no one," shouted Jaeger defiantly.

"Mr. Harris called you about this case, correct?"

"I think he called me, yes."

"Did you not discuss your disability? Isn't that what motivated you to testify here today, to ensure that the Army would be there when you needed them?"

"Objection!" bellowed Harris.

"Sir, I'm only here to... I'm just here to... "

Lindquist trumped Harris' bellow with his own, "Counsel!"

Nick, knew the poison of doubt was already working. "Withdraw the question. Thank you, Mr. Jaeger."

Nick changed direction.

"And it is no coincidence that, at the time you went blind you were manufacturing denatured alcohol on your farm?"

"What's that got to do with it?"

"You are well aware that the consumption of denatured alcohol causes blindness, aren't you?"

"I never drank it. Why should I?"

"What did you make it for?"

Harris rose from his chair again. "Your Honor, this whole line of questioning is collateral. It has nothing to do with this case. The witness has denied the allegation put forth by Mr. Castalano. I say let's move on."

Lindquist furrowed his brow. "I agree. Counselor, he denied drinking it, so move on!"

Nick walked back to his chair and fell into it hard, tucked his hands beneath his ass, breathed in deep and exhaled long. "No further questions."

Lindquist looked at Harris. "Counsel, redirect?"

"No, sir."

Lindquist turned to Jaeger. "Sir, thank you for your testimony today. You are free to go. Marshal, let's take a five minute break."

While Nick was sitting in his chair, a man holding a VFW service cap walked through the gate of the well to where Nick sat.

"Mr. Castalano, remember me?" he whispered.

Nick looked at the man, trying to place his face. "No, you look familiar, but no. Where do I know you from?"

"I'm one of those guys the VA sent you to destroy in 1980. Remember me, Agent Orange?"

"Mister? What's your name, sir?"

"Jenkins, VA denied me, and you... "

"Yes, now I recall. But, Mr. Jenkins, I'd nothing against you. I was just doing my job."

"You know, doctors givin' me six months now—multiple myeloma they call it."

"I'm truly sorry, but... "

"No need to be sorry now, but people like you are a disgrace—anybody ever tell you that? Did anybody ever tell you that you kill people—veterans? That you kill veterans, and that you're a fucking government goon?"

"Sir... " Before Nick could say anything more, the man walked off in the direction of the gate. Nick studied him for a moment and, for an instant, wondered what he had done. Whether he played a role in this man's fate.

When the Jaeger's left the room, Julie followed them to the foyer. "Mr. and Mrs. Jaeger, I'm Julie O'Conner. My brother was in Camp 13. And when you mentioned Conner, I thought that maybe you were talking about him."

"Ma'am, I'm afraid I told them all I know," Jaeger answered humbly.

"Well I can tell you what he looked like. I even have his pic... "

Jaeger smiled. "Nah, that can't help. He seemed like a regular guy."

"I was hoping that... "

"I'm afraid I can't be of any help. Good meetin' you."

A Judge Of Oral Hygiene

TEN MINUTES AFTER ADJOURNING COURT, Lindquist was sitting in Dr. Pendergrast's dentist's chair. The doctor, a portly man, waddled over.

"Okay, Joe, open up." After forty-five years of poking around people's mouths, he showed little bedside manner as he peered through the spectacles that sat comfortably on his red, bulbous nose.

"Joe, the abscess perforated the bone, draining into the surrounding tissue." He put his hand on a swelling on Lindquist's neck and said, "Does this hurt?"

"It's tender."

The doctor reached under Lindquist's jaw, felt around, moved down his larynx, and squeezed. "Does this hurt?"

"A little."

"You should have gotten here when you first felt the tenderness in the gum. Infection like this floods the bone, washing it away like soap. I'm going to have to take the tooth. There isn't enough bone left."

"Do whatever you have to."

"Well, we'll give you some nitrous oxide to dull the pain. I have to go up there and scrape the bone, after I remove the tooth. You're going to have a gap if you smile too wide, but there's little I can do right now. If you want a false tooth, I can build a bridge later."

Lindquist's chair vibrated and his ears buzzed. His head dropped below his knees, and a dental assistant with a fair amount of cleavage moved beside him. He closed his eyes. "Take a deep breath, Mr. Lindquist," she said, in a calmingly squeaky voice.

Within seconds he went from admiring long hair brushing tops of flourishing breasts to hearing, "Joe, wake up. We're done, Joe."

Lindquist looked over and saw Pendergrast on a stool next to him.

171

"Joe, I felt this lump in your neck, and I want it looked at."

Still drowsy, Lindquist came back, "Probably a swollen gland right?"

"I don't think so, but I'm not the expert. I'd like you to get it checked out. Probably nothing, maybe related to the infection, but I want to be sure."

Uneasily, Lindquist asked, "What else might it be?"

Pendergrast knew what else it might be. " I don't know, but go see, Doc Reichhart over at the North Avenue Medical Center. He's an oncologist, and he'll let us know if it's nothing or something we need to deal with."

"Oncologist! You mean... "

"Joe, I don't mean anything. It's a lump for God's sake. It could be anything. I don't remember seeing it last year. So let's not read anything into this. Let Reichhart tell us what it is."

Later that day, Lindquist sat in his easy chair as the sun set, feet on the foot rest, his tabby Red squeezed between his hip and the armrest. He rubbed the knot of flesh on his neck to which he had paid no mind over the past several months. He pulled out his journal and wrote:

A witness today reminded me about the winter of '44, the one that shaped my fear—the kind of fear I saw in my father's face every time it rained hard, the kind of fear that I felt when the doctor told me Mattie had a week to live. The kind of fear I now feel toward what the doctor may say about the lump. Fear, will I ever conquer it?

He closed his eyes, and December '44 flashed before him. The rain had turned sleety, thawed mud thickened and froze in a diabolical cycle. Where the wind blew hard, and snow packed itself into all corners of the foot-soldier's life. The enemy left behind twisted wire, booby traps and mines. Winter settled into daily routine, and the troops found refuge in burned out farmhouses, barns, pillboxes and foxholes. But such refuge did little to ward off pneumonia, trench foot. frostbite. The day before Christmas, while patrolling in the mountainous Ardennes, his squad took a wrong turn down a deserted road that turned into a forest opaque with sharp-sided hills and deep rapids. Eventually, they came to a no-name village. When they heard the distant, strained growl of diesels they found a small cottage where they laid low spying in the direction of the increasing sound. Finally, a brown tank came into view, escorting a dozen armored half-tracks and a column of ragtag foot-soldiers from the retreating 1st SS Panzer Division.

When the tank came within a hundred yards, it moved out of position and swiveled its turret toward the cottage. VROOM! A fast whistle followed a delayed thud. The first shell hit next door. The house collapsed into a pile of seventeenth century rubble. The turret groaned a few more degrees to the right, where the squad hid. Before the next round, Privates Joe Lindquist and Robby O'Halloran ran down a cobblestone alley to an abandoned rectory. The tank pounded the cottage until it too turned it into a pile of stone, marking the spot of another burial ground.

The tank twisted its turret toward the small church attached to the rectory. VROOM! A whistle, a wait and a thud. A bronze bell and its wooden headstock tumbled through the belfry. Its clapper clanging one last time.

Hearing three more shells, the privates burrowed deeper into the corner of the cellar. Fifteen minutes later, VROOM! A whistle, nothing and then, a thud. The first floor of the rectory splintered into grains of sawdust and a thousand shards. Joe looked up at two precariously hung beams and beyond that, the dome of a placid night sky. The tank stopped shelling. A five-minute pause, and then a shell screamed in. The beams came down and wood, masonry, and shattered wine bottles covered Robby to his waist.

"You okay?" His body slumped forward. "Robby, you all right?" Lindquist pulled himself out of the rubble far enough to see his friend leaning forward. "Robby, you all right?" The soldier did not answer, his chin resting between the open lapels of his burgundy stained overcoat. Blood spurted lazily from the side of his neck.

Lindquist shut his eyes, but he could not shut out the sound of crashing cymbals, the oversized pounding drums, concrete, exploding glass—unwrapping his senses only to be reset by the whistle of the goddamn shell. VROOM! Aged wine or Robby's blood—maybe both—painted the ancient walls purple.

When he heard the tank move on, Joe pulled a heel of gray bread from his overcoat and drank from a decapitated blue bottle. An hour passed and he stared, trembling through the gaping hole at the half-hearted moon, at the ominous apparitions of war. He was a man who would someday judge other men's intentions. A man who someday would sit in his armchair, with his red tabby and a legacy of dreams about tanks, hard earthy sounds, Robby O'Halloran's corpse, bread and wine, outlines and accidents that follow missed turns in the road, perhaps giving new meaning to the phrase: *In vino veritas.*

Searching For Answers

BARE-CHESTED, WEARING JOCKEY SHORTS and wool socks, Jack reached for the pack of Lucky Strikes on the stovetop. The phone rang. He tapped out a cigarette and put it to his lips. He fumbled the match, lit the cigarette and released a cloud of blue smoke as he ambled over to the phone.

"—ello," he rasped.

"Jack? You 'wake? Geeze, it's nearly noon!"

"Julie?"

"Guess where I've been all week," she snapped.

"Where?" He took a deep drag, letting the smoke out little by little.

"Goddamn court, that's where! Thought you were supposed to be there!"

"Couldn't make it," he answered, sounding like he could not care less.

"You mean you've been goddamn drunk!"

"Why'd you call?"

"I heard some things that made me feel like dying," she replied, signaling in her tone that she wanted sympathy.

"What the hell are you talking about?"

"Jack, what do you know about my boyfriend Roger?" she asked, shifting to a prosecutorial voice.

"What? Roger who? What're you talking about?" Jack put his thumb and index finger around his mouth and slid them down his chin.

"Roger, you know... the guy I used to date."

He took a deep drag. "For Christ's sake, are you crazy? That was thirty years ago. Are you feeling all right, or what?"

"Jack, you know I never forgot him," she said.

"How the hell am I supposed to remember what happened thirty years ago? I can't tell you what happened last week."

"I'm comin' over."

Jack exhaled smoke through pursed lips, letting out a blowing sound.

"What's that?"

"I farted. Don't you have to go to work or something?"

"I gotta get to the bottom of this."

"You're crazy, you know that? You're goddamn crazy," he barked.

"You must have made the connection when you returned from the war. I talked to you about him. I remember it like yesterday. We were in the gym at school. I'm comin' over later."

Jack hung up, grabbed a tumbler from the sink and went to the liquor cabinet to pour himself a stiff *Seagram's 7*, no ice. He walked to the front room and flopped on the overstuffed couch. A picture Julie had taken of him and his mother when he returned from Korea in late 1954 lay over the fireplace in a bed of dust. He remembered that he had arrived home dressed in a new army shirt, canvas duffle bag slung over his shoulder, and had stood in the kitchen doorway watching his mother through a screen door. She had aged a dozen years since he had kissed her that morning at the train station just over four years before. Her housedress was faded and frayed, her knees and elbows more boney. Then, jolted by an emotional current coursing through her tiny frame, the frying pan she held flew into a kitchen cabinet, and she flung her head back. "Jack!"

Two deep-set gray eyes peered back from a pasty, sunken face squeezed dry. "Yes, Mom, it's me." He opened the door and Mary ran into his embrace, weeping for all the years that had washed away.

"You didn't tell me you were coming," she said, patting her hair as if in a strong wind. "I hardly recognized you, hardly recognized my own son... lost in that, that uniform."

"It's a size too big," he laughed.

"Oh, my son, Jack, Jack, my son, you'll never know, you'll never know. I prayed every night." She hugged him again.

"I know. It's okay," he whispered to comfort her.

Mary moved away, the two sizing one another up, readjusting memories. Jack looked into Mary's eyes and knew what she must have seen: a thin, tired, delicate man, not the strong boy who had left when the train pulled out of the station. Mary put on a pot of coffee. Jack sat down at the yellow table that had witnessed three generations of Prados in happier times.

"They wouldn't tell me where you were." Mary patted a napkin in front of her.

"Let's not talk about that now."

She started for the fridge. "I'll heat up some soup."

"Terrific, it'll be the best I've eaten in years. What is it?"

She reached for a large ceramic bowl. "Pasta *fagiole*, your favorite."

"Well, not sure about that. All I ate was soy beans, half-cooked, and sorghum, a ball about the size of my fist."

Hesitating, she offered, "I can cook a... "

Jack smirked. "Oh, no, just kiddin', Mom, the *fagiole*'s good."

They talked about his trip home, where he had boarded the Marine Adder, a one stack transport out of Pusan that landed in San Diego. After a half dozen military hops, he had reached Long Island where he hitched a ride. Then Mary began to fill in the weightier events that had occurred during his time away, notably the passing of Nonna Rosa.

Jack scanned the once familiar room. For all the ways their lives had turned, the room where Nonna Rosa had spent her days had changed little. A large woman who dressed in flowing flowered housecoats, her graying hair wrapped in a swirl pinned to the top of her head. She washed her cherub-like cheeks with nothing more than Ivory Soap—a woman as plain as her kitchen. Before college, Jack spent most of his time in that kitchen, listening to the radio, doing homework. Every so often he would look up from a book and let his gaze sweep past the pantry on one side, the back window, the porcelain sink, the gas stove with double kerosene-fired heaters and the small Frigidaire. The kitchen had a resonance all its own: the radio, penetrating sounds from Julie's violin, boiling water, oils in the frying pan, the mechanical innards of the gray enameled tub swooshing clothes. Sometimes Nonna would waltz around the kitchen like a portly ballerina. And at some point, like a jukebox out of money, the music would stop and Julie would emerge from the pantry, pour a cup of black coffee and return to her "music room." If the windows were open, the percussive crack of wind filled bed sheets on the line called attention to a kind of freshness that was left in the residue of his later childhood. On the day he returned from war, the wind blew hard too, the grass that had always grown high rustled furiously, a broken clothesline flapped from side to side, waiting for someone to put it to work again.

When Jack asked about Julie, Mary told him that she had taken ill in '51 and that she no longer played violin. "I don't think it's so much the hand. It's her heart. It's broken. That guy Roger she dated never came back. She works at St. Pats, at the school."

Jack said nothing and walked over to the rear window to look out.

After three bowls of soup, Jack set out to surprise Julie at work. At the principal's office a plump young woman with insect eyes lifted her head when Jack walked through the door.

"Can I help you?"

"Yeah, I'm looking for Julie O'Conner."

"You her boyfriend?" she asked coyly.

"Nah, her brother."

"Oh, you're Jack. In the Army. Julie showed me your pit'cher." The woman grinned through her nicotine-stained teeth, waiting for his reaction.

"Right," Jack cracked, careful not to show the slightest interest.

The secretary's eyes lifted over Jack's head to the clock. It was 2:30. She turned back to Jack and scanned his brown ribbon-less shirt. Jack saw her give a faint smirk. "Probably in the gym. Out the door, take a left."

The echo from the leather heals of his military shoes ceased when Jack opened the heavy steel door that led to the combination auditorium/gym. He heard sloshing from someone mopping the floor. He walked across the gym to the edge of the stage from where the sounds were coming and boosted himself onto the elevation. He peeked behind the red, heavy curtain and in the corner, dimly lit by a 60 watt bulb, a petite woman in a gray smock swabbed the floor. She had a mop stick twisted beneath her upper right arm, which she managed to push back and forth using a rotating wrist movement. "Yo, Julie! Julie, that you?" he yelled.

Even before she turned, her jaw had dropped. "Jack? Jack, you're home!" The mop fell.

Jack ran to hug her, thinking how Julie and his mother were as close as he had been to any woman in years. Julie, likewise, had not embraced a man since the night Jack left for Hamilton's farewell party.

"How've you been?" she cried, stepping back and beaming.

He glanced down at her odd foot position and quickly turned his attention to the sparkling lime green eyes he had remembered as he had languished in prison.

"Good, good, real good. Got in about two hours ago, stopped by the house. Mom looks good, little tired. Is she seeing Dad?"

"Not often, but when they do, you know it's never good. Mom wastes so much time in the past. She doesn't let go." Jack showed no emotion, and she changed the subject. "How are you? You look skinny."

"Well, yeah, I haven't been eatin' in the best restaurants." He laughed.

"I imagine, but how much *do* you weigh? Can't be more than... ."

"One-twenty, more or less."

"Wow, I wouldn't 'a known you, Jack, if I saw you coming down the street."

"Forget me, how are you? How's your leg? Mom said you were sick." Jack grimaced.

"It's fine. The doctor figures that I'll limp a little from now on. My foot, it's getting so I can almost get it off the ground, but," she hesitated, "it doesn't matter."

"You always had that stick-to-it-ness. You'll get there."

"Yeah, I know, but it's my hand." Pushing her hand toward Jack she said, "See, I can't move these two fingers much."

Jack ran his finger lightly over her wrist, and then pulled her close. Julie sobbed as he gazed over her shoulder, out the grimy gym window where the wire mesh ran crisscross, looking to the green lawn and beyond to the maple trees that were turning red-yellow. He turned his head in the direction of the older, brown and white three story houses beyond the trees—the ones that were freshly painted. The place looked like it did before he left, quiet and reserved, where the gardens and hedges still lifted spirits, where his baby sister ran down Willa Street, a non-stop chubby toddler, always the center of attention. Where it went unnoticed that she'd changed from a talkative five-year-old, to a shy seven-year-old, to a skinny, introverted nine-year-old, until finally in her mid-teen years, she'd withdraw for long periods as she worked her music to near perfection.

"Have ya seen any of the old crowd?"

"Nah. And that guy I used to date, Roger, well, he never made it back," she said somberly. She rubbed her arm across her face to dry the tears.

"Oh? Julie, I'm sorry." Jack felt edgy, biting into his lower lip. "Ya know I lost a lot of good buddies over there." He turned away pursing his lips. The hands on the wall clock pointed at 3 p.m., and the school bell clanged. The sound of the students's noisy dismissal filtered into the gym. He faced Julie again. Her eyes glistened in the mid-afternoon light that poured through the wired window. When it was quiet again, Jack interrupted the long reflective moment, "Could ya play me somethin' on the piano?"

Julie smiled ear-to-ear. "I don't think so. Was never that good on the piano. You know the violin was my thing."

"I'm home, Julie. Come on... one time, for me?"

Julie thought for a moment and then ambled over to an upright in the corner of the room, lifted its oak keyboard cover and sat down. "I haven't played... for a couple of years."

Barely twenty-six, Julie sat in a janitor's smock, her hair carelessly wrapped in a brown bun, and her delicate white hands resting on off-white and chipped ivories. The notes sounded sharp as she mapped out the approach for something resembling a melody with her good hand and a low note with a few good fingers. High notes haltingly pinged off the soundboard, then burst into a minor scale—a deep D-flat in the left hand resonated with a voice weakened by years of longing: "You'll never know just how much I miss you." Though tears streamed down her cheeks, Julie suddenly appeared younger than she had the moment before. The music transported Jack back to a mansion of debutantes with coquettish smiles, and if Jack had had any intentions of telling Julie what he know about Roger, he decided to bury them then and there.

***

After talking to Jack on the phone, Julie went home. The heat stifled the apartment, so she decided to pack a small overnight bag and sleep in Jack's spare room. About nine that night, she took the bus to Willa Street, crossed the street, walked past the row of faded brown and white three story houses that hadn't been painted in a generation. The day had threatened thunderstorms. It was close to dark and the houses appeared older than usual. Except for a relative few, most people rented. The once well-kept lawns were now hardpan. The flowerbeds of her childhood were gullies of stagnant rainwater. The maple trees along the sidewalks were fat around the trunk and full of brown and shriveled leaves. Everything on Willa Street was reflective of everything else, so the hard brown dirt made the dented aluminum garbage cans at the curb appear fatter than normal, the fatter garbage cans made the street look narrower and the narrower street pushed back the clock.

When she arrived at the house shades were drawn, same as a few days before when she had kept Jack from blowing out his brains.

"Jack, you here? Where are you?" Her eyes adjusted to the outline of familiar objects and odd shadows that haunted the hallway. Even though it was warm outside, the air conditioning made her shiver.

She stopped before the hall mirror, which reflected bloodshot eyes held in place by gray, puffy bags and a crease emerging at the bottom of her nose and outlining her mouth before finally disappearing beneath her chin.

She pressed against the flesh that joined her jaw to her throat. She went to the kitchen to shut off the air conditioner, ran upstairs, searched the rooms and returned to the living room to flop in Nonna's overstuffed chair. In an ashtray on the end table, a long-ash cigarette had burned itself out. Her eyes moved over the knickknacks and the pictures on end-tables. Slowly, the room darkened and the images and bric-a-brac of a life passing too quickly disappeared into oblique shadows and silhouettes. Jack never showed.

***

Earlier in the day, Jack had showered and dressed, grudgingly intending to go to court as ordered in the subpoena. He planned to answer much in the way he had seen on T.V. when the witness "can't remember." But as he was leaving the phone rang, and a man on the other end who identified himself as Mr. Travers and was connected to the case, told him he did not need to appear as indicated in the subpoena. The caller mentioned he that wanted to meet Jack later in the day. Jack felt relieved and although the caller refused to tell him specifically why he wanted to talk, Jack agreed to meet at the Silver Streak Diner at 8:30 that night.

About twenty minutes past eight, Jack was walking toward the diner when a dark blue Chevy four door pulled alongside him, two men in the front seat, window down. The driver asked, "Yo, buddy, you Jack O'Conner?"

"Yeah, why?"

"I'm Bud, Bud Travers. We spoke."

"I was going down to the diner."

"Figured we'd grab a beer someplace on Barnum. Hop in."

They looked like cops, mid thirties. Jack climbed in. Travers said reflexively, "This is Steve Jones." The man looked straight ahead, making Jack feel all the more wary.

Jack leaned forward in the seat and asked anxiously. "What's this about?"

"Let's wait till we get there," Travers said guardedly. Jack saw Jones looking at him through the rearview.

"You cops?"

"Sort of. We work for the government, US Government."

182

Jones was wearing a summer suit with a white shirt and open collar. He was a big tall guy with light colored hair—hard for Jack to judge his height, but had to be over two hundred pounds. Travers, a smaller, swarthy man, sat sphinx-like.

The car turned down Barnum, drove about a mile into the rear of a dirty brick building with a sign: *Prince Harry Bar and Grille*. The parking lot was dark with two cars parked against the building. Being familiar with the place, Jack breathed a little easier . As Jack opened the door Travers rested his arm on the back of the seat, "Wait, before we get out, let me tell you why we wanted to talk."

Jack slid behind the driver's seat. Travers had small, steely eyes reminiscent of a Doberman. "We've been following the Girardin case and have reason to believe that this Art Girardin guy is a flake... and— "

Jack interrupted. "Wait, let's start over. Who're you guys?"

"We work for the government, like I said," Travers replied in a tone that riled Jack.

"But the government's big."

"Steve and me, we're part of DIS."

"And what's that?"

"Defense Intelligence Service," Travers responded, sounding like a cop.

"Army, Navy, what?"

"Defense."

"Ok, so what's that gotta do with me?"

"You can't help the situation, especially, if some shyster lawyer gets you on the stand, twists your memory—you know, making you look like a whatcha-call-it turncoat."

Jack's face began to flush. "Look, Mack, I don't like the way this is startin' off."

"Aw'right, leave that aside."

"Get to the fucking point."

"Bottom line? We're gonna buy you a ticket for a vaca', down south a few weeks," said Travers.

"Leave tonight," Jones snickered.

Jack grinned cautiously. "Are you guys shittin' me?"

"Nope, dead serious." Travers pulled his thin lips back, like a dead man grinning.

Jack did not like the way Travers said it.

"Well, I'd have to think it over."

Traver's tightened his jaw. "Ok, you got about two minutes, and Mr. O'Conner, I might add... little choice."

"Look, Travers, I ain't got no beef with you guys. I don't even know who the Christ you are. I'm not even sure I'd help Girardin's side, but I don't like being told I gotta do anything."

"Jack, we're trying to do this quick and professional. I'm told you're a smart guy, so I decided not to beat around the bush," he said, his face relaxing.

"Who told you?" Jack asked, showing concern.

"That's something we can't discuss, but we'd pay for the entire trip. Wanna take a girlfriend, we can arrange that, too. But be fast. Tomorrow, latest. Come on, all expenses."

"I appreciate that, but I ain't making no decision tonight."

With that, Jack left the car and walked toward the bar. Just before he reached the rear door he felt a large hand grab his shoulder. He swung around: it was Jones, all 6'4", forty waist.

"Wait a minute buster, get back in the car, so we can work this out."

"Fuck you." Jack shook off his hand and reached for the bar door. Jones' beefy forearm corralled his neck. Jack yelled, "What the fuck you doing, you fat bastard?" He struggled, but the giant had him in a bear grip. Travers came around the front.

"Look O'Conner make it easy on yourself."

"What the fu—?" Jack screamed.

Before he finished his expletive an air-deflating blow slammed into his solar plexus. As he gasped for air, a fist came across his jaw. He remembered nothing else, until he woke up in the middle of the night, smelling like gin, uniformed cops on each side. When he saw the uniforms, he bolted, but they tackled him. He swung at them and they cold cocked him.

Dungeons Here and There

WHEN JACK HADN'T APPEARED IN COURT ON MONDAY according to the subpoena the sheriff served the morning he walked back from the diner, Nick was not overly concerned, because Jack actually knowing Roger Girardin had seemed like a long shot. But Jaeger's testimony changed all that. The O'Conner he had testified as helping him out of a jam, may well have been Jack Prado O'Conner. On Thursday, Nick had Mitch tell the oversized sheriff to leave a second subpoena ordering him to court on Friday. When Jack failed to show Friday, the first item on Nick's weekend "to do" list was to find O'Conner. He had to determine if he needed Jack to testify about Jaeger's unlikely claim that Girardin had died on the ridge. He called Jack's phone Saturday and Sunday. He sat back wondering what to do next, flipped open a phone book, found Prado, and called a half-dozen names, none related to Jack. But on the seventh call heard, "Yes, Jack Prado. He's my husband."

Bingo! "Is he there?" Nick asked.

"No, he's not."

"Will he be home later?"

"No, I don't think so, he doesn't live here anymore."

"Can you tell me where I might find him?"

At first, Anna wasn't interested in talking about her husband, especially to a lawyer, but reluctantly she volunteered that Jack had been depressed, drinking hard, passing out.

"I learned he was arrested Friday night. Police told me he was drunk at the rail yard, on the tracks. You know, at the far end of Willa Street. Claimed they yelled out. He ran, slugged a cop."

"Is he in lock-up at the police station?"

"I don't know. All I know's he's in jail."

185

Nick ran Jack down at the county jail, but decided to wait until Monday morning to catch him at the arraignment.

***

On local maps a small rectangle points to the red, granite courthouse on the corner of East Main and Hill Street. It was built in 1848, a time when "Victorian" stood for more than an architectural style—especially to convicts sentenced to hard labor or the gallows. Nick went into the prosecutor's office and asked to see Jack's arrest report. He learned that later in the morning he would be charged with resisting arrest, assaulting an officer and criminal trespass. The judge would be familiar with the place, the rail yard where the inebriated homeless had sought refuge in abandoned boxcars for decades. Depending on his view of cops, the railroad, the homeless and the man standing in front of him, he would decide whether to set the bond so high Jack would be held over for trial or to let him walk. In either case, to be disposed of down the line, an immaterial artifact on one scale-pan of a balance beam held by none other than that blind woman called Justice. After reading the file, Nick proceeded to lock-up to find Jack.

Off the central rotunda, marbled busts of past jurists led the public to three courtrooms, a dozen offices, two Lysol-laden lavatories and a maze of oak planked dark hallways. Nick, in pinstriped suit and with briefcase in hand, walked down one hallway to a steel door, behind which was a stairwell to the catacombs below the courtrooms. To get into the stairwell, Nick had to know the jailer—who only admitted lawyers, cops and clerks. In the forty years on the job, the guard never had to decide whether judges were permitted below.

"Who you here for?"

"A Jack Prado? No, make that O'Conner, Jack O'Conner."

The guard put his un-calloused hand behind his extended derrière to retrieve a chain with a key. Nick passed through the opening and hesitated for a few seconds, before the tunnel-like flight of smoothly worn granite stairs that disappeared into darkness.

On the first landing, Nick encountered a rancid bouquet of alcohol, sweat, urine, feces and vomit. At the bottom of the stairwell, the air thickened, water dripping along one side into a fetid puddle. Nick could no longer hold his breath. A few six-by-six cells held two prisoners each, one fourteen-by-fourteen cell held eighteen. Another held a solitary man accused of murder, another a woman, and yet another a man sick beyond drunken heaves. No vacancies. A somber, living tomb, where except for the erratic groans and moans of self pity and despair, the tenants hear no evil and see no evil, and on this day were oblivious to Nick's presence.

As Nick got closer to his destination he detected an undercurrent of broken mumbling.

"Cracker Jacker, what're ya gonna do, those blind will one day see you, please, leave me the sea... Jack, Jack, Jack be nimble, Jack be quick, All work and no play. Easy Mac, cracker Jack... he's a prick."

Nick saw a man sitting on the edge of the bunk, his elbows on his knee, head on his hands, swaying slightly back and forth.

"Jack. Jack O'Conner?"

The mumbling stopped. Jack's head snapped up, his face drawn and unshaven. A shiner, a swollen right cheek, a split lip and bloodshot eyes—maybe from crying, or maybe from years of drugs and alcohol. Nick could not be sure. He had met many men in this place, most with faces summing up a past of brutal self destruction; a self-defeatist life of several interminable lifetimes.

"Mr. O'Conner, my name's Nick Castalano. I'm an attorney."

"Not O'Conner—Prado. You my lawyer?"

"No, I represent a man who's trying to find out what happened to his brother during the Korean War. You were in Korea. Right?"

Jack put his head down taking a couple of short quick breaths. "I don't need this shit right now, mister." He cupped his face, rubbed his eyes. "That was a thousand years ago."

"Well, Mr. Prado, only a few questions."

"Not now. I don't want to answer any fucking questions. Beat it!"

"Mr. Prado, promise I won't take much of your time."

"Look, I ain't got nothin'."

"I need to have you look at something—tell me what you think, that's all. We can do it here or I can have you brought before a federal judge. Have it your way."

For a few seconds it was quiet except for the sounds of a woman sobbing. Jack closed his eyes. "Get me out of here, and I'll talk as long as you want."

"I can't, Mr. Prado. I may have to call you as a witness, and I can't very well be your lawyer, too." Nick omitted that there was always the possibility that Jack would be an adversarial witness, one that he might have to rake over the coals.

"All right, then if you want, let's talk after I get out of here, but listen up, I ain't going be no witness."

"Tell you what, Mr. Prado, I'll wait for you upstairs. When the arraignment's over, we can talk?"

Jack looked at Nick. "You think I'll get out today?"

"Can't say. They'll probably ask for bond. Have you been in trouble before?"

"Never. First time."

Nick returned to the upper world and walked through the double door entrance to the arraignment court, the drainpipe for the criminal justice system. He would wait to see if Nick walked out a free man. Now that he had finally found him, he did not want Jack slipping through his fingers. An hour passed before Jack, represented by a public defender, appeared and in just a few minutes more, the judge pronounced the only words that mattered, "You are free to go, sir, on your own recognizance. Don't leave the state. Next case!"

Nick met Jack on the way out, and the two went to a small conference room where Nick occasionally met clients. Plaster walls lathered and troweled in the last century were gray and graffitied, but otherwise retained their smooth hardness. The place whiffed faintly of feces from the infrequent bum who used the room to nap, defecate and leave. In the center was an oak table carved with hundreds of initials and two folding chairs for defendants to discuss past faults and divine their future with an advocate licensed to contribute to their fate.

With a stubble beard, Jack reeked from a combination of halitosis, alcohol, urine and body odor. Nick walked over to a frosted window, forced it open and let in the siren sound of an ambulance stuck behind a fender bender, opting to talk over the racket rather than take the stench. Jack stood waiting, his arms wrapped around himself.

"Have a seat," he said in a loud voice.

The men sat across from one another. "I noticed the prosecutor referred to you as O'Conner, yet you go by Prado, which is it?"

Jack exhaled, moving restlessly in his chair. "My mother's maiden name is Prado, I prefer that, but my legal name is O'Conner. You can refer to me as Prado... Man, do you have a cig?"

"No, gave it up."

"Is this gonna take long? I am dying for somethin' to eat." Jack rotated his head like he was trying to release a crick in his neck.

"No, this won't take long. Tell me, did you know a Roger Girardin when you were in the service?"

Nick could not be sure if he had seen a shudder run through Jack—the man shifted constantly.

"Not sure, maybe... maybe, vaguely," Jack said in a way that did not give Nick confidence he was ready to cooperate.

"He was from Bridgeport."

"Like I told ya, maybe."

"Well, if you knew him, would it have been while you were a POW?"

"Don't remember him there." Jack folded his swollen lower lip under his upper teeth.

"When then? When'd you know him?"

"Might have been a guy that was with me in the 24th."

"He never returned from Korea... "

"Mister, could have been MIA, KIA. Lots of things happened."

"Like, maybe he didn't come back with the other soldiers?"

Nick saw Jack's jaw stiffen. "What're you driving at?"

189

Nick raised his hands, palms open. "Hey, it's no business of mine. But, those couple of dozen guys that decided to stay on with the Chinese after the POW exchange were called turncoats. Right? It's possible Girardin defected, isn't it?"

"I don't know about him, but I didn't. I was too sick to come back. It's this kinda bullshit I'm tryin' not to get mixed up in. I got a wife and kid, and they shouldn't be hearing this crap, like I was a... a traiter or somethin'."

"Jack, I know what the guys went through that came back after the POW exchange. It wasn't deserved. I, for one, believed they *were* brainwashed. So, I'll do everything in my power not to get into that."

"Well, that would really fuck me up, job-wise, you know."

"Yes, I know."

"Well, I'm risking a lot talkin' to you."

"Yes, and I know that."

"More than you know, Mac. More than you know."

"I have some maps of a POW camp. Can you look at them?"

Nick removed his jacket. Sitting down again, he reached for his briefcase, removing several yellowed, folded documents and unfolded one marked B-2.

"Do you recognize this?"

Jack looked at Nick, then at the map. He reviewed the lines on the paper for about thirty seconds. "It's the layout of the camp I was at." He pointed to a blue set of lines at one edge of the paper, "The main road came in here. We came and went by that road. And here's where the barracks were, all over here—a little town. Not really barracks, huts more like, where we slept."

Jack stopped. He had added nothing that Nick did not already know. Nick rolled out the next map, marked B-4 in the upper corner. "Do you recognize this one?"

"Well, it's the eastern end of North Korea near the... Yeah, here's the Yalu, here's the border. Manchuria."

Nick pointed to a line, "Do you know what this is?"

"Looks like a map of the route south."

"Anything else you recognize?"

"No. Look, Mac, it's been a long, long time." Jack scratched the large lump left by the billy stick.

"How about these, B-3 and B-1?"

"Well, B-1 looks similar to B-2, think it's probably Camp 13. B-3, I don't know what area that's referring to."

"Over here, on B-2 these hexagonal marks, what do they stand for?"

Jack's eyes slid to where Nick pointed. Beads of sweat had formed on Jack's forehead, and he rubbed his hands along his legs. "Don't know."

"Think hard... I was hoping you could tell me."

Jack rose from his chair. "Look, I got a splittin' headache."

"I just need a few more answers."

"They might be anything," Jack avoided Nick's gaze. "Camps, caches, you know, ammo. Or even minefields. Who knows? Hexagons within hexagons. Hexahexagonagon. Ha!"

Nick could see the man was nearing the edge again and changed tack, asking more about Jack's life after the service. Jack said he had worked for Hamilton Helicopters after he came home from Korea. Nick asked how he had gotten the job, and he mentioned that he knew the owner.

"Did you know that the owner Trent Hamilton was also a POW?" Nick had read this in the local newspaper.

"No, no I had not."

Nick found Jack's answer curious, figuring that if he knew the owner when he came back from Korea, he would know that they both shared the uncommon experience of being POWs. However, while Jack's responses were mostly nods or a flat out "no's," he seemed to have returned to a level of rationality.

"Jack, a guy named Jaeger testified that you and Girardin were patrolling one morning, late November '50. Claimed you'd saved his life when you killed a sniper. Recall that?"

Jack looked confused. "No, ain't got no memory of saving anybody. Can hardly save myself. Ha! Never was on no patrol with Girardin neither. Guy's got it wrong."

"I need you to say that in court."

"Do I have a choice?"

"Not much, I'm afraid."

***

Nick, Kathy and Mitch met over lunch at Zorba's. Without asking, Big Sally slid Monday's meatloaf special in front of Nick. She also brought a couple of burgers for Kathy and Mitch.

After interviewing Jack, Nick had sent Mitch out on a fact-finding mission to gather some basic information on Trent Hamilton—since he was, after all, a POW—and because Nick felt uneasy about Jack's answer.

"So, Mitch, what'd you get?"

Mitch swiped the hair out of his eyes and recounted what he had gleaned from the local library newspaper stacks. "Well, they're local high flyers, as we know: Hamilton's CEO of Hamilton Helicopters, the family business. Sister's married to a senator."

"Okay, yadda yadda, and what we don't know... "

"Well, the town gave Hamilton the hero's welcome when he came back from Korea, tickertape, the whole nine yards."

"He'd been a POW, right?" asked Kathy.

"Yeah, we knew that, but better than that," returned Mitch.

"Interesting choice of words," quipped Kathy.

Mitch ducked his head, but knowing he had their full attention, he took a bite out of his burger. Nick and Kathy watched and waited as he chomped.

"Well?" asked Nick.

"Guess where." Mitch replied, licking his fingers.

Kathy winced. "Camp 13?"

"You got it. Busy place, old Camp 13."

"Excellent work, Mitch."

"All right, so court tomorrow?"

"Yeah, all right," Nick conceded. "But find O'Conner's military records this afternoon. Kathy can play point man for a while."

But wait," Kathy interrupted, "let me get this straight. Three local boys, this Hamilton fellow gets the ticker tape, Prado is a turncoat, and Girardin never comes back? Wow. At least you can't blame it on the water."

"So what's this Prado guy like?" Mitch asked.

192

"More importantly," Kathy added, "what was his recollection of events?"

"Recollection of events," mimicked Mitch.

"Vague," answered Nick. "A lotta 'don't remember,' or 'too long ago.' But it was more than that. The guy seemed rattled."

"Can we use him?" asked Mitch.

"We have to, to rebut Jaeger, but what happened in Camp 13 isn't something the guy's giving up easily."

Mitch slurped his coke, inspecting the ice melting at the bottom. "What's his beef?"

"Can't tell. He's not being straight. Like I said, this thing about Hamilton—you'd think he'd have mentioned it, even if he wasn't in the same POW camp. Just the idea they were both POWs. Then again, he's troubled by the possibility that his time in Korea after the POW switch will come out. That he'll be called a commie or a traitor or something. It was a bad time. And he's definitely an alkie, but it goes beyond alcohol. He can't think straight. I've seen that. And people don't like to get up in front of a lot of strangers and bare their souls. It's terrifying."

Gumshoes and Secretaries

AFTER LUNCH, NICK SENT KATHY to research Hamilton Helicopters stories at *The Bridgeport Post* where she found dozens of articles about the company that she summarized for Nick — its government contracts, work force and local influence. From the early 40s until the Hamilton's takeover in '52, pay had been fair, layoffs rare, business cyclical. It had a foundry, which aged men years before their time—most working until 62. It hired whole families, workers complained little and, although lines between management and workers had been razor sharp, workers had a job for life.

When Trent took over in the early 50s, the first casualty was the friendly atmosphere between workers and management. The end of the Korean War collapsed the spare parts business and the company downsized. A '53 *Wall Street Journal* analyst wrote that the company needed, "A cultural sea change" to stay competitive. Two years after his return from the war, Trent Hamilton had installed management loyalists, including Jack O'Conner, who assumed a middle management role half-heartedly. He ran a less than tight ship — far from meeting Trent's expectation of affording no quarter to foot-draggers — but Trent did little to change Jack's work ethic, figuring he achieved his objective: keeping Jack close and beholden.

Hamilton's management philosophy was described by a *Bridgeport Post* editorial as:

"... a biological determinism, where the success of the company (Hamilton Helicopters) depends not on innovation or product integrity as much as on forced ranking bottom up, where the lower ten percent are routinely replaced by better prospects on the theory that evolution produces the best management team. Hamilton divided competition into two kinds, those prepared to lose it all in taking what they wanted and those who refused to risk it all and falling

short. Hamilton's attitude, 'Take what you want, pay for it, say thanks and move on.' The attitude a hunter takes. No sentimentality."

Beginning in '65, Hamilton started recapturing the technology that had been stolen by renegade ex-licensees setting up competition throughout the world. Hamilton's lawyers sued, bribed and put a heavy hand on U.S. embassies for help. With that mission accomplished, Hamilton regained dominant positions in Brazil, Congo and India.

Nick did not know what to make of the information on Hamilton Helicopters. His concerns were more immediate: if O'Conner were linked to Roger in some way, and O'Conner and Hamilton were linked in wartime, was it possible that Hamilton knew Roger, too? Nick wondered what Hamilton would say if he were asked outright, "Did you know Roger Girardin?" Rather than cold call, he asked John Santos, the ex-FBI agent he used from time to time, to make contact. Santos met Nick that night at the law office.

"John, see if he remembers Girardin. It's a long shot, but maybe we'll get lucky. If Hamilton knew what happened to Roger, we could get to the bottom of this pretty quick."

Santos went to Hamilton's office the next morning, flashed his old F.B.I. badge at the coiffed receptionist, and asked for Hamilton. In the next instant he was greeted by a sentinel in stilettos and a tailored suit, who put the ex-cop under the lamp rather than the other way around. "Who are you, and what do you want with Mr. Hamilton? If you need answers, put it in writing, address it to our lawyers Kramer and Fish." But John did not come away empty handed, he learned that Hamilton was on a trip, and was not expected back for two weeks. He asked where. "We don't give out that information. Please leave, now."

When Santos gave Nick the news, he replied. "While we're waiting for him, get some G-2 on his non-public activities." Santos lined up a few people willing to talk. One described Hamilton as the "alpha male," another as, "cunning and careful."

195

A so-called friend from the country club met Santos at a diner before tee-time, while it was still dark. Surprisingly, he said, "His father taught him how to con people."

"Con? Strong word. How's that?"

"Guy creates the illusion that you're like him, ambitious, high-spirited. Gets you to identify with him, his cause. Keeps that billfold just out of reach. Gets you to believe your fortunes are tied to him."

"Are they?"

The man did not answer.

An executive fired three months earlier spoke by phone, breathing hard. "Rude, scrapped with the foreman, the union, even the workers, if he saw something he didn't like. When he felt he'd won, he'd rub your nose in it... ."

"Why did you quit?"

"I didn't. Had a heart attack. Retired me, what they used to call 'fired.'"

"Do you know anything about Hamilton's overseas operations?"

"Not much—a division in Brazil, India, has ties in Washington. Don't know much more than that." The man added, "He visits the plants a few times a year."

"Why is he successful?"

"Man lives on the edge, a gambler."

"Gambles what?"

"Against getting caught, always tryin' to slip through, skirting the edge."

"Like?"

The man exhaled into the phone. "Mister, I think I've said enough."

"Well, doesn't sound like anybody I want to be friends with, not an ounce of some redeeming quality."

"Except for the orphanage."

"The orphanage? What's that?"

"He started an orphanage and some kind of adoption service for Chinese and Korean kids sent to the states by some overseas missionaries."

"What's his role?"

"Chairman and a big, big donor. I mean seven-figures big."

The two men were silent until the man remarked, "Hear he may run for governor."

World Travesty
August 1983

AS THE PLANE DESCENDED INTO CALCUTTA, Hamilton peered out the 747 first class upper-deck. The man sitting next to him remarked, "The city's just like the rest of the third world—dirty. Just bigger." It was 2 a.m. local time when the chauffeur headed for the Tan Mahler Hotel where a new moon and an occasional run of ghee lights brought from the shadows mile after mile of homeless wrapped in white linen. Hamilton, having traveled the route many times, eventually bored of the view and closed his eyes.

The next morning, over eggs and a few slices of specially ordered bacon, he read the Asian edition of the Wall Street Journal. A trend line showed futures on an incline. He picked up the phone and wired a two word telegram to his broker: *Sell aluminum.* He put his toast into the egg's yellow center, stuffed it in his mouth and casually gazed out the window—following one-armed, pickpocketing wafts horsing around and giggling before they struck the mark. He went back to the article, where it said his associate John Walker Russell was in line for Secretary of Defense. Hamilton met Russell, then a CIA operative, through Hamilton's former army boss Andy Johnston twenty years ago. Shortly afterwards Russell and Hamilton formed a profitable alliance, where Hamilton supplied inside information to Russell in his CIA capacity, and Russell reciprocated by helping Hamilton export technology, especially when U.S. export licenses were almost impossible to obtain. In time, the "business" from Russell's point-of-view deserved more than simply G-2, which only benefited his employer. Russell wanted his cut, access to a Swiss bank account in which Hamilton would deposit a small percentage of the funds from each export transaction. Reading the newspaper, Hamilton surmised that the level of scrutiny Russell would get being elevated from Undersecretary to the top Defense post would be intense, and he wasn't happy, since any detection of their relationship would result in embarrassment or worse. After all, he had his eye on the governorship.

After breakfast, Hamilton proceeded to meet his Far East contact. In the next few minutes he found himself part of a moving wall of people and decided to slip down a side street where the hubbub transitioned to a relatively stilled picture, where women quietly went about chores in brilliant saris of vermilion, turquoise blue, brown, white; each forehead smudged scarlet, aquamarine or soot black to symbolize one or another blessing, demon inoculation or simply to adorn her face. A man rummaged through a garbage heap, another darted around it, almost run down by a bicycle. Hamilton noticed a light skinned woman sweeping the sidewalk: a fifty-year-old woman lost in a seventy-year-old body, with arms only slightly thicker than her broomstick. She swept briskly. He stepped around the miniature dust devil that swirled in her wake, then reached into his pocket and pulled out a twenty dollar bill. He slipped it into her hand.

Hamilton came to the two-story frame that bore the number 96, the place where he would meet his associate. This kind of meeting was not typical for a man of Hamilton's position. People in-country did his bidding, but this convocation was classified as "sensitive—highly confidential." Hamilton knew he could maintain a defensible position if the meeting were ever exposed for what it was. Officially, the organization he dealt with was Crawford, Singh and Sons, Ltd., a subsidiary of a larger Indian concern. Hamilton walked up two flights and into a room that was crowded by a desk, four chairs, a floor fan running on high speed, two Indians and a Chinese man.

The Chinese man smiled widely. "Hello, Trent, excellent to see you again."

"And, you too, Tat Wah. Three years, right? What have you been doing?"

Trent had known the man for thirty years, and though he had gained weight since last time, he would recognize him strictly from his short, wide shouldered, stocky appearance and his hallmark white Palm Beach linen suit, gray fedora, highly polished black shoes and ebony cane.

"Yes, three. Been going between Shanghai and Hong Kong." He tapped his cane into his hand.

"What's been your focus?"

"Erecting tire plants. Planning to export because the economy's sunk. That "Intellectual Revolution" stunted growth. Now we turn policy to entrepreneurship."

"Well," Hamilton started in a sympathetic tone, "we had our rabble rousers... protesters, civil rights."

Through with small talk, Tat Wah asked, "What do you bring today?"

Hamilton's beefy hand opened his briefcase, grabbed and laid before the men engineering plans for an optical guidance system that could aim handheld missiles at low flying targets. It was about the size of a large camera: ten pounds. How Tat Wah would use the device, Hamilton could only guess. A forerunner of the product had been used to pan cameras in U-2 spy planes that photographed Cuban missile sites. It had remained classified, and, understandably, the U.S. was reluctant to license it for export. Russell knew how to get things done, however, and four weeks earlier, he had given Hamilton the green light to meet with his foreign connections.

The matter of interpreting drawings was left to the Indian engineers. Tat Wah and Hamilton went outside. Taking a long drag on his cigarette, Hamilton said, "Look around— isn't this a despicable place?"

"Yes, though no fault of ours."

"It's a good place to do business," Trent breathed confidently.

"Yes, labor is economical." Tat Wah tapped his cane, scanned the neighborhood. "As far as Calcutta's misery goes, we play no part in it."

Nearly two hours had passed before the Indians went in search of the two men, and reconvening, the engineers affirmed the integrity of the drawings. Tat Wah picked up the phone and called Hong Kong. Hamilton heard him wire $2,000,000 into a Swiss bank account with a designated account number. After lunch, the men returned to the cubbyhole, where Hamilton called the Disraeli Bank, which confirmed the deposit.

"Well, Tat Wah, as always, well... not always." The two men smiled reservedly in the way men familiar, but distant, do.

"Excellent seeing you, Trent," the Chinese smiled warmly, adding, "We are survivors, are we not?"

"That we are, Tat Wah. See you when I have something."

The American empty handed, pockets full, and the Chinese, plans in hand, bowed toward one another and went separate ways—one east, one west along the side street.

Prequel to Reckoning

WHEN JACK LEFT THE COURTHOUSE after his interview with Nick, he had a five-day beard, pants soiled at the knees and a torn shirt. On the bus ride home he squirmed, obsessing about his jail time, past and possibly the future. He arrived home close to four, jumped in the shower, then wolfed down a peanut butter sandwich he found in the refrigerator. With a full belly and body scraped of three days grit, he laid down on the couch, beer in hand, closed his eyes and like all other attempts at sleeping lately, he thrashed, mumbling about his upcoming court appearance and what he failed to tell Nick. He had his own theory of what the map symbols meant, because he knew where he had seen them before. The lawyer did not need to know what he knew about marks on a pad in a Progressive day room when he dealt with a Chinese interrogator.

The next morning the sun beamed into his window partly shaded by the hundred-year-old oak in the backyard. He walked to the Silver Streak for a cup of joe. After downing two cups, reading the local headlines and avoiding eye contact with Mol the flirty waitress, he walked to the rectory to see Father Ryan. He knew the priest was an early riser because he served the six o'clock mass. He rang the bell. A haggard looking nun with a thin, sharp nose answered. Pulling her black cardigan taut over a starched, white blouse, she asked, "Can I help you, young man?"

"Sister, is Father Ryan in?"

"No, my boy, earlier he went over to the veteran's home to give last rites."

Jacked twisted his lips and then walked past St. Patrick to the green park bench with a brass plaque that read: *Purity, Innocence, Sympathy. PIS* he mumbled to himself as he surveyed the stone rectory. At six, the church bell announced the recitation of the Angelus. He closed his eyes, bowed his head and put his hands over his ears. Eventually the bell stopped clanging, the noise giving way to screeching black birds sitting on the telephone wires across the street. He walked to the granite stairs into the basilica where a mildly obese priest shuffled up the left side on his way to the confessional. The first in line for confession was a woman with beagle-like, flaccid cheeks wearing a red pullover sweater and blue scarf. Next were two old men, one flour white, the other a jaundiced yellow. When the last of the penitents departed, Jack opened the curtain, kneeled before the shuttered wire separating him from God's ear and said, "Father, the noise has returned."

"What's that, my son?"

"The ringing, screeching it's come back."

"My son, it's completely silent here. Perhaps you need to see a doctor?"

"I'll be all right."

"Proceed, then."

"Bless me, father, for I have sinned, it's been two weeks since my last confession."

On Jack's walk home he noticed a strange car parked beyond his house, smoke pouring from its exhaust. He looked out the front window several times to see if it had left, and eventually dismissed his concern.

Starring An Eye Witness

WHEN THE CLOCK OVER THE JURY BOX struck 10 a.m. Lindquist assumed the center of the judicial prefecture he'd command for the next several hours. In his usual way, he glared at the crowd through the drugstore half-glasses resting over his spacious nostrils. He rubbed his neck below his jaw nodding to Nick, "Counselor, call your next witness."

Again, the already sweltering courtroom had no vacancies. Julie, and now Anna, Jack's estranged wife, eyes front, sat quietly, dressed in the black dress she had worn to the half-dozen funerals she had attended, including her son's. Like her sister-in-law, she wore little makeup, her expression calling her out among the reporters as not simply a woman with little to do, but someone with an interest in the proceedings.

"Your Honor, plaintiff calls Mr. Jack Prado O'Conner to the stand." Jack was sitting between Julie and Anna. Gaunt, cheek swollen, lower lip puffy, a knob on the back of his head, he brushed past Julie and the other spectators, each moving their legs sideways. As he made his way down the center aisle, the crowd observed a narrow, six-foot-tall man tucking his shirt into wrinkled pinstriped pants. He felt hundreds of eyes tracking him across the well, his heart pounded, his hands trembled as he imagined how his personal history would unfold before strangers, while someone out there was watching his every move. He regretted that he had refused to go south.

In a hushed voice the clerk instructed him. "Stand here, in front of the witness box." He felt the judge take his measure, and wondered what he thought about his bruises. He stared ahead, mouth agape, so that Amy Dusseldorf, the reporter from the local paper, would note: "*A man who stands tall, weathered... looks like he's spent years drinking... cheap whisky... and last night got the shit beat out of him."*

"Please raise your right hand, sir," shouted the clerk in his soprano voice, chin jutted forward.

Jack had the urge to throw up. He raised his unsteady hand.

"Mr. O'Conner, state your full name and address for the record."

"Jack Prado O'Conner, 320 Willa Street, Bridgeport."

"Be seated."

Nick began with a lilt to his voice. "Good morning, sir. Is it Mr. Prado or Mr. O'Conner?"

"I prefer Prado. It was my grandfather's name. I go by that name."

The stenographer, who since the trial started had changed her hair color from gray to brown, spoke in an official capacity for the first time. "Sir, you'll have to speak up, or get closer to the microphone. I can't hear you."

"Mr. Prado, you're here under a subpoena, correct?"

When Jack leaned into the microphone the spectators heard the barreled voice of a heavy smoker. "Yes, sir."

"Are you married, sir?"

"Yes," Jack answered, a slight quiver in his voice.

In the split second that it took Nick to get to the next question, Jack blinked rapidly and made eye contact with the two darkest pools of light in the room: Anna's deeply-set perfectly round eyes. He had looked into them hundreds of times, telling her she was the only one who could save him, like the time he practically poisoned himself drinking a fifth of scotch following their son Will's death. Hyperventilating, he breathed heavily.

"What's your wife's name?"

"Anna." Jack's eyes turned dewy.

"Does she reside at your address?"

Jack's eyes shifted. "No, we're separated."

"Sir, can you repeat that, I could not hear you," squeaked the stenographer.

Regaining his composure, Jack muttered, "We're separated now." He saw Anna avoiding his glance.

"Sir, you enlisted in the army in May 1950, is that correct?"

"Yes, sir."

"Did you enlist alone or with a group?"

"Well, I graduated college as an ROTC officer and had to serve a term of enlistment."

"Did you enlist with others from your class?"

"Yes."

"Local boys?"

"Yes."

"Remember their names?"

"Yes."

"Can you tell us who, if you remember?"

"A friend, a guy named Trent Hamilton."

The name Hamilton stopped Nick in his tracks. He looked down at his yellow pad. Sirens from a fire truck going by outside the courtroom let Nick take time to regain his composure.

"Where do you work, sir?"

"I'm unemployed. Used to be a manufacturing manager for companies around town."

"What companies were they?"

"Well, the last company full-time was HH, I mean Hamilton Helicopters. Until '72, then, after that I consulted for... "

Harris, exasperated, interjected. "Your Honor, I object to Mr. Castalano's line of questioning. I fail to understand the relevance."

Lindquist exhaled audibly. "I assume this is introductory, but Counsel, please move along."

Nick nodded in deference to the judge. "Well yes, your Honor, I think I'll tie this up if I'm permitted some latitude."

"Very well, Mr. Castalano, but before the evidence is closed you'll have shown us its relevance."

"Mr. Prado, please provide a brief summary of your involvement with Hamilton Helicopters."

Jack grabbed the pitcher and poured a glass of water, which he drank. He then rested his hands on the witness box and rested his head on his chest, thinking about where to begin.

***

The week after he returned from overseas he called Trent, and they exchanged what had transpired since they had last seen each other during the war. Trent told Jack that he had a job waiting at HH, but made no overture to meet socially. It wasn't until six months later when Jack started work at HH that he and Trent met up. Again, neither of them spoke about Korea, or old girlfriends, keeping the discussion to what Jack would be doing in the Assistant Plant Manager role, a nice place to start a career.

Jack understood Trent better than any man he knew— perhaps with the exception of his own father. And, he knew Korea would only open a wider circle of misgivings for both of them. Not to mention that the new job also paralleled Jack's new relationship with Anna and neither man needed to go there, either.

***

What Jack knew was that one January in '55 he spotted Anna walking among a crowd of window-shoppers near Walgreen's Drug Store. He yelled out, waving his arms. Through a breathy condensation he saw her cross the street with a big smile on her face. They talked over coffee. She asked him about Trent. He said he'd spoken to him by phone, but hadn't seen him and as to Tracy he'd not seen her since he'd left for Korea. She told him that she wasn't married, but had a son, William, who was about to turn four. The reunion led to a phone call the day after that in-turn led to coffee the following week. The day before Ash Wednesday, they went on their first date to a movie and afterward, to a local pizza joint, where a man with a goatee put a nickel in the juke and pushed, "*Wanted*" by Perry Como.

"Jack, that's my favorite song." She watched for his reaction. Jack showed none. She made small talk: why her hips had broadened, why she'd let her hair grow over her shoulders, what she wanted out of life. Jack was skinnier than she'd remembered, thin faced, quieter. His hair glistened black and she thought him especially handsome, but he'd lost that Montgomery Cliff innocence the girls once teased him about, retaining, she thought, the actor's shyness.

After that first date they saw each other regularly. Easter came in early April that year and after mass, the couple went behind the church to take pictures of Will in his three-piece suit, brown fedora, scarf blowing in a light breeze under a full sun. Anna, with one hand, held the top of her blue wide-brimmed hat that had rested on the bun of her hair, and with the other hand motioned to Jack to stand next to the boy. Flicking aside her bangs, she focused the Brownie on a man and boy each missing part of themselves, snapping pictures that showed a child, chest out, a man his arm around the boy's narrow shoulders. The couple sat on the bench near the rose garden while Will ran after pigeons pecking left over rice from a wedding. She snuggled close to Jack, her big-brim folding against his head. "You know, when Will was born his father wouldn't come forward." She paused. "It was Trent."

"I figured," he said coldly.

"Jack, I never told him."

"Somebody must've... but it's none of my business."

"I knew he would've never accepted he was the father. I moved on."

Jack grabbed the knot in his tie. "Anna, let's not talk about it."

She removed her hat, unfastened her bun, letting her hair fall over her shoulders. He rested his hand on her thigh and kissed her cheek.

"A guy kisses a girl, but it doesn't mean anything," she said.

Jack pulled out a cigarette, lit it, throwing the spent matchbook in front of them.

"Anna, give me your hand." Jack squeezed it tight. He blinked rapidly as he looked ahead.

***

"Mr. Prado, did you understand the question?"

"My first assignment at Hamilton was to assist the Plant Manager. I was assigned to production control, the department that schedules operations along the manufacturing line. The job entailed planning and distribution of materials and methods at different points and times."

"Mr. Prado, when you say Hamilton Helicopters, does it have any relation to Trent Hamilton, the man you enlisted with?"

"Yes, his family owned the company. He got me the job."

***

If the entire story were relevant, which to the court it hardly was, Jack had a good job which abruptly ended in 1972 for reasons he did not have to account for in court. And he did not have to account for the details of the life he led after work—some might say the authentic one. When Anna and Jack had married in '55, they moved into a cold-water flat across the street from the South End River. Every six hours, low tide exposed its tar stained banks and blanketed the air with the smell of bunker fuel and dead fish. For Jack, having recently spent three-plus years in a POW camp, it was home sweet home. For Anna, it was a starting place, and if Jack could make his way with a little help from Trent, she would get to where she felt she was always headed: Fairview. For now, on the other side of the river was the Hamilton Helicopters' flight line and at any given hour—even deep into the night—they could hear the chop, chop, chop of the whirling blades, discomforting sounds if one focused on them. In decades to come, that same sound would haunt the memory of the men who left their youth in a Vietnamese rice paddy. One such ship would one day crash and in a significant way would lead to Jack's quitting Hamilton Helicopters and all it represented.

By now Nick had raised in Jack all those memories from when he had returned in '54, and he worried that Nick might delve into the cloud of suspicion under which he returned. Even though the charge of commie sympathizer was never an issue between Trent and him, he couldn't immediately work at HH until his discharge status was upgraded. So Trent's family pulled out the stops for the eventual security clearance that followed, for reasons which Jack could only speculate: past friendship, moral debts unpaid, for obligations assumed, for secrets kept.

In all respects, Jack and Anna's life hadn't been different from the lives of other young families in the urban east from the mid-fifties forward. In '57 Mona was born.

By '58 the couple had saved enough to buy a small six-room colonial on the west side of town. A '49 Chevy sedan got Jack back and forth to work. During the day, Anna worked at a small variety store a block from home. Anna and Mona spent time together at Girl Scouts. During the summer Jack and Will would throw a baseball before supper. Winters, the two of them hibernated in the cellar, working on a massive toy train village. Jack watched his son's mind work through his hands, moving from boyhood into adolescence. He watched him use the drill press to slowly bore its way through wood or sheets of steel on its way to making a soapbox racer. The days he and Jack spent in these places spoke volumes about the closeness between the man and the boy standing in peace on the solid ground called home.

***

Nick proceeded to take Jack through the preliminaries of when he enlisted, the units he was assigned to, where he fought in the fall of '50 and where he ended up at the beginning of '51.

"Mr. Jaeger testified that you and another man saved his life on or about November 27, 1950. He testified that he'd been on a scouting mission and, in the course of trying to kill an enemy soldier, he did not realize he himself was a target. He testified that a man with a name sounding something like yours came to his rescue. Do you not recall such an event?"

"No, sir, never saved anybody's life scouting."

Harris, muttered under his breath loud enough for Townsend to hear, "Goddamn it." Lindquist raised his head and looked over at defense table. Harris avoided eye contact.

"Mr. Prado, do you recall November 24 or 25, 1950, for any reason?"

"Yes. Was with a rifle company, patrolling the north shore of the Ch'ongch'on River, maybe 50 miles south of the Yalu, near a little town called Unsan. Maybe west of it, actually. Snowed all day. Shortly before dark—this is late

210

fall, it gets dark early—and just before it got dark, the Chinese struck."

"What happened next?"

"We were committed back to our battalion area... to hold the line."

"And did you?"

"No, the battalion retreated, company by company leap-frogged three, two, one," he replied, illustrating, by rotating one hand over the other. "The Chinese hit again. Ran us out of our positions, dawn next morning—mass confusion."

"Did you continue to fight?"

"They'd surrounded us; we started regrouping around the first battalion area, three, four miles away." Jack's voice weakened, he swallowed hard, reached for the pitcher and observers like Anna heard the reverberating clink of the glass. Jack's hand trembled. He blinked rapidly and proceeded to mumble. "And Captain, Captain Klein, either Klein or Stein, Mine, Captain, Captain, Oh Captain... Klein."

"Excuse me?" Nick blinked. His key witness wasn't going to lose it now, was he?

"Sorry, Company Commander Klein shouted, 'Men, we're surrounded... use escape evasion, every man for himself.'"

The words, "every man for himself" bounced off the plaster walls. Nick waited a moment before asking the next question. He saw Jack recompose himself.

"Would you say that your unit became fragmented? During this... "

Jack's eyes moved up and left and not letting Nick finish. Jack continued, "Dove into a ravine. Ravine. Ravine, two guys... hidin' in a bramble ravine."

"How long'd you stay?"

"Maybe two or three hours, it seemed forever. Below zero, snowing. We heard 'em coming."

"You heard who coming?"

"Someone speakin' Oriental."

"What did you do?"

"We weren't sure what to do. They could've been ROK."

"What happened, next?"

"Bayonets, all directions."

211

"Were any of you wounded?"

"Not really, I'd twisted my leg." Jack pointed down. "No more Jack-be-nimble, you know."

"Right." Nick gave Jack a piercing look, but he seemed calm. "Could you walk?"

"Sure."

"Where'd they take you?"

"You have to imagine it was total, mass confusion. They were picking us up all over. We're not talking a small city block, we're talking miles wide, squatting us down in the snow after they searched us, put us up in a little draw 'til dark."

"Did you and the other men stay together?"

"For a while, but some of us split off into groups, about ten guys each."

"What happened next?"

"Air strikes, plus artillery." Jack observed Nick begin to rub his hands together and shift uneasily in his chair. "But, too late. In fact, we killed our own."

Jack took a gulp of air. Inwardly, Nick willed him to continue, just finish accounting for why he could not have rescued Jaeger.

Jack continued, "Nobody had no idea where we were. That's how it happened. Started to get dark, pulled us out of different draws, marched us in circles all night. Few took off their boots, toes froze, lost 'em, had to wrap their feet in rags from long-johns. Next morning they'd put us in another ravine, kept us there till dark."

"Sir, are you telling us that it was impossible that on November 27, 1950, you were on a scouting mission, as Mr. Jaeger claims?"

"I am saying that I was already a POW."

Lindquist saw Foster lean over and whisper something to Harris, who kept his eye on Jack and shook his head in agreement.

Nick, irritated by the mumbling from the defense table, looked over, then put his hands in his pocket, and walked out from behind the podium. "Did you eventually reach an encampment?"

"We stayed goin' 'round in circles, round and round like a merry-go—"

212

"How long," Nick intercepted.

"—Uh, couple of days and then started north."

"Where'd you sleep?"

"Marched us every night and put us in Korean rooms or whatever was available at night —I mean in the daytime. We was marched to the Pukchin-Tarigol Valley collection site. Then marched 'til we got to Sinuiju, near the Manchurian border."

"What happened when you got near the border?"

Nick returned to the podium and turned several pages in his trial notebook.

"They put us in a bean camp, soybeans and bran. Lot of men already there."

"How long?"

"About a week. Then marched us along the Yalu."

"Destination?"

"Pyoktong, a camp on the south bank of the Yalu. Stopped marching early January '51, at what later came known as Camp No. 13."

"Did you go to any other camps while a prisoner?"

"No, sir, stayed until February '53 when... "

"You're, of course, referring to the end of the war, right?"

"Well, sir, beyond that."

Jack waited for Nick to ask why he did not return with the other soldiers.

"And during this time, did you meet a soldier named Roger Girardin?"

Jack rapidly blinked several times in succession. "Never!" And, of course, with that answer Jack once again knew that he needed those sanctimonious voices to speak to him about sanity, secrets and sins of omission.

Nick saw Jack's eyes blinking fast and thought there might be something Jack was holding back. Perhaps, Nick thought, he hadn't asked the right question.

"And, Mr. Prado, I take it from your answer... let me phrase it differently, did you *ever* meet a soldier named Roger Girardin?"

Jack listened carefully and heard the word "soldier" in the question. "Can you please repeat that?"

"Did you ever meet a soldier named Roger Girardin?"

213

Jack listened, his head cocked, and heard the word "meet" in the question. He had known Roger before he was a soldier, met him as a civilian, not as a soldier, at least not a meeting that could be ever discovered. He swayed back and forth.

"Mr. Prado, an answer please?" Nick asked after not getting an immediate response.

"No, sir."

Jack looked down at his notepad, not sure whether to press Jack on what seemed an emphatic "no." He decided to go in a different direction.

"Mr. Prado, you and Trent Hamilton were in ROTC. You both went into officer's training school together?"

"Yes, sir."

"Did you see much of him there at the training school?"

"Yes."

"Did you see him in Camp 13?"

Nick noticed that he looked at someone in the crowd and hesitated. "Not that I can remember."

"When you returned home, did you see much of him?"

"Except occasionally at work, our paths didn't cross... you know, worked in the same place, but he was upper management."

"Thank you, Mr. Prado, I have no further questions at this time. Counsel, your witness."

Harris rose, "Mr. O'Conner or is it Prado?" he asked with a smirk.

Jack ran his hand through his hair. "Told Mr. Castalano, I prefer Prado."

"Well, before you arrived today a Mr. Jaeger testified that you and Private Girardin saved his life on or about November 27, 1950. He testified that he'd been on a scouting mission and in the course of trying to kill an enemy soldier he didn't realize he was himself a target. He testified that you and Private Girardin came to his rescue. Do you not recall that event?"

"No, sir, I can't say that I never saw a Private Girardin then."

Nick rose from his chair. "Your Honor, Counsel is mistaken and mischaracterizes Mr. Jaeger's testimony. He did not testify that this man sitting before us was the Connell or O'Conner he referred to."

Harris wrung his hands. "Your Honor, I apologize, but I thought I heard him say O'Conner or Connell, and I therefore assumed it was this witness. I got turned around on this. Nevertheless, I think that the question's proper, but please strike it. I will rephrase."

"A day or so ago a Mr. Jaeger, Thomas Jaeger, testified that he was with a regiment near Kunu-ri close to the Ch'ongch'on river." Harris made a fist in each hand. "Were you in that area at any time?"

"Yes, I believe so, near the middle of November."

Harris hammered his fist into his hand and raised his voice. "You were in retreat... right?"

Jack rubbed his chin with the back of his hand. "Yes, movin' south."

"Mr. Jaeger testified that two soldiers, a Conner or an O'Conner and another man, Jardin or Girardin, saved his life from a sniper. Would you remember saving a man one early morning on a ridge in the Kunu-ri area, November, 1950?"

Jack looked over at Nick. "No, can't say I can remember something like that."

Harris stepped forward, blocking Nick's line of sight. "Mr. Jaeger claims that the Girardin man was killed by a sniper, and that he had a conversation with the Conner or O'Conner man shortly afterwards. Is it possible that he was talking about you and that the dead man was Roger Girardin?"

"No."

"But, you were captured right about that time Jaeger claims he might have met you, correct?"

"Yeah, so were thousands of others."

"And from the sounds of your story, you were understandably traumatized?"

Jack blinked repeatedly. "I wouldn't say that."

"Is it possible that you had a lapse of memory surrounding events shortly before and during your capture?"

Jack sat silent, unable to control his blinking, something Harris interpreted as a sign that Jack was evading the truth.

"Sir, it may have played out differently, isn't that right?"

"Anything's possible, sir." Jack blinked several times.

Harris stretched his arm in the air. "Didn't you tell our investigator, Mr. Devaney, that it was possible, but you weren't absolutely sure if you remembered Girardin?"

Jack snapped, "When?"

Harris raised his voice. "When he called you at home just last Thursday."

"I don't remember what I told anybody. I started remembering this stuff, I think, when I first talked to Mr. Castalano yesterday." His voice trailed off. "Maybe I read about him in the newspapers, I don't know."

Harris picked up a document browned with age. "Mr. Prado, were you sympathetic to the North Korean's point of view?"

"Objection. Your Honor, Mr. Harris' question lacks specificity. What "point of view" is he referring to?"

"Sustained. Mr. Harris, please qualify your question."

Harris read the document to himself, the one he had waved in front of Jack. "Mr. Prado, are you familiar with the word Progressive to describe a POW who was sympathetic to communist propaganda?"

"Yes, sir, I am."

"Well, were you a so-called Progressive?"

Nick saw Jack stiffen, but he seemed to hold his own. "No, sir, I was not!"

"Is it not true that you signed a statement that the U.S. and its allies were murderers?"

"I don't recall."

Harris's questions were coming quicker now. "You informed on your fellow soldiers did you not?"

Jack's lips tightened. "That's a bald faced lie."

"Isn't it true that you were held over by the Communists after the war ended, after the POWs were repatriated?"

"If you mean that I returned from Korea in '54, yes, yes, I was detained."

Harris spread his arms, raised his voice, "Is it not true you were detained because you chose not to come back with your comrades?"

"No, sir!" Jack protested, his voice also louder. "I was left behind because... because I'd been forgotten, left to rot in a cell."

"And when you returned, you were given a dishonorable discharge, is that not correct?"

"No, I—I didn't receive a dishonorable, sir."

Harris paused for effect. He picked up a paper from the lectern and turned to Lindquist.

"Your Honor, may I approach the witness?"

Lindquist shook his head yes, curious why a difference of opinion existed on what seemed a matter of record. Harris, cool and in control, approached Jack, "Sir, I am handing you a document marked Exhibit 101 Defendant Army for identification. Do you recognize that paper?"

"No, I don't."

"Well it's captioned with your name, is it not?"

"Yes."

"It's a discharge paper, isn't it? What is the number in the left hand bottom?"

"It says DD 214. But— "

"Sir, if you would please give me the document."

"But—"

"One moment, Mr. *Prado*," Harris interjected.

Harris took the document and handed it to Nick. "It's the official record, certified."

Scanning it, Nick handed it back to Harris who gave it to Lindquist. He did not look at Mitch. He would have his head later for failing to find it.

"Your Honor, I'd like to enter this as a full exhibit," continued Harris.

Lindquist looked at Nick. "Any objections?"

"Relevancy, where is Mr. Harris going with this?" He could only watch as the credibility of his witness was put under scrutiny.

"Overruled, I will allow it."

"Mr. Prado, please take this document marked Exhibit 101, and tell this court if you wish to change you testimony regarding your discharge."

Jack scanned the document. "No, sir, I don't wish to change anything. That was a—"

Harris cut Jack off. "Is it not true, sir, that you were given a dishonorable discharge from the United States Army as indicated on that form?"

"That was a mistake!"

"Yes, it was upgraded, am I right? After some period. Isn't that right? Wasn't that what the Army did for all those who collaborated? Changed their status some years later?"

As if washing his hands of Jack, he turned from the lectern, "Your Honor, the government has no further questions at this time, but we reserve the right to recall Mr. O'Conner or Mr. Prado, as the case may be."

Lindquist looked in Nick's direction, "Any redirect, sir?"

Nick knew there was no territory to be regained at this point by questioning Jack further. "No, your Honor."

"Ladies and gentlemen, let's recess until 2 pm."

Nick walked down a hallway to a payphone farthest from the lobby—he needed privacy. The phone was in use. As he flipped the pages of his pocket calendar, he heard the caller explain, "I'll be there at five to work the shift. My brother just finished up." When she hung up and turned, the caller stood facing Nick.

"Ma'am, I'm sorry, are you Jack Prado's sister?"

Taken by surprise, she clutched her bag tighter to her chest. "Yes, Julie O'Conner."

"I'm Nick. Nick Castalano.

"I know, nice to meet you." Julie found herself caught between Nick and the phone.

"Nice to meet *you*. I didn't know Jack had a sister."

"Well, yes, only the one." Julie tried sidling around Nick, who was blocking her path.

"You've sat through the entire trial, haven't you?" Nick shifted his weight to the right, blocking Julie's escape.

"Why, yes."

Anticipating Julie's move to the right, Nick shifted back to his left. "Special interest in the case?"

Exasperated, Julie took a deep breath and looked up at Nick. "Roger Girardin was my boyfriend."

It was Nick's turn to be caught back-footed. "Roger Gir —!" How much more information had Jack failed to mention? "This is quite a surprise." Moving his jacket out of the way, Nick put his hands on his hips.

Julie's lips quivered. "Mr. Castalano, I don't know if I should be talking to you."

"Why's that?"

"Well, is Jack in some kind of trouble?"

"No, Ms. O'Conner, I'm just trying to get to the bottom of ... "

Julie blurted out, "Roger and I were very close."

"Didn't Jack know you were dating Roger?"

"Of course. We were all kids together, we hung out. I mean, Jack and his girlfriend Tracy and her brother Trent."

Nick raised his eyebrows. "Why wouldn't Jack mention you dated Roger?"

"Maybe he didn't think it was important."

"You heard me ask if he ever met Roger, and he said no."

"Mr. Castalano, you asked him if he met the soldier."

Nick swore inwardly. It was splitting hairs, but here was a spectator pointing out the problem with his question. "And his girlfriend, this Tracy, is she Trent Hamilton's sister?"

"Yes, she is."

"Did you know Trent?"

Julie cocked her head. "Am I being questioned, Mr. Castalano?" Julie returned. "I said, we hung out together. Trent had a bit of a mad crush, but we never really... dated. Then, he and Roger got into some teenage trouble, and they parted ways. May I go now?"

Nick raised his hands in mock innocence. "Just one more thing. What was he like?"

"Who? Roger?"

Nick saw real warmth spreading across the woman's face, but tears blurred the emerald green eyes staring up at him. He dropped his hands.

Pyoktong

DAVID BRADSHAW, A CRUSTY SIXTY-YEAR-OLD BLACK man listening to the hum of the engines on Continental Flight 807 from Atlanta to Hartford tried to remember his service from beginning to end. He recalled passing through Fort Benning, Georgia, where he had entered boot camp at the lowest rank in a hierarchy that extended from the President through a complex network of generals, colonels, majors, lieutenants, warrant officers, noncommissioned officers, corporals, privates first class, privates and basic recruits—the last position reserved for him and his kind. And his kind on July 25, 1948, was that of a Negro recruit in an all black outfit one day before Truman signed Executive Order 9981 stating, *"It is hereby declared to be the policy of the President that there shall be equality of treatment and opportunity for all persons in the armed services without regard to race, color, religion, or national origin."* Private Bradshaw RA34018221 thereafter represented a fully-integrated asset in a military accounting journal, his serial number—signifying a soldier's existence— stamped in his mind and worn around his neck as two small metal tags, one to be inserted in his mouth and the other sent to his kin, forever linking identification and death in the enduring certainty of a small stainless steel tablet. He knew about dog tags, having put many in soldiers' mouths, and others in the walls of huts where many were never found.

Bradshaw rented a Ford Escort, drove sixty miles to Bridgeport and booked a room at the Holiday Inn. The next morning he walked to court early, a black man in a black suit, white shirt and the flowered yellow and green tie his wife had bought him ten birthdays ago. Except for the clerk, he was alone for nearly half an hour before the usual crowd trickled in. He surveyed his surroundings, making himself feel comfortable in a strange place, a habit he had acquired growing up in a small Georgia town. He thought about his wife and their two children, married now, and the quiet retired life he led, spending most of his day in his garage with his vintage '59 Dodge and Hemi, a mongrel canine. By ten, the courtroom was abuzz with conversations that were hard to listen in on. The first few reporters noticed the large middle-aged man and making assumptions based on race and dress, assumed he was a witness.

Lindquist had woken up at six feeling dizzy. Things seemed to improve after his usual orange juice and English muffin. He arrived a few minutes before ten and, without delay, asked Picolillo to open court. Holding his hand to his neck he peered over his wire rimmed glasses and barked, "Call your next witness, Mr. Castalano."

Upon hearing his name called, Bradshaw rose and carried himself across the room like a wiry gray-haired warhorse. After the formalities of being sworn in, Nick established Bradshaw as having been a POW. Although every man's experience of being captured was personal, for the sake of judicial economy, Nick dispensed with the generalities and details of war with which Lindquist had now become familiar.

"After you were captured, where'd they march you?"

Bradshaw answered in a gravelly Georgia accent, "Yes, sir, t'was north."

"And where'd you stay to get some rest?"

"They put us in a room at daylight. In the night you'd get out and form lines, start marchin' again."

"Did there come a time when you were marched to a POW camp?"

"Yes, sir."

"Did you know at that time that it was known as Camp No. 13?"

"No, didn't know. It's not like they declared "this is Camp 13." They gave us no camp numbers. It was maybe through the Red Cross we found out it was Pyoktong, and was Camp No. 13."

"Was your company, that is the unit of men that had been captured initially... did they tend to stay together until you came to Camp 13?"

"No, 'cause t'was many of us, we were scattered out. Don't really know how many men was on the march I was."

"Did you meet a man named... strike that... how many men, if you know, were at Camp 13?"

"Really... don't know how many men were there at the time I was. Whenever we reached Camp 13, with the men that we'd picked up at Pyongyang, there was, oh maybe thousand of us in that one group."

"Now, was this particular camp, Camp 13 that you described, was it on any body of water at all?"

"Backwaters of the Yalu."

"You say the backwaters—what do you mean?"

"On toward the west coast of Korea there's a hydroelectric dam that's built 'cross the Yalu. Behind that dam for miles there're backwaters, where the water floods the valleys, and so forth, in the backwaters."

"What could you see? Could you see other land across the water?"

"Oh, yeah."

"Was it a lake, or was this water flowing?"

"Well, all I can tell you is t'was strictly a backwater. Don't know of any that you have up here. In Georgia we have Clark's Hill. It's a reservoir. And it's all water backed up behind the dam."

"Mr. Bradshaw, while you were in the Army did you become familiar with map reading?"

"A fair amount," he replied confidently.

"Can you tell the court what training and experience you had in map reading?"

"Well, I learned as part of my NCO training, early 1950. And I led a small platoon in Korea where you read maps all the time. Orientation and map reading, that's what got us from place to place."

"Your Honor, may I approach the witness?"

Lindquist waved his hand. "Go ahead."

Nick handed Bradshaw several 11 x 17 inch sheets of paper. "I'm going to show you some diagrams and ask you if you can identify them for us, please."

Bradshaw reached into his jacket pocket for a pair of wire rimmed glasses and gingerly placed the temples over his ears before taking the documents and laying them on the small ledge in front of the stand. He leafed through them. A minute passed. He pulled off his glasses.

"You have several maps here, sir."

Lindquist interrupted, "So that the record will be complete, why don't you have them marked for identification? Then when the witness refers to something, we'll have something in the record that he's referring to."

Taking the documents from the ledge, Nick asked, "Clerk, can you please mark these separately?"

The clerk stuck small, yellow markers on each of the four sheets.

Nick handed the stack back to Bradshaw. "I'm going to show you Plaintiff's Exhibits B-1, B-2, B-3 and B-4 and ask you if you can identify any or all of these exhibits, please."

Lindquist interjected himself again. "This is the first time you have seen these, Mr. Bradshaw?"

Bradshaw's sunken eyes turned toward Lindquist. "Yes, sir."

The witness adjusted his glasses. His head moved over the paper. "Exhibit No. B-1 seems to be." He paused, ran his hand over the paper to smooth it out flat, "Could be a rough schematic of Camp 13, though I see lots of differences from the way I remember it."

"How long were you in Camp 13?" Lindquist probed.

"I left spring '52... possibly changes took place after."

"What else can you tell us, looking at Exhibit B-1?" asked Nick.

"Well, sir, the camp in Pyoktong had rolling hills like Georgia—was really part of a village cut in two to make the prison."

With grit from his '59 Dodge embedded deep beneath his yellowed finger nail, Bradshaw pointed. "At the small area here that somebody must've tried scratchin' out... this might be what we called 'The Point' where we buried our dead."

"Can you tell us what that arrow points to?" asked Nick, indicating on the map.

"That would head towards 'Death Valley' about ten miles north, toward the east coast, the men of the 2nd

Infantry named it 'Death Valley' 'cause they'd lost so many guys there from starvation."

"Mr. Bradshaw, please hand me B-2."

Bradshaw leafed through the pile. "This map here looks like B-2 was."

"The number again, please?" Harris asked.

"I'm sorry, I mean B-2 looks like Camp 13, and there's 'Death Valley' again and the army escape route down the east coast. But Camp 13 had a, a main road coming down, like it showed on B-1."

Nick made a mental note of a possible army escape route.

"Can I look at B-1 again?" Bradshaw requested.

"Yes, go ahead," Nick replied.

The witness pulled up B-1 and handed it to Nick, who held it up for Bradshaw and Lindquist. Harris had to move to see the map. Bradshaw pointed to a strip on the map.

"This was the road that came through the camp and led down to the river. As you came into the camp here, you had the officers' company here. Right next to the same side of the road you had the sergeants' compound. Across here was the place they took us for brainwashing. Down in this area here they had the colored, which are listed here, but actually it was all Turks."

Lindquist turned to Nick. "Excuse me, if it's important, Counselor, anybody reading the record will simply see that he testified, 'Here was so and so,' and they'll never know what the witness pointed to unless you describe it as you go along."

Nick clarified the record. "Let the record indicate that the witness pointed to the lower left hand corner of Exhibit B-1. He described the middle, the third portion in the lower two quadrants of B-1. And then, finally, the right hand lower half portion of Exhibit B-1."

Harris walked to the center of the well. "If I can be heard, your Honor? He seems to be testifying from these maps, which are not in evidence. They've been marked for identification, and I'm waiting for an offer, at which time I would object."

"Mr. Harris has a point, Mr. Castalano."

Lindquist moved his head around like his neck was stiff. He grabbed it and then looked over in the clerk's direction. "Gentlemen, let's take a five minute recess."

Nick walked back to Mitch, "The maps are a problem. They have to be authenticated and considered relevant before they're allowed into evidence. The person who drew the maps might verify their authenticity but it might have been anyone, American, Chinese, North Korean... "

When court reconvened, Nick continued, "Your Honor, based on the stipulations with Counsel, whatever had appeared in the record before the Army Board for the Correction of Military Records would be considered an official government document and automatically admissible. But, Mr. Harris objects to the court considering new evidence, evidence he claims wasn't provided to the Army when Arthur Girardin first requested the reclassification. We claim that because the government had these maps in the government archives or in some other branch of the huge bureaucracy, the government must be charged with their constructive possession and therefore had imputed knowledge. Our position has been that Girardin wasn't required to collect every document in the government's files."

Lindquist tracked Harris's moves to the center of the well. Harris parted his suit jacket and put his hands on his hips. "It's not fair to present evidence that Girardin failed to present to the Army Board. This has been our argument for the past year. I don't think they have been made part of the earlier record, your Honor. That's the basis for my objection. They clearly weren't presented to the Board when it entered its decision."

Lindquist winced. "True, Counsel?"

"Yes, your Honor, but that's not the point... "

Harris cut Nick off. "Mr. Bradshaw indicated that they might be this and possibly that. He didn't prepare them. And it looks like because he didn't, he doesn't have personal knowledge."

"Your Honor, it's because the Army Board for the Classification of Military Records was so deficient in their examination of the facts at the hearing stage that Girardin's rights to due process were violated and that the court should hear the case from the beginning. This is a *de novo* proceeding, as far as we're concerned. So that we can get it on the record, I offer B-1 into evidence as a full exhibit. If Mr. Harris still has an objection, I'd argue that the witness has testified sufficiently, in terms of what this map fairly represents."

Lindquist twisted his mouth in one direction and the other, finally taking over. "Well, I suppose. Mr. Bradshaw, do I understand B-1 is, as you testified, a rough sketch? In other words, you aren't vouching for whether it's one inch equals forty feet, or one inch equals sixty feet? Just a rough sketch that you're referring to for the purposes of giving a general picture of what you remember of the location where you were housed and restricted in this prison camp, Prison Camp No. 13?"

"Yes, sir. Rough sketch of Camp No. 13."

"Mr. Bradshaw, does sketch B-1, depict a reasonable likeness of the layout of Camp Number 13 in October 1951?"

"Sir, this isn't, you know, a contour map. But, yes, generally I'd say this is a map of it. This road here... "

"What road are you referring to?"

Nick held up the map so Lindquist could see what Bradshaw pointed to. "This one here that says *'To Company 2.'*"

"At the extreme left hand of the exhibit, diagonally drawn across the road, *Company 2*. You believe that is in the proper location and place?"

"Yes, sir, generally speaking. It says here, *'To NCOs.'*"

Lindquist turned to Harris. "If it were offered solely as a rough sketch, Counselor, would you still object? And he might identify it as actually depicting the layout of the camp as he remembers it, as a rough sketch? Would you still have the same objection?"

Harris lowered his voice an octave, "No, your Honor, but I strongly reaffirm that it was never before the Board. So what is its relevancy to this proceeding, which is limited to a review of what was in front of the Board?"

Lindquist responded, "I don't know either. However, I presume Counsel must have some reason. Counselor?"

"Several bases, your Honor. Number one, some maps were provided by Admiral Sturgen. It is our opinion... " Nick trailed off in his response.

"By whom?" Lindquist snapped.

"Art Girardin at the very beginning of his investigative efforts obtained them from Admiral Sturgen. That puts them in the hands of the Government."

Harris countered. "No, your Honor, that puts them in the hands of the UN Armistice Commission, which isn't the Government or the Army Board."

Nick responded sarcastically. "He was an admiral in the U.S. Navy, for God's sake."

Harris shot back. "Serving with the U.N.! I've been trying to make this point."

"Gentlemen, let's calm down." Lindquist's dizziness returned. His stroked the lump on his neck which began to throb persistently. "Technically you're correct, Mr. Harris." Lindquist ran his hands over his scalp. "Look, we're in an unusual situation. Mr. Castalano, you started to state your claim. It was in possession of the admiral. For what purpose?"

That Nick did not know. "Your Honor, the maps are relevant because, through the Swiss emissary, we used them to communicate with the North Koreans, when I asked them if they might find Roger Girardin's remains. Their response was a little unclear, but it was taken as indicating that they weren't going to help."

Beads of sweat formed on Lindquist's forehead. "So what, what does that have to do with relevancy, Counselor?"

Nick felt part of the case hadn't yet fully revealed itself; for instance, why did map B-2 have a route leading away from the POW camp with hexagon symbols marked along the way?

"One, this witness will testify that he observed Roger Girardin at some point in time. It may help the Court in having some understanding as to where he saw him, because he did see him on several occasions around the camp."

After nearly forty-five minutes wrangling, Lindquist thought he had heard the clearest statement on the usefulness of the maps, but it was also when the room began to spin. He brought his hand to his head until it stopped. "I'm inclined to let the maps in because it adds some tangibility to something that happened so long ago. All right. For the purpose of it being a rough sketch or a schematic of Camp 13 in 1951, identified as such by the witness, although he did not create or make it, it might help the Court to understand where the witness saw certain things."

Lindquist turned to Harris. "You've been awfully quiet. Any objection?"

"Your Honor, I do think that they will prove to be superfluous. Exception."

"Exception noted, the Court will allow it, then. Exhibit B-1, a full exhibit."

Lindquist pressed against his neck, "Counsel, can you find an easel to put the maps on, so that we can all see what the witness is referring to. You know, in fact, this would be a good place to stop."

Suddenly, as if catapulted by some demonic force, Lindquist jumped up from his seat and hollered, "What are we watching?"

The exclamation reverberated off every wall, the crowd watched in horror, stunned as the judge scanned the room side-to-side in a spellbound state. Had the judge lost his mind? In the next second, Lindquist fell to the floor behind the bench. A woman in the back of the courtroom screamed. The stenographer jumped overturning the transcription machine.

"Oh my God!" A reporter yelled, "Call an ambulance."

Lindquist's secretary Alice opened the door behind the bench to see the judge's body sprawled. Picolillo, having seen hundreds of boxers knocked out with their eyes wide open, knew the judge was in another world, one of seizure, clenched teeth and dilated eyes bulging out of their sockets. He turned the judge onto his back and started compression, two times each second. Mitch, who had put in hours as a lifeguard at the local pool, tried to find a pulse. Alice, seeing the whites of his eyes turn crimson, repeated, "Oh no, oh no... " Ten minutes later, paramedics had pushed their way through the crowd, finding their patient spread-eagled—a clerk, two robed judges and a stenographer hovering covetously.

A Beautiful Season

NICK FELT THAT THE DAY HAD SUCCEEDED in one respect: beating him to a pulp. The administrative judge suspended trial indefinitely pending Lindquist's return—if he returned—so Nick had no way of knowing how much downtime there would be. At least a few weeks, judging from the fiasco that had gripped the courtroom. That night he went home feeling moody. Diane, in a flowered house dress, her long blond ponytail draping the nape of her neck, went unnoticed. When he told her about Lindquist's collapse, the pressure of getting the maps in, she understood. But Nick's funk did not end with the events in court that day. It had occurred to him that his law practice was in limbo for the foreseeable future. This grand plan to switch to representing veterans wasn't working out as expected.

Later that night, unable to sleep, he went to his study, where he usually picked out something dry to read—something to put him to sleep. Instead he grabbed an electronic chess game, which was smart enough to keep him from winning. Every so often, after moving a chess piece in response to the computer, he jotted down the sequence of court events back to the first day of trial. He wrote down the possible moves Harris might make, but the rules of litigation were more complicated than chess. Sometimes rules were made up, did not follow convention, or there were just too many exceptions, and if there were enough of those, then in reality there were no rules. Was it possible that his opponent, like the electronic chess set, could actually beat him? He scanned the books on his shelf: *The Old Testament, All Quiet on the Western Front.* He especially liked the cover of *Mutiny on the Bounty*: a clipper ship with sails unfurled. It reminded him that he had always wanted to learn how to sail—buy a boat, spend time with his son fixing it up, take Diane out sailing once in a while. Come to think of it, they hadn't left the kids with her parents for a weekend alone in years. It would be good for them. He missed her, having her to himself, even if it were only for a weekend. When did they stop doing that, he wondered. Out of single malt, he poured himself a stiff glass of twelve-year-old Dewars.

Diane opened her eyes around two and noticed Nick gone. She went to the study, where Nick was pouring his fifth shot. "Honey, it's late."

"Diane!" He looked at his wife standing at the door—beautiful, pristine, sleepy—and was just sober enough to realize he was too drunk to make a respectable approach.

Her hazel eyes narrowed. "You've been drinking."

"Couldn't sleep," he slurred. "The case is driving me crazy. I just can't figure why they've dug their heels in so deep on this. It's no skin off their nose, just give the goddamn reclassification."

"Things will look better in the morning," she added, too tired to engage in the kinds of existential questions Nick loved to grapple with at two in the morning when he was "three sheets to the wind."

"I suppose, but you know, sweetheart, justice isn't one man's battle—it's every man's, not for one man, but for all men. I don't understand why everyone isn't pulling in the same direction?"

The Möbius Strip

LINDQUIST HAD BEEN COMATOSE FOR FIVE DAYS when a conclave of doctors, those on duty and those from the long night in the emergency room gathered around his hospital bed to remove the breathing machine and see if he regained his sensibilities. Ventilator unplugged, IVs disconnected, a doctor shook him vigorously. He did not stir. The doctor shook him again, and Lindquist took a shallow breath and opened his eyes—baffled that his wrists were tied to a bed, above him an array of monitors with phosphorescent green traces that swept across video screens, and that except for his sister Klara and his secretary Alice, the room was full of strangers who stared at him like an alien.

The seminal medical event, the one that had choked off blood flow, had every potential to erase the trillions of impulses that had flowed into his sensory pathways and impressed themselves into the billions of nerve endings in the course of what Lindquist called his life. Although the results of an EEG were guarded to slightly positive, for at least the next few days he appeared childlike. It was possible that the brain reverted to an earlier stage in life, but he would never know because, as the neurologist explained to Klara, the brain doesn't report to itself what goes on in its mysterious cosmos. In the days that followed, a rational attitude began to emerge, one where he displayed his usual temperament, demanding more than a sick man should—especially one who eight days earlier had, by all measure, died.

Two years after Peter Lindquist had moved from Vermont to Boston following the tragic death of his wife, he married Jenny Revere Svenson, a woman who would raise Joe until college. Klara was born the year following their marriage, so Joe was Klara's big brother, and she saw Joe's recuperation as her responsibility.

"Joe, I don't like seeing you in bed like this, in a hospital no less. But, I do love seeing you every day. Like we're kids again."

"Yeah, but we didn't spent time enjoying each other as kids, we were self-centered brats, going from pillar to post."

Klara smiled. "Happily, we're close, now." She changed the subject. "Joe, when you passed out, did you see anything? You know a light or a sign? They said you'd died."

"No, don't think so, no light. But you know, Klara, I did see my life pass. The life measured from the moment I took my first breath until those last ones. I saw no flash, no long tunnel, no light at the other end, but as I was passing out... felt calm. It's like in that final moment I resolved things that might've troubled me. In a split second, I realized that I was only those things that I'd touched, the places I'd breathed, the people that I'd loved."

Lindquist, admiring her gentle look, waited for his sister's response. She had a pretty face and seldom wore make up, was a big-boned woman, though not being self-conscious of her size, and she did little to hide it. "Klara, am I making sense?"

She kissed him on the forehead. "I love you Joe, and yes, you make a lot of sense."

Chess Games

A FEW DAYS LATER, NICK LEARNED THAT THE TRIAL would resume in September. Nick enlisted Mitch and Kathy in picking up the lines of inquiry he'd abandoned when the trial had first begun: people that might shed light on issues he had no answers for. There were still many questions, not the least of which was what happened to the over four hundred POWs that had never been heard from again. Another question was whether there had been sightings of American soldiers in North Korea, China, or the Soviet Union. And, finally what certain hexagonal symbols meant, if anything. What had Jack called them? "Hexagons within hexagons." His quest for answers had ended when the trial drew near, and he had to prepare witness examinations. But, with the break in proceedings he would have time to resume the investigations.

Following the suspension of trial, he called Bob Cousins whom he had met the previous summer at an ABA International Law Section meeting. Nick remembered him saying he had Korean connections. He asked if he knew any college students in Seoul who would be willing to work at the archives there. Cousins did not know anyone offhand, but put him in touch with Henry Kang, a forty-year-old Philadelphia businessman. Nick told him about the case and what he was after. Kang indicated he would call back in a few days after seeing what he might do. The Korean meanwhile did his due diligence and discovered Nick had something of potentially considerable value that he could use to his benefit. Kang called Nick, arranging to meet in Atlantic City over the weekend. Nick spotted Kang from his description: 5'7", wide shoulders, brown leather flight jacket, dark glasses, jet black crew cut. They went to the *Gambler's Den*, a restaurant at *Caesar's Place* Kang frequented when he came to town. Nick learned that Kang had been one of five students who, during the 1959–1960 student protests in Seoul, invaded the presidential Blue House forcing President Syngman Rhee to resign. For his service, Kang was considered a genuine patriot to whom the country extended a lifelong calling-card into all echelons of the government.

"Nick, the kind of information you are asking about would probably not be found in the archives, and if it were, it'd be classified. And of course any classified information would only come with a very steep—prohibitively steep—price."

"How much are we talking about?"

"It's not money, Nick. The Koreans need something more essential."

"And what's that?"

"Access."

"Access to what?" Nick asked naïvely.

"To power, Nick, in D.C."

"Why's that? They have an embassy, lobbyists, don't they?"

"Nick, let me explain it this way. Do you play chess?"

"Yes, in fact I do."

"Are you good at it?"

"I'm no Bobby Fisher, but I play a good game."

"Me too, someday we will play."

"So what's this got to do with chess?"

"When you are trying to deal with Washington, it is like chess. You need a full complement of pieces on the board at all times. We lost our knights, our rooks, our bishops a few years ago. To achieve our objectives on an ongoing basis, we need people to clear the way. We need access."

Seeing Nick's face, he rushed to assure him. "No, no, do not get me wrong, all on the up-and-up. For the right contact we could pay, that is, *offset* the cost of your efforts, even pay for you to go to Korea yourself. If I could offer the Koreans someone who could do some lobbying for us, that is, for them."

"Yeah, but who'd you think I know that can help?"

"Well, Mr. Cousins tells me you have a colleague who worked in Washington. One that was well connected, someone you could put us in touch with."

Kang was referring to Seymour Freedman, Nick's friend who had retired in the late 70s from government, most notably as Chief Counsel to the House Judiciary Committee. The two men met at a cocktail party at a time when Freedman was moving from Washington to New York just after he had married for the fourth time. Freedman, the first guest Nick laid his eyes on when he walked into Hannie Azan's crowded living room that winter Sunday in '79, was overweight, with drooping jowls, flabby chin and a red lumpy nose plastered to a large balding head. Nick's enduring memory of that day was not Seymour's anatomical features, but that the left side of his shirt hung outside his pants, free beneath his open suit jacket, which with every turn, revealed an opened fly. But Nick quickly learned that despite his slovenliness, the man had a keen intellect, spoke impeccably—up close and fast—engaging responders who felt the power of his conviction.

Before Nick left for home that afternoon, the man dropped dates, names, places and historical happenings, all while lighting a succession of fresh white cigs from the rapidly diminishing butt gingerly held between his yellow stained fingers. Freedman proved more than a fast-talking, chain-smoking neurotic who had lived in the luminosity of a former stellar federal career: he had grand theories on politics.

Nick called Seymour to explain what the Korean wanted. Seymour asked a lot of questions.

"I want to meet him to better appreciate who the man is, what's his game." In late August, the two men drove to Atlantic City, and since Seymour had an appetite for oysters, they met Kang at the *Old Oyster Barn*. After introductions, Kang got down to business. "Mr. Freedman, I have been retained to enlist someone who could meet with the highest echelons of the Korean government with the view toward helping them with several problems."

"When you say high echelons," Seymour paused. He squinted his eyes and looked at the man hard. "Relative to the president, what do you mean?"

Kang turned his head away, avoiding Seymour's intimidating stare. "I cannot disclose that or be certain how high up." He made eye contact. "But be assured that for your help— with access to the right people here—the very highest echelons of the Korean government would make it worth your while."

"Why me?"

"Let me speak frankly. You are an important man, Mr. Freedman. You know Washington inside out. I know your reputation. We need someone that can repair considerable damage." He slowed his speech. "You will remember the scandal involving congressional payoffs in 1976."

"How well I remember. Nick, you may not remember, but the Korean intelligence operatives had been accused of funneling bribes to some thirty members of Congress." He added, "And the Justice Department made it stick."

"We have come to know this unfortunate time as Koreagate," Kang said addressing Nick. "The central figures were a man named Park and his Korean friend, an ex-elevator operator in Congress."

"You mean the operator who once had a crush on Karl Gabler, the seventy-year-old Ways and Means Chair?" Seymour quipped.

"Yes, that one."

"Oh yeah, how could I forget her." Seymour laughed. "The press was all over the halls following the election and Karl was being hounded because he had put his hat in the ring for Speaker. Well, Karl wanted time with, I've forgotten her name now, but the Korean elevator girl. One of my staff actually caught him in the copier closet with her one night."

"Yes, that must be the same one. And of course you know that Congress censured Rohban, John McDougal and Buddy Wilson. All of them."

"Christ, later Dick Pajewski was jailed," Seymour added, "I knew all that, but I left Washington in '79, so I missed a lot, too."

"Well, you can understand that Koreagate has had some long term dislocations. We cannot gain admission to any government offices. We need help."

By the end of the meeting Freedman had accepted an invitation to fly with Nick to Korea, for a fee of three thousand dollars and all expenses paid for each of them.

Freedman's interest was clear. The connection included the prospect of bringing in a fat retainer representing the Korean government. For Nick, it had the added attraction of releasing the pressure building up between him and Diane. With the case on hold, Nick had spent too many hours considering his crumbling prospects with a bottle of scotch until finally, one night, Diane had had enough. "Maybe you shouldn't have taken a case against the government. After all, you had a good record with them on those VA cases."

"Yeah, but it was like shooting fish in a barrel."

"They liked your work, Nick, and they paid. So maybe it wasn't the most exciting thing in the world. But do you think they're ever going to send you another case?"

It was a question that did not bear answering, but when the silence between them became overpowering, Diane gave up. "I'm going to bed."

Ten days later, Seymour and Nick were in Korean Airlines Business Class, traveling to Seoul. Freedman's presence had more importance to the Koreans, and it was no surprise that when the men arrived, the first order of business was for them to ascertain what he would be willing to do on their behalf. Nick had no illusions that Freedman was the key to his success. The day after arrival, the two men were picked up at 9 a.m. by limousine at the Marriott Hotel. Three Koreans dressed in black slacks and black leather bomber jackets waited in a second limo. The pair of limos sped out of the compound and onto more heavily trafficked thoroughfares, before turning down quieter streets and, finally, into a complex of empty back alleys. The cars stopped before one of a narrow row of two and three story gray masonry houses.

Freedman, with Nick behind him, followed a man sporting a light blue turtleneck under his jacket. The accompanying men were all about 5'5", broad shouldered and small waists. Freedman muttered, "Strongmen... KIA." Nick glanced over his shoulder. Freedman was more accustomed to "cloak and dagger"—having followed seedy men, like the man in the blue shirt, when he had worked protocol in the Kennedy White House. Reaching a second landing, the two Americans looked fleetingly at one another and then at the KIA men, before climbing the last flight of narrow wooden stairs. Freedman removed his jacket. His shirt was soaked. He paused to catch his breath. The men finally reached the top floor and entered a small, three room apartment with white walls. They were seated at a dining room table that accommodated six, filling the space. Seymour sat at the head, his backside halfway into the hallway, Nick and four men fit like clams on each side of the table. At the far end sat Jang Jun-Hwan—thin faced, crooked teeth, a man in his late sixties, distant. A minute passed during which everybody, except Nick, lit a cigarette.

Jang smiled, looked around the table, and finally spoke, "Can I offer you a glass of orange soda?" A man in a black jacket put tall heavy tumblers on the table and filled them from a quart bottle. "Sir, please indulge me. I need to be certain who you are, or rather who I am told you are, as impolite as that may sound. Can you please tell me, by way of example, what you did in Washington and a few of the people you claim to know."

Seymour gave Jang a five minute recitation of the sort that he would give if he were a job applicant. When Seymour finished, Jang nodded and turned to Nick, whose summary took roughly a minute. Following the Americans' disclosures, Jang's question was more pointed. "Mr. Freedman, I am less interested in who you know on a professional level, than who you know on a personal or friendly basis. With whom do you socialize?"

"I've had a long political life as a White House aide in the Kennedy, then Johnson Administration and finally the House of Representatives... by 1968, I got to know on a first name basis the power brokers—you know, Kennedy family, three Secretaries of State... "

"Yes, but how well, and among these, what gentlemen in particular, Mr. Freedman?" Jang was still not satisfied.

"Well, Kip Karigan, Majority Leader in the House of Representatives. His daughter had a drinking problem. Called me at two in the morning to get her out of jail. Drunk driving. There are many examples like this."

"Ok, Mr. Freedman, I understand." Jang turned to Nick. "And, you Mr. Castalano?"

239

"I know few people, in Washington that is. I went to school with Giacomo Locke, Congressman Joseph Rodham's top aide. If he were here he would have a million stories, but I'm afraid I have none."

The Korean screener listened but did not ask Nick to elaborate. "Gentleman, I need to excuse myself. I will return shortly." Jang rose, bowed politely in Freedman's direction and left.

"He's reporting what he heard up the line," Freedman remarked.

Jang returned half an hour later. "I apologize for the delay. Let me ask you, Mr. Freedman, do you have any reservations helping our government find someone who will listen to a problem we have with delisting—that is being unauthorized to export certain weapons systems to allies in Africa."

"I'd have to know more. It sounds like someone already did business in an impermissible way."

"Yes, that is the allegation, so to speak. Nevertheless, we need to put the pieces back."

"Well, it'd do no harm to see if there were someone who might listen to a reasonable explanation. I think I can do that," Seymour replied.

Jang once again dismissed himself. It was nearly noon when he returned. "Gentlemen, we would like to escort you to our next destination, if you would be so kind."

"Where'd that be?" Freedman inquired.

"We would like you to meet a few of our representatives at the Ministry of National Defense."

Nick and Seymour looked at each other, turned toward the door and saw a man in black motioning them to follow back to the limos. The cars sped off, lights flashing, overtaking vehicles at speeds topping 150 kilometers. In fifteen minutes they had reached the Korean Ministry of National Defense.

The doors of the limo swung open. Soldiers with M-16s slung over their shoulder guarded the entrance. The men exited the car and were escorted into a marbled lobby the size of a small office building. A man in an officer's uniform approached with his hands extended. He smiled and addressed the Americans in barely understandable

English, "Give me passports." The two gave up their passports, and another man in fluent English asked each of them to stand against a green sheet before he swung around a large box camera mounted on a tripod.

The Americans were given badges with their names and picture, which they affixed to their lapels. Nick quipped, "Must mean something like VIP." A soldier escorted them up a flight of wide stairs, along a short gray granite hall and into a cavernous sitting room with a red and white oriental rug. At one end was an oversized oak desk. A score of chairs lined the walls. A diminutive gray-haired man stood behind the desk. Freedman entered and the man came walking in his direction, aided by a cane. Nick looked down and saw the man was wearing a prosthetic. Handing his business card to Freedman, he declared, "I am Oh Jin Woo, Korean Minister of Defense." Behind the Americans a troupe of ten men filed in, consisting of generals, colonels and civilians in dark business suits. One man introduced himself as the CEO of Daesun, the largest Korean electronics conglomerate.

The first ten minutes were spent introducing each other. The defense minister made salutary remarks that lasted another ten minutes, followed by Seymour, who responded like he had been dispatched by the U.S. State Department. Seymour ended by smiling widely for the minister. The Koreans turned to Nick. He offered that he had been a veteran and without any official imprimatur, he extended America's appreciation for Korea's commitment in Vietnam. The officers smiled gratuitously and Nick turned his attention to the minister.

The minister spoke about how grateful he was that the Americans made the trip. After another forty minutes of ritual speeches, during which jet lag and boredom combined to make Nick's eyes droop and his head bob, the minister concluded. He smiled at Seymour. Then with good cheer and in perfect California English, asked, "Will you gentlemen join me tonight?"

"Yes, I'd hoped that we could attend a traditional Korean dinner, a *kisaeng?*" Seymour winked knowingly at Nick.

The supper was fit for a Korean emperor and the music for its royal court. Generals, colonels and businessmen and the cast of characters from the earlier meeting were in attendance. In a large circle, each sat with a pair of young women. The night was filled with food; live music for dancing was supplied by an accordionist and singing drummer. By the end of the evening, no one could stand, neither Minister, General, chefs, hostesses, nor their esteemed American guests. Nick felt jovial, careless—the trial was another world away.

Dawn was breaking over Seoul's Han River when Nick and Seymour, each joined by a hostess, stumbled toward the limo that would return them to the Marriott. As the car drew away from the hotel entrance, Nick discovered the unbearably young, unbearably beautiful Rachel Choi, her alias for such occasions, standing next to him.

"I go to room," the woman said in barely understandable English, as she gripped his arm.

"Not with me. I go alone," Nick answered firmly, trying to disentangle himself. He saw Seymour disappear into an elevator with a girl equally young, equally beautiful.

"No, cannot do. Must go," was her reply.

She looked at Nick on the verge of crying.

"Must go or get fired. Please take me... to room. So they see me go."

Nick caught on. "All right, come stay for a little while, but then you go. Yes?"

"Yes."

Nick and she stood perfectly still as the elevator accelerated to the sixth floor. Nick opened the door to his room, removed his jacket, loosened his tie and sat at a overlooking the Han River snaking its way through the city. Earlier in the day, he had set up his chessboard, and changing focus from the dark outline of the river, he slid white king's pawn K-3 to K-4. He felt Rachel watching him, and then saw her extend a small, delicate hand to black queen's bishop sliding it diagonally to the far side of the board: checkmate.

The unexpected move raised Nick's eyes. "You know how to play?"

"Yes, little."

"Where'd you learn?"

"University, go to university, learn English, learn chess."

"Are you a student?"

"Yes, student now, earn tuition working for Minister."

Nick began understanding this cultural exchange on a new level. "I'm impressed. You seem like a smart girl."

"Thank you, Mr. Nick."

"No. Call me Nick. But you must be going, Rachel, now."

"Can stay if you would like me, Nick."

"Don't think that'd be a good idea."

"Ok, I call desk for taxi?"

Nick listened without comprehending to the melodies of Rachel's voice as she spoke into the phone. Bidding him goodbye, she left. As he watched her shut the door, he thought, "If she's a day over eighteen, I'm a drunken sailor."

The next morning Nick and Seymour began a series of meetings with the Koreans to discuss the kind of support they needed. The calendar on Nick's watch read 9/8. In a windowless room on the second floor of the headquarters, they sat across a glass top table from Lee Dae-Ho, a two star general, and Park Dong-Min, a full colonel. The men discussed terms of engagement which, if successful, would begin Freedman's representation. Seymour did most of the talking—to do with trust, control over the various matters, assurances that if he represented the government that there would be no illegal schemes, payoffs, espionage or other high crimes that foreign agents need to "wet the bed over." The Koreans afforded no comfort, responding evasively. Freedman could not get the unqualified answer he needed. Seymour had told Nick earlier what he had to hear, but the Koreans could not, or would not, speak for their larger constituency. Freedman remained stoic, but in his usual way chain-smoked—after each deep drag on unfiltered Chesterfields, he'd let the cigarette burn into a large, tenuous ash that would hang until the slightest air current tore it off. And it would fall onto his pin striped suit or the general's Persian rug. It was Freedman's way of telling the men that he did not give "two shits" if he represented them. After four hours, the meeting ended in a stalemate as to how the representation would play out.

The next day the Americans were summoned to Colonel Park's office to discuss what Nick hoped to find in Korea. They were joined by Yoon Sung Min, an undersecretary from the Korean State Department. Nick summarized the Girardin case and a laundry list of questions, indicating that he would settle for a few crucial leads.

"Colonel Park, I'd like to know how to read several maps that I've brought with me. In particular there are some marks that I think could be important. And, of course, if anyone has information about whether any Americans were left behind, I would like to know that, too. And, if there were American's left behind, why? Lastly, but importantly, do you have any records concerning a soldier by the name of Roger Girardin or his whereabouts?"

The Colonel scribbled notes in a black bound notebook. "Mr. Castalano, I am not sure we can help, but we will do our best. Do you have any more questions you can share with me and secretary Min at this time?"

Nick reached into his leather briefcase and pulled out a manila folder from which he removed and unfolded three maps. "I think these are maps of Camp 13. You must be familiar with this camp along the Yalu."

"Yes, notorious for inhumane conditions during the war."

Nick turned over one of the maps. He waited until the colonel and the secretary perused it before pointing to a hexagon. "What do these symbols mean?... burial grounds?"

The two Koreans each made notes. The Colonel said, "Mr. Castalano, we have no answers right now. But if we could get a copy of these, we will get back to you if we find something that may help."

After the meeting, the Americans were driven back to the hotel. That evening, there was a knock on Nick's door.

"Hello, Nick."

"Rachel!"

"Come to pick up package from downstairs for my boss, and I wanted to see how you doing. Are you invite me? We play chess?"

Nick eyed her up and down. A white flowered dress fit tightly around her neck and tiny waist before falling below her creamy white knees.

Nick stepped out of the way. Rachel walked over to the table where the chess pieces sat from the night she parried Nick's errant move.

"How's school?"

"I take one course, English."

"What's your major?"

"Don't have major."

"How old are you?"

"I... twenty-one."

"Wow, just a kid."

"Kid?"

"Yeah, very young woman."

"You have drink, Nick, beer?"

"Kentucky whisky, it's on the bar."

Rachel got up, unwrapped two tumblers and poured a generous portion of whisky, a splash of water.

"Let's play game, Nick. I take white, you black."

Nick smiled. He looked beyond Rachel and at the dresser where a single white gardenia rose from a thin vase and then turned to the window and saw the Han River as a black ribbon separating the city. "An odd start, but okay."

Rachel arranged the pieces while Nick watched, sipping his whisky. She moved the white king's pawn to K-3. He mirrored her with his black king's pawn to K-3.

She moved the queen diagonally to the edge of the board.

Nick thought for a moment, then moved the queen's rook Q-4.

She quickly moved the king's bishop diagonally to the edge of the board.

The board began to reel as Nick made a swipe for his knight. It had become so difficult to stay focused, and he felt so tired. Rachel's face, beautiful, young, blurred and loomed, then blurred again. Nick could feel the room tipping.

"Mr. Nick. Easy. You want I stay, Nick, no worries."

"Yes, but no. It's best you go." He thought he may have hurt her feelings as he walked over to the bed. He saw her

245

unhurriedly leave her chair grabbing the sequined purse she had hung on the back. In slow motion, he watched her move toward the door before he fell back, eyes closed.

"Good night, Nick. Nick, good... "

Nick did not respond.

The next morning the Americans sat in the windowless room again. Nick's head was in his hands.

"You all right, Nick?" asked Seymour.

"Yeah, too much whisky."

"Not a closet drinker, are you?" Seymour jibed.

Nick tried smiling. He was about to mention Rachel, and how he did not remember getting into bed, did not remember undressing, but Colonel Park and General Lee entered and extended a curt good morning.

Lee addressed Freedman. "Sir, I would like to start today's meeting with a list of matters we had hoped that you could help with."

"General, sir, our earlier meeting left unresolved if the representation could meet my requirements."

"I assure you that we will meet your requirements." The general paused. "But these things take time, as you, a man of great experience, know." He paused to sip from a cup. "I need not restate our need for contacts in Washington, such as you could provide. We might consider you, exclusively, to help us soften the effects of poor past judgment."

"General, some "poor judgments" are considered crimes by our government."

"But hopefully you could broker a political solution to our alleged arms exports to Africa—that is if they conflicted with U.S. Export Law. Delisting denies us important access to armaments essential to our security."

The men spoke around the details once again, and within the hour the meeting concluded when the general announced that he had to attend a scheduled meeting. The Americans returned to the hotel, Seymour saying, "I am getting bored with the pace at which the Koreans do business."

On September 12, at approximately 8:30 a.m. Freedman received a call from the administrative assistant to the Chief of Staff to the President of the Republic of Korea. She requested a meeting at 11 at the Blue House. A car would pick them up at 10:30. When they arrived they were escorted to a conference room with pink and white flowered wall paper and several porcelain vases sitting on highly polished mahogany tables. A large octagonal table sat in the middle of the room atop a white and blue Persian rug. At least fifteen minutes passed before two men walked in, one of whom was Colonel Park. "This is Mr. Yoo, Chief of Staff to the President of the Republic of Korea." Yoo, extending both arms, palms upward, said, "Please be seated." He indicated that he had been fully briefed and that he would try and answer any questions Nick had. Nick again sketched out the case.

When Nick finished, Yoo nodded to Park who supplied the Americans with a synopsis of the war, particularly the October through December timeframe. Nick knew the history. But Park covered a more detailed account of events that were experienced by the ROK in conjunction with units of the 19th Regiment, especially in the vicinity of the village of Pakch'on and the Ch'ongch'on River between October 25 and November 27, 1950. They suggested that the information would be useful in putting the Girardin disappearance into a battle context, since he was last seen in these parts November 25, 1950.

Park spoke like an historian. "Mr. Castalano, I understand that the man you are looking for was in the 8th Army 24th Division, 19th Regiment, Company C. Our records show that therefore he was near the Ch'ongch'on River valley, which varies in width from six to thirty kilometers depending on who's measuring." Park went on for fifteen minutes without taking a breath. Nick took notes. Then all became quiet, signaling that Park had finished.

Nick asked, "Mr. Park, do you have any information about the maps?"

"We obviously have many thousands of such maps. We were able to confirm the ones you produced are of Camp 13. The one actually labeled Camp 13 shows a road near the camp area which looks like a long road for troop movements leading to a crossing point into Manchuria, and the symbols seem to coincide with our intelligence reports at the time of major minefields we may have laid later in the war. Our maps do not show such fields, but an analysis of our records indicates that those were areas where the U.N. forces were targeting such ordinance. I am afraid I have nothing further at this time."

"Thank you, Colonel," said the Chief of Staff.

"Sir, once again, could you tell us if your records tell you anything about the soldier named Girardin in Camp 13?" Nick asked.

"Well, there was one entry in an intelligence record that indicated that if we encountered a Private Roger Girardin or Sergeant Joseph Johns, we were to return them to Seoul CID, in connection with a classified report. Other than that we... "

Yoo raised his hand and then quickly completed the sentence for Park, "... we have nothing to report. No, we have no other record. Maybe you need to inquire at the U.N. Armistice Commission."

"Do you know if there was any unit mentioned?"

"No, a rather superficial document. I wish I could share it, but it is classified," Yoo countered.

Yoo lit a cigarette, blowing smoke in Seymour's direction. Seymour took a deep drag on a short butt and doused it in his coffee cup. Yoo rose from his chair and opened his arms, signaling to Park that the meeting was over. He extended a handshake to his guests wishing them a safe trip. "Colonel Park and I have to attend a meeting now. If you have any further questions, feel free to direct them to my attention. You have my card."

In the weeks following the return to the U.S., Freedman made several trips to the Korean Embassy in Washington to entertain whether to represent the government. In the end, he applied for foreign agent status and set upon representing the ROK in the U.S. His first assignment had to do with illegal arms exports.

Machines Do Not Lie

ON THE PLANE FROM KOREA, NICK MULLED over Park's comment about the long road for troop movements leading to a crossing point into Manchuria. Yoo had obviously cut Park short. There was plainly more information than Yoo, or more accurately, the Korean government was letting on. The fact that the symbols coincided with minefields, and that the U.N. forces were targeting the area for ordinance was also curious. Stopping in the office on the way home, he left the map with a note in big black letters for Mitch: *Find an expert on signs, symbols, and hexes!*

When Mitch had seen Nick's note to find out about signs, symbols and hexes, he took the most obvious first step for a recent post-grad: he called his friend, Bill Norgren, who was writing up his PhD in Mayan Hieroglyphics and asked if he could be pointed in a direction to figure out what the hexes meant. Norgren suggested that it could be some kind of language, a hieroglyph or ideogram he was unfamiliar with and passed Nick onto his friend Barry Eisenberg, a PhD linguist at Fordham University who knew something about codes and semiotics. Mitch faxed a portion of the map to Eisenberg who returned the next day. "I figure that the hexes might be a take-off on the symbol that is associated with the first Chinese character set. The legendary King Fu Xi from over 7000 years ago invented an ancient symbol referred to as the eight hexagons."

"It's no surprise they're Chinese in origin," Mitch reasoned. "They were found on a map that may have been drafted by the Chinese. But what do they signify?"

"That I can't say. You may also want to see what databases might show the existence of the mark in other contexts."

"Like what?" Mitch asked.

"I don't know, maybe religious, political, corporate logos for instance."

Mitch turned to Skip Repetski, a friend who specialized in trademark law asking if he could figure out if the hexes were some kind of logo. Skip called Mitch the next day. "The search turned up several hexagons as logos for everything from diapers to aircraft parts, helicopter parts at one time."

"Can you tell me who registered the mark for helicopters?"

"Yeah, a Hamilton Group."

The mark Skip had found consisted of a hexagon within a series of diminishing hexagons. He took a magnifying glass and compared it to the ones on the map. "They look the same. You know the aspect ratio, each side of a hex is the same length, and the relative size of the interior hexes to each other is very close. But maybe you don't have to take my word for it."

"What do you mean?"

"There's this guy Henriques in AI over at computing who's big into patterns, he might be able to tell you more," he said, writing out a number.

On the phone, Mitch told Henriques that Skip had suggested he talk to him about a pattern problem, but he was unsure why, exactly.

"Well, I work on systems that improve on automatic fingerprint identification and hand writing analysis," Henriques responded. The next day, a note Henriques left with the receptionist admitted Nick to the scientist's lab. The name on the door read: *Golois Logic For Optical Pattern Recognition,* or simply *GLOPR*, was the software program that, among other things, did statistical pattern recognition —that is, how close one image matched another.

Henriques looked up from this desk. "Mitch?"

"John? Thanks for taking the time to meet with me."

"So, let's see what you got," said Henriques.

Mitch showed Henriques the two symbols. "I need to know whether two symbols are precise matches in the mathematical sense. In other words, might you tell me whether they were authored by the same draftsman?"

"As a linguist might determine plagiarism?" Henriques asked.

"Yes, that sounds good."

"In theory, I can. We do something called pattern recognition—not like a human does, but by reducing an image to its mathematical representation. It's a branch of topology."

"Like mapping? Okay, and in plain English?"

"Let's assume that if these were drawn by different artists, there'd be variability in the drawing. We try and find out if the variability is due to random variations of one individual or more than one. If the variations are small it would tend to point to one artist. The idea behind *GLOPR* is to electronically scan the specimen images of the two hexagons, the ones from the maps and the ones from the trademark search. The computer will perform a shape analysis deciphering the images' mathematical properties in the geometrical sense. For example, there are spaces between the hexes as they recede into smaller and smaller hexes. We can measure the spaces, we can measure the aspect ratios. This means measuring the actual outer and inner shapes of each of the embedded hexagons, their areas, the line lengths, the areas of the spaces between the hexagons and even the texture, as well as highlighting any distinguishing features, such as curves, ridges and craters that are apparent."

"So you're saying it will say to with what degree of mathematical certainty the two images were drafted by the same person?"

"Right, or at least you can talk about similarity in a statistical way. It'll take a few days to carry out the analysis."

The following Monday night Henriques called Mitch with the result, "The tests are nearly conclusive: the same individual probably—within a certainty of ninety-eight percent—drew the hexagons on the map and the ones produced for the logo."

251

The Paper Camp

FRIDAY, SEPTEMBER 23rd AT THE STROKE OF TEN, Lindquist returned to the bench, open-collared, loosened tie, fresh red scar starting below his jaw and ending under his shirt. Ed Armstead, the CBS radio reporter, observed that Lindquist appeared ten pounds lighter, cheeks sunken, eyes more deeply set behind the specs that rested loosely on his nose. The judge moved forward, positioning himself to look into the witness's face as best he could. The witness chair was already occupied by David Bradshaw, who had flown in from Atlanta the night before. Lindquist warned in a stern, but weak voice. "Sir, you are still under oath. Proceed, Counsel."

"Mr. Bradshaw," Nick began, "When you sat in that chair nearly six weeks ago, I showed you a map referred to as Plaintiff's Exhibit, marked B-1for identification, and asked if it fairly described an area you were familiar with. If you could step up to the easel to my right, let's go through that again, please."

Bradshaw walked to the side of the easel where two thumbtacks fastened the map to a flip chart. "Yes, by looking at this, part of this area here might be what was considered the escape route down the eastern edge of the peninsula. It begins in the backwater of the Yalu and goes south for about ten miles. Whoever drew this has the Yalu River written in here, but that would not be the Yalu River. It would be the backwaters. The Yalu River would be off to the left hand side of this."

Nick understood the testimony to confirm what he had learned from Colonel Park.

Lindquist leaned forward. "It is really the backwaters of the Yalu River, is that it?" he asked, barely audible.

"Yes, sir. That's what it'd be. This speck of an area over here's where we buried 1,800 to 2,500 men."

Nick flipped the page on the easel, where two thumbtacks fastened the map B-2.

"Let me now draw your attention to Map B-2. Would you know what that hexagon within a hexagon figure means?" Nick asked, making sure Lindquist was paying attention.

"It seems to mark some kind of station or point of interest."

"Have you ever seen such a mark?"

"No, not a six-sided figure like that, but different mapmakers in intelligence units use their own marks to point things out."

"Mr. Bradshaw, do you recall seeing any wounded when you arrived in Camp 13 in December?"

"There were many wounded. There were many sick."

"Was it the practice of the soldiers other than trained medics to look after the wounded?"

"As well's we could. Dysentery, that's what killed most, that an' starvation. Lots were dying from wounds that they got at the time of capture. Had no medical. Had no surgical tools, no medicine. Without, you know, sulfur, for instance, small infections start going gangrenous. We had a doctor by the name of Bohannon, but he'd done nothing, had nothing to treat us."

"Did you participate in treating any of the POWs while you were in Camp 13?"

"I dug shrapnel out, I dug bullets out and anything else I could do to help."

"In tending the wounded in January '51, you say you were digging out shrapnel and bullets... on a steady basis. Did you ever have occasion to tend anybody with stomach wounds?"

"Stomach wound, no. A side wound, yes."

"On what occasion did you tend a person with a side wound?"

"Sometime after we got to Camp 13. I'd say maybe ten days, two weeks after I was at Camp 13—I have to explain something here. We were losing a lot of men every day, dying. Death was something we took for granted. Every morning we gathered them up, stacked them —usually they'd freeze during the night. Minus zero, wind constant. We'd stack 'em six feet high. A death room. A lean-to, really. Those we couldn't get in the room, we stacked them

253

outside. Then in early spring, after it warmed up a bit, we'd get as many as we could, take them across that inlet, to a finger of land, scrape the snow and put the bodies there, cover them with the snow, say a little prayer."

Nick saw the judge lift his pen. "What did you do with the medals or tags?" asked Lindquist, again moving away from the emotional moment, objectifying the stacking.

Bradshaw turned. "The dog tags, sir?"

"Yes, the tags."

"Anytime I handled a body, and if he had dog tags, I would take one of them," he answered.

As Bradshaw answered, the judge wrote furiously. "Didn't they all have dog tags?" Lindquist asked.

"No, sir. Some men'd lost them, sometimes the enemy took 'em. For souvenirs, or who knows what. But those that did have 'em, I'd take one for myself, and the other I'd put in the man's mouth. Stayed in his mouth when we buried him. Later on, the Chinese found out that some of us was keeping 'em, and they had shakedown inspections. I kept hiding mine. Later when they transferred me to another barracks, I couldn't get to my hiding place. Tags must be still there."

Lindquist wanted specificity. "Where are they?" he asked skeptically.

"Had 'em hid in a hollow I'd dug in one of the shacks. At the very top I'd dropped 'em. Far as I know, they're in what's left of the camp."

"Thank you, Mr. Bradshaw, proceed." Bradshaw picked up on where Nick had been going before Lindquist's detour. The judge picked up his pen and started writing.

"Late January we was stacking bodies, to get back to your question, and there's this man lying right next to the death room. Most of these shanties, they'd one, sometimes two, what you'd call rooms to live and sleep. We slept on the floor. I was in a room sixteen feet square, ten men. Lot of 'em had the little sheds on the other end. Anyway, this man was laying there, sprawled really. And, one of the guys who was helping with the bodies said, 'I guess he'll be one of the ones tomorrow.' I asked, 'What's wrong?' He said, 'He's wounded... bad.' I asked, 'Well, can't they do nothing?' And he said, 'Nope.' I just looked at him."

"He'd a large wound, here," Bradshaw explained, soberly pointing to his right side. "The wound already turned black. Rotting. Stinking. Man's on fire. I asked, 'Is there anything else wrong with him?' Guy didn't know. Well, I'm no doctor. I ain't had no medic training... But I read a lot. I 'membered some of the old things we used back home."

Nick felt that the subject of life and death was coming alive. The maps gave bearing to where men buried their atrocities. Yet, in the next instant, Lindquist again interrupted. Nick raised his hand off the lectern, giving the judge one of those 'I-can't-believe-it-looks.'

"Where's Dr. Bohannon, whatever his name was?" Lindquist asked.

"Up in the officers' compound. Occasionally they'd let him exam the men, all he could do was look, nothing to work with."

"Wouldn't he have the same tools you had?"

Bradshaw faced Lindquist. "If he'd seen the man, yes, sir. They'd take Bohannon to a certain building, he'd have sick call. The only people that got over were those who could walk. Those who couldn't, didn't see him."

Nick hesitated before asking his next question, largely to let the absurdity sink in. Seconds ticked off the clock over the jury box. "What happened next?" Nick asked.

"I went to the latrine, reached down, and scooped out a handful of feces with maggots. I wrenched them from the feces best I could, and placed 'em into the boy's side. I took a rag and tied it up. I felt that I couldn't hurt him, because he was too near... well, figured that day that he would've gone ahead and died."

"When'd you see him again, I mean, after you put the maggots in him?"

"Later on, after the ice melted. Guards would let us go to the reservoir after they segregated the companies—three companies with barbed wire between them, wouldn't let us mingle. I was in Company 1, mostly black, a few whites. Company 2, all white from everywhere; Company 3, American white and British. Then there were the Turks. Like I said, I was in Company 1. After the river thawed, they'd let us go down, wash clothes, and take a bath. And

255

after the water warmed some, they'd let us swim. During the first summer, 'round June, the Chinese came in, issued us what they called a student uniform—a white shirt, Mao hat, tennis shoes, pair of white shorts. Lots of us took the Chinese stuff, like paper and dip-type pens, to write propaganda. A lot of 'em took the ink, wrote their names, drew pictures of their states, anything they wanted to, on their shirts."

Bradshaw told the tale like some good ol' boy sitting on his porch telling war stories; his lazy Georgia drawl spoke a simple account of how he remembered what, where, how he came to see it. "One day, water was warmer. Was down there swimmin', some washing clothes, killin' lice, and this boy walked up and said, 'I think I owe you a heck of a lot,' I asked, 'Whatca mean?' He said, 'Think you saved me.' Couldn't remember. He said, 'You'member puttin' maggots in a man's side?' He raised his shirt. I saw the scar. Could put your fist in it, the scar toughened like leather. He'd wrote his name on his shirt, '*Girardin*—G-i-r-a-r-d-i-n.' Told me he'd been with the 24th, remembered he'd been wounded and left for dead, and then captured... around the spot where his unit had gone to pull out the 1st Cav."

The judge notated his pad, lifted his head and waved his hand in Nick's direction. He had no questions. When the emotion had subsided, Nick asked, "Did you see him again?"

"Yes, I did, but we couldn't get together just anytime, because the guards didn't want socializin'." Bradshaw answered, anticipating Nick's question. "The last part of August, it was one of the last times we'd go to the water. If the guards knew that you were from one company, and you were trying to talk, or you're talkin' to another company, they'd split ya up. Tried to keep us segregated. While I was at the river we'd sneak a few, you know, slip a few words. Becomin' real familiar? No."

"Now, can you describe this person's physical appearance?"

"It's hard. First time I saw him he was on the floor. I'd guess he weighed maybe 120 pounds. Skin, bones. Soft eyes. Next time was summer. Heavier, not much. Shorter than me."

"How tall are you?"

"Five-eleven, close to six. I say he was—well—you couldn't say how big the man was, because none of us weighed more than 120, 130 pounds."

"Do you recall the color of his hair?"

"Maybe brown or sort of dark."

Nick held a manila folder with a big green "X" across the front. He removed a picture. "Let me hand you a photo, marked for identification as Plaintiff's Exhibit 106. It's of Roger Girardin, taken just before he departed for Japan in 1950. Is this the man you attended to and then saw on the river?"

Bradshaw studied the picture that had been blown up to the size of the manila folder from which it was removed.

"Sir, is this the first time you have seen this picture?"

"Yes, sir," Bradshaw answered with sureness.

"Mr. Bradshaw, do you recognize the man in that picture?"

"I am sorry, I don't."

"Thank you for your honesty."

Lindquist addressed Nick. "This would be a good place to stop, Counsel. Mr. Harris and Mr. Castalano, see me in chambers to discuss how much time we'll need this afternoon. Clerk, please see me in chambers."

The marshal hollered, "All rise. This honorable court is in recess until 2 p.m."

As had been his habit, Harris rushed out of the courtroom to report to Russell. He picked up the phone, said hello, pressed the speaker button and put the receiver back into the cradle. Before he had a chance to tell Russell he was on the speaker, the man bellowed, "Harris, did you know that fuck Castalano subpoenaed Hamilton?"

"Shit, no."

"Shit, yes. Harris, you are in no way to accede to that clown's attempts to have Hamilton appear."

"Sir, it is not in my purview to tell Castalano who he calls."

"Remember that chess game I told you about? Well maybe it's time to call 'check.' You understand?"

Harris answered, "I don't think that'll work, but let me try to change his mind."

The response on the other end was predictable, "Let me know, or we'll handle it from our side."

Before court reconvened, Harris walked over to Nick. "Nick, a word?"

Nick glanced around, "Sure."

"Look, is subpoenaing Hamilton really necessary?" Harris stood so close that Nick could see a vein pulsing near his temple. "I can't for the life of me understand why he needs to be brought in. He's an important guy. Might be the next governor. Is it worth entangling him in this crap? Frankly, this is going nowhere, even if you prove the man was a POW. I have said it all along, MIA, POW. So what?"

"Are you offering a change of classification if we were to leave Hamilton out?"

"I don't know if we would go that far, but suppose we did?"

"Well, how much would you be willing to tell us about what happened to him?"

"Nick, honestly, we don't know."

"Would you concede for purposes of assessing damages, that he lived another four or five years after the war ended? The family is entitled to something."

"Come on, Nick, you know we couldn't arbitrarily do that. It'd open hundreds of suits from people claiming they're entitled. And I think we're getting ahead of ourselves. Right now, this is about quashing Hamilton's subpoena."

"Quashing it! Are you crazy? He's my witness. You don't represent him."

"Look at it like a good game of chess, Nick. You like chess, don't you? You see, playing the game right can sometimes make the difference between a good business and being stuck above Zorba's, Nick." Harris smiled, showing all his teeth.

"What are you talking about?" bluffed Nick, but vague, discordant images of whisky tumblers, a white gardenia, a chess board, a river, were already floating through his mind.

"Does your wife know you like to play chess?"

Nick stared at Harris for a moment. Were they talking about what he thought they were talking about? The pulsing along Harris's temple had subsided.

"Fuck you, Harris."

At 2 p.m., in his lazy baritone the marshal shouted, "All rise. Court's back in session."

Lindquist appeared in the doorway behind the bench, tired, "Please be seated." His eyes fell on Nick, "Proceed, Counsel."

"No further questions of this witness."

Harris chimed in, "Your honor, I have just a few questions for Mr. Bradshaw."

"Proceed."

"Mr. Bradshaw, you are not a medical doctor, are you?"

"No, sir."

"But, you claim that you can cure people of various ailments, true?"

"No, sir, I don't."

"Sir, isn't it true that you were accused by the local district attorney, in your state of Georgia some years ago for holding yourself out as a physician of sorts?"

"Most of that was made up by him."

"You ran an ad in your local paper, claiming you could cure rheumatoid arthritis, true?"

"Yes, sir, but that was 20 years ago, and—"

"Sir, the local district attorney had you investigated."

"Yes, I think that I'd told him I had these cures I learned from my grandmother."

Harris scored. "I have no further questions of this witness."

Nick, slightly stunned, stood up. "Your Honor, the witness is free to go."

Lindquist announced that trial was being recessed until the following Wednesday because of an unplanned appointment. What he did not disclose was that the appointment was at the Sloan-Kettering Cancer Center.

As the crowd was leaving the courtroom for the day, Nick turned to Art Girardin. "Despite Harris's shots at Bradshaw, I believe that based on Bradshaw's testimony and the reports from the '53 Panmunjom interrogations, we've proven that Roger was a POW."

"Yeah, but what about Jaeger?"

"Okay, contradictory, and the judge has to decide between Bradshaw and Jaeger. They each have their problems."

"And O'Conner, what about him?" Art asked, skeptically.

"His testimony proved nothing, tangential maybe, to indicate a larger context to the story," Nick attested, though inwardly he felt something had been "off" in the witness's testimony.

"You saying we should stop now? Is that it? But, what about my brother?" Art asked pointedly, his large, beefy face noticeably red as he leaned forward, both paws on the table.

Nick came back forcefully. "We've been through this before, Art. My aim, if you recall, was not to solve the mystery of your brother's fate, or why the goddamn government wouldn't acknowledge he was a POW. This suit only considered the narrow issue of whether Roger was a POW, period."

"So what you are telling me is you want to throw in the towel," Art badgered.

"I'm saying we can rest at this point, because I think that on the strength of Bradshaw's testimony we have your brother in Camp 13."

"Yeah, technically, you're right. But what happened, Nick? Don't you want to know? We're talking about a person, a human being! My brother. Could have been *your* brother, anybody's brother. What the hell happened?" Art searched Nick's face.

Nick knew Art was right, but he also knew that Art was unaware of what was going on behind the scenes. Even Nick knew that he himself did not know the half of it. He was just beginning to realize how far the government was willing to go to make sure some secrets stayed that way.

And did Mitch's discovery about the symbols mean Hamilton Helicopters was involved, too?

"Art, we have gone over this before. How far do we take this?"

"Nick, if there is one iota of a chance in finding out what happened, now's the time," Art implored.

"Yes, but at what cost? The money long since ran out."

"That's the difference between this case and the Agent Orange ones, huh? As long as you got paid you worked until you made sure those guys were completely screwed."

"Goddamn it, Art, I resent that. I've given you one-hundred percent, pay or no pay. And what I did for the VA is no business of yours."

Art now sounded apologetic. "You're right, Nick. I'm sorry, you didn't deserve that. But if we can collect from the government back pay or whatever, it's yours. I'll pay what I owe, and sign whatever you want. I promise, you got my word. I just want an answer."

Nick conceded that they were as close as they were ever going to get to discovering what happened to Roger—and hundreds of other soldiers like him—but he needed time to weigh up his next move. He was flat broke. "Let me think about it."

X-Rated

WHEN NICK ARRIVED IN COURT AT 9:50 ON TUESDAY morning, Mitch was waiting for him beside Art Girardin. "Someone left you this on the table." Mitch slid an envelope across the table: *For Attorney Castalano only.*

Nick wedged his finger under the lip of the envelope. Inside, a packet of black and white photos were tied together with an elastic band. He vaguely heard Mitch say something about similarities and topologies and something that sounded like glop, but his attention was focused on the photos. The first was of Nick lying on his back, his shirt unbuttoned, with Rachel, naked, porcelain body, one arm lying on his hairy chest, white leg over his, looking like what he imagined she would look like naked: not a day older than sixteen. There was no need to see the others.

At precisely 10 a.m., the marshal shouted, "All rise. Court's back in session."

Nick slid the photo back into the envelope, looked over towards Harris, who refused to look him in the eye. He had no choice but to collect himself and proceed. Lindquist stood in the doorway behind the bench, looking exhausted. "Please be seated." His eyes fell on Nick and Harris.

"Gentlemen, Judge Fox had an unexpected emergency this morning, and I have agreed to take over his motion docket for the next day or so. I will ask that these proceedings be... " Nick hardly heard Lindquist because the blackmail was absorbing his concentration. Nick hurried out of the courtroom to the pay phone. "Seymour, Nick. Yes, fine, fine. I need to talk to you real quick, in person. Can we meet at five, say on the park bench in front of the Elias Howe monument at Seaside Park? Ok, good. Well, I need some help, and you're probably the only guy... yes, has to do with the trial."

Park Benches and Private Places

LATE IN THE AFTERNOON, NICK MET SEYMOUR on a park bench adjacent to the ocean seawall. Over the sound of crashing waves, Nick thanked Seymour for the impromptu meeting.

"To what do I owe the unexpected pleasure, Nick?"

"I'm in a jam, Seymour. Looks like someone got annoyed when I subpoenaed Trent Hamilton."

He handed Seymour the envelope of photos of Rachel and Nick. "Little present waiting for me yesterday."

As Seymour fumbled open the envelope, he asked, "Wonder why they're so goddamned concerned about this guy testifying?"

"I think it's because he might run for governor, and they don't want him exposed to anything that'll screw up his chances."

"I see," said Seymour, as he rifled through the pictures. He smirked. "Lovely as I remember her, or rather, imagined her."

Nick grimaced, "You think it's funny, and I'm having nightmares."

Freedman took a long drag on a shrinking Lucky, puckered his lips and smiled wryly.

"You know, there's probably not one clean defense contractor in these United States. Every one of them has something buried. Hamilton could prove to be the exception, but I doubt it. Hell, recently they clipped Whitlsey Jet Engines for sending engineering drawings to Japan without clearing them through U.S. Export. Didn't get an export license. Not even the Reds. Deep shit. It doesn't take much to step in it."

"You know, I was about to rest my case. I've taken this as far as I need to prove Girardin was a POW. But you know what? I'm pissed. Fucking pissed. And that they would go this far tells me there's something real big at stake here. How quick can you turn the screws?"

"How about I start cranking tonight?"

Nick was surprised by Seymour's enthusiasm. "Tell me what I owe you for this."

"The Korea connection is the best thing that's happened to me since I left government. You owe me *nada*."

"Then tuck in your shirt, and zip up your fly, for God's sake. What'll people think?"

Freedman smiled, stepped on his cigarette butt, stuffed in his shirt and fixed his pants.

***

That night Nick went home, and as had become routine, he could not sleep. Listening to Diane sleeping, he played out the possibilities. What if the photos were made public? How would he explain to Diane? Over and again without discovering a new way out, until he began to doze. He remembered when Jamie had got lost on a field trip to the Grand Canyon the year before. As Nick feel into a deep sleep, Jamie appeared walking the floor of a canyon of maze-like wonder, a three dimensional world with circuitous trails leading to more trails folding back on its mysterious geometric beauty that had turned deadly. Together, they walked on one of a thousand switchbacks in a desert of brown dust and an ruby sun hanging high in the western sky. A buzzard screaming, "Jack, Mac," flew over vertical crimson cliffs winding for miles from where they saw thousands of marching troops. Hexagons on an unfolding map, a river, that snaked into a blind canyon, wooing them into the canyon's umbilicus, penetrating her inner parts. Nick, his mouth cotton-dry, tried desperately to call out to his son, warn him of thousand footfalls, of minefields, of errant slips, of one's fragile mortality, but each step sank deeper into a sandy earth, and the boy vanished, lost. The night skies twisted beneath a spiraled path in an endlessly alien world, until, finally, step by step, he reached a rim and Jamie turned and smiled, and the sun's rays showered Nick, himself prostrate as if praying to some pantheistic god.

264

Upended

IN THE SHORT TIME SEYMOUR WAS ON THE CASE for the Koreans, they were beholden: he'd managed to pry open doors in Washington that had been shut tight by their indiscretions, both "export and sexport" as he put it. "You don't work in D.C. for a score of years without knowing where the bodies are buried," he told Nick when they met at Zorba's. "Now let's step back and see where Harris is going with these photos of yours. First of all, somebody out there doesn't want Hamilton testifying—probably the man himself."

Nick interrupted, "And so... "

"Let me finish. If you don't call off the dogs, they're dropping the dime over the photos. You need to tell them what you know, and what you're willing to bury if they back off."

"Well, what do we know that will get them to do that?"

"Not a lot, but remember: like blindfolded chess, they don't know how the pieces are arranged on your side. We can bluff our way out."

"Don't keep me in suspense. What the hell'd you find out?"

"Big man Hamilton makes two or three trips a year to India. According to the export records, Hamilton Helicopters uses Mitchell Exporters out of Brooklyn to ship parts to Calcutta, which through an importer are delivered to Crawford, Singh and Sons. Assumption one, Hamilton sees Crawford when he's in India."

"Not enough there," Nick said.

"No, you're right, but my contact—none other than Colonel Park—tells me Crawford, Singh and Sons is a PRC front." A Cheshire cat smile crossed Seymour's face.

"Un-fucking-believable! Hamilton's selling to the Reds?!" Nick could hardly contain his excitement. "Who's Crawford? I mean, who're the principles?"

"Only thing we know is the guy that interfaces with the Chinese is out of Hong Kong, Cho Tat Wah."

"Who?" Nick could not believe he had heard correctly.

Seymour was ready. "Not who. *Wah.* Yup, rings a bell, doesn't it? Cho Tat Wah."

"Wow." Nick was flabbergasted. "Shit, Hamilton's in bed with Cho, commandant of Camp 13." When he had recovered his composure, he asked, "And after this, there's a 'second of all?' You said, 'first of all.'"

"Oh yeah, right," Seymour responded. "Second of all, don't think this is just about protecting Trent Hamilton's political ambitions."

Nick grimaced, "What're you saying, Seymour?"

"Think, Nick. Who risks most if it comes to light that Trent Hamilton has been cozy with Cho Tat Wah?"

"You mean since Camp 13?"

"Oh, that may have been the root, but no, I mean when Hamilton and Cho Tat Wah linked up in the late 60s, these despicable bastards needed a confederate right here in the good ole U.S. of A.—someone who knew how to turn the crank to make the wheels go round. Things don't happen like this unless all the parts are engaged. All at a price, I'm sure."

"Have anyone in mind?" Nick asked.

"Not a clue... yet."

Nick sat back, the enormity was beginning to sink in.

Freedman lit up a cigarette. His eyebrows moved nervously. "Nick, here's what I suggest. You call Harris, tell him you want to meet. Only the two of you. Do it off-campus. The coffee shop next to the courthouse. Get close to him. Whisper in his fucking ear. You tell him that you're about to subpoena records from Mitchell Exporters that will trace parts to Crawford. Since he knows you were in Korea, you tell him that you got a witness at the highest level of the Korean government that will testify or supply an affidavit that Crawford's a Chinese military front."

Nick thought he saw the flaw in the strategy. "Yeah, but if I were to try and get into this at trial, he would have objected on relevancy grounds. It's collateral... presuming, of course, Hamilton would deny the connection between HH and Crawford. Harris'd know this."

Seymour blew smoke in Nick's face. "Nick, you're missing the goddamn point. These guys can't risk it. The downside's fucking explosive. I know this is BS, but he can't take that chance. If they went through the trouble of tracking you down in Korea, they know you met with the ROK, they know I was there for Christ's sake. They know who I am. They're not going to risk it."

He took a deep drag. "They know that they better not miscalculate what we can do."

"Yeah, I suppose you're right." Nick shook his head slowly.

"Even if you couldn't get it in at trial, they'd be afraid of *someone* raising the matter before the Commerce Department. The last time I checked, Red China's still on the *"Commerce Control List"* as a country that requires a license. And for military use parts? Well, there're no such licenses I know of. This ain't a case of being de-listed at the defense department, it's jail time, espionage, all that shit." Freedman scripted it like he was screenwriting for a James Bond movie.

"So, I tell Harris I have this info. He'll be shit-faced when he figures his own skin's in the game. He'd have knowledge of possible criminal activity, espionage... he's a federal fucking lawyer working for the Justice Department. He's going to have to deal with that. Second, he'll figure that if they continue to hold the pictures over me that this thing can blossom into something that might bring Hamilton and his company to their knees."

Freedman lit another cigarette. "Checkmate, as we say."

Tightening the String

IN '67 JOHN PARKERSFIELD, CONNECTICUT'S JUNIOR senator, met Tracy Hamilton, by then an attractive, thirty-seven-year-old, unmarried socialite. Parkersfield found her lovely, charming and well informed about business and politics. Despite being married, Parkersfield often invited Tracy to dinner when he visited Palm Beach alone. The following year he filed for divorce. Six months later, he and Tracy married. The year was 1969. Parkersfield followed his young millionaire wife back to Fairview, and in 1972 Parkersfield left politics and went to work for HH as a lobbyist, helping the Defense Department put Hamilton into foreign markets. Meanwhile, Tracy remained, together with Trent, co-chair of Hamilton's Board of Directors.

After Harris met with Nick, he called Russell to tell him that the attempt to intimidate Nick had failed. In fact, it had backfired—big time. Russell called Trent about the scenario Nick had painted for Harris. Trent, in turn, called a meeting to prepare Tracy and her husband for any potential blow-back if he could not keep things from mushrooming. What Tracy and Parkersfield knew about Crawford was that it was the company's agent throughout Southeast Asia, nothing more. Trent had intentionally kept it that way. What Parkersfield and Tracy did not know was that Russell pulled the strings, allowing the technology to fall into the hands of Crawford. Russell had his own special password to a sub-account at Disraeli Bank of Zurich, for those occasions when a deposit was made on behalf of an Indian subsidiary by a Hong Kong limited liability corporation.

Trent knew Russell had no limits when it came to stopping anyone dead in their tracks if it threatened him or his account. If the Girardin case continued to draw

Hamilton closer, Russell himself might be dragged in. And he was still considered a dark horse for the Secretary of Defense. As he said to Trent, the entire matter was "... spinning dangerously out of control," adding, "something extraordinary might have to be considered." Russell's protection of Hamilton only ran as deep as the protection the man afforded himself. If anyone, including Hamilton, was a liability, then he needed to be separated out, and he would move swiftly to do so.

Respite and Tranquility

LINDQUIST HAD NEVER MET TRENT HAMILTON but knew him by reputation in state politics and as a Yankee patrician whose pockets were lined with old money. Such a man was consulted before anything politically important happened, such as who ran for high state office. Certainly Hamilton would be a factor in which district court judges were nominated for the Second Circuit Court of Appeals. Yes, Lindquist knew well how much a judge was willing to exercise his power in the face of forces that influenced the course of a career.

Nick looked at his watch. It was nearly 2:30 p.m. The afternoon crowd streamed into the courthouse. Harris sat, head on his chest, hands alternately pulling on his fingers until they snapped—resigned to the inevitable blowback from Hamilton's appearance. Lindquist called the afternoon into session and instructed Nick to proceed.

"Your Honor, plaintiff calls Mr. Trent Hamilton to the stand." Nick had never laid eyes on Hamilton until now, following the 6'4", steely-blue eyed, big headed man with the thinning crop of light brown hair as he opened the gate between the gallery and the bar. He wore an Armani gray tailored suit, French cuffs, gold links and a smooth, red silk tie with a perfect Windsor knot. He strode across the well, the sounds from his fresh leathered soles snapping off the walls like a drum roll announcing the man about whom people spoke in the same breath as 'our next candidate for governor.' He assumed the stand and stoically faced the crowd. The clerk swore him in. Nick began in a moderately cordial tone. "Mr. Hamilton, thank you for taking time out of your busy schedule to help us with this matter, the matter regarding Roger Girardin."

Hamilton stiffened his jaw. "I will help where I can," he answered, barely able to contain his rage.

"Mr. Hamilton, can you tell the court your occupation?"

"I'm the CEO of Hamilton Helicopters," he snapped, staring menacingly at Nick.

"Located where?"

Hamilton's face showed a tinge of red. "Our main location is here in the south end of Bridgeport."

"And how long have you been with the company?"

With a slight lift of his jowl, he answered. "Since, well, since my family bought it around 1950."

"Sir, you are a veteran of the Korean War, are you not?"

Trent sat back in the chair. "Yes, June '50 to October '53."

"Mr. Hamilton, I am going to ask you some questions about your service. You should know that I've had an opportunity to review your impressive service record, which I mention because if you need to refresh your memory on a point I have the record here."

Hamilton's face relaxed, the redness disappeared. "Thank you, I do not think I will need it."

"What outfit were you with?"

"The 8240th Army Unit Headquarters X Corp Intelligence. I also was with a unit that did special forces type work."

"Weren't the special forces started in'51 or '52?"

"Yes. In 1950, we actually were part of a program that later on, in '52, was formalized. I believe, but don't quote me here, part of the program became the Psychological Warfare Center at Fort Bragg, North Carolina. I was with CIC, or the Counter Intelligence Corp."

"Were you part of any Army division?"

"The 8240th combined with command recon activities, which assumed responsibility for behind-the-lines activities, that is intelligence and special operations."

"What did special forces—or I guess CIC—do, exactly?"

"We had different kinds of missions. For example, training partisans in sabotage or laying anti-personnel mines behind the lines. Other missions included operations to contact prisoners in POW camps, establishing escape and evasion routes from the camps. In some instances we worked with the CIA in covert ops."

"Were there any other assignments, such as unusual investigations, covert activities against insurgents?"

271

Harris inserted himself into the proceedings. "Your Honor, please remind the witness that he is not to offer testimony regarding any confidential or secret military operations or information."

Lindquist understood, the government having stressed this in the early days of the litigation. "Yes, Mr. Hamilton, if you believe that any question will require you to divulge any state secret, please tell me in advance and we will retire to my chambers for further inquiry."

Hamilton nodded. "Yes. Well, sir, I was about to say, 'nothing comes to mind.'"

Nick continued. "So you worked behind the lines?"

"Yes, we had various missions, mostly behind the enemy lines." Hamilton answered.

"There came a time when the enemy captured you, is that not true?"

"Yes."

"Can you tell the court what led up to your capture?"

"Yes, it happened on my second mission behind the lines. August '52. A squad of about ten paratroopers parachuted in near the Yalu River Estuary, a bunch of islands there. Raining. We were to surveillance what we could of troop movements and supervise the ROK laying of minefields on a road of strategic importance to the enemy."

As with all the previous witnesses, the room became eerily stilled when the subject turned to the events leading to a soldier's capture. "We worked laying mines for a few days. But, apparently, one of the chutes wasn't buried well after we'd landed. The Chinese spotted it. The area became infested with NK. One by one, we were captured. I held out for a day or two but was eventually found."

"What happened next?"

"Tied my hands behind my back, marched off a few miles north to what I later learned was Camp 13."

"When you got there, did you see anybody from your unit?"

"No, the men were segregated—officers in one place, noncoms and grunts in another."

"Did you not find it odd that you didn't see anybody from your squad?"

"At first, but after a while you don't think about it."

"Did you consider that maybe they were killed?"

"Yes, I suppose things like that go through your head, but I would've heard that if it were in the minefield area." Hamilton no longer showed signs of his earlier outright fury.

"You joined the service with a man named Jack O'Conner, is that not so?"

"Yes, that's right." Hamilton looked at his hands.

"And did you go to Korea with Mr. O'Conner?"

"No, sir. Jack and I joined up as ROTC officers. But Jack was, well how'd you say it? Washed out."

"Did you see Jack after that in either the U.S. or in Korea?"

"Yes, sir, in Korea."

"Where and under what circumstances?"

"We were POWs in the same camp, although we rarely saw one another. I was an officer and being that he was enlisted... well, I saw him from a distance, and we'd wave, but that was it."

"Did you see Mr. O'Conner after the war?"

"Yes, I gave him a job after we got back from Korea. Maybe 1955."

"Does he still work there?"

"No, he left several years ago. Think he quit in '72–'75 timeframe."

"Do you maintain any connection, now?"

"No, when he left I lost touch. Actually I hardly ever saw him even during the years he worked for Hamilton."

"Sir, you were in Camp 13 from the time of your capture through your repatriation in September 1953?"

"Yes, sir, I was one of the last to get out of the camp," Hamilton answered, a hint of snootiness in his tone.

"Why is that, sir?"

"Because I was, informally at least, the administrator of the Americans.

"What do you mean informally?"

"The Chinese put me in charge."

To provoke Hamilton, Nick asked, "I would have thought the highest ranking officer would've been in charge?"

273

"Well the highest rank was in charge of the troops, but I was in the dayroom. I spoke Chinese," he answered smugly. Then with an air of accountability he continued, "They'd funnel various things through me. I'd communicate them to Colonel Levine. He was the highest ranking officer among us, until he was transferred. But for most purposes, you might say I was the lead man."

"And when was he transferred, if you know?"

"Don't recall."

"But you stayed, did you not?"

"Yes." Hamilton looked at his watch.

"Who precisely put you in charge. What was his name?"

"Don't remember."

"What was his position?"

Hamilton offered little. "Commandant, maybe."

"What was his rank?"

"Not sure, equivalent. Colonel maybe."

"Again, do you know why they selected you to remain?"

Not intending to be overly cooperative, Hamilton remained brusque. "I could only speculate."

"Speculate then."

"Objection," yelled Harris.

Nick came back quickly, "Strike that. Why did you believe that they kept you?"

Irritated now, he answered. "I spoke Chinese, and in that way I could act as a go between."

"Did you get to know most of the troops in the camp?"

"Well, some, but there were too many. But I've always been good with names, and even if I don't remember them now, if you were to mention someone I might recall."

"Roger Girardin."

Hamilton looked into the crowd, past Nick. "No, not him, not at Camp 13."

Nick waited for a second to see if the witness blinked, but instead Hamilton reached for his pitcher, poured a glass of water and turned the glass around—inspecting the water's clarity. Nick slowly turned to Harris, but he refused to return his look or to see Nick's raised eyebrow. But there wasn't much Nick could do about it.

"Sir, if you saw Roger in Camp 13, you would've recognized him? Is that true?"

"Objection, your Honor, speculation."

"Strike that."

Nick handed Hamilton a photo. "Sir, here is a picture of Private Girardin just before he shipped out to Japan taken the summer of 1950. Do you recognize that man?"

Hamilton studied the picture. "I have never seen this man."

"Sir, did you not know that Roger Girardin dated Jack O'Conner's sister before the war?"

"He may have, but that was thirty years and two wars ago. I can't be expected to remember that far back, and in any case I did not socialize with Jack's family."

"Mr. Hamilton, did you know any men named Girardin while you were in the service?"

"There was one, his name was Milton. Pronounced his last name Jerdin, but I think he spelled it with a soft "G." I'm not absolutely sure on the spelling. Ran into him. I do not have a clear recollection of which it was."

"Mr. Hamilton, did any government lawyers brief you on this point?"

"Mr. Harris may have mentioned the name, but that's it."

Harris reached for his glass, tipped it over and spilled water on his paisley tie. He quickly brushed it off . Nick and the judge looked in his direction. He stood up and pulled out his silver pocket watch. "Your Honor, defendant would ask that we take a short break at this time."

Lindquist's eyes moved to the wall clock and agreed, "Yes, Counsel, we have run over our usual morning break."

Trent and Anna stood up at the same time. She looked at him leaving the witness stand to stretch his legs. She saw him look toward the back of the courtroom where she was sitting and recalibrated the image she'd carried for thirty years. Although now he had the full grown body of a fifty-seven-year-old, he still resembled the boy she had known. She asked Julie, "Do you think he recognizes me? He's looking over here again. I don't think he... "

275

Instead of answering Anna, Julie asked, "Why do you think that Jack and Trent never picked up on their friendship after they came home?"

Anna never told her sister-in-law that William was Trent's son, and naïvely she did not think that Jack told her either. "I don't know, guess some things don't last." Anna knew their separation was not a simple one, not of boys growing into men, men going to war, diverting lives due to career choices or geography. No, they separated because their lives were so intertwined. The plain fact was that they had a friendship, which was inseparable in college, and then afterward, based on mutual self-interest —parasitic perhaps—winding around one another, growing like tangled banyan trees in a hairy contemptuous swamp over the course of many years, too complicated even for close friends to understand or untwist. She could not see what had played out in Camp 13, but she saw the fleeting guilt in Trent's eyes for his transgressions before he joined the Army in that instant when their eyes met and he hesitated and quickly turned away. She found it hard to believe that he was the man to whom she gave the sweetness of her youth, but she never regretted it either. After all, as she often thought, without Trent, Will would never have been born.

Red Hot Cold War

THE SUMMER OF '68 FOLLOWING HIGH SCHOOL graduation, Trent's other son, William O'Conner ventured to California partly to spread his wings and partly to join in one war protest or another—there were hundreds to choose from. Before leaving, he told Jack "Most of these kids being drafted are victims of the power elites who prey on boys, poor kids, most with no way forward." He and the many young men and women like him were not bystanders: they stood against war and the establishment. They searched for an answer to why America was in Vietnam or why blacks were burning down ghettos. Many ended up finding a new direction, a new despair, or a new drug: marijuana, cocaine, heroin or LSD. William tired of the California scene, returning in September '69 to attend St. Johns University. But the following year, he quit—partly because he could not afford it and partly because his grades were dismal. He returned to Bridgeport. By the following January, he had yet to enroll in college again. In early March, he received a draft notice ordering him to report for a physical on April 26. He immediately tried to enroll in college and reapply for a deferment.

Jack was working for HH when Will told him about the draft notice. Trent was spending most of his time at the bank. Jack rarely, if ever, ran into him. He made two attempts to have Trent, an influential member of the draft board, help with the deferment. His old friend and boss did not return the calls. Finally, Jack went to the bank in late March and asked him to pull some strings; after all, he was Chairman of the local draft board. Trent was polite to his old college buddy, war buddy and senior employee of one of his major investments. And although they never spoke about it, there was the paternity connection. They parted on a hearty handshake, and Jack thought that he had succeeded in postponing Will's military service. When Jack learned that William's deferment did not materialize, he tried calling Trent, and discovered to his grim disappointment that Trent was in India selling helicopter parts—in all likelihood returning too late to do anything to divert the army's intention to induct Will.

***

When Jack could not reach Trent, he went to Father Ryan in hopes that he had some advice. After explaining his situation, Ryan did not think he could be of much help, explaining that he had received one or two calls a month about the draft, and after a few attempts at exerting a subtle ecclesiastical influence on a particular member of the draft board, the bishop told him to keep his nose out of things that weren't God's business. Jack sat, head bowed, ready to accept the inevitable.

"Vietnam, Father, Vietnam. What in hell is it?"

Ryan kept his feelings in check rather than make Jack feel worse than he did. He did not answer.

"Father, it's odd that soldiers hate war, what it stands for, more than anyone—unless they're insane. But they also justify what they've done when it's over."

"Yes, and many of those—especially when they get old—will tell you service during war was their greatest achievement. There's this need to justify why we've been put on this earth."

The men sat quietly. "What should I do, then, just accept Will's situation?"

"Jack, Will knows a little about mechanics. Send him down to the Army recruiter. I know the guy. I'll call. Let's see if they won't take him. Send him where he'll be out of harm's way."

***

Will was trained at Fort Wolters in Texas to fly helicopters. By the time he had graduated from flight school, he had gained a reputation for knowing about helicopter mechanics, owed in no small measure to working summer's at Hamilton Helicopters. Instead of being shipped to Vietnam, he was sent on a temporary duty assignment to Japan where he worked with Fuji Heavy Industries outside of Tokyo. They were developing

278

modifications to the Huey UH1-J, a derivation of the craft he had learned to fly. Six months after arriving in Japan, he received orders for Vietnam.

In 1970, Warrant Officer William O'Conner went to Vietnam to fly helicopters, while Anna and Jack watched the war, like the rest of America, through the nightly news projected on the TV.

Irrevocable Truths

IN THEIR UNIVERSE, A TWENTY-FIVE watt bulb in the middle of the room supplied illumination when the lights dimmed on the tiny Christmas tree lamps that shone through the cellophane windows of little cardboard houses. The Lionel train ran in a continuous circle. All was well in the manufactured town Jack and Will had assembled in the basement. Upstairs, the doorbell rang.

Anna answered and an army chaplain asked, "Mrs. O'Conner?"

"Yes?"

"I am here from the Army and regret—"

Anna screamed.

But, the truth, having been suddenly coiled, irrevocably wound into every fiber of her existence and could not be unwound, by Man, Nature or God. Jack, hearing her shrieks, ran upstairs from the cellar. When the chaplain left, the parents remained clutched until their mind, spirits and bodies deflated. They talked, sobbed, bawled how they would make it through the night, how they would live on. How they would tell their daughter Mona that Will was dead.

Sometime after the second hour, Jack went back to the cellar. The train was still circling. He remembered the hours that turned into days that turned into years. Will and he laid track. They built neighborhoods. They made platforms of plywood to satisfy their passion for railroading. They built trestles from tiny balsam beams—a quarter inch wide and three inches long—piece by piece, each a truss in the trestle engineered for the locomotive to make its way up the grade. Plaster sidewalks a quarter-inch high curbed streets dotted with cardboard houses. The leaded inhabitants living affluent lives raising children —posed in a solitary positions. A rubber brontosaurus and a plastic dragon Will had placed in the town square and left there by Jack so he would never forget Will's sense of fantasy—or as a reminder that dinosaurs and dragons might stave off enemies that could disturb the sanctuary of Toyland. Here, even the appearance of movement was an illusion; the locomotive's headlight cast on a wall never went anywhere, except in Jack and Will's imagination. Yes, here life was static. What the man and boy could not control in life, they controlled in the miniaturized train towns sprawled across the basement. This would be the land Jack would fashion. If he were God.

At a friend's house for the night, Mona would be told when she returned in the morning. Having called Mary, Charlie and Julie, Anna went to bed. Jack consumed half a fifth of J&B by 10 p.m. About 11 p.m. he felt the urge to tell Trent. Drunk as he was, he drove north to Fairview, heading for the mansion—a place he had not seen since the night the Hamiltons threw the farewell.

The hills and valleys were now grey images on the eastern side of the Ford as it climbed the final quarter mile of the long hill, past a vacant roadside stand that led to the drive at the foot of the mansion's front steps. The moon was high in a sky filled with cirrus clouds. It called to mind his youthful memory of the yellow color that had bathed the Hamilton estate the night he said goodbye to Tracy. He parked in the same place he parked twenty years earlier. He walked to the front entrance. Jack heard music and remembered the sounds of twenty years ago. A butler greeted him.

"Yes, may I help you?"

The butler took Jack's measure. Eyes bloodshot. A drunken man in a worn out flannel shirt struggling to keep his balance.

"Tell Trent Jack O'Conner's here to see him."

"Sir, he is not available right now."

"Tell him that Jack's here," he repeated. "He'll wanna see me."

"Wait here."

Trent appeared at the front door.

"Jack, what the hell you doing here?"

"Will is dead!"

Jack could see a flicker of doubt cross Trent's face, but it was gone in an instant—the perfect host was back. "What! Oh God, Jack... I am sorry, so sorry. What happened, for Christ's sake? Come in, let's go to the library."

It wasn't what Jack wanted, how he had thought it out in his mind, but he could not think it all out anymore. He followed Trent into house. Musicians surrounded a piano, people mingled with drinks in their hands. His eyes glanced beyond the players. On the veranda, guests were caught up in small talk. Maids in white housedresses circulated. Things were as he'd pictured it so many times since that last night so long ago.

In the library, a Doberman stood next to an easy chair. "He's okay, long as I'm here," Trent said as he poured two drinks. Coolly, he asked, "How's Anna taking it?"

"Anna?" The thought inflamed Jack, "For Christ's sake, man, your son just died."

"Look, Jack, you're upset," Trent said, "Nothing's going to bring the boy back."

"The boy! The boy? His name's William, William. That's his name... Trent... remember? William. One of the dozens you left in your wake—like Anna, like Dawn, Roger... me."

Trent cocked his head. "You keeping score, Jack?"

"Yeah, I've kept score. I've kept score goddamn it."

"Who the hell is Roger, or Dawn?"

"Trent, you killed them, don't you remember? You killed 'em, and... you can't even remember their names. Goddamn—can't even remember their names."

"You're talking crazy, Jack. I never left anyone in any wake, and certainly not you, for Christ's sake. You'd still be in Manchuria, buried, if it wasn't for me. Or behind some press on a factory floor, if I didn't prop you up all these years!"

"Fuck you, Trent!" Jack screamed. "You, my great benefactor, my great savior."

"Jack, calm down or you'll have to leave. I have some important people out there."

The room went silent. The vacuum of non-response was filled by the muffled sounds of the music and the din of cocktail conversation behind the oak door.

Jack put his face in his hands and began to sob. "No, nothing's going to bring him back. I know. But you could've kept him from going in the first place."

"Me? Me, Jack... I had no control."

Jack looked up at Trent now standing by the bar. "You've always been in control, you were on the *fucking draft board*," Jack howled.

Jack's face was beet red, the wild-eyed look of a man about to explode. Trent reached into his breast pocket and pulled out a leather wallet. He opened it and reached for a pen on the bar. "Jack, I have to get back outside, but let me help you and Anna out—there'll be expenses."

Jack sneered. "You bastard, you goddamn bastard. You always have a way of skating free. But, you're not free on this one. You're not free. I don't want your fucking money, you hear me? You're not free," he yelled, in full rage as he catapulted from his chair, hitting Trent square in the chest. Knocking him against the bar, knocking two stools to the floor. "Keep your motherfuckin' checkbook." The doberman stood up, but stayed put.

The library door opened. Jack spotted Tracy dressed in a sequined crinoline cocktail dress, walking quickly, Grecian-like, toward the central foyer. He had not seen her since the night before they had left for the Army. She stopped at the doorway, half hiding behind a man in a black dinner jacket. With fire in his eyes, Jack gazed at her and figured she did not recognize him. Then she turned her lips pretentiously in the way she had twenty years earlier, and his heart jumped. She reached into her purse for her glasses, but he was already heading for the front door. He turned to take a final look as the crowd drew closer, and he saw Tracy putting her glasses back in her purse.

***

Six-months after Will's death, Jack lay in a hospital bed, staring at a flaking wall. His eyes shifted to a fan wobbling off-center over his head. An ebony brown orderly, with snow white hair, stood a few feet away and asked in a Jamaican accent, "Heh mon, you comfortable?"

"Yeah, but where the hell am I?"

"VA hospital."

"VA? What the hell am I doin' here?"

The orderly walked toward a door with a small wire mesh window. "Doc will be in, in a few minutes."

Ten minutes later a balding, middle aged man in a white smock walked in.

"Jack, good to see you're awake. I'm Doctor Kaspersky."

"Why am I here?"

"You were admitted last week after an episode. Remember?"

"Remember what?"

The doctor filled in the details. A week earlier, Jack had complained to Anna he hadn't slept in days, kept awake by nightmares where men threatened to chop off his hands. The dreams were as real as if he were awake. "Jack, your wife said that over the past few weeks she's heard you talking to someone in the basement, where you have toy trains. You took an axe to the layout. Destroyed it. You're suffering from a psychosis. Probably something brought on by your son's death. Treatable, for sure. We have you on a new medication."

Memories Fast Forward

NICK'S BULL-LIKE RESOLVE TO GET TO THE BOTTOM of Girardin's whereabouts, focused on Hamilton's evasiveness. "Did you know of any POWs that did not return, sir?"

"Yes, I suppose I knew many," Hamilton said coldly.

"Do you know if any soldiers were murdered, shot, hanged, committed suicide? Or died while working at the camp—you know, heart attack, appendicitis... blown up in a minefield?"

Hamilton looked down, biting his lower lip. "Well, let me think, we had a few suicides and a fight in the Turkish barracks. Someone was killed. But no, I did not know of any odd deaths. Many died of pneumonia, dysentery. Most GIs died before I got there—this happened after they were first captured. Late '50, the whole of '51."

"What about GIs trying to escape?"

Hamilton's eyes shifted side-to-side, "No, not that I recall."

"Do you know if there was an escape route leading from the Camp 13 south?"

"Could have been."

"I am going to show you Plaintiff's Exhibit B-1, which had been previously marked for identification. Look at the easel. Have you seen anything like this map before?"

Hamilton glanced at the map. "Please feel free to walk over." Hamilton walked to the easel. He studied the map.

The crowd shuffled, a few coughed and others whispered. The noise steadily increased until Lindquist brought the gavel down. "Quiet, please."

After roughly two minutes of doodling on his yellow pad, Lindquist pulled his eyebrows together. "Is this the first time you have seen this, Mr. Hamilton?"

Hamilton blinked several times before glancing at Harris, "Yes, sir."

Nick caught the contact between the men and moved around Hamilton to put another map on the easel.

"Have you ever seen this map?"

Lindquist interrupted again. "Number, please?"

"B-2, your Honor."

Hamilton, moved his finger in the air from side-to-side. "It shows an obvious route leading south from Camp 13, down the east coast."

"Would you know what this hex mark means?"

Hamilton kept his eyes on the map. "No."

"Have you ever seen such a mark?"

"No."

Lindquist felt tired. He turned to Nick, "Counsel, are you going to be much longer?"

"Yes, sir, a bit. But given the lateness of the hour, I can recall this witness when we reconvene tomorrow?"

Turning to Harris, "Any objection, Counsel?"

"No, your Honor."

"Mr. Hamilton, can you be here tomorrow at ten?"

Hamilton pulled his lips taut, "Fine, yes, I can be here."

"Very well, this court is adjourned until tomorrow morning at ten."

As Nick and Mitch walked toward the exit, Mitch mentioned to Nick, "I never saw Hamilton before, but he looks vaguely familiar."

"Probably saw his picture on TV or in the newspaper when you were at the library."

"Maybe, more recently than that... I have to think about it."

***

During Hamilton's testimony Harris had been slipped a note that Russell wanted a call as soon as possible. He and Foster rushed upstairs, closed the office door and had the secretary put the call through.

Foster yelled into the phone anxiously, "I have you on the speaker, Mr. Secretary."

Before Harris could finish saying hello, Russell bellowed, "Listen, the goddamn papers turned up."

Harris looked at Foster, "Papers? You mean the orders? I thought they were secret."

"Yeah. Well, somebody is playing fucking games with us."

Harris looked out the window. "Do you have a copy?"

"I do."

"What's it say?"

"Turn the speaker off and pick up the goddamn phone."

"Go ahead," Harris said.

"Well it says:

'September 30, 1950, CIA, U.S. Embassy, Seoul: Top Secret. Arrest without delay Private Roger Girardin and Staff Sergeant Joseph Johns, 1st Battalion, 21st Regiment, 24th Infantry Division. Confiscate all cameras and film... '"

When he finished reading, Harris said, "Well, we're going to have to bring this to Lindquist, get it under the standing secrecy order." He expected no argument on the necessity for disclosing.

"Bullshit. It doesn't exist, you hear me?" hollered Russell on the other end.

"Sir, but... "

"Harris, it does not exist. Do you hear me? Do you have the slightest idea what we are trying to steer clear of?" Russell demanded.

"Yes, Mr. Secretary, but... "

The phone went dead.

***

What Russell had refused to share with Harris was that following a briefing in Seoul, the Barclay Task force, Lieutenant Colonel Barclay, Captain Reiner and CIA operative Perrone set out for points north in the direction of the Eighth Army's 24th Division. By the third week in November, they had reached the Ch'ongch'on River. The ice that had formed in large swaths had begun to bridge the opposing banks. The ice, rain, snow and the sub-zero winds blowing in from the Asian hinterland solidified anything that did not move. The three men eventually arrived at 24th Division Headquarters and informed the brass that they were there to return Privates Johns and Girardin to Seoul for questioning.

Complicating the assignment was that the NK and the CCF were fiercely defending the valley and the surrounding hills. The 8th Army, 24th Division, 19th Regiment was taking heavy casualties and started falling back. The month of November slipped away. The CCF rounded up more and more Americans, and when it was clear that the U.N. forces were in full retreat toward the 38th parallel, the three man posse headed back to the embassy in Seoul. They reached their intended destination a few days before Christmas. Notably, the men were not relieved of the powers that went with the mission to arrest and, if necessary, keep Roger Girardin and Joe Johns from telling anyone of the atrocity they had witnessed. In fact, when they returned to HQ, they debriefed an entire squad of intelligence officers in the hope of expanding the search rather than abandoning it. One of the officers at the debriefing was Trent Hamilton, who recognized the name Roger Girardin and could only imagine that it was the guy he knew from back home —a guy with whom he had a score to settle, and now doubly so.

In closing, CIA operative Robert Perrone said, "And remember, confiscate any film they may have in their possession, regardless of how the apprehension goes."

"Suppose they're not in a position to be returned?" Hamilton asked.

The CIA operative answered assertively. "Use your discretion. These men cannot and will not fall into enemy hands, period."

"What's that mean, exactly?" Hamilton persisted.

"Do I have to paint a picture, Lieutenant?"

Out of the Blue

AFTER NICK LEFT COURT THAT DAY HE WENT back to his office to catch up on some work. As he turned the key, the phone rang. Nick figured Diane wanted to know when to expect him for supper, but when he answered a man started shouting something barely comprehensible about being a vet. Nick considered hanging up, except between mentioning the Girardin case at the top of his voice and moments of labored breathing, he said his name was Kenny Preston—the man, besides Montoya, on the Broadbent list who was unaccounted for. The man sounded drunk, although claimed he was sick, but what he told Nick could have a potentially explosive impact. He decided to accept the man's claims at face value, until Nick asked him what he had done before he had gotten sick.

The man slurred his answer, "Twenty-t'ree years was a... milling machine operator."

"For who?"

"Aah, t'was a... Hudson Valley Machine Shop, near Albany."

"Can I ask what's ailing you?"

"Cancer, goddamn cancer caused by the metal."

"What do you mean, 'metal?'"

"Worked beryllium, made parts for copters, companies like Bell, Sikorsky and a company down your neck of the woods—Hamilton."

"Hamilton?"

"Yeah, same company as that guy that testified at your trial."

"Do you remember him from Korea?"

"Not sure, but his company signed me a death warrant; they knew those parts caused cancer, those sons-a-bitches."

Nick thought about Preston's timely call, his possible motivations, but had to go the next step.

"Mr. Preston, if you can get here by Monday, I'll put you up overnight. Is that possible? And, depending on how things go, I might like you to testify on Tuesday. What do you think?"

"My daughter will drive me down Monday morning. Should get there around noon."

Nick, was feeling buoyed by the call, but when Preston hung up, Nick heard a click in the receiver that sent a chill through his body.

An Unscheduled Summit

ART GIRARDIN BELIEVED THAT THE GOVERNMENT had conspired for political reasons to cover up his brother's disappearance, along with that of the other 450 missing POWs. Nick, while he still wasn't one hundred percent convinced, was more interested in *motive*. Nick knew the CIA had intervened on more than one occasion when he had subpoenaed records he thought had bearing on the case, but he did not know *why* the CIA maintained its interest in a matter that occurred thirty years ago. In more than one instance, like the Broadbent report, Harris claimed a state secrets privilege. Lindquist reviewed documents, *in camera*, denying Nick access to most of the documents. There were a string of coincidences that defied explanation, such as Sonny Reiner's untimely death a mere three days after meeting with perhaps Army agents. Could they all be coincidences? Nick wondered. But for all the thousands of documents Nick reviewed for the case, and for all the witnesses he interviewed, none was more revealing than a meeting with Ambassador J. Rufus Jefferson, from the U.S. State Department earlier that week.

Seymour Freedman had invited Nick to a joint regional National Security Agency/American Bar Association meeting at the Carlisle Hotel in New York City. Much to his surprise, the meeting host introduced the ambassador by saying that he had been a negotiator at Panmunjom in 1953. After a talk on the subject of Chinese and American strategic interests, he made an abrupt exit, telling his audience he had to testify in Washington the following morning. Nick ran out and cornered him in the lobby, telling him in a nutshell what the Girardin case concerned. The ambassador was to the point.

"A large number of POWs were not returned. Why? Well, that's complicated." He told Nick that the particular

291

answers he needed were not in the United States. Being the diplomat that he was, he hinted that there were venues where Nick would find others more open.

On the ride back to Connecticut that night, Nick told Freedman what Jefferson had told him. Freedman said that he was planning a trip to Seoul to exercise a long standing invitation to the Blue House. "Nick, the people you're dealing with are powerful and rich. They use bogeymen that end in'ation.'You know, we fight for nation, democratization and monetization. Be careful, Nick, these men are treacherous; they don't give a rat's ass. They have a lot to protect and hide."

Freedman told Nick that he had met with the highest levels in the government during his visits to Korea. "They were pleased with my efforts to link them up with the right people, especially after I fixed the licensing problem. They also feel indebted to you Nick. After all, you orchestrated all of this—at least, in the beginning.

The next day Freedman called Nick to tell him that they had been invited to the Korean Embassy in D.C. the following week to talk to Jong Lee, one of Yoo's administrative assistants.

Freedman and Castalano boarded Amtrak to Washington the next week and met with Jong Lee who opened the conversation.

"Yes, the ambassador was correct, many men were not returned. As the Armistice approached, the North Koreans were increasingly agitated over the U.N.'s unwillingness to force the 40,000 North Korean POWs and defectors to return home. Korean soldiers on both sides had families on both sides of the DMZ. Given a choice, many of their soldiers desired to remain in the South. The NK accused the ROK of breaching the deal with the POW repatriation. When Big Switch came, the North Koreans retaliated and refused to release hundreds of U.S. soldiers. Our governments kept this secret since the Armistice."

Nick slumped in his chair, stunned that Lee would so matter-of-factly reveal something Nick couldn't get anybody to talk about for years.

"When we reached the Armistice in June '53, casualties were almost three million dead, over one-hundred thousand American casualties, thirty-five thousand dead. We did all we could, but short of resuming hostilities, the subject was best left to the post-war negotiations, which failed."

"You have no idea what happened to them?" Nick asked incredulously.

"Some of them, not all. We know that at least sixty men were executed at a place called Death Valley."

"And you're telling me that our government knew this?"

"I am afraid so. But I must caution you: this cannot be disclosed at this time, since it would present an embarrassment that even your Mr. Freedman could not fix."

Nick offered what he knew. "South Koreans opposed the truce negotiated by the U.S. and its allies. I read that in June '53, nearly twenty thousand North Korean POWs stormed the barbed-wire fences. Security had apparently disappeared. The soldiers quickly mingled with the locals who were quite willing to provide shelter. The allies, concerned that the North would call off the Armistice, issued their own spin on what happened. General Clark's headquarters released a press report calling it '... a breakout and not a release by their guards.'"

Seymour slid his hand through his hair. "Yeah, but, what we didn't know was that the North Koreans saved face by retaliating, by refusing to release a number of allied POWs. Outside the U.N. Security Council members and Korea, the rest of world never came to know this other piece of the story, did they, Mr. Lee?"

Lee didn't answer Freedman's largely rhetorical question. "Mr. Lee, do we have any idea where they ended up?" Nick asked.

"The North Koreans were incensed, believing that the president of South Korea had ordered anti-Communist prisoners to be freed, defying the U.N. structured armistice for reasons that, as they put it, were too obvious to explain. They steadfastly refused, even to this day, to acknowledge that they'd kept the hundreds of soldiers."

"Were all the men they held back only from that development?" Nick asked.

"No, there were others not repatriated. Mainly from Camp 13. We have gathered other information that indicates that U.N. soldiers, likely Americans, had mined Kuneri, near Hung Nam and Ham and near Camp 13. Special operations oversaw the laying of these and other minefields." He handed Nick a report. The government had blacked out most of the information. "I have a report we confiscated. It's classified secret. I have the translated copy. You can read it, but unfortunately it must stay here."

Lee handed the report to Nick, who read the part that included names he recognized.

The interrogator indicates that Lieutenant Trent Hamilton, RO 10435789 was Special Forces April 20, 1952, when his squad of seventeen men was dropped into the Yalu River Estuary islands. Once in contact with Man-O-War was to provide radio contact with Skatefish and then train partisans. The second phase was to include contacting prisoners in POW camps and establishing E&E routes. Assignment included survey troop movements, create maps of the various landmines/landmarks and supervise the laying of minefields. Jump succeeded, but radio contact failed two hours after insertion. Subject speaks Mandarin. Subject cooperative. Signed Colonel Cho Tat Wah, CCF, PRC, October 1952. (Translated 1955.)

The aide half-speculated. "I have studied the entire record. My opinion? Hamilton could have been caught with the maps, or that Hamilton detailed the location of the minefields. My conjecture. What is not conjecture: further intelligence indicates that many POWs used in mine clearing operations were killed, and those that weren't ended up in Death Valley."

"So is this where the allied POWs that weren't repatriated were last located?"

"Yes, we believe so. Anyone not accounted for ended up there. Where they went from there is anybody's guess."

"Do you know if Roger went there?" Nick asked.

"We do not. For some reason, those that survived the mine detail were only known to the enemy... as were the four or five hundred sacrificed for the escapes that occurred in Seoul in June."

"So you're telling us you don't know what happened to the ones that ended up in Death Valley?"

"There were secret negotiations after the war between North Korea and the U.S. envoy in Switzerland, but they never resolved the matter."

"Meaning what?"

"Meaning those men were left behind."

"Meaning that's what the government is trying to cover up."

The End Comes

JACK HAD EVERY INTENTION OF WATCHING NICK grill Hamilton for the second day. At 8:30 a.m. he was still in pajamas. He stumbled into the living room, flicked on the TV and fell back on the front sofa, confused, mumbling, "8, 7, 6, 5... 8, 7, 6... 5, 8, 7... 6, 5... " Cartoons blasted from a kid's morning show while he hummed a ditty that went, "I hear the dogs a-whispering for me to come and listen." A chicken in the cartoon squawked while being chased by a fox. He laughed. He looked out the window to see if there were any strange cars up the street. There was. A late model four-door, maybe a Ford, he thought. He took a swig from the bottle of gin he held fast in his right hand. "The godless devil's soul for all you ask of me... " Jack chortled.

***

While Mitch waited for the trial to resume he took some pictures from an envelope that Art Girardin had received from his father several weeks back. The pictures were gruesome. Photos of dead bodies, bulldozers, military vehicles, cars and men in the vicinity of piles of dirt. When Art showed them to Nick, Mitch and Kathy, no one knew what to make of them.

Holding one photo of a man standing next to a car, Mitch turned to Nick, "Look at this picture. Tell me what you see?"

"Soldiers shooting the breeze next to an army sedan."

"Yeah, and who's the tall guy remind you of?"

"I dunno."

"Umm, what do you think Kathy?"

"Who's it supposed to be?"

"All rise." Picolillo yelled.

"Your Honor, the plaintiff recalls Trent Hamilton to the stand."

296

Lindquist advised Hamilton, "Sir, you are still under oath."

"Your Honor," Nick began. "Based upon certain answers Mr. Hamilton gave, I would like to cross examine Mr. Hamilton as an adversarial witness."

"Would you like to be heard, Mr. Harris?"

"No, sir, no objection."

"Proceed, Counsel."

"Previously, I'd shown you Map B-2, is that not correct?"

"I'm not sure."

Pointing to the map, Nick asked, "On that easel, there's Map B-2. Tell me if you recognize the hex symbols along the route I'm pointing to. Come closer if you need to."

Hamilton did not move. "Think I already testified to that... no idea what those marks mean."

"Sir, is it not true that Hamilton Helicopters used such a symbol as a trademark for parts?"

"May look similar," Hamilton conceded.

Nick handed Hamilton a copy of drawing. "I show you Plaintiff's Exhibit 96. It's a logo or a trademark. It's identical to the mark on the map, isn't it?"

"Similar."

"Can you explain the striking similarity?"

Harris stood up. "Objection, speculation."

"Sustained."

Nick handed Hamilton another document. "Please look at Plaintiff's Exhibit 98, a certified copy of the trademark application for Hamilton Helicopters showing the hexagonal design. Note the trademark was granted by the U.S. Patent and Trademark Office, in 1955. Note that the design is a series of hexagons within hexagons." Nick gave Hamilton a moment. "Look at page two... is that your signature, Vice President, Hamilton Helicopters, Inc.?"

"Looks like it. I don't remember signing this."

"But you did. You're not denying that, are you?"

"Saying I don't recall. Would you remember something signed thirty years ago?"

"We have established the striking similarity of the registered trademark for Hamilton Helicopters and the marks on the map B-2, did we not?"

Brushing Nick off, Hamilton responded, "If you say so."

"If you don't recall signing the trademark registration form, isn't it possible that you forgot you'd made those marks on that map almost thirty years ago?"

Hamilton paused. His jaw jutted forward. "I don't know."

Nick raised his voice. "You don't know what?"

Hamilton pursed his lips. "If I forgot, it means 'I don't know.'"

Nick followed up immediately. "So it is possible you made those marks on Map B-2?"

Harris catapulted from his chair, yelled, "Argumentative, your Honor, the witness testified he didn't know where the marks came from."

Lindquist leaned forward turned in the direction of Hamilton. Calmly, he said, "The witness will answer."

Hamilton's face flushed pink. He coughed. "I... don't remember."

"So if you don't remember, sir, it's possible you did make the marks." Nick said smugly.

Hamilton leaned forward. Stared at Nick threateningly and shouted, "No, I did not, do you understand, no, no, no!" The room echoed 'no, no, no,' and Nick waited until it dampened into silence.

"Mr. Hamilton, does the name Cho Tat Wah ring a bell?"

Hamilton hesitated and looked at his hand. 'No, what kind of name is that anyway?"

"Mr. Hamilton, I will ask the questions. Would you not remember the Commandant of Camp 13?"

"No, why should I?"

"Because previously you'd testified you were the ostensible spokesman for the POWs, so it seems logical you'd remember your counterpart?"

"Don't remember."

"And you never met a man by that name in civilian life."

Hamilton glared at Nick. "No."

"Would it refresh your memory if I asked you had you ever met someone with that name in India?"

"Objection," shouted Harris. "What does India or this name have to do with this trial, your Honor?"

"Overruled, please answer the question, sir."

"No, it doesn't."

Nick knew he was getting close to breaching the agreement he had with Harris, not to disclose Hamilton's nefarious trading operations in India in exchange for deep-sixing the photos of him and Rachel.

"Sir, let me call your attention back to map B-2. You previously testified that you did not know how those hexes got there. But, is it not true that you supplied information to your captors as to the very mine locations you and your men laid before you were captured?"

"No, that's not true."

"Is it not true that you supplied information to Cho Tat Wah the commandant of Camp 13, as to the mine locations?"

"Objection! First, it has not been established that a man by that name was the commandant of Camp 13, and this witness said he didn't know this man."

"Sustained."

"Sir, does the name Bud Rawlings mean anything to you?"

"Why, yes, he was with my company until this past year."

"His position, sir?"

"He worked in sales."

"International sales, the executive-in-charge, in fact. Is that not true?"

"Yes."

"I am handing you an affidavit, signed by Mr. Rawlings regarding what he knows about Hamilton Helicopters in India. I ask you if this refreshes your recollection of the name Cho Tat Wah?"

A minute passed before, Lindquist interjected himself impatiently, "Well, Mr. Castalano, do you have any question pending here?"

"Yes, sir. Mr. Hamilton, does that affidavit refresh your memory as to who Cho Tat Wah is?"

"Well now, I do recall doing business with a Chinese man by that name. I called my contact Cho."

"But you do not deny, based on your refreshed memory, that the man's name is Cho Tat Wah, do you?"

Hamilton hesitated and twisted his lip. "I do deny it, since I do not know a man by that name."

"Sir, was Cho Tat Wah not the commandant of Camp 13?"

"I said, I don't remember."

Nick looked over at Harris who by now was fuming. "Your Honor, may Counsel and I approach the bench?" asked Nick.

"Yes, to this side please."

Nick went to the side opposite the witness chair. "Judge, I believe that this witness has answered untruthfully and... "

Lindquist cut Nick off mid-sentence. "Counselor, I hope you have a good faith basis for that claim."

"I do, your Honor."

"Proceed, Counsel."

Nick walked back to the podium while shouting the question at Hamilton. "Mr. Hamilton, do you still deny that given that the hexes are identical to your trademark, and given that you knew where the mines were, that you did not draw those hexagons?"

"I do not know what you are implying!"

Nick turned to face Trent. "Isn't it true you assisted Cho Tat Wah, the man you now do business with in India, and... strike that, isn't it true you assisted Cho Tat Wah, the man you now do business with in India, in locating the mines, so they could be cleared using your comrades?"

"Objection, argumentative, and it has not been established he is doing business *in India* with this person."

"Overruled, answer the question, sir," Lindquist swiftly ordered.

"That is a scurrilous accusation," Trent shouted.

"You will answer the question, Mr. Hamilton," Nick said calmly.

"How could I possibly... ?"

Nick grabbed a copy of the previous transcript. "You previously testified that, and I will quote you here, 'They'd funnel various things through me. I'd communicate them to Colonel Levine. He was the highest ranking officer among us, until he was transferred. But for most purposes, you might say I was the lead man.' Was that not your testimony?"

"Something like that, yes, but I was no traitor."

"I'll let others judge that, sir."

"Objection."

"Withdrawn. Your witness, Mr. Harris."

"No questions, your Honor."

Claymores and Mongrels

ART'S EYES WELLED UP WHEN NICK SAID, that after talking to Preston, he would continue with the case. Even Diane had surprised Nick with a show of support, "They hadn't come this far to turn back without more answers," she said. And Nick was still fuming over the blackmail attempt. He had Mitch call Jack to remind him that the subpoena was still in force. In the back row, Julie, Anna, Jack and Father Ryan sat quietly.

Lindquist turned to Nick. "Counselor, do you have another witness?"

"Your Honor, two more. The first is Mr. Kenny Preston, a man mentioned in the Broadbent report as having remembered Private Girardin. Until now we'd been unable to locate him. He's been laid up in a veteran's home in upper New York State for the past year. His daughter was kind enough to bring him here today. Although we did not schedule his testimony, I think that our examination of this man will be brief."

"Mr. Harris, any objection?"

"Your Honor, hearing an unscheduled witness this late in the trial may be prejudicial."

"I understand your concern, but under the circumstances I'm willing to hold open the taking of testimony for an additional week for rebuttal following this witness's examination. Mr. Castalano, call your witness."

Nick pushed Preston, a man lost in a wheelchair, to the front of the witness box and turned him so he faced the crowd. When he took the oath everyone bent forward to hear a weak voiced, gray faced man with eyes like hollowed out caves. He looked like he had recently undergone chemo. Nick quickly established that Preston had been a POW in Camp 13, and was familiar with Girardin, having been in the same hut.

302

"Mr. Preston, you told Mitch LeBeau yesterday, the man sitting over there at Counsel's table, that there came a time when you and other POWs were detailed to clear mines—anti-personnel mines?"

Preston looked up and to the left. "Yeah, late winter of '53," he said in an voice louder than that with which he had given previous answers.

"Do you have a month or... ?"

"No, can only tell you... the last winter spent."

"And what exactly did the detail involve?"

"We were told that routes south of the camp were mined with claymores."

"Would you explain what a claymore is, sir?"

"A landmine. Set off when you push a little plunger, like if you step on it."

"How were you selected for this detail?"

"Don't know, orders came from the commandant."

"Do you know who that was?" Nick asked.

"Yeah, name was Jo or Cho."

"Did you not tell me on the phone on Saturday, that the man's name was Cho Tat Wah?"

"I may have, but the meds sometimes make me forget what I say," he smiled.

"Were there guys from around the camp?"

"About fifty or sixty. Only remember guys from my hut."

Nick studied Preston's face for an instant. "Okay, sir, if you can, please recall how many men were on each crew to clear these mines."

"About a dozen, more or less, in my crew. We had about fifteen guys."

"Remember who stayed behind?"

"Only remember a few."

"Did Girardin go?"

"Think so, can't be sure."

"Do you recall how you were told of the detail?"

He shrugged his shoulders. "When they came an' got us, we didn't know what they were up to. But it wasn't unusual that they'd line us up, bring us to the dayroom where they'd try an' brainwash us."

"Any other details you went on?"

"When they wanted us to move dead bodies across the river to the burial place or dig latrines... when it got warm. We had things to keep us busy. Didn't give it much thought."

Nick continued. "Were there any rumors what they'd planned?"

"Nope, they come got me, rounded us up."

"Where'd the rest of the men come from?"

"Around the camp, fifty, seventy-five guys."

"When we fell out in the yard, there were lines of men. I fell in the back of one of them. It was cold, dark, nobody shootin' the bull."

"What happened then?"

"Waited. Waited, freezing, must've been five below, wind blowing... eyes almost froze. Most of us had light jackets. Then they gave us these heavy coats, like U.S. issue."

"And, did you know who the enemy guards were? Did you recognize them?"

"They were Chinese, if that's what you mean."

"Yes. Tell us what happened next."

"They marched us out of camp."

"Can you describe what a clearing operation was?"

"We were put into units of two to four men, and at some point, the guards put us in a long line."

"What happened next?"

"Marched to where we were put on hands and knees, crawled around with these pointy rods." Preston demonstrated by bending his fingers on both hands, walking them in the air in front of him. "We poked the ground, about four feet, maybe five, in front of us to see if we hit somethin' hard. It was a crazy idea," he said, pointing to his head and twirling his finger.

"Aside from it being potentially deadly, why was it crazy if someone wanted to blow up a claymore?"

Preston sighed, "The ground was covered with snow, Mister. Though, someone may have tried clearing it—small truck, maybe even shoveled by hand."

"How'd you know where to start poking?"

"The Chinese had a map they were goin' by. I think it musta showed where the mines were."

Nick stepped toward to the easel. "Mr. Preston, if you will, would you please bring your chair over here? This is map B-2 for identification. It's been established as a map of Camp 13. Is this the layout of the camp to the best of your recollection?"

Preston studied the map for maybe thirty seconds. "More or less."

"Do you see on that map the place you were detailed to clear mines?"

"Yes, sir. See all these little hexagons?" he said, without hesitation.

"Yes, I see," said Nick, now on the receiving end of the question.

"Where these hexagons are?" Preston said, breathing hard. "This is where we cleared mines." He moved his hand along the section of road shown on the map.

"What was the road like?" Nick asked.

"Well the road they were trying to clear was pretty narrow, lined both sides with a ditch and woods."

"What was the procedure—if that's the right word?"

"Well, the idea of poking the metal rods and digging around places that looked suspicious didn't really work, so they put us in the woods—to get out of the wind, I guess. Then, we were waiting in the woods when they called the first team and put them into a ravine along the road. Took about six, eight guys at first. We didn't know what they were up to. We lost sight of them pretty quick."

"Did you know where they went?" Nick asked.

"Not at first. But later, when our turn came, we found out," Preston said with a grimace.

"What'd you find out?"

"Give me a second to catch my breath."

In the back row, Jack sat mesmerized by Preston's testimony. Every so often, he affirmed Preston's statement with a shake of the head.

"Yes. You okay? need a break?"

Preston shook his head "no" and continued. "Lashed us, about three or four on a side, to these logs, to drag them down the road."

"Why were you dragging logs?"

"Plan was to explode the mines."

"Wouldn't your weight explode the mine if you stepped on it?"

"Maybe and maybe not. The snow distributes your weight over an area, and anyway we were mostly pulling from the side of the road."

"What happened next?"

Preston came back quickly. "Whatcha think? Some of the logs exploded. When a mine went off it blew 'em to kingdom come."

Preston looked at the crowd and saw a man in the back row—Jack Prado O'Conner—nodding his head in agreement.

Preston continued, "Piece of wood hit my shoulder like a fastball... dislocated it."

"It disabled you, then?"

"Wasn't life threatening, but I couldn't go back. Saved me from the detail after that."

"Do you know anyone who died?"

"Only half of us marched back. The first day, that is. In the end, only three or four of us were left back at the hut. Learned that the guys that'd completed the detail either died or were moved someplace."

"Remember the names of the guys that were in the hut in the end?"

"Jameston, me, another guy came in much later, Mexican guy."

Nick looked over at Lindquist—it looked like his eyes were shut. "When'd they let you go?"

"After a full day, it seemed. My shoulder was aching pretty bad. Yeah, I came back from the drag and rested alongside the road in the ravine."

"Did you return other days?"

"Not me—shoulder you know—but the guys that were okay, yes."

"You knew Roger Girardin from Camp 13, did you not?"

"Yes, sir, was in my hut for a while."

"Did you see Roger Girardin on the detail?"

"Don't know. Later that first day, must've been late afternoon when we were marching back from the detail, there was a body alongside the road. We was walking close to the other side. Looked like one of ours was just lying there. On his side."

Nick wanted to make sure that Lindquist heard Preston say that he'd seen the soldier. "So you did see a GI on the ground?"

"Yeah... "

Wanting a more definite statement, he pressed, "You seem unsure."

Preston responded defensively. "Well, was thirty years ago... but yeah, probably forty, yeah, forty feet away, on his side, wasn't moving."

"Might you recall if you thought that he was wounded or dead?"

"Wasn't sure what to make of it. Too far away, but it wasn't a good sign. Boy was hurt, or worse." Preston brought his lips back, his chest labored in every breath, and he contorted his face.

"Was there anybody next to him?"

"A dog... few feet away."

"A dog?" Nick asked surprised.

"Yeah, big, brown mother... big, standing next to him."

Nick took a drink of water. "Now, why'd you remember that?"

"Don't know, just popped up," Preston said apologetically.

Nick inhaled and let his breath out slowly. "Did you see Girardin again, after that day?"

"Never. Not after that. Didn't see him in the hut that night."

"Did you imagine he'd died?"

Harris rose up, "Objection, calls for speculation."

"Overruled."

The courtroom went silent. Preston looked around, but did not answer. Lindquist looked at his watch.

"Did you imagine he had died, sir?" Nick repeated.

Preston grabbed his wheelchair's arm rests. "Don't know," he mumbled.

"So is it your statement that you never saw Roger Girardin again?"

"Nope, never saw him again."

"Do you remember meeting a Jack O'Conner in Camp 13?"

"Not sure, sir."

"How about Trent Hamilton?"

"Yes, I think he was a translator."

"What else can you tell us about him?"

"He owns a helicopter company."

Nick looked at Harris. "Counselor, your witness."

Harris rose from his chair, twisting his ring around his finger. He looked down at his two colleagues.

"Mr. Preston, how long have you known about this attempt to locate Roger Girardin?"

"Maybe two or three years, read about it in my VFW magazine."

"Why did you not come forward before?"

"I don't know, guess because I took sick."

"How long did you talk to Mr. Castalano the day you called him?"

"'bout an hour."

"And how long did you talk to Mr. LeBeau or anyone else from his office?"

"Talked yesterday morning to Mitch over there, maybe 'nother hour."

"This is an important case, as far as you are concerned, right?"

"I'm not long for this world and need to set things straight."

"Isn't it important that we be sure about what we say here?"

"Yes."

"You want to... do the right thing, true?"

"'Course."

"This story about blowing up mines... sounds... if you'll excuse me for saying so... *incredible*?"

Preston just stared at Harris.

"How can a log blow up a mine? You have to step on it, don't you—you know, apply direct force?"

"I suppose. I ain't no mechanic, just saw what I saw," Preston said sheepishly.

"Well how'd they tie the chains to the logs?"

"Don't exactly remember."

"Were there many chains?"

"Think so."

"How many men pulled?"

"Mighta been four or six."

"A chain for each man pulling, is that how it worked?"

"Yeah, something like that."

"Wouldn't they get in each other's way?"

"No, we was strung out."

"Why was none of this mentioned in your interrogation report when you were released?"

"Was so many years ago, maybe I did tell 'em."

"Is it possible that under the stress of being a POW, you came to imagine that all of this happened?"

"No, sir. Saw what I saw," Preston asserted.

"Is it possible that under the stress of being ill, you have come to imagine this?"

"No, sir."

"Are on a medication?"

"Morphsul."

"That's a morphine. Pill form, correct?"

"Think so."

"Makes you drowsy?"

"Sometimes."

"Clouds your thinking?"

"Sometimes."

"Ever hallucinate?"

"What?"

"You know, dream while you aren't sleeping."

"No, sir, never did that."

"And isn't it true that the first time you heard the name Cho Tat Wah was in this courtroom today?"

"No, sir, aah, well to be honest, like I said, I don't... "

"You're not sure, are you? You're not sure you ever heard the name before. You're just trying to follow Mr. Castalano's lead, aren't you, trying to do the right thing?"

Nick jumped up. "Your Honor, compound question, and Mr. Harris is testifying—he's not letting the witness get an answer in edgewise."

Harris interjected before Lindquist could rule. "Strike the last question. Sir, without prying into your personal life, can you tell us why you're on medication today?"

"Pain."

"I assumed so. But from what?"

"Cancer, sir, cancer. Cancer caused by poison metal."

"Poison metal. I don't understand—can you elaborate?"

"Metals used in 'copters. I used to machine stuff that caused the cancer."

"You're not involved in any lawsuit because of your illness, are you?"

"Worker's comp, that's all. But the 'copter companies are the ones that caused my sickness, no doubt."

"You hold these companies responsible for your cancer?" Harris asked with a hint of sarcasm.

"Yes, sir, all those 'copter ones."

Harris turned to Lindquist. "Your Honor, may I have a moment to confer with my colleagues?"

Lindquist looked at the clock over the jury box. "Proceed, but make it short, please."

Harris and his cohorts put their heads together; Nick imagined the conversation had to do with the mention of helicopters. He figured that Harris wanted to ask more, but the first rule of cross examination is not to ask a question that you don't already know the answer to. Harris walked back to the podium.

"Mr. Preston, may I ask if you have ever met Mr. Trent Hamilton?"

"No, don't think so."

Harris breathed a sigh of relief. "Do you know who he is?"

"Only what I read in the papers last couple of weeks, when he testified here."

Now Harris had a bonus question he could ask—one that could not hurt, but could potentially help. "But, sir, you claim that helicopter companies like Mr. Hamilton's are responsible for your cancer, isn't that true?"

"Yes, sir, that's true."

"Isn't it true that you have come here to testify because somehow you believe your testimony will reflect poorly on Mr. Hamilton?"

"Sir, that's ridicu—"

"In some way to get back at his helicopter company?"
Nick jumped up. "Objection, argumentative."

"Withdrawn, no further questions."

"Do you wish to redirect, Mr. Castalano?"

"No, your Honor."

"Have you any more witnesses?"

"Yes, your Honor, plaintiff re-calls Mr. Jack Prado."

Lindquist looked at the marshal, "Let's take our lunch
break first."

***

Harris opened the door to his second floor war room
and was greeted by the secretary. "Mr. Harris, this
envelope was on my desk, addressed to you."

Harris opened it. There were a dozen photos of people
in a pit—obviously dead— bulldozers, a U.S. Army vehicle
with men inside. One picture contained an arrow someone
had penned in, pointing to a man leaning against a car.
His next move was to have the secretary put a call through
to Undersecretary Russell.

"Russell, I have a dozen photos somebody dropped off
—you know, like the ones we talked about... There's an
arrow pointing to a guy, a second louey, looks like. Well
not sure... Yes, sir, I'll get to the bottom, ask what they're
looking for."

***

Following the break, Jack assumed the witness stand.
As he looked out at the crowd he realized that the stiff shot
of gin he had for lunch would not control the shakes that
coursed through his body all morning or quench the
memories that like a fire-breathing dragon had been
wakened from a thirty year sleep by Preston's testimony.

"You already testified in this case, so you're still under
oath. Do you understand?" Lindquist warned.

"Yeah... ah, yes, sir." Jack responded, nervously.

"Your Honor, plaintiff requests permission to treat Mr.
Prado as an adversarial witness at this time."

Lindquist raised his eyebrows. "Well, Counsel, I
suppose you have your reasons. Permission granted,
unless Mr. Harris wants to be heard."

Harris frowned. "No, the government has no objection."

"Mr. Prado, you previously testified you were in North Korea from late 1950 until after hostilities ended, is that not true, sir?"

Lindquist noticed Jack's hand tremble when he dabbed his brow with a brown paper towel. "Are you all right, Mr. Prado?"

Jack did not respond.

"Are you all right, Mr. Prado?" Lindquist repeated, louder now.

Jack's lungs grew tight, his heart pounded. "Can I have a minute?"

Lindquist shook his head slowly. "Is that enough time, Mr. Prado?"

"Yes, thanks." Jack blew in and out, trying to control his breath. Droplets of sweat had formed on his forehead. His hands were shaking again.

"Can we resume, Mr. Prado?" Hearing Lindquist, Jack opened his eyes. A hundred people were watching, including Father Ryan. And Julie.

"Yes, yes, I'm fine."

Nick continued, "I'll try and be brief. I'm going to show you Plaintiff's Exhibits B-2, which you've seen before, correct?"

"Yes, you showed me some maps when we met."

Nick tacked B-2 to the easel. "Can you identify what this is a map of?"

"As I stated before, I cannot definitely say."

"But you have seen the marks placed on this map before?"

"What marks?"

Nick pointed to the "hexagons within hexagons" marked along the road. "These hexagons."

"Never tied to a map, no."

"Have you ever seen such a mark before, in connection with anything?"

"Sure, I've seen that kind a mark before. Plenty of times."

"Mr. Prado, it is not true that this mark was the trademark for S-84 Hamilton Helicopter in the mid-1950s when you started working there?"

312

Jack felt his breath shorten, his legs turn gelatinously weak.

"Are you all right, Mr. Prado?"

Jack's lips tightened.

"Mr. Prado, I asked a question... " Nick paused and turned to the stenographer. "Madam Stenographer, please read back my last question."

"Question: 'Mr. Prado, it is not true that this mark was the trademark for S-84 Hamilton Helicopter in the mid-1950s when you started working there?'"

"Sir, please answer the question."

"Yes, come to think of it, Hamilton used that mark."

"Mr. Prado, would you know why these marks were drawn on this map?"

"No, sir."

"Your Honor, if I may, I need to confer with my colleagues for a minute."

The judge raised his eyebrows, took a deep breath, let it out slowly, "Yes, go ahead."

Nick walked over to Kathy and whispered, "Prado knows what the little 'hexes' mean. Let me have that line we drew up yesterday." Nick returned to the lectern.

"You know Trent Hamilton, do you not?"

Eyes wide open now, Jack answered, "Yes, I do."

"And knew him before the war?"

Jack hesitated. "Yes, sir."

"And while you were in Camp 13?"

"Uh-huh."

"And knew him after the war?

"Uh, yeah."

"You went to college with Hamilton?"

Nick saw Jack looking for someone in the crowd. "Yes."

"You went to ROTC with Hamilton?"

"Right."

"You joined the Army together?"

"Yes."

"You were cashiered out of the officer ranks when you were involved in an automobile homicide?"

"No, that's not... " Nick saw Jack unnerved. "That's not true, it didn't happen that way!" Jack shouted.

Harris did not like the speed with which Nick was buzzing through the cross-examination. "Objection! What does this have to do with this case, your Honor? Mr. Castalano is impugning the character of a man that has nothing to do with this case!"

This slowed Nick down.

"Withdraw the question," Nick replied.

Lindquist squinted. "Sir, unless you have a good faith basis for calling into question anyone's reputation in my courtroom, I will sanction you, keep that in mind."

"Mr. Prado, please tell the court how many times you saw Hamilton when you were in Camp 13?"

"A few times."

"In what kind of situations did you run across Lieutenant Hamilton?"

"I would often see him on the grounds walking from his barracks to the day room."

"Isn't that where the North Koreans and, later on the Chinese, ran operations."

"Yes, sir."

"Why would any POW go to the day room?"

"Every day there were indoctrinations and just about everyone had to attend at one point or another. The commies were trying to get us to, well, to believe that America was evil... that communism was good."

"Was this voluntary?"

"No, had to."

"And isn't it true, that you were indoctrinated so well that you didn't return with your fellow soldiers after the war?"

"No, that was not the reason I returned late. I was sick."

"You mean physically?"

Jack hesitated. "No, a breakdown."

"Were there other American soldiers that were with you after the POWs were repatriated in August 1953?"

"Yes, there were a half, maybe a dozen, yes, a dozen or so that I knew about."

"And in this courtroom, Mr. Harris showed you your DD 214 indicating you received a dishonorable discharge!"

"I did, but it was changed."

Nick took a breath. "Is it not true that Mr. Hamilton was instrumental in pulling strings to get your discharge upgraded?"

"Yes, sir, the company I worked for."

"You couldn't work at Hamilton Helicopters with a dishonorable, could you?"

"Couldn't get by the security clearance, no."

"Let me go back to your contact with Lieutenant Hamilton in Camp 13. You say you observed him in the day room?"

"Occasionally, I did."

"And what would he be doing?"

"It's been so long ago, I don't recall any particular instance."

"But is it not true he had been friendly with one or more of the Chinese in charge?"

"Had that feeling, back then."

"Were there others in the camp that believed Lieutenant Hamilton was friendly with the Chinese?"

"Yes."

"How did they come to that conclusion?"

Harris jumped up. "Objection. Calls for hearsay."

Wanting to hear more, Lindquist ruled quickly. "I will allow it. Please answer, Mr. Prado."

"Hamilton spoke Chinese, and for some that was enough."

"And what would be the talk among the other POWs?"

Harris quickly rose from behind his table. "Objection—hearsay."

"Sustained."

"Mr. Prado, I am going to show you Map B-2, and ask you when was the very first time you saw such a map."

"I saw it in a dayroom, in Camp 13."

"The room that the Chinese used to grill the POWs in?"

"Yes, sir."

"Did the map have the little hexagon symbols on it?"

"Can't be sure after all these years."

"And you did see Lieutenant Hamilton in the dayroom?"

"Yes, sir, on occasion, as I indicated to you."

"Did you know if the Chinese or the NK ever used POWs to do anything connected with military operations?"

315

"No, not really."

"I don't mean take up arms, but did they enlist or force POWs to be used as cover for them?"

"Yes, that they did, like when we were force-marched from where we were captured, to our final destination—to the camp. Many times we were put out in front, in case they were fired upon, or when our planes were overhead."

"Any other times, after you were in the prison camp?"

"Like Mr. Preston said, groups were forced to clear minefields."

"I am going to show you Plaintiff's Exhibit ABR entitled *Summary of Interrogatory Respondent, John Millers.* Please read it to yourself, sir." After a minute, Nick asked Jack, "Mr. Prado, please tell the court what the memo refers to."

"Corporal Millers, in August 1953, tells a U.N. interrogator that there were rumors of POWs being used to clear minefields in North Korea."

"What, if anything, can you tell us about those kinds of operations?"

"The U.N. had laid land mines at some point south of the camps. At least, that's what I recall. Supposed to be escape routes."

"And, sir, is it not true that the very map you have in front of you shows the minefields designated with the symbol we have been referring to as a hexagon?"

"Don't know that for sure."

"Is it not true that the symbol on the map is the same symbol that Hamilton Helicopters used as a trademark?"

"Yes, similar."

"And, sir, if it is the same symbol, the only individuals who might have made those marks are either you or Lieutenant Hamilton?"

"Objection, calls for speculation!" Harris shouted from his chair.

"Sustained. And Counsel, I expect you to stand when you address this court," Lindquist admonished Harris.

Jack continued, "I do not understand your reasoning, I did not... "

Harris interrupted. "You need not answer, Mr. Prado."

Nick turned to Lindquist. "Your Honor, either this witness or someone at Hamilton Helicopters would have made the marks—otherwise how could they be the same? Especially coming after the war in the form of a trademark?"

Harris abruptly rose to his feet. "Same objection. It's only speculation on this witness's part if and whether Hamilton Helicopters or Hamilton himself knew anything about the maps, the symbols or the so-called minefields."

Lindquist did not address Harris's objection. He wanted to know what he could on this score. "Please answer the question, sir."

"I don't know. I didn't know the Hamilton trademark at the time. I came back in '54 after Hamilton bought the company. I thought his family bought it during the Korean War. I don't know... "

Nick stopped the witness short. "You do not know what?"

"I, I don't know if Hamilton knew the POWs were clearing minefields."

"Was Roger Girardin one of the men assigned to clearing the minefields?"

"He may have been, not sure."

"Sir, you are evading a responsive answer. Need I remind you that you are under oath? Is it not true that Private Girardin was one of the POWs ordered to clear the minefields?"

"I only knew what was being rumored!"

"And what was that?"

Harris stood up again. "Objection, the answer calls for hearsay!"

"Your Honor, I am asking whether there had been a commonly understood reason for the disappearance of dozens of POWs, Private Girardin among them. And given that no records exist on this point—or at least the government has not produced any—this witness may have a recollection of what was commonly understood among the troops."

Lindquist's face was flushed from either the heat or a persistent neck-ache. "I will allow it since I am hearing this case, not a jury. And I can decide whether it is reliable or not. Please answer, Mr. Prado."

Begrudgingly, Jack answered. "We took it that GIs were being used to clear minefields. Girardin may have been one of them."

"And can you tell us what else you know about this activity?"

"Don't know much. We were told that the POWs were used to clear the fields, some of them never came back. At least not to our camp."

"You testified, 'We were told.' Who are the 'we'? And who told you?"

Harris jumped up. "Ambiguous."

Nick understood, "Who are the 'we?'"

"'We' were the guys."

"And who told you?"

"Don't remember exactly."

Nick continued to press Jack about 'who' and 'what' he knew concerning the mine clearing operation, but Jack was tighter than a drum.

"Is it not true that Private Girardin was one of the POWs ordered to clear the minefields?"

Jack put his hands to his face.

"Sir, do you need some time to compose yourself?" Nick asked.

Jack nodded his head yes.

"Can we make it five, your Honor?" Nick asked.

While the court recessed Julie remained in her chair, stunned, repeating Jack's confession: "We took it that GIs were used to clear minefields. Girardin may have been one of them." It was certain that Jack was with Roger and certain that he had kept it from her throughout the years. It wasn't rage. Rather, she felt stung by the cruelty of his reticence—his cowardice. How could she face the man, the only man that she trusted to tell the truth? She tried to make sense of it, remembering how he went to Korea a wide-eyed, inquisitive boy ready to fight the red menace and had returned a quiet man, impossible to penetrate.

As people made their way out of the courtroom, Jack stayed in the witness chair to avoid facing Julie. His eyes were shut, and he mumbled, counting backward, remembering something that had long been trapped in a screed of subconscious, the place where his darkest dreams lay dormant. Suddenly, his trembling body felt like it had been transported back in time, back to Camp 13.

Rituals

WHEN THE CHINESE CAPTURED JACK, THEY FORCE-MARCHED him and a half-dozen men from Usan to Pyoktong. Fifty miles times seventeen-hundred yards times three feet. In the odd miles he counted every step forward and reversed the count in the even ones, discounting the pain, forcing his legs like clubs of dead meat to pound a path through deep snow, beneath the cover of trees, beneath smoke filled clouds that hung just above the hilltops, through empty countryside, villages. One guy that kept falling behind finally quit, the men hardly noticing as they forged their way north. Another comrade, bared feet turned blue-black, refused to stand after a short break, and as the men pulled away, they heard the unmistakable shot of his execution. Weeks later, the band reached a town nesting in the security of three side by side hills and the Yalu, and cordoned off by a barbed wire fence, inside of which lay a maze-like collection of muddy village roads and stucco-like dirt shacks, some tiled, unclear where one ended and another began. Jack passed burned out buildings, square foundations and an inner compound surrounded by more wire fence, where he later learned his captors lived and officiated. In the distance, brick smokestacks rose out of larger factory-like buildings like slender, red test tubes, belching smoke, smudging the icy skies.

Two guards shoved Jack through the door of a one room hut—thatched roof, hardpan floor resembling something he'd seen in pictures of Native American adobes. Inside, packed like canned fish, were 15 men, weeks unwashed, greasy lice colonies roaming freely through overgrown beards, multiplying and sapping blood. When Jack stumbled in, the wheezing and coughing men hardly noticed. It smelled like a crapper. He found a tiny vacancy. Every now and again diarrhea-stricken men bolted for the latrine; the weaker ones would curl up and shit their pants.

His comrades told him he would be fed a bowl of millet and sorghum and sometimes a ball of soybean, twice a day. Over time, many would contract beriberi, rickets and dysentery and eventually die. A week after he arrived, the guards kicked open the door and dumped a kid, delirious, foul smelling pus oozing from a gangrenous leg wound. He stayed in a coma, death's rattle disquieting the darkened quarters for several nights until he became silent. Jack helped stack his body behind the shanty, where it would stay until the spring thaw. The man on Jack's left had the pasty orange and yellow look of jaundice. The following week Jack dragged him to the stack outside too.

In late spring, hushed lilies grew in the woods, on the hills and near the shore. The place could be mistaken for a rustic vacation spot, except for the death and dying still rampant inside the huts. Men exhausted by famine could not lift their arms to keep the flies from feasting on their faces. Beriberi and rickets kept them from using the latrines. And then the shouting started. Chinese held indoctrination sessions outdoors, every morning for hours until noon. They would scream and rant until the POWs recited slogans or chorused that particular day's message: *the Americans were capitalists engaging in war crimes.*

Jack reverted to counting numbers, adding, dividing, multiplying and occasionally mumbling odd results. One night he turned to Arsenalt, the guy next to him, and said that he had a recurring dream where, like a character in "Alice in Wonderland," he dropped into a rabbit hole to feel no pain, a comfortable fairy-like world where he blinked his eyes backward, counting the seconds contained in a year to the cheers of faceless bystanders. Eventually a fellow inmate, tired of his nonsensical ramblings, told him to shut up or they would throw him outside. From that point on Jack kept his dreams and newly emerging visions to himself, although it could not stop the numerological mutterings over which he had no control.

In May, the men were allowed to walk to a shallow inlet to bathe, wash clothes and cut their beards if they had something mildly sharp. Jack kept to himself—or perhaps more accurately, the men stayed away from him because he lived in another world where he held imaginary conversations. He kneeled next to a pool of water and stared at himself. His face was thin, although a good likeness of his civilian self, something that could not be said for most of the men. Then he heard, "Jack, Jack O'Conner!"

Jack stood up and shot back. "Yeah, who're you?"

"I'm Roger, from back home."

Jack's mouth fell open, his eyes blinked uncontrollably. "Holy Christ."

Roger grinned from ear to ear and Jack embraced him in a bear hug. "When'd you get to this retreat?" Roger asked.

"They caught me 'round end of November, the Ch'ongch'on River valley. You?" "Yeah, me too, Ch'ongch'on River. November. How you doing? What's the matter with your eyes?"

"Nervous twitch, got worse when I got here."

"When was the last time you heard from Julie?"

"Not sure, maybe October. You?"

"Last letter I got, was... early November."

"How'd she sound? Say anything about my mother?"

The men's excitement gradually subsided, the conversation turning to small talk, until Roger said, "Say, you know your friend there, Hamilton, I could swear that I'd seen him back in Suwon... yeah, saw this guy standing next to a car, next to this mass fucking grave, weird... really sickening."

"What?"

"Well, at the time the guy only looked familiar, I wasn't sure it was him, and it all looked pretty threatening, so I went on my way... it was some time later it sank in—it hadta be him. Just thought it was too much of a happenstance."

"Where're you now?"

"Up behind the day room. You got any room?"

"Yeah, we had fifteen, then four passed this winter, dysentery," Jack replied, eager to have Roger join him, and then added, "Why?"

"We're shoulder to shoulder."

It was the better part of an hour later, when they went separate ways. As Jack walked back to the hut, Montoya asked, "Who were ya talking to?" Jack did not answer, walking dead ahead, in another world.

The summer passed into fall, and it was snowing for the first time when Jack saw Roger walk into the hut, a big grin on his face. Jack startled himself out of a gloomy daze. "Roger, where the hell'd you go?"

"No place. They changed our routine, so I never saw you by the river again."

"What brings you here?" Jack asked.

"Overcrowding. Few of us had to move. Figured a good time to jump over."

"Well, have a piece of floor. Right here," Jack said, patting the ground beside him. "Montoya, no problem, right?" Montoya looked at Jack, but said nothing.

In '52, snow fell from mid-October on and confined the men to their huts. Jack had run out of things to talk about, and fell into long periods when he slept or sat quietly. In early December, it snowed every day. Under his breath, Jack continued to repeat things that did not make sense. His twitching got worse. One day, Jack recited the same thing for fifteen minutes. "My eyes blink goodbyes to flies who despise our lies, and spies on what's in our cries."

"Jack, knock it off! What the fuck are you saying anyway?" Montoya asked.

"It's a gospel, for my ministry," he answered contritely, not wanting to offend.

"What ministry, for Christ's Sake?"

"I'm doing what God wants, to carry His word into the backwater of no-man's land among the men, our tribe," Jack explained, trying to rationalize.

"Jack, my amigo, get some sleep."

It was close to Christmas when he started telling his cellmates that he was visited by an angel who told him to gather the "Believers" and hold mass. And Jack noticed that Roger, who had of late chosen to have absolutely nothing to do with him, decided to join his enterprise. "Roger, how about me making me an altar? It'd keep you busy."

323

There was a ban against holding religious ceremonies, but over the next few weeks, Jack watched the hut cadre steal pieces of wood and string and assemble a small altar —not more than a wooden board on two short stools and a small cross placed on its bare surface. Meanwhile, Jack's ramblings continued. "Shall slew the snake in his track, bury his body in tamarack." But no one asked Jack what he was saying, long since accepting that he had crossed over.

When the men finished building the altar, Jack called his "congregation" together and despite the men's collective opinion that Jack was a little crazy, all eleven of them kneeled— except Roger, who Jack saw watching from the far corner. They recited the Our Father. The wind howled, and snow blew through the clapboard cracks. For a while they had forgotten the hell they were in and raised their voices singing a few familiar carols. During "*God Rest Ye Merry Gentlemen*" the door burst open. A cold blast of air blew the floor mats against the far wall. Three billy-stick-carrying guards ordered everyone face down. A guard swept his hand over the makeshift altar, leaving it in a pile of rubble. Two men grabbed Jack by the scruff of the neck and threw him into the snowy night. "Out, Out," they ordered. Jack screamed, *"Kyrie eleison, Kyrie eleison!"* Once outside, the guards pummeled him into unconsciousness.

For the next few days, in a four-by-four cell off the day room, Jack slept and ate, pissing and shitting in a milk pail. And there were two brief appearances in the dayroom, sitting across from a Chinese interrogator demanding he renounce the war. It was during the grilling that he had first seen those little hexagonal diagrams on a sheet of paper lying next to the soldier. On the third day, he overheard Colonel Cho, the CCF commandant of the camp speaking Chinese to a man with a familiar voice. In a swift rush of excitement, Jack realized it was Trent Hamilton. Jack waited. When it sounded as if Cho had left the dayroom, Jack called in a soft voice, "Trent, Trent."

Jack thought he had heard something, but nothing happened. "Trent, can you hear me... ? I'm here... next room," he called in a loud undertone.

In the next instant, Cho and Trent walked in. Trent was in an officer's combat uniform —crew cut, day old stubble, but otherwise in good shape.

"Jack!" he clamored, hardly able to get the words out. "You're the last guy I thought I'd see." Beneath Jack's eyes, Trent saw two blood-dried, hollow black shadows. His face had a deep scratch that went up and over a purple lump on the side of his head. His left eye was swollen like a jawbreaker. His cheeks were sculpted around two bones, making them appear jarringly transparent. Long matted hair stuck to his head under the glue of dried blood. His khaki wool pants were pinched at the waist by a black electrical cord, a white pullover shirt made from flour sacks hung on an undernourished frame beneath his opened field jacket. It wasn't the guy Trent remembered from a rainy night when a dead woman was about to take the wheel in a car impaled on a telephone pole.

"What're you doing locked up?"

"Ask that fuck next to you," Jack answered in a raspy voice.

Infuriated, Cho hollered something in Chinese.

"He says we can't talk. I'll make contact," Trent said coolly.

Later that night, Trent returned to Jack's cell. "Jack, Jack," he whispered.

"Trent?"

"Yeah, they got me sleeping out back in a shed, can't talk long, but wanted to catch up."

The men talked about family and briefly about their experiences following their separation at boot camp. "You'll never guess who's here," said Jack.

"How the fuck do I know, who?"

"Girardin, you know, the guy my sister dated. He was up at your place once."

"Girardin, how could I forget? That bastard ratted on me—remember the car thing?"

"Oh yeah," Jack chuckled.

"Laugh, all you want... but if I see him... he's toast."

A sound came from outside, and the men went silent. "I better get back," Trent warned.

The next morning before six, two guards took Jack from the four-by-four cell to a seven-foot deep, three by five hole covered by a rotting oak door. They pushed the cover aside and shoved Jack backward. He fell onto a floor rife with dog bones. Unsure about what he stepped on, he leaned against the wall until his legs gave way, and he fell on his back. A china-blue sliver of daylight came through a crack in the center of the cover. Eventually the sky turned cobalt black; the temperature plummeted. He started walking up and back, before a rush of diarrhea forced him to the pail. He curled up, trying to stay awake, fearing he would die from overexposure. About an hour later a wool blanket and a tarp fell into the hole. He wrapped himself, fell asleep. Next morning, a guard lowered half a bowl of millet. It went this way for three days and nights, and on the fourth day his meal did not come. He felt he would die from hunger, thirst, the dryness in his eyes. He had shortness of breath —like he did after beatings from his father or the prison guards. He curled into a fetal position, his eyes opening and closing and producing a stroboscopic view that encircled him. Then it happened. He imagined he faced the dirt black wall where a man—exactly like himself, but a civilian—looked through a green stained glass window. He heard a deep, low voice.

"Jack, my man, who dropped you here?"

"Dunno, slipped in from nowhere," he answered, wondering where the voice came from.

"Jack-Be-Nimble, where are you?"

"Right, right here," he sobbed, adding, "I don't understand."

"Jack-Be-Quick. My brains blew. I'm on the other side... I flew."

"Tell me, what is it you say?" he begged through sobs.

"Soul drifted one way, body another."

And so it went, hearing an incomprehensible ghost, but answering best he could. In due course, Jack slept, waking the next day to the sound of the sliding cover and a sub-zero blast of air. A guard handed him a bowl, half rice, half water. Then he heard the voice again.

"Jack, you've dried, died."

He faced the wall. An image, twisted eyes, stared back. A voice coming from deep inside, "With neither soul nor love you're ole, caught in a murky fold. Tipping man, one end points to heaven and the other hell, a swirl, a slow whirl, gyrating, rotating 'round you can't see, out, in, up, down, crack a light, look, you can't reach it, can you... went by... my, my."

Jack listened spellbound. "Another chance, missed, pissed, can't choose fast to outlast the list. Ha, ha. Don't lose sight of it. Get your timin' right so you can fight. Don't slide. Hide, hurry, options are... narrow, big arrow."

And it went this way, talking nonsense, isolated, until the guards dumped him back in the hut, delirious, malnourished, his sour smell adding to the gut wrenching odor that already saturated the shadowy quarters. He lay twisted, doubled over at the door like an old drifter coughing up dry air. He felt Roger and Montoya drag him to a spot between them. Someone removed his clothes, laid them out flat to dry, and checked his body. Except for the evident mud and caked feces, there were no misshapen bones or bruises. But his hands and finger joints were swollen to almost twice their normal size, nails thickened, yellowed, several split to the cuticle. Montoya saw Roger bring in a heap of snow, melt it and bathe Jack, inch by inch. The men watched. They had never seen one man wash down another man. Someone brought back an extra portion of soup and in a week's time Jack seemed to regain strength—although he had a raging cold. Roger on one side, Montoya on the other, he felt secure.

In the weeks that followed Jack contracted something that made his hands puffy and more ominous, and he had a wound on his leg, hardened by a pus oozing scab. His mind was far from right—not that it was by any measure before his incident in the pit—but Roger was more concerned about the leg infection. A blizzard blew in from Siberia, giving Roger the opening to make a run to the storeroom where the Chinese kept medical supplies. Guards were safely indoors, and by staying in the shadows and the cover of snow blowing at 70 miles per hour, he had the opportunity he needed. The storeroom was unlocked, and he easily retrieved a bottle of alcohol and clean gauze.

327

He was confidently on his way back to the hut, when he felt a blow from behind from a baton-swinging guard, who dragged him to the dayroom. There he saw commandant Cho, and standing next to a wall map, a prisoner that looked like a matured Trent Hamilton. The man glanced at him and turned away. A Chinese interrogator asked him what he was doing, and Roger confessed he was looking for medical supplies, which was corroborated by the evidence the guard found after he clubbed him. Roger thought that he would be put in the lock-up behind the dayroom or maybe even the hole, but the Chinese, for reasons he could not fathom, dragged him back to the hut.

But Roger was right: it was Trent, and Trent had recognized him. And it was something that would haunt Trent throughout the winter that lay ahead.

Two nights later, Jack relapsed, rambling, in a daze, a fever, his leg on fire. A bright moon shone through a small crack in a window covered with boards and revealed Jack's swollen, ashen face—open-mouthed, struggling to scream, eyes wide, trance-like, staring into the abyss. He felt Roger lift his head on his lap. He felt him press his fingers over his eyelids and close them, as he had seen done for more than a few dead men.

"Sleep, Jack, sleep. This will end."

Jack's mouth grimaced shut.

Just before Jack passed out he heard Roger say, "Today, I saw patches of green across the river—two boys sitting on the shore like a painting, like Homer's *Boys in a Pasture* I once saw in a museum, a long time ago."

A Brother, Dead or Alive, Unclaimed

JACK LOOKED FOR JULIE IN THE BACK OF THE COURTROOM. Their eyes met. He took a deep breath.

"Mr. Prado, before the break I'd asked if it were not true that Roger Girardin was one of the men assigned to mine clearing. But more directly, let me ask you, Mr. Prado, do you know what happened to Roger Girardin?" Nick asked, his shoulders noticeably slumped.

"I once believed I'd killed him!"

Doubting what he had just heard, Nick asked for confirmation. "You? I'm sorry, Mr. Prado, please repeat that?"

The courtroom stilled. Jack planted his face in the palm of his hands. Nick asked quietly, "Mr. Prado, why did you believe you killed Roger Girardin?"

"It's a long story," Jack said, sounding completely spent.

"You knew Roger before the war, did you not?"

"Of course," he answered, as if everybody knew.

"He was your sister's boyfriend?" Nick asked, guardedly.

"Yes," he answered sheepishly.

"Did he die? Are you sure?"

"I'm sure."

"How did it happen? How did that poor boy die?"

"It comes back to me like a dream remembered. I'd really forgotten, put it far back in my mind, until I heard Mr. Preston. Sometime, late winter '53, they sent a few of us to clear mines, like Mr. Preston said. A bunch of us, me and Roger. Don't remember the other names. I was out of it most of the time. A zombie—I felt like a zombie. Guards gave us iron rods, pickaxes, you know. We had to stab the ground, looking for mines, because it was snowed over."

"Was Trent Hamilton there?" Nick asked.

"Don't know. Don't see him when I try to remember. But I see the dog that followed him. Strange, I don't see Trent, uh, Mr. Hamilton. We were in teams of two or three. Teams were two, three hundred yards apart. I see me and Roger away from the rest, poking around a mound next to some woods. All of a sudden, an explosion. Guard went down—blew his leg off at the knee. Dead, I figure. I see Roger, too. He's about ten feet from me... on the ground. When I get to him, he's bleedin' from the gut. I put my hand on his coat. It's warm, wet. He's in shock. I figure... still able to know what was goin' on. Asks me, how bad. I don't know. 'Don't let me die like this,' he begs. Blood soaks his coat. 'Can't do it,' I tell him. 'Do it... do it before they come, don't let me die like this.' I'd been in a fog. I don't know what to do. If his gut's opened? The worst. You die, slow. Hear men yelling, getting closer. I see the dog."

Lindquist looked to the back of the room where Julie sobbed openly. "I am afraid I will have to ask the marshal to escort out anyone who may be interrupting these proceedings."

Nick waited until the courtroom quieted down. "Trent's dog?"

"Yeah, the mongrel."

"And Trent?"

"Like I said, no. But I'm confused. I turned Roger on his side. The guard with no legs had a rifle. I ran over got it, ran toward Roger. It's hazy. Thought I heard a shot."

"What do you mean 'thought you heard a shot?'" Nick asked, measuring his words.

"Well, gunfire, but somebody cold-cocked me. Maybe I imagined all of it."

"Did you fire the weapon?"

"Don't know."

"Was the weapon aimed at Roger?"

"Maybe."

"Was it your intention to kill him, as he begged?"

"Don't know."

"What happened then?"

"I came to in the cell in back of the dayroom."

330

"Were you grilled?"

"No, left alone. About a week later, brought me out. Bunch of Chinese, maybe five, sitting at a long table. Cho was there and Trent, too—he had the brown dog. Asked me what happened. Trent translated. Told them much as I remembered. Claimed I'd shot him. So I figured I did but couldn't remember."

"Shot Roger?" Nick repeated what he had heard. "You figured you'd shot Roger?"

"Yes, yes, shot."

Stubbornly, Nick wanted Jack to add an element of doubt that he had shot the boy. "But you don't know for sure?"

"No, no, don't know for sure."

"You did not defend yourself?" Nick shouted.

"Told them I saw someone else. Between us, I'm not sure."

"They didn't believe you?"

"Guess not."

"What'd they say?"

"They ordered me to be shot," Jack gulped.

"Did they say you killed him?"

"No, don't think they actually said that, no. Said I shot him. I remember they didn't say I killed him. Next I knew, I was hauled off by half-dozen guards. Walked for a day, toward Manchuria. Crossed the Yalu, over one part that still had ice. Asked if I was going to die, nobody talked."

"Where'd you end up?"

"A holding cell."

"How long?"

"'Bout a year, don't know, seemed like that. Finally, me and about two dozen other guys were taken back to Panmunjom, and the U.N. took us from there."

"Did you tell the army what happened? When you were released?"

"Told them I thought I might have fired at Roger. Told them up to the point he was wounded, and the rest, yes."

"When you came home, why didn't you tell people around you what'd happened? Why did you keep everything to yourself? Tell anyone?"

331

"'Cause, when I came back, the Army knew what I'd done. It was still a crime to fire your weapon at your own— you know, to kill a soldier. No excuses. Was told by this Army lawyer. Asked a lot of questions about other guys I knew there. If I was ever in Death Valley. A lot of questions about Roger. Asked if he ever told me about any killings of civilians, infiltrators."

"What are infiltrators?"

"You know, North Koreans dressed sometimes like civilians." There was a moment of silence.

"Did Roger ever tell you anything about civilians being killed?"

"Yes, and he thought the Army was involved. Said he'd taken pictures."

"Anything else about the pictures you can remember?"

"Said he thought one of the guys looked familiar."

Harris jumped up, "Objection, hearsay, move to strike that last answer."

"Sustained, stricken."

"Did he tell you who he thought that guy was?"

Harris jumped up again, "Objection, hearsay."

"Sustained."

"Tell us what happened next."

"They'd let me go if I didn't talk about what happened."

"And that's why you didn't even tell your sister, Julie?"

Jack remained silent.

"Mr. Prado, is that why you didn't tell Julie, your sister?"

"Figured Julie didn't need to know. Painful not knowing, but knowing? Was worse. Afraid how she would've taken it, you know —me being accused of killing Roger. I was afraid if she learned that... "

Nick focused on Hamilton. "What about Hamilton? He knew Roger was killed?"

"Yeah, he knew, he knew."

"Do you think he helped in your life being spared?"

"He would've helped if he could have. He always said, 'Ridley guys stick together.' He was friendly with Cho, but he wouldn't let me die." There was a long hushed moment.

Nick turned to Lindquist, "No further questions, your Honor."

Harris's two associates shook their heads in tandem, signaling that Jack hadn't hurt them —at least, not insofar as the main objective, keeping under wraps the Task Force mission and the fact that over 400 POWs were left behind after the final repatriation. Harris, though, could not leave it where it was, "The government has a few questions of this witness, your Honor."

Rather than walk to the lectern, he preferred to attack the witness from behind the security of his table. "Mr. Prado, sitting here testifying today, I noticed that you were swaying back and forth. You seemed to, in fact, doze off at one point. Are you well, sir?"

"Yeah, sure."

"Well, if you are well, let me offer an explanation as to why we saw you dozing off. Sir, you are inebriated? Drunk, aren't you?"

"No, I ain't. I have this condition," Jack said.

"Are you telling this court that you had nothing by way of alcohol before you came here today?"

Jack was silent, looking down at his lap.

"Sir, we need an answer."

"I don't think it's... it's none of your business."

"Your Honor, would you please direct the witness to answer?"

"You will answer, sir."

He looked at the crowd. "So I have a shot to calm my nerves." He grinned, shrugged his shoulders. "So, what's the big deal?"

"Sir, you didn't walk a straight line when you came across the courtroom today, is that not true?

"I walked okay."

"Did you drive here today?"

"No, I didn't."

"You are not sober enough to drive are you?"

"I don't drive."

"Are you currently facing charges in Superior Court of resisting arrest, assaulting an officer and criminal trespass for walking along the railroad tracks?"

Nick turned to Art. "Oh, shit!" He said and stood up. "Your Honor, allegations such as this are not relevant."

"I agree, Counselor, move it along," Lindquist responded.

Harris defended his line of questioning by trying to tie Jack's arrest to his admission of having a drink before he came to court that day. "You were drunk that night, weren't you?"

"Objection."

"Sustained."

"I noticed you muttering to yourself Mr. Prado. Isn't it true that you've been diagnosed as a paranoid schizophrenic and on occasion exhibit delusional tendencies?"

"No, that's not... "

"Aren't you under the care of a psychiatrist?"

"Yes, I see someone from the VA."

"Are you capable of separating your dreams from reality?"

"Objection, irrelevant."

"Sustained."

"Your Honor, records obtained from the army and the VA tell us that this witness has a long history of delusional tendencies, and we suggest that his testimony here today about seeing Roger is simply another manifestation of that illness."

Lindquist turned to Nick. "Counsel, would you like to comment?"

"No, sir, I think that the Court can well determine Mr. Prado's ability to testify accurately and truthfully today."

"Very well, the witness will answer the last question. Clerk, please read it back."

"Are you capable of separating your dreams from reality?"

Jack hesitated before answering in a weak voice, "Yes, I'm on medication and don't have those problems."

"But you were not on medication in Camp 13, were you?"

"No, sir."

"So it's possible that all you now remember may have, in fact, been yet another delusion?"

"No, that's not... "

"No further questions of this witness."

***

Nick turned to Art and shook his head. With mouth turned down, Art raised his arm as a sign of success. Nick smiled faintly at Mitch and Kathy. He turned to the crowd, then Lindquist. "Plaintiff rests, your Honor."

"Mr. Harris, are you calling any witnesses?"

"The Army does not plan on calling anyone, your Honor."

"Then you rest?"

Lindquist, face wan and drawn, looked at the lawyers and spoke in a quiet voice. "Gentlemen, this concludes the trial portion of this case. I will expect your findings of fact and conclusions of law on my desk no later than two weeks from today." He sat up, grabbed the temples of his glasses and moved them to the bridge of his nose, before looking at the crowd and saying loudly, "Thank you both for a well conducted trial."

When the gavel came down and court adjourned, Julie looked for Jack, but he had disappeared. Julie's mind raced, stunned by what she had heard Jack tell the court. She boarded the bus to Willa Street and Barnum Avenue, its diesel engine warbling and emitting a cloud of black smoke before the driver's brake forced the strap-hangers to pitch forward. Two sets of accordion-like doors opened with a *shisss* from its underbelly—the end of the line for Julie and the bodies spent in the south end factories. She walked to the old house, where she found the sink empty, fresh linens on the beds. The house had been vacuumed. Out back, garbage cans were filled, a box brimming over with spent bottles of beer, hard liquor. A bundled pile of newspapers had a note: *"For recycling."*

She sat in her grandmother's chair, thinking about Jack's small talk and slowly cooled down. She thought about how Jack was not completely to blame. After all, she ignored the signs, the ones Father Ryan talked about. She wanted Roger to materialize in a world that she knew did not produce miracles. Neither Jack nor she ever mentioned what ailed them, what lay buried in their hearts—as much her fault as his. Maybe because they had no name for it. Rather than talk about it, they carried the weight of it—

335

each year stooping lower than the year before, each year further narrowing their gaze into the unsounded future. For Jack, the weight became heavier and heavier until unbearable: a pending divorce, out of work, alcohol, delusions, dark impenetrable things he carried. Anna and she would talk about what bugged him, but they had no choice but to leave it where it was, each year letting it compress his space a little more, each year making him smaller and smaller in a world that did not notice. She could not hold Jack responsible for wanting to keep the pain of Roger's death from reaching her. In the truest sense, it was an act of devotion.

Extra! Hear All About It

AMY DUSSELDORF'S BYLINE ON PAGE ONE IN THE morning edition of the *Bridgeport Post* caught Nick's attention first. Lindquist had yet to decide the case, but she jumped the gun, detailing the Girardin case from the beginning—including Jack's startling testimony the day before. The story told the unsolved mystery of POWs lost in war. It mentioned that Trent Hamilton, a businessman, philanthropist and prominent politician, was a POW at Camp 13. Dusseldorf wrote that during the trial witnesses testified to a mark on maps detailing mines along a road near Camp 13 and that the marks appeared "*surprisingly similar*" to a trademark of Hamilton Helicopters used a year following the Armistice. Trent Hamilton and his family still owned a majority interest in the company and, based on U.S. export records she obtained, it also indicated that an agent of the current company in the Far East appeared to have the same name as a North Korean guard identified in connection with the atrocities at Camp 13. Nick knew Freedman's hand was all over the story. In his excitement to share the story with Diane, it wasn't until twenty minutes later, when he turned the front page over, that he read below the fold:

The medical examiner ruled early this morning that the death of a Bridgeport man hit by a train on the New Haven Line was an accident. Authorities identified the victim as Jack O'Conner from a dog tag he wore around his neck. It was later confirmed he resided at 320 Willa Street. O'Conner died of multiple traumatic blunt injuries. The medical examiner is investigating why the victim, apparently on his way to Washington D.C., fell from the southbound platform. The spokesman said that the medical examiner's office is conducting an autopsy and routine toxicology tests. On Thursday evening, about 10 p.m. the engineer of the 10:03 p.m. Grand Central to Bridgeport

Express reported seeing someone on the tracks. Police are asking anyone who witnessed the fall to call 203-333-7000.

***

Later that morning, Hamilton called Russell to tell him Jack had been killed, but Russell responded with some news distressing to each of them: the U.S. House of Representatives, Veteran Affairs Committee leaked to the Pentagon that its staff was looking into Korean and Vietnam POW/MIA matters again and was making a trip to interview Kenny Preston. "God knows where this will go once the committee gets it," Russell groused. "And this is not completely for posterity; these assholes are always looking for blood—maybe yours, Trent, maybe mine, if I can be tied to this fiasco... keep that I mind."

"Yeah, this fucking "fiasco" may already have screwed any chance at putting my hat in the ring," Hamilton complained, with a tinge of self-pity.

"That's the least of my worries," Russell added, sounding a more ominous note.

"So, what's the answer?"

Russell had no answer, but said unyieldingly, "I'll handle it from here."

***

The night after hearing about Jack's death, Father Ryan offered a few words during a novena for the good nuns and a few devout parishioners, "We may think God does not hear our prayers. He hears, but all God can do is give us the signs so that we may act where it may be impossible for Him to exercise his will." The parishioners did not know what to make of his remarks.

Father Ryan met Julie at the house on Willa Street. He sat on the overstuffed sofa that had lost all its tension, giving him the sensation of being stuck in a hole, and drank a whisky and water Julie had mixed. Julie lifted the blinds, and in light from the street lamp, she could see Jack's calico swishing its tail, probably at the rats that now inhabited the demolished house across the street. She thought about how Jack, Roger and she, each in their own way, were no different from the cats and rats with whom they shared this place: born of parents, lived and died—

We Were Beautiful Once

natural machines, that for a time overcame to produce the things essential for life, each in their own way moved by fear, hope, turning life's gears, reeling-in dreams, desires, devotions, hates, pushing against the next barrier. Were their lives directed by accident, fate or neither? Or were they like an unavoidable liquid force, drawn to a common ground, avoiding obstacles, hidden forces conspiring to channel their essence into the unfathomable ocean, the end of their journey? To what end, what purpose? She walked to the fireplace mantle and lifted the tin frame with the picture of her and Roger on the beach. "Someday, I will learn the truth, Father. This story has not ended."

After consoling Julie, Ryan returned to the rectory and his soundproofed study where he drank more whisky, smoked cigarettes and wrote:

We who possess the human soul bear an inborn capacity to love and to kill because we have been programmed to guarantee the survival of our kind, our species. The recurring thought of this fact of nature consumes us above all else. We do that which maximizes the chance that our blood will endure another day, a week or indefinitely. It drives us to love, it drives us to hate; it drives us towards civility and barbarity—we employ all methods, sometimes all in the same event—as the soldier who kills his comrade to show how much he loves him.

339

The Last One Standing
December 2004

TWO DECADES AFTER JACK'S ENCOUNTER WITH the train, Mona's son, Ned, stepped on a land mine in Iraq. A funeral was held at St. Patrick's where Monsignor Ryan, pastor emeritus, gave the sermon, which in part reflected on the young man's life, and in part on what Ryan learned about life from the vantage point of the corner of Barnum and Willa. In his inimitable way, the priest's sermon ended with a philosophical observation that Julie once again found hard to follow.

"In our quest to discover who we are and what potential lies ahead, we each take different paths, deciding whether to go left or right at countless forks along the way, and when we reach the end we come to see that we have traveled but one inevitable journey."

Following the funeral services, Anna and Julie invited mourners to refreshments at their house on Willa Street. Julie smiled warmly. "Thank you for coming, Father. Your sermon touched me deeply."

Heads bowed, Julie and Ryan stood looking down at a blue, hooked living room rug while breathing in a bouquet taken from the funeral parlor. Visitors in the adjoining room chatted, clinked glasses. A moment later, a shadow caught Julie's attention. A man with a heavy white mustache in a dark pin-striped suit, blue tie, stood in the double French door to the outer hallway. Their eyes met as he walked toward her.

"Julie, I do not know if you remember me. I'm... "

The man nodded. She extended a frail hand. "Of course, you're Nick, Nick Castalano. How could I not remember you?" she said, her voice quavering.

"I didn't know Ned, but I wanted to express my condolences," he replied, taking her hand.

"Oh, Nick, thank you. It's been probably... twenty years, right?"

"Yes, twenty years, Julie."

"Monsignor Ryan, I'd like you to meet Nick Castalano."

Ryan carried his cane in his right hand, so he extended his left, which had a slight tremor. "Hello, Nick. You were the lawyer... "

Grasping the man's hand, Nick finished the sentence, "The Roger Girardin case."

Julie glanced over at Nick. "Gentlemen ,if you'll excuse me, I have to get something out of the oven." The men watched her hobble into the hallway.

Searching to break the silence, Ryan, arms folded, turned to Nick and asked, "Are you still in practice?"

"No, retired last year. I do a little teaching at the law school. Left the practice to a younger man, Mitch LeBeau, good fellow—once an intern of mine, specializes in veterans' rights. And you, Monsignor, I remember you were the pastor at St. Patrick's."

"I retired, too, two years ago," Ryan said with satisfaction. "I was ninety this year."

"God bless you." Nick pursed his lips and put his hands in his pockets. The men were quiet again, until Nick asked, "How long have you known the O'Conner family?"

The priest raised his white, bushy eyebrows as if calculating. "Oh, from the time Julie was about ten—back when the war started, the big one."

After a few minutes of silence, Ryan excused himself, and was later seen exiting the front door. Another ten minutes passed, when Nick turned, feeling someone at his elbow. It was Julie. Her soft pale eyes were moving from side to side.

"Nick, can I trouble you for a very, very big favor?" she asked, barely above a whisper.

Nick lowered his eyes, tilted his head forward and, with a note of empathy asked, "What's that, Julie?"

"Well, with Ned passing," Julie hesitated, "and, so much of my life having changed because of one or another war... " She hesitated again. "Well, I was wondering if you'd would sit with me to talk about Roger and Jack."

She raised her eyebrows, calling Nick's attention to the lime green eyes he remembered from over two decades ago. Nick squinted apologetically. "Julie... I don't know much more than what you heard in court, years ago."

"I know that, but I have spent most of my life trying to make sense of what happened. I'm old now, and you'd think it doesn't matter anymore. But with Ned going, it simply makes it all the more... "

Appreciating that she would not take no for an answer, Nick agreed to sit down sometime after Christmas.

On the last Sunday of the month following the New Year, Nick visited Julie. He sat on the overstuffed sofa across from Julie, separated by the stained maple coffee table and a bottle of red wine. The blinds were drawn, keeping the afternoon sun from imposing on what was a room still in mourning. Julie fixed her eyes on Nick. "Can you tell me anything outside of what I heard in court those years ago?"

Nick began to recount details that Julie already knew. He seemed a bit reluctant to go beyond the record and, after fifteen minutes, said, "Well, I am afraid I don't recall more than that."

Julie smiled almost imperceptibly. "Nick, tell me if I am right in assuming that if I talk to a lawyer their lips are sealed forever?"

Nick nodded his head. "Yes, if you tell a lawyer something, it's protected by the attorney- client privilege."

"So if I tell you something, it will stay between us, here in this room, right?"

"Yes, I suppose, but what's so secret, Julie?"

"Before I pass away, I want someone to know what I have lived with for almost twenty years."

Nick seemed befuddled. "You're making this sound ominous. What would you like to tell me?"

"Nick, when Jack died, I never believed he committed suicide. I know it appeared he did. And to tell you the truth, a few months before... he was ready to blow his brains out. But in the end, he was going to set the record straight. I think that you know something here. I think that you know that he was on his way to Washington."

"Well, yes, he had an appointment with Senator Skidmore's staff, but the authorities didn't find any foul play. So the assumption was that Jack decided, at the last minute, to end it all. He did have a good deal of alcohol in him at the time."

Julie continued. "Be that as it may, I started thinking after he died that Trent was the one who should have been punished. He was Will's dad, you know. Never once asked about him, never once offered one single dime when the kid wanted to go to college and couldn't afford it, never stepped in when he was drafted. And, not to tell you how Jack sacrificed for Trent. Trent would never have been an officer if Jack had not taken the blame for that poor girl's death. And I know that he was mixed up in Roger's death, somehow. Otherwise how come he was so friendly with that Chinese guy?"

Nick felt Julie was rambling now, but he let her get it out of her system. She started to sniffle, and the two sat quietly until she regained her composure. "I learned that Trent took the train from Washington to Bridgeport twice a month. I also learned that he'd arrive Friday nights at around eleven. I went to the station on at least a half-dozen occasions after dark and found it completely dead—except for this blind vagrant who sat on the ground, knees drawn up, arms crossed, head down. But lost my nerve every time I went, and never stayed long enough to meet the train. And so, one day, figuring I needed moral support, I talked Father Ryan into walking me to the station to meet the train—the one from D.C."

"For what reason?" Nick interrupted, although he was afraid he knew where this might be headed.

"I wanted to talk to him about what he knew. Maybe give him a piece of my mind. Truthfully, I don't know now."

Nick added, "Trent was a dangerous man—that's what I'd been told."

"Yes, I know. But in any case we waited, Father Ryan and I, 'til the train came. He got off. We waited along the ramp leading to Asylum Street not far from the blind man. It was December, one year or so after Jack died. Here he came, long cashmere camel coat, a brief case. When he got

343

about ten feet from us, Father Ryan yelled, 'Trent Hamilton!' He stopped, startled. 'What do ya want?' he shouted. And I shouted back, 'Answers.' Then he took his brief case—you know, he held it by the handle and swung it over his head—and charged Father Ryan. He was a big man. I was scared and went back and fell down. And the next thing I knew he was beating him with the case, when all of a sudden... "

Nick interrupted again, "He was shot!"

"Yes, I took out a small gun that belonged to Jack. I heard this shot. He fell back. Father and I ran."

Nick knew Trent had died the year following the trial, but had suspected it was a professional hit, connected to his illegal export operations. But Julie? Father Ryan? He was stunned.

"I threw the gun over the bridge," Julie added matter-of-factly, as she stared beyond Nick. Next day, I read in the paper that the police thought Trent was murdered by some toughs. Father Ryan and I kept quiet. I never told anyone. 'Til now."

Julie walked to the fireplace mantle and lifted the tin picture frame that held the photo of her and Roger, taken the last time she had seen him. She studied the photo. The greyed-out coat she remembered was navy blue. His arm wrapped tightly about her waist. Her hand, still good, was wrapped between his fingers. She turned to Nick.

"Roger and I," Julie said, her voice low, rasping. "We were beautiful once. Weren't we?"

Acknowledgments

I want to express my gratitude to those individuals who have helped make this book a success through their inspiration and suggestions: particularly to my wife, Susie, for her insights and to Cara Morris and Lynn Hargrove, discerning reader/critics; to editors Eugenia Kim and Rosvita Rauch who patiently plowed through many drafts; to tireless copyeditors Elizabeth Renfrow and Allyson Gard; to the dedicated team at Sunbury Press for all their thoughtful expertise, including Lawrence Knorr, President and Publisher and Tammi Knorr, VP of Marketing & Author Relations.

Made in the USA
Lexington, KY
20 February 2013